The
LONDON
GIRLS

OTHER TITLES BY SORAYA M. LANE:

The
LONDON
GIRLS

SORAYA M. LANE

LAKE UNION
PUBLISHING

Text copyright © 2022 by Soraya M. Lane
All rights reserved.

Published by Lake Union Publishing, Seattle

www.apub.com

Amazon, the Amazon logo, and Lake Union Publishing are trademarks of Amazon.com, Inc., or its affiliates.

ISBN-13: 9781662504044
ISBN-10: 1662504047

Cover design by The Brewster Project

Printed in the United States of America

*For Victoria & Sophie, my 'Dream Team'.
Thank you for your enthusiasm, your incredible
ideas, and for always believing in my writing. I
couldn't do this without you.*

This is no war of chieftains or of princes, of dynasties or national ambition; it is a war of peoples and causes. There are vast numbers, not only in this island but in every land, who will render faithful service in this war, but whose names will never be recorded. This is a war of the Unknown Warriors; but let all strive without failing in faith or in duty, and the dark curse of Hitler will be lifted from our age.

Winston Churchill, 14 July 1940 (by radio broadcast)

PROLOGUE

LONDON, 29 DECEMBER 1940

Smoke curled through the air, threatening to choke Ava as she slowly opened her eyes. She reached out a hand, fumbling in the dark, clawing at the ground as she tried to drag her body from the hard road beneath her.

Where am I?

She blinked, the black skyline in the far distance punctuated by large, rising clouds of white smoke that she knew could only mean one thing. *Bombs are falling on London.*

The ringing in her ears was so loud she could barely think; a high-pitched scream that made it almost impossible for her to piece together what had happened.

Ava finally hauled herself up, frantic now as she realised she'd come off her motorcycle on the road and could be hit by a vehicle at any moment. The blackout meant that the roads were the most dangerous place to be as night fell, with most vehicles forced to drive without lights. She couldn't remember what had happened, how she'd ended up on the ground, her body flung so far from her bike. Had she hit something? Had a bomb been dropped near her?

I was riding straight and then . . . Her mind felt like a sieve, unable to piece together the moments that had left her on the ground.

She searched for her torch, barely able to see as she shuffled across the road. Eventually her foot connected with something hard and she bent to collect it, grateful to discover it was what she'd been looking for. She turned it on, banging it against her leg when it didn't immediately work, and then suddenly there was a pool of light around her, illuminating the crash. *There was a tree.* It all came rushing back to her then: the explosion that had sent her careering sideways; the fallen tree trunk she'd seen too late; swerving across the road, her front wheel clipping the trunk and sending both her and the motorcycle flying up into the air.

Ava's breath caught in her throat, rasping as she hurried to inspect her bike. She wiped at her face, eyes stinging as she hauled her motorcycle up, her light positioned between her teeth now, and desperately tried to start it. But it was a waste of time; the front wheel was pushed back into the frame, and even if she could have started the engine, she never could have ridden it. It was a mangled mess.

She hauled the motorcycle off the road, arms screaming in pain as she used all her strength to move it, hoping it would look salvageable come morning, and she checked the satchel across her body, sliding her hand inside to make sure the document was still there. Her head was spinning and she lifted her hand to it, wondering if perhaps she'd hit it. When her hand came away sticky with blood, she realised there was a good reason for how woozy she felt. Her head had started to pound and she was finding it difficult to balance, let alone walk, her ears still ringing and making it almost impossible to think. She stood in the dark, her light turned off now for fear of being seen from the sky as more booms echoed out, more than she'd ever heard before, and she tried to ground herself, tried to keep her feet steady as she focused on breathing in and out.

You deliver those documents, even if it kills you.

Ava had never forgotten the words relayed to them during their training, and as she set off down the road on foot, her canvas satchel firmly across her body, bombs falling behind her and wreaking havoc on the city she loved, she wondered if it was to be her last dispatch. Every time she was sent out with a memo, she knew she was carrying an order or piece of information considered crucial to the war that was highly time-sensitive; they all knew they were risking their lives every single time they set out. She'd just been lucky up until now.

She forced her legs into a run, like a newborn foal trying to gain its balance as she stumbled along, determined to do her job even if it took her all night. How much time had passed? She wracked her brain, trying to remember where she'd been, how long she'd been riding for before the crash.

Devonport. You were trying to get to the shipyards at Devonport, in Plymouth. You know the route like the back of your own hand. You can do this.

She stopped a moment, turning her light on to get her bearings again. She was still miles away, but so long as she could walk, if she could just keep moving, she could still make it before morning. *I'm not going to let anyone down. I can do this.*

Another boom sounded out so loudly that she felt it reverberate through her feet, the ground shuddering with the force of it as she propelled herself forward again, as she refused to accept defeat. But in that moment there was something scaring her more than the bombs; she could smell smoke, and it was becoming thick in the air, filling her nostrils, sending a shiver down her spine as she realised what was happening.

London wasn't just being bombed. It was on fire.

If ever there was a night she was in danger of losing her life, it was tonight.

PART ONE

CHAPTER ONE

AVA

Ava stood in front of Norfolk House, running one palm down her tailored navy uniform to smooth any creases. She'd caught the tube and then walked from the station as she did every morning, and she wished she could have lingered a little longer in the morning sun. Two weeks ago she'd been moved from the Navy section to a temporary posting, on loan to a dashing general who had a penchant for working late into the night. The hours were long, which meant she was frequently exhausted, but she'd loved every minute – working so closely with a man like him wasn't exactly a hardship. Her heart skipped a beat as she walked, the way it always did when she knew she was about to see him.

She squared her shoulders and entered the building, which was already a hive of activity. There were men and women from all three services stationed there and it didn't seem to matter what time of the day she was there, it was always busy – war never slept.

'Morning,' someone called out as she headed for the stairs.

Ava smiled at a fellow Wren, their fashionable Women's Royal Naval Service uniforms setting them apart from the other working women in the building. She knew it was the not-so-secret reason why so many young women wanted to join the Navy – because the uniforms were so smart – and she'd heard the waiting list was a mile long now. If only she could tell them all just how much work the job actually was, it might reduce the list by half. But she knew many of the girls would still apply, simply because they weren't likely to encounter any objection from their parents. It had certainly been that way for her; her mother loved bragging to her friends that her daughter was a Wren, and her father had been more than happy for her to join. As far as they were concerned, it was the most prestigious posting a woman in London could have.

Ava smiled to herself as she pushed open the door to the section she'd been assigned, walking through to General Armstrong's office. She hesitated, lifting her hand to knock on the open door before entering. As he did every morning, her boss waved her in before she even had the chance to tap her knuckles against the wood, somehow sensing her presence – it wouldn't have mattered if she'd arrived two hours early, she would bet he'd already be there.

'Good morning, sir,' Ava said, making her way to her desk and setting her things down, lingering just a moment longer than necessary when she felt him watching her.

'Morning, sailor.'

She giggled, feeling a familiar heat in her cheeks as his eyes appraised her. He'd said it so many times now that she shouldn't still find it amusing, but for some reason she loved the way he called her *sailor*. In the beginning, Ava had wondered if he simply couldn't remember her name, and it wasn't lost on her that, despite being part of the Navy, she was never going to see the water, but she loved their little morning joke all the same.

'Sir, the Chief of Staff's conference begins in thirty minutes,' she said, forcing herself to keep a straight face. 'I have all your notes from yesterday evening ready for you.' She slowly walked around

8

and then leaned over him, straightening the papers on his desk. 'Would you like a cup of tea beforehand?'

General Armstrong sat back in his chair, and she could tell his eyes never left her. 'You always seem to know just what I need,' he said. 'But a half-teaspoon of sugar today, sailor. Just don't tell my wife, she'd be furious if she knew.'

'Your secret's safe with me,' Ava said with a smile. *Sugar in your tea isn't the only secret I'm helping you keep from your wife; I doubt she'd appreciate the way you're looking at me right now, either.*

Ava left her bag by her chair and quickly headed to their staffroom to make his tea with the requested half-spoon of sugar instead of his usual carefully measured quarter. He had a secret jar that she'd taken on her way past his desk; she'd never asked where it came from although she guessed the black market, as he always managed to keep it more than half-full. She'd missed being in the Navy section with the other Wrens to start with, but the general had certainly made her time with him interesting. Whenever she was around him, her pulse raced and her stomach fluttered; for her it had been love at first sight. The moment she'd walked into his office – his dark brown eyes never leaving hers as they were introduced, his hand holding hers a second longer than was polite – she'd fallen for him. She knew in her heart that he felt the same, especially when he came up with excuses to keep her late each night, always offering her his driver to ensure she got home safely. As far as she was concerned, it was only a matter of time before he told her how he truly felt – surely he didn't lend his chauffeur-driven car to just anyone? She only hoped he made his feelings clear before her time working for him came to an end.

Ava was back at her desk within minutes, shuffling papers and making sure she had everything for the meeting, in between quick gulps of her own hot drink. From the moment their meeting began, she'd be taking notes and typing, the day always a blur of preparing for the next meeting of section heads, and as much as she knew the general liked her, she was also well aware of his expectations when it came to her work. The more she did for him, the more secret smiles she received when they were alone.

Soon they were making their way downstairs, Ava following a few steps behind the general as he greeted countless people by name until they were ushered into the large meeting room. There were as many women as men seated, all with pens poised to begin taking notes in shorthand. Despite the glamorous uniforms, the Wrens stationed at Norfolk House were doing little more than secretarial work.

The meeting began like it always did, and Ava did her job quickly and efficiently, barely digesting what was being said as she recorded everything for the general, until one particular memo caught her attention. She looked up with interest.

'The Navy has settled on the absurd notion of recruiting *women* as motorcycle dispatch riders, to deliver memos throughout England,' one of the men in attendance said. 'It's causing quite the stir amongst some of the ranks, but we do need to free up more men to be posted offshore. They're proposing to recruit from our existing Wrens, although I don't expect they'll have much luck. What kind of woman would volunteer to be out in the dark of night riding a *motorcycle*?'

Some of the other men chuckled and spoke amongst themselves, as if it were the most ridiculous idea they'd ever heard, but Ava sat ramrod-straight, her attention suddenly razor-sharp. She could barely restrain herself from interrupting to ask more. She knew that women were flying planes and doing all sorts of unexpected work to free up men for service, but Wrens riding motorcycles? Now that was something she most definitely wanted to know more about! Her parents would be furious with her for even thinking it, which was one of the reasons she liked the idea of it so much, and she also liked the 'out at night' part. Independence wasn't something often extended to her by her father, but these women would have the cover of *work* to keep them out at all times. She chewed on her bottom lip as she thought it through, imagining the freedom such a job would afford her.

'We'll be circulating the memo presently to see what interest there is, but we're expecting only a handful of capable riders to apply. I doubt it'll be a position that's easy to fill, although from what I'm told there are a few speedway riders they've already begun with.'

'Women capable of riding motorcycles? I'd say it will be an impossible position to fill!' someone called out. 'What next? Shall we send them to the front lines too?'

Ava glanced at her general, desperately hoping he'd say something in support of women, but when he looked up, he seemed to find the idea as absurd as all the other men in the room did. Her heart sank. She'd somehow hoped he'd think differently.

'Good luck to them,' he muttered. 'They're certainly going to need it.'

'Meeting adjourned,' the bushy-moustached admiral in charge announced. 'See you all this evening.'

The meeting over, Ava filed her papers and followed her boss, upset with him for making it sound as if no woman would be capable of such a job. She glanced around at the other women to see if anyone else looked as excited as she felt, exhilarated by what had been announced, but no one so much as returned her gaze, all busy with their own workload and trotting after the men they were taking notes for. Typical; something exciting was announced for women, and everyone just carried on as normal, without a second thought.

I could do it, though. Excitement built inside her as she hurried down the halls, her low heels clicking as she failed to keep up with the general's long stride. *I could apply to be one of those women. There's no reason why it can't be me. What an adventure it would be! And then I'd be free to sneak off before or after my shifts to see him without anyone knowing my whereabouts.* All this time she'd been worried she wouldn't be able to see him any more when her time working for him came to an end, but this would certainly give her the opportunity.

'Sailor, I can hear you thinking all the way back there. What is it?'

She looked up, surprised to see that the general wasn't even looking at her as he spoke. Did he have eyes in the back of his head?

'Something on your mind?' he asked.

'Nothing, sir. Just thinking about the, ah – the notes I have to prepare for you.' She grimaced, knowing how easily he'd see through her lie. *Will he think it's a good idea, once I explain it to him?*

When they reached his office, the general blocked her way, frowning as he looked down at her.

'I wouldn't like to see you get hurt, sailor. Motorcycles are death traps,' he said. 'Besides, it'd be a disappointment to lose a girl like you to such an unladylike job. I'd miss seeing you around the office, and it would be such a shame for you to give up that uniform when you fill it out so nicely.'

Ava blushed at the comment. 'Sir, you're a married man! I don't think your wife would appreciate you being so forward.'

She'd had to say it, even though her stomach was dancing. *Is he teasing me, or does he truly want to be with me?* She had to know.

'Ava, my marriage is all but over. It's merely a formality.'

She gulped. 'You're truly free to do as you please?'

The general laughed. 'Do I look like a man who needs permission to do as he pleases?'

Ava gazed up and into his dark brown eyes, his hair perfectly combed from his face, the smell of his oaky aftershave filling her nostrils. She lifted her chin defiantly, despite her nerves at being so close to him, despite not being entirely certain of herself around him. 'No sir, you do not.'

She was well-used to men who liked having the upper hand – she'd grown up with one after all – but the general had certainly surprised her with his directness.

'So, can I stop worrying about you running off and riding a motorcycle?'

'You'll barely see me once I'm back downstairs, so it won't matter what job I have,' she said, trying to sound bright, not liking that he was telling her what to do all of a sudden. She hoped her attempt at lightening the situation would work. 'I think riding motorcycles sounds like quite the adventure actually, and you haven't even seen me in trousers before. You might find you like it.' She didn't have the nerve yet to tell him why the job might work to their advantage, hoping she hadn't read the situation wrong.

'I doubt very much that I'd prefer a pretty girl like you in trousers,' he muttered.

He didn't say anything else, but she could sense his disapproval resting like a heavy cloak over her shoulders. Ava settled into her chair, ignoring it as best she could, and began typing up the notes from the meeting, at the same time trying not to get carried away with her thoughts. But a motorcycle dispatch rider? A shiver of anticipation ran through her as she imagined herself on a bike, racing around London delivering messages, being free. Before the war, her aspirations hadn't amounted to more than finding a dashing man to marry and escaping the tense atmosphere of her parents' house, but now she found herself loving the freedom of having a job and doing things she'd never dreamed of doing before.

She smiled to herself as she typed, forcing herself to slow down lest she make an error and have to redo the memorandum all over again.

Somehow, she needed to find out more. Perhaps she could create an excuse to go back to the Navy section and beg the other Wrens to find out information for her? Surely she wasn't the only one excited about the opportunity?

'Sailor?'

She cleared her throat and glanced back. 'Yes, sir?'

'Have you ever actually ridden a motorcycle before?'

Ava kept her composure, not even turning to face him. She was surprised he was still thinking about it. 'No sir, I haven't.'

'Well, good, that's one less thing for me to worry about. I doubt you'd even stand a chance.'

Ava let out a long, slow breath, not wanting him to know how badly she wanted it, or how much she hated being spoken to like that. As a child, she'd liked to defy anyone who underestimated her, and nothing had changed since then. But she refused to let his words sting, not before he knew one of the main reasons she was considering it in the first place. He'd shown her so much respect in the past, which was why his rebuke about her abilities hurt all the more. It was only days ago he'd told her she was so pretty and clever, and now he suddenly didn't think she was even capable of learning something new! *Just say it. Tell him why you really want to do it.*

'Do you remember when you asked me to meet you late one night, and I had to decline?' she asked, turning in her chair and keeping her voice low.

His smile told her that he definitely remembered; it had been her first Friday on the job, the first time she'd wondered if he was possibly as smitten with her as she was with him.

'Well, imagine if I had *this* job? I'd have an excuse to be out every night if I needed one. My parents wouldn't know a thing about my whereabouts, and I'd be free to do as I pleased after dark.' She lowered her voice to a whisper. 'I have to admit, it's one of the reasons I was so immediately drawn to the job.'

14

She noticed the way his eyebrows raised, as if he was suddenly far more interested in her idea, and a little thrill went through her as she imagined saying yes to him next time he asked and arriving at his townhouse. She bet he wouldn't doubt her ability to ride a motorcycle if it meant she was more available to see him.

'Back to work,' he said, going back to his own papers. 'We still have a full morning ahead of us. But it's certainly sounding far more promising now that you put it that way.'

'Will you give me leave to apply then?' she asked, holding her breath, hoping she hadn't pushed him too far.

His eyes met hers and he nodded, but she knew what his long gaze meant. His permission was clearly in exchange for her saying yes next time he asked her to visit after hours, and it sent a shiver of anticipation through her body.

Ava fought against a smile as she went back to her typing, wondering how difficult it would be to apply, and then how difficult it would be to convince her parents to let her take part. Her father would likely explode; his temper was a beast at the best of times.

Riding motorcycles sounded like more fun than she'd ever had in her life before, and if it gave her something exhilarating to do each day, then as far as she was concerned, she'd be a fool not to apply. She closed her eyes for a moment and imagined the general opening his door to her, the look in his eyes as she stepped into his home after dark. Perhaps then he'd finally make his move and show her exactly how he felt, or even invite her to stay.

—— ⁂ ——

Ava hurried downstairs, her heels beating a fast clack on the hard floor as she rushed into the Naval section, head down as she made for the tea room. On her way she saw some of the other Wrens look up and she inclined her head, beckoning them to follow her. From the corner of her eye she saw two of the women rise, whispering excuses as they followed her, and she only hoped that none of their superiors noticed her and questioned her presence. She had no good reason to be downstairs, and no excuse prepared, either.

She paced in the small room, her mind racing as she waited for someone, *anyone*, to join her. All she needed was information, and she'd thought of little else as she'd bided her time, waiting for an excuse to leave her office.

First through the door was Lucy, whom Ava had completed her training with earlier in the year.

'Tell me what you know about the new recruitment,' Ava said hurriedly. 'The female dispatch riders?'

As Lucy went to open her mouth, Catherine – another woman Ava had known for months – stepped through the door, closing it behind her and turning with a big grin on her face.

'Is this what you're looking for?' Catherine asked, producing a piece of paper she had concealed inside her jacket. 'I had a feeling you'd be crazy enough to want to apply.'

Ava reached for it, her heart skipping a beat as Catherine placed the memo in her hand.

'You're welcome,' Catherine said. 'Although you owe me a favour, all right? This isn't supposed to be distributed until tomorrow.'

Ava nodded, tucking the paper behind her back when the door opened, but it was only another Wren who'd come to see what all the fuss was about.

'What are you lot whispering about?' she asked.

'Ava here wants to ride motorcycles,' Lucy said. 'I don't think we're exciting enough for her any more.'

They all laughed, but Ava ignored them. She stared at the memorandum in her hand and slowly read the words, excitement building within her. They were looking for motorcyclists, and it appeared that they were first wanting to recruit women who already had experience; however, they were prepared to provide training if required, and that was the part she couldn't stop rereading. She had not the faintest clue how to ride a motorcycle, but she was certainly willing to learn. How much harder could it be than sitting astride a horse, anyway?

She took a big breath and looked up at the other women in the small room, who were all watching her, as if waiting for some big announcement. They likely all thought she was mad.

'Well?' Catherine asked.

Ava glanced at Catherine, then Lucy, and then the other woman, whose name she couldn't remember.

'I'm going to apply,' she said, surprising herself with how convincing she sounded.

'You're not!' Lucy gasped.

'I am,' Ava said firmly. 'Can I keep this?'

'No.' Catherine groaned when she tucked it into her pocket anyway. 'Ava, no!' she cried. 'I'll have to type it all over again.'

'I'll bring you in lunch tomorrow to say thank you,' Ava promised. 'Please?'

'Fine. But it had better be something good.'

Ava gave her a quick hug then spun around to make the cup of tea she'd come for. She had the general's secret stash of sugar in her pocket and she pulled it out, not realising immediately that the other girls had all gone silent.

'Where did you get all that sugar from!'

She slowly turned, seeing Catherine's arched brow. 'Ah, it's the general's. He keeps a personal supply.'

She watched as Catherine moved closer and took down a cup, holding it out. 'Half a teaspoonful. For the memo.'

Ava looked down at the jar, knowing it wasn't hers to give but also knowing that he'd never find out. She sighed. 'Fine. But if I disappear, you'll know why. He's very protective of his sugar.'

'How *is* it going with the handsome general?' Catherine asked, waggling her eyebrows. 'You're the envy of everyone being put on his service, you know.'

Ava shrugged, as if she hadn't fallen head over heels in love with the man. She'd certainly done her fair share of fantasising about smoothing her palm down his jacket lapel as he kissed her, and with the idea of this job rattling around in her head, her anticipation had increased tenfold.

'I can't complain,' she said nonchalantly. 'But I'll be finished with him soon, and this sounds far more exciting that sitting here at a typewriter all bloody day. Give me an adventure any day of the week.'

Catherine laughed at her, and Ava finished making the tea, walking back to her office as quickly as she could without spilling it, the memo burning a hole in her breast pocket. Despite her outward confidence, she was nervous. Being a Wren had changed her life; it meant she could leave home for long stretches every day instead of being so tightly controlled by her parents, not to mention she had her own income, which she'd never had before. She would hate to lose what she had, but surely it wouldn't affect her existing position if she wasn't accepted?

Tomorrow. I'll apply tomorrow. Although she had a feeling that applying wasn't going to be the most challenging part of her plan; now she had to tell her father.

She'd waited all night to tell them, but it wasn't until Ava's mother rose to collect the dinner plates that she finally cleared her throat to speak. Her father reached for his glass, sitting back in his chair, his eyes fixed on his daughter. They weren't unused to her speaking her mind at the dinner table, but usually it turned into an argument that had her father threatening to send her packing. She took a deep breath.

'I wanted to talk to you both about a new, er, *promotion* that I've decided to put myself forward for.'

Her mother sat, still holding the plates she'd collected. 'Oh? What kind of promotion?'

'As you know, my work for the general comes to an end next week,' she said.

'You'll be back in the Navy section after that?' her father asked, reaching for the newspaper he'd left folded beside him while he ate. He glanced at her over his glasses, before seeming to switch his attention to the newspaper, clearly disinterested.

'The Navy are actually looking to recruit women for quite an extraordinary new role,' Ava said carefully. 'They need Wrens to become motorcycle dispatch riders, delivering important memorandums all over England by the sounds of it.'

'Absolutely not!' her mother cried, dropping the plates to the table with a clatter as she looked at Ava in horror. 'Of all the hare-brained things you've said in your life, this, this—'

Ava looked to her father, thinking for one naïve second that he might support her, before he began to laugh. 'Ava, that's the most hilarious thing I've heard all day. A motorcycle rider? Your mother's right, it might be your most hare-brained idea yet.'

She reached for the edge of the tablecloth and clenched her fingers around the starched fabric. 'Regardless, Father, I'd still like to apply.'

He set the paper down then, and she clenched the tablecloth even tighter. 'My dear, what exactly makes you think you'd be capable of doing this job? Please enlighten me.' He sat back and smiled. 'Perhaps your ability to balance on a horse?'

Ava didn't tell him that was exactly what she thought. 'I'm also very capable at driving your motorcar,' she said, hating the quake in her voice.

'The answer is no,' he said, picking up his paper again. 'No daughter of mine will be gallivanting around on a motorcycle. It's unseemly.'

Ava looked at her mother, who just shook her head, lips pursed as she rose with the plates. They'd been delighted when she'd come to them and asked if she could become a Wren – it was something to boast about to their friends over dinner parties, after all. *Dispatch rider* clearly didn't sound anywhere near as prestigious.

'Father, if you'd just—'

His fist hit the table with such force that the remaining plates and cutlery jumped. 'I said no!' he roared. 'Do not question me. Go to your room!'

Ava straightened her shoulders and levelled her gaze on him, even as her stomach clenched with fear. She'd pushed him to anger many times, but she'd always known when to back down. Tonight, she'd already decided not to take no for an answer, regardless of the consequences.

'I am a woman of twenty years, with a prestigious job working for the Navy,' she said quietly. 'I think I'm well past being told to go to my room, don't you?'

The glass tumbler that he threw came within an inch of her forehead. If she hadn't been so used to his temper, and so adept at ducking, she would have no doubt sported an ugly scar for the rest of her life.

Her father's face was red as her mother ignored the shattered glass and rushed to the drinks cabinet to fetch him another Scotch, his eyes dark as he leaned forward.

'Unless you want to find somewhere else to live, Ava, you *will* do as I say,' he said. 'If I tell you to go to your room, you go!'

Ava rose, leaving her mother to clean up the mess as she walked to the door.

'Defy me on this matter and you'll never set foot in this house again, do you hear me?'

She turned, resisting the urge to tell him that she didn't need his damn permission, instead addressing him in her calmest voice.

'Father, this is something I feel very strongly about,' she said. 'Women are desperately needed to fill these roles, to free more men up for service, and I'm prepared to step up and do my bit. They're expecting Wrens to come forward if they're either experienced or capable of learning, and I'm certainly capable. It also doesn't change the fact that I'm a Wren because I would still hold that title, if that's your primary concern.'

'Then let them take someone else's daughter,' he muttered, downing the new drink her mother had brought him. 'As far as *I'm* concerned, this conversation is over.'

Ava turned on her heel and went to her room, closing the door and flopping down on to her bed. With or without their permission, she was going to apply. This was the last time she was going to let him tell her what to do.

CHAPTER TWO

OLIVIA

Olivia hurried into the tea room, glancing at her wristwatch as she pushed open the door, almost colliding with a group of women standing in the small space.

'What's going on in here?' she asked as she elbowed her way through. 'Did I miss my invite?'

She reached for a cup, beyond tired and desperately in need of tea before she started work for the day. Sleep wasn't something that came easily these days; between the long hours of work and then nights worrying about sirens or hiding in bomb shelters, there wasn't much chance for shut-eye. She lifted the kettle, keeping an ear on the excited chatter behind her as she started to pour the boiling water into the teapot.

'Haven't you heard?' one of the women asked.

'Liv, they're recruiting women to be motorcycle riders, and one of our Wrens is applying this morning!'

She narrowly avoided spilling boiling water on herself, setting the kettle down and tuning in properly to the conversation. 'When did you hear about all this?'

'Apparently they need dispatch riders to zoom all over London delivering messages, because they're running out of men to do it,' Lucy said. 'Can you believe it?'

'And who's this girl who's applying?'

'Her name's Ava,' Lucy said. 'She's as crazy as they come, that one. I bet she'll do just fine. In fact, I heard a rumour she was having an *affair* with the general she works for!'

There was a gasp from another Wren, but Olivia didn't react. She wasn't one for listening to gossip, but she did want to know more about the new job.

Her eyes travelled around the room, settling on a piece of paper pinned to the wall. She walked over and tugged it down, scanning the memo, her eyes widening as she read the call to action. *Experienced motorcycle riders preferred.* Her pulse quickened. *I could do this.*

'Can I take this?' she asked no one in particular.

Olivia forgot all about her much-yearned-for cup of tea and hurried out of the room, leaving the gossiping Wrens behind as she strode down the hall to her superior's office. *I need to do this, before I lose my nerve. Just do it, just walk in there and ask him outright. How many other Wrens would have as much experience on a motorcycle as me?*

She paused outside his office, taking a moment to consider what she might say. As she was preparing herself, a petite brunette walked out, her smile so wide Olivia couldn't help but notice it. She looked familiar, but then so did a lot of the girls – there were so many of them working in the building now, but it was only the Wrens she'd been through training with or sat beside that she knew by name. The woman passed with a wink, and Olivia was left wondering if she'd also applied for the position.

'Can I help you?'

Olivia looked up and saw the admiral's secretary watching her, and she squared her shoulders, quickly smiling and forgetting the girl in the hall.

'Yes, I'd like a moment of the admiral's time if he's available?'

She received a curt nod in response. 'He has five minutes. Keep it brief.'

Olivia walked in, clearing her throat as she tapped on his door. 'Sir?'

He looked up and waved her in. 'How can I help you?'

'Sir, I'd like to apply for leave,' she said.

'Leave for?'

Olivia squeezed her hands together, hating how nervous she sounded. 'Leave to apply for the position of motorcycle dispatch rider.'

She held out the memo, half wondering from the puzzled expression on his face if he even knew what she was referring to.

'You're the second young lady to ask me that question in the past ten minutes,' he said, stroking his thick grey moustache. 'Please tell me I'm not about to lose all my Wrens to this new' – he paused – '*enterprise?*'

She shook her head as she realised that the brunette must have been the one the others had all been talking about. What was her name. Anna? No, *Ava*. 'No sir, I don't believe there's many women wanting to apply. In fact, I think it's the exact opposite.'

He nodded. 'Well then, permission granted. I don't want to lose any of you, truth be told, but I suspect it'll be much harder to fill the dispatch positions than find willing new Wrens to work here.' He sat back, appearing to study her. 'You know how to ride a motorcycle?'

'Yes, sir, I certainly do.'

'Well then, I wish you all the best. It sounds like you're exactly the type of young lady they're looking for.'

He went back to his work then, dismissing her as his gaze returned to his papers, and she turned to leave, her hand flying to her mouth in an attempt to mask her excitement. But as she did so, she came face to face with another young woman, sending her files flying as they collided.

'Oh, I'm so sorry!' Olivia gasped, grabbing hold of the woman's arm to steady her, before dropping down to collect what she'd knocked to the ground.

The woman dropped down too, looking mortified as she scrambled to collect her fallen papers. They'd managed to flutter all around them, scattering in every which direction.

'It's fine, I shouldn't have been waiting so close to the door,' the woman murmured.

'You're here to apply too?' Olivia asked.

'For the dispatch position? I don't know about applying yet, I thought I'd try to find out more information perhaps, but . . .'

Olivia touched her hand, smiling as she stared into her eyes. 'You go straight in there and ask for leave to apply,' she said encouragingly. 'I've just done it, and there's another one of us too, a Wren named Ava – she's applied as well. It'll be great fun if we all get in, but if you're anything like me, you'll need to act quickly before you lose your nerve.'

'You really think I should?'

'I really think you should,' Olivia said firmly as they faced one another. 'I'm Olivia, by the way.'

'Florence,' the other woman said, holding out her hand.

'Well, good luck, if you decide to do it,' Olivia said. She needed to go and find this Ava, to see if she knew any more about what they were getting themselves into. 'I think we'd have a heck of a great time if we got in.'

'Yes, you're right. I just . . .' Florence's voice trailed off. 'It's daunting, I suppose. That's all.'

'Florence?' Olivia said as she turned back around. 'If you do decide to apply, why don't we meet downstairs after work. We could have drinks, or maybe even dinner out? I'll try to find the other Wren who's volunteering, see if she wants to meet too?'

'I'd really like that,' Florence replied, and Olivia noticed the way she stood a little straighter, as if she were suddenly more confident about applying. 'See you about six then?'

'Six it is.' Olivia smiled as she walked away, glancing at her watch and gasping when she realised how late she was. Her boss was going to be furious with her!

But as bad as she felt about her tardiness, there was an excitement building inside her that hadn't been there for a long time. A flutter in her stomach, the thrill of anticipation, the memory of what it had been like to ride a motorcycle when she was younger. It had been years, but she knew she could still do it.

Up ahead, Olivia saw a brunette standing talking, and she rushed over to her, surprised to find that it wasn't who she was looking for. 'I'm so sorry, I thought you were Ava.'

'Ava?' The Wren smiled. 'She's up working in the Army section this week.'

Olivia smiled her thanks and headed for the stairs to see if she could find her. She was already late, so what was another five minutes? She forced herself to slow as she entered the Army floor, trying to catch her breath from running up the stairs as she stopped by the first desk with a secretary sitting at it.

'Do you know where I'd find Ava?' she asked. 'She's a Wren, and I believe she's temporarily working on this floor.'

'In there,' the other woman replied, inclining her head without looking up.

'Thanks,' Olivia said, continuing on and pausing outside the office she'd been directed to. 'Ava?'

The brunette she recognised from earlier lifted her head and Olivia walked in, glancing around to make sure she wasn't going to disturb anyone by talking. 'Can you meet for a drink after work?' she whispered. 'To talk motorcycles?'

Ava's eyes widened, her lips parting into a full grin. 'You applied too?' she whispered back.

Olivia nodded. 'There's another Wren as well. I thought we could all meet.'

'Count me in,' Ava said, before groaning. 'Will you wait for me if I'm late though? My general works long hours, he seems to lose all track of time.'

'We'll wait,' Olivia said, as a broad-shouldered man, presumably the general, entered. She couldn't help but remember the gossip from the tea room; he was incredibly handsome, with his thick dark hair and broad shoulders, but a good sight older than Ava, although Olivia could see why the other Wren might find him attractive.

Olivia nodded to him and quickly walked out, before breaking into a trot as she rushed downstairs to her own office. If she were late for the Chief of Staff's meeting, she'd be fired before she even got the chance to become a dispatch rider.

You'd be so proud of me, Petey. She smiled as she ran down the stairs, thinking of her eldest brother. She loved all her brothers to pieces, but Pete was six years older than she was and he'd always been her favourite. He was the one who'd scooped her under his arm and taken her on all sorts of fun adventures, including, much to their mother's horror, teaching her how to ride a motorcycle. Her other brothers had done everything they could to get away from her, to *not* include her, but not Peter.

'What time do you call this!' her boss barked, the moment she entered the room. 'And where's my bloody cup of tea?'

She forced a smile, lowering her head demurely and darting to her desk.

'Sorry sir, I had some, ah, *delicate* issues to attend to.'

Olivia knew it was cruel – the poor man turned as red as a beetroot – but it did stop her from having to explain why she was unusually tardy. She'd grown up in a house full of men, which meant she knew exactly how to use her femininity when she had to.

'Well, don't let it happen again,' he blustered.

She slipped into her chair, quickly gathering what they needed for the meeting. His bloody tea could wait until later.

———— ❧ ————

Olivia had only been waiting a few minutes when Florence appeared, her cheeks pink as if she'd been hurrying. Her face broke out into a warm smile the moment she saw Olivia, and she found herself smiling back, as if the other Wren were an old friend.

'You made it!' Olivia said. 'Does that mean you applied?'

Florence sighed. 'I did. Something about what you said gave me the confidence to go ahead and do it, although I've doubted myself ever since.'

'And?' Olivia asked.

'And he gave me leave to apply! Although he did frown when I told him I had no past experience. I mean, what woman working here would have experience riding a motorcycle, for goodness' sake?'

Olivia shrugged, not wanting to make Florence self-conscious about her lack of practical experience by admitting her own.

'Did you find the other Wren?'

'Ava?' Olivia asked. 'Yes, although she said she might be late.'

They chatted a while, about work and how sore their wrists and hands became from all the typing and shorthand they had to do, and as they were running out of small talk, the building almost empty of workers, Ava appeared. And just like that, Olivia knew she'd done the right thing in asking her to join them.

Ava might have been petite, but her presence was anything but small.

'Sorry girls, you must be so bored, waiting for me all this time.'

Olivia shook her head and Florence did the same. 'Not at all,' Olivia replied.

'Come on, I have a car for us!' Ava said, beckoning for them to follow.

'She has a *car* for us?' Florence said.

Olivia was about to answer when Ava called out, waving her arms to get them through the door.

'The general *always* has a car waiting for me,' Ava said. 'It's his way of making up for all the late nights.'

Florence wondered for a fleeting moment whether perhaps there was another reason the general always made a car available for her, but when the black car pulled up at the kerb and the driver got out to open the door for them, the thought slipped entirely from her mind. She'd never had such a luxury before, and the driver was frightfully comical, with his bushy eyebrows arrowed in surprise, likely at the sight of three women instead of his usual single passenger.

'Freddy, can you take me somewhere different tonight?' Ava purred, batting her eyelashes at the older driver. 'We need to let our hair down, so I was thinking the French House, in Soho?'

She turned to look at them, and Olivia nodded. She wasn't exactly up to date with the best places in London to go for drinks – she'd been expecting they'd find their way to a local pub – but she was happy with Ava taking the lead.

'I just don't want to be out too late,' Florence said. 'I know we've had two nights now without a bomb, but . . .'

'Me too,' Olivia quickly agreed. 'I'd hate to be caught out in it.' The thought of a bomb falling when she was on an open street put the fear of God into her.

Ava nodded. 'Of course. Freddy, would you be able to come back for us? Perhaps in an hour? The general won't need you until midnight, of that I'm almost certain!'

Freddy grumbled something as he started the engine, and Ava sat back with a satisfied-sounding sigh.

'So, tell me everything,' she said, then laughed. 'Sorry, where are my manners! I'm Ava.' She held out her hand.

'Florence.' Olivia sat back as the two of them shook hands across her.

'How long have you been two been Wrens?' Ava asked.

'Six months,' Olivia said. 'Although I've only been at Norfolk House for a couple of months.'

'I'm quite new to all this,' Florence said. 'It's one of the reasons I wasn't sure about applying for the role so quickly.'

Ava waved her hand in the air. 'The Navy are *desperately* looking for plucky girls to become riders, and I'll bet there aren't many of us.'

'The girls in the tea room looked at me like I was stark raving mad when I told them,' Olivia shared.

'I know, they thought I was crazy when I told them, too,' Ava said. 'But it'll be an absolute adventure, don't you think?'

Olivia looked out of the window, pleased that it wasn't dark yet as she listened to the other two talk. She'd never been scared of the dark as a child, but now, with the Luftwaffe targeting them night after night and destroying so much of the city she loved, the dark terrified her. It was almost a relief when dawn broke each day, even if it did mean viewing the carnage from the evening before.

It didn't take long for them to reach the French House, and they all bundled out of the car as Ava called out her thanks to the driver. Seconds later they were through the doors and inside a room panelled in dark wood, the air hazy with smoke and the bar propped up by men in uniform.

'How about I find us a seat, and you order the drinks?' Ava said.

Olivia nodded. 'What do you girls feel like? Gin and tonic?'

'How about champagne?' Ava suggested. 'We are celebrating after all, aren't we?'

Olivia wasn't so sure they were celebrating quite yet, but she hadn't drunk champagne since a friend's wedding and it wasn't like she went out for drinks very often. She jostled her way to the bar, trying her best to ignore one leering soldier and smiling politely at a well-dressed older man in civilian clothes who made space for her. Florence appeared at her side then, and she appreciated the help carrying the drinks over to Ava, who'd found the perfect spot for them in the far corner of the room. There was no music playing, but the noise was loud with so many people talking and laughing in a small space, and Olivia found herself half shouting to be heard.

'I can't believe so many people are out on a Wednesday night!' she said, looking around at the crowd gathered. 'I thought it would be quiet.'

'It's all the men home on leave. I suppose they want to make the most of their few nights of freedom,' Florence said.

'So long as they don't come over here and expect us to entertain them!' Ava said, making a little snorting sound when she laughed, which made Olivia and Florence erupt into giggles.

'Cheers,' Olivia said, holding up her glass and clinking it against the other girls'. 'It feels a bit too early to celebrate, but I can't stop thinking about it all.'

'Oh, we'll get in,' Ava said, grinning as she set her glass down. 'Do you think we'll get to keep these uniforms though? I'd hate to give mine up.'

Olivia glanced down at hers, instinctively running her palm over the navy fabric. 'I hope so. If I'm completely honest, it's my favourite part of the job!'

They all laughed and sipped their drinks again, then Ava spoke.

'So, what do your parents think of all this? Or haven't you told them yet?'

'I'm actually sharing a flat with another Wren and four nurses,' Olivia said. 'My family has a country house and they'd much prefer me to be there, tucked away from all the danger, but it's been lovely having some freedom. They already hate my being in London, so I figure there's little point in telling them what I'm doing, unless I'm accepted.'

'What about you, Florence?'

Olivia noticed the hesitation on Florence's face, the way she glanced down at her hands before replying, looking awkward. 'They'd be fine with it, I'm sure.'

Olivia was going to ask more, but it struck her from the way Florence had said it that perhaps she hadn't told hers yet, either.

'Mine are less than impressed with the idea,' Ava said, rolling her eyes. 'I've decided to just carry on without telling them I've actually applied for now. Otherwise I might be calling on you to see if you've room for another in your flat!'

Olivia smiled. 'We're already two to a room, but the sofa is always free.'

Ava grinned back at her. 'I was only half joking. I might actually have to take you up on that.'

'I heard today that we'll be summoned in groups,' Florence said. 'Apparently they want to try us out, see how we go, before deciding who to ask back for training.'

'Look, how hard can it be?' Ava said with a casual shrug. 'I'd say it'll be as easy as riding a bicycle.'

Florence didn't look convinced, and Olivia was going to reply but decided to keep her mouth shut. She knew that riding a motor-cycle was *nothing* like riding a bicycle, but if she said that, then it would be admitting her experience, and she didn't want to sound as if she were bragging.

'Do either of you have a sweetheart, or should we be looking for some handsome fellas tonight?' Ava asked, her eyes wide as she took another sip of her champagne.

'Not me, I'm taken,' Olivia said, holding out her hand and grinning as the girls oohed and aahed over her ring. It was only small – three modest diamonds set in a thin gold band – but she loved it. 'I haven't seen my Leo in months, but we're hoping to get married once the war is over.'

'You lucky thing,' Ava said. 'Although be pleased you're not married already. He'd probably stop you from applying for the new position if you were.'

She was going to tell them that Leo loved that she could ride horses and motorcycles well enough to keep up with any of the boys, but that would mean disclosing her past experience, and she still didn't want to do that.

'How about you, Florence?' Olivia asked. 'Do you have a sweetheart?'

Florence shook her head. 'Not me.'

Olivia couldn't help but ask Ava, secretly wondering if perhaps the rumours were true and she *was* having a romantic liaison with the general. 'No fiancé waiting in the wings for you, Ava?'

Ava's conspiratorial grin told Olivia she was definitely one to watch. 'I do have a man,' she said, in a voice barely louder than a whisper, making Olivia and Florence both lean forward to hear more. 'He's gorgeous, much older than me, but I can't say more. It's a little complicated.'

'What kind of complicated? He's not married, is he?' Florence asked.

'Let's just say that he won't be for much longer. He's made it very clear that he wants me, not her.'

'I know we've only just met, but Ava, please be careful,' Olivia cautioned. 'A man who will betray his vows – well, I'd just hate to see you get hurt.'

'Don't be silly, he would never hurt me.' Ava waved her hand in the air as if to dismiss her words, and Olivia glanced at Florence, who looked as alarmed as she felt. Perhaps the other Wrens' misgivings about Ava weren't quite so far-fetched after all. 'But thank you for your concern.'

They sat a moment in silence as more people came into the bar, but Olivia's thoughts were interrupted when a man approached them, his accent thick as he smiled and spoke.

'Ladies, could I buy you a drink?'

Oliva sat back and looked to Ava, who immediately seemed to revel in the role of flirt.

'Do you have any handsome friends?' Ava asked.

The man looked over his shoulder, before turning back with an empty look. Clearly, he didn't.

'Sorry, we're discussing work,' Ava said. 'We have *very* important jobs. Perhaps we'll come and find you later.'

The man looked perplexed, and when he left them Ava burst out laughing at the same time as Florence's face fell.

'The poor man!' Florence said. 'He looked absolutely crestfallen!'

'He'll be fine,' Ava said. 'Look, he's already found someone else to ask.'

Sure enough, their would-be suitor was leaning in to talk to another young woman, which did make Florence feel a lot better.

'Girls, this could be one of our last nights of freedom!' Ava said, finishing the rest of her champagne in one gulp. 'In a few weeks' time, we could be racing around on motorcycles all over England. We need another drink!'

Olivia swapped glances with Florence again, before looking at her watch. She still wanted to leave before it was too late; she was terrified of not making it home before the witching hour when bombs began to fall.

'Maybe just one more,' she heard Florence saying.

'Olivia?'

She sighed. 'All right, but just *one* more.'

Ava slung an arm around her shoulders on one side, and Florence's on the other. 'We're going to be formidable, the three of us,' Ava declared. 'We're going to be handpicked for these jobs, I just know it.'

'I wish I shared your confidence,' Florence said.

'Me too,' Olivia murmured, as Ava rose to go and get their drinks for them.

'She's something else, isn't she?' Florence shook her head, and Olivia sighed.

'She certainly is. Don't you just wonder where some people get their confidence from?'

'I have a feeling it wouldn't matter what she set her mind to, she'd believe in herself,' Florence said. 'I'm only worried she might not make the height or weight requirements, although I don't want to be the one to tell her.'

'Don't want to be the one to tell me what?'

Olivia and Florence both jumped in surprise, not having noticed Ava arriving back at their table.

'You were fast! Where are the drinks?' Olivia looked past Ava, wondering if the barman was carrying them for her.

'I didn't even make it to the bar,' she said. 'The barman called out that the next round is on the house. Now, what was it you couldn't tell me?'

Olivia glanced at Florence, shrugging her shoulders as if to tell her she may as well just say it.

'Well . . .' Florence began.

'Come on! What is it?'

'I'm worried you might not meet the weight requirements of the medical.'

Ava just shrugged. 'Nonsense. I'll refuse to take my coat or shoes off, that'll add a few pounds, and I can always put some rocks in my pockets. Trust me, it won't be the first time I've had to do something like that.'

By the time their drinks arrived they were all laughing, imagining Ava with her pockets full of rocks as she stood on the scales. Olivia barely knew her, yet she had a feeling she wasn't joking about the lengths she'd go to when she set her mind to something.

'We're going to have the best of times, girls,' Ava said, leaning in towards them. 'Doesn't it seem so much more exciting than sitting in an office, typing all day?'

Olivia grinned at Florence, buoyed by Ava's confidence. It was most definitely rubbing off on her, and deep down she knew that her motorcycle-riding skills should make her suitable. If she could tear around on the grass after her brothers and keep up, then surely she could deliver messages by road?

'Do you think we'd be riding at night?' Florence asked.

'I'd say we'll be riding whenever they need us,' Ava said. 'Imagine the adrenaline, racing around in the dark!'

'Perhaps we'll be divided into shifts,' Olivia said. 'I'd say they'll need us all the time.'

She and Florence both squeezed Ava's hands back when she reached for them, before they all took another gulp of champagne. Olivia was still excited, but thinking about what they might be signing up for . . . She sipped her drink again. It was certainly daunting.

'To the best damn motorcycle-dispatch-riders-to-be in London!' Ava announced. 'Just imagine what we're going to be doing for the war effort. This is our chance to have the adventure of a lifetime.'

Olivia clinked her glass first with Ava's and then Florence's, wishing she shared some of her new friend's confidence. But Ava wasn't wrong; she bet they *would* have a fabulous time together, and they would be doing something incredible for the war effort.

If we get the chance.

CHAPTER THREE

FLORENCE

'Here, have some toast, and I still have some of your favourite marmalade left if you'd like some?'

Florence smiled at her grandma and sat down at the kitchen table. Sun pooled on the wooden top, and she reached out to touch a sprig of fresh flowers sitting in a glass jar. 'Thanks, Grandma. I'd love that.'

She'd learned not to protest when her grandmother offered her something special; it was her way of looking after Florence, trying to feed her and lavish love on her as if it might somehow heal her broken heart. Florence looked up as her grandmother set a plate in front of her, then took one of the pieces of toast and pushed the plate away.

'I'll only eat it if you have half,' she said. 'I know it's your favourite, so you can't say no.'

Her grandmother threw her hands in the air but eventually took the toast, and they both sat back, eating slowly, enjoying the last of the tangy marmalade. They wouldn't have nearly enough sugar to make it this year, so it was going to be a lot more tart than usual, even if they saved up the rest of their ration from now until next summer.

'You know, I rode a motorcycle once,' her grandmother said. 'I went out with a young man and he put me on the back of one. My mother forbade me from ever seeing him again once she found out!'

They both laughed at the thought, and Florence had the overwhelming sensation of wanting to wrap her arms around her grandma to keep her safe. She was a spritely old thing, whippet-thin and with a strength that often surprised her, but she was Florence's only remaining family member and that made her determined to protect her.

'Your mother on the other hand, she'd be proud to see you on a motorcycle. She'd be cheering you on, I just know it.'

Florence wasn't quite so convinced her mother would have been encouraging her, but it was a nice thought. She'd have done anything to feel her mother's arms around her, to listen to her soft voice, feel her warm lips brush the top of her head as she passed her at the dinner table. If Florence shut her eyes, she could almost hear her voice, the way she'd sung softly under her breath as she listened to the radio in the kitchen; she could see the house she'd grown up in as if it still existed.

She quickly blinked, as if it might help to erase the memory. It never did, but for some reason she always tried.

'Tell me about these other girls. Are they nice?'

Florence swallowed her toast, which had gone dry in her mouth as she'd lost herself in memories. 'They're lovely, although I've only met them once. Ava seems like she's not scared of anything, and Olivia is confident too, but in her own way. They both seemed like a lot of fun.'

'If you all make it through today, why don't you ask them around for a cuppa? I'd love to meet them. There's nothing I love more than company.'

Florence rose, taking the rest of her toast with her. 'Thanks, Grandma, I will.' She pressed a quick kiss to her grandmother's cheek, but as she was pulling away, strong fingers laced around her wrist, holding her in place.

'Flo, are you all right, love?'

She took a deep breath. 'I'm all right. It's just . . .' Her voice trailed off and she couldn't get the words out. 'It never goes away, does it? Sometimes it feels like it was only yesterday.'

Her grandmother's fingers released her and she received a pat on the hand instead. 'People tell us it'll get easier, but it doesn't. The only thing that we get better at is hiding our pain.' She let out a sigh. 'I never want to bring it up because I don't want to upset you, but if you ever want to talk . . .'

'I know I can talk to you,' she replied.

'Well, you just keep that chin up today and show those fellas exactly what you're capable of, you hear me?'

Florence couldn't stop herself from laughing. 'Yes, Grandma, I'll keep my chin up.' She had a funny feeling her grandma would get on brilliantly with Ava, and she half wondered if she would have applied to be a dispatch rider herself if she were a few years younger. Her grandma was as fearless as someone half her age, and despite everything they'd been through, she still seemed to get up each day and manage to hold her head high. Recently she'd been told she was too old to be an air-raid warden, and she'd been furious at being turned down.

'I'm proud of you, Flo,' her grandmother said, and unexpected tears shone in her eyes. 'What you're volunteering for, after every-thing you've been through . . .'

Flo took a deep, shuddering breath as unshed tears gathered in her eyes, too. 'I think it makes me want to do it more,' she mur-mured. 'It's made me even more determined to help, to do my bit. It can't be for nothing, everything we've lost, it just can't be.'

'Well, good on you, my brave girl,' her grandma said, smiling brightly as she blew Flo a kiss. 'You go get 'em.'

Florence said goodbye and grabbed her jacket, quickly buttoning it as she hurried from the house, her grandmother's encouragement ringing in her ears. It had been three weeks since she'd applied, and today they were to report to the ATS Training Centre in Camberley for a test drive and an interview, and although they'd been told to wear *appropriate* clothes, Florence was most comfortable in her WRN uniform so she'd decided to wear that. The skirt might not make motorcycle riding that easy, but then she didn't exactly have any suitable trousers to wear, and there hadn't been any instructions on what was classified as appropriate.

The clouds parted above her and suddenly bathed the road ahead in sunshine as she walked to the station, and Flo smiled up at the sky. When the weather cleared for her, she sometimes liked to pretend it was her family looking down on her, sending her luck, making her feel closer to them somehow. But today, after her little talk with her grandma, the unexpected sunshine only made her miss them more instead of comforting her.

I miss you so much, Mum. Sometimes I can't get that night out of my head, it's like I can still feel it, still smell it, still taste the ash in the air. And when I wake in the night, tangled in my sheets and damp with sweat, it's like I'm there, stuck in that moment, reliving it over and over again. And that's when I realise that you're actually gone. That you're never coming back. That you'll never hug me again, or talk to me late at night by the fire. That Dad will never be there to walk me down the aisle when I get married. That you'll never see my children, that they'll never know their grandmother.

Flo fisted her hands, nails digging into her palms. *Today is not the day to go down memory lane. Today is my day to shine, to do something for the war that will make a difference. Today is my day to make you all proud.*

She quickened her pace, as if she could outwalk her memories. But it turned out that walking them off was as useless as trying to blink them away.

———— ⁓⁓ ————

'Good morning, Wrens!' came a booming voice, attached to a hulking great man in uniform who was striding across the field towards them. He was perhaps in his sixties, but his voice belied his age.

They'd all arrived within fifteen minutes of one another and Florence had naturally moved to stand with Ava and Olivia, who, like her, were dressed in their smart WRN uniforms. There were two other girls standing slightly away from them, but the poor things were wearing dresses, and with the wind starting to rise, she was certain they'd be regretting their choice of outfit. She glanced at the groups of Navy boys who'd gathered nearby, their eyes wide at the sight of women waiting on the field. She hoped they wouldn't be too amused by the driving skills displayed – knowing they were there watching wasn't going to help her confidence any. Surely they wouldn't be allowed to loiter once the training commenced?

The booming-voiced man caught her attention again, drawing her gaze from the younger men. He seemed to pause as he approached, looking first at the two women in dresses, before sighing loudly and continuing his walk towards the group. He seemed less than impressed.

'Good morning, ladies. I'm Commander MacIntosh,' he boomed. 'But you can call me Commander Mac.'

'Good morning, sir!' they all replied in unison.

'You're here today because you've expressed interest in becoming motorcycle dispatch riders, and I'm here to see if you've got what it takes.'

Florence swallowed, her throat suddenly dry as sandpaper as she listened. Nerves that hadn't been there before unexpectedly hit her stomach, and she had to fight to keep her shoulders square and her chin raised high. Her bottom lip had started to tremble too, and she clamped her mouth shut tight to stop it.

'Up until recently men have exclusively filled this role, but we urgently need them to dispatch messages at the front lines, and we can't get them there fast enough,' he continued. 'Some months ago, we recruited a handful of true pioneers in British motorcycle racing, to see if women had the skills to replace our men. I'm pleased to say that those women have paved the way for you all.' He paused and considered each one of them. 'It's because of them that you're even getting this opportunity.'

Florence tried not to shuffle her feet, but as she found herself the object of Commander Mac's scrutiny, she started to get nervous all over again. Why was he staring at her? Had she done something wrong? Had he noticed how nervous she was?

'You,' he said, pointing at her. 'Name?'

'Wren Hughes,' Florence said, clearing her throat to try to project her voice more loudly. *Why is he calling me out before anyone else?*

'You've ridden a motorcycle before?'

'Ah, no sir. I haven't.' Her voice faltered as she answered the question. Surely he'd seen her application and would have already known that? She'd made it very clear that she had no experience when she'd filled out the form!

'You're up first,' he said, seeming to disregard her answer as a loud noise reverberated through the air and a woman came roaring towards them on a motorcycle.

Florence jumped at the noise, but Olivia's hand caught hers, calming her as they watched the performance before them. The woman rode in a big lap around them, going fast on the grass before turning sharply and eventually coming to a sudden halt nearby.

'Ladies, I'd like you to meet Theresa Wallach,' he said, waving his hand towards the woman, who climbed off the bike and tucked her hat under her arm, giving them all a quick nod. 'Not only has this young woman previously ridden from London all the way to Cape Town in South Africa, she's also used to riding a hundred miles an hour when she's racing. So, when I say you're up against the best, I mean it.'

What the heck am I doing here? Florence had the overwhelming feeling that she should be making an excuse and leaving, but she forced her feet to stay rooted to the spot. The other girls were inexperienced too; he was only trying to frighten them, to make them see how good they had to be, wasn't he? There were only a handful of female motorcycle racers in London, *surely*, so that meant their recruitment pool had to be particularly small. There's no way he could ever expect them all to be this good!

'Show her what to do,' he said. 'This one is up first.'

'Yes, Commander,' Theresa said, giving Florence a quick smile.

Florence forced herself to walk closer, ignoring the doubt in her mind as she listened carefully to what Theresa was saying.

'This here is a 350cc Royal Enfield WD/C motorcycle,' Theresa said, her body angled so that they could all hear her. 'They're excellent for navigating our roads at the moment, because they're both nimble and fast. Now this is how you start a motorcycle, watch me carefully.' She made it look so easy, and when she gestured for Florence to step closer, she hesitantly moved forward. If only she could have seen one of the other girls go before her, so she had longer to figure it all out.

'You need to sit confidently on the bike, balancing yourself like this in the middle of the seat, and with your hands here.' Theresa demonstrated, showing her the correct position, before indicating that it was her turn to try. Florence stepped forward and did as she was told, feeling slightly better now that she was actually giving it a try herself – perhaps it wasn't going to be so hard after all, if she stopped worrying so much. All she needed to do was listen to Theresa and follow her instructions, and she was thankful at least that her feet comfortably touched the ground, which made correcting her balance that much easier.

'Good, your position is great,' Theresa said. 'Now, to start her up, just like I did. The hardest part is getting the hang of how to kick it down, and for those of you who are smaller, you'll have to jump down hard on it. Once you're in gear you can slowly ease off the brakes, and then you're away! But I suggest you start out slow to get a feel for her; it's easy to go too fast and then panic, and before you know it you've got a motorcycle on top of you!'

A motorcycle on top of me? Oh Lord.

The sound of the engine wasn't something Florence was used to, and she found that it was the noise more than anything else that set her teeth to rattling with nerves again. Well, that and the terrifying pep talk she'd just received. She glanced up and saw Theresa watching her, smiling encouragement, and further afield the commander, only his face was hovering in a frown. She gripped the handles more tightly.

'You can go whenever you're ready, just remember to ease off the brakes slowly. Don't go too slow though, or you'll find it impossible to balance.'

So do I go fast or slow? What happened to starting out slow! Florence kicked down to start the motorcycle, taking five tries before she finally got it, cringing as she held the clutch and put it into gear before lurching forward. But Theresa's words of encouragement gave her the confidence she needed, and she attempted to go faster then, believing it would make everything easier for her as she continued to wobble over the grass. *Fast but not too fast. Just stay steady. You can do this.*

Flo grinned as the bike steadied, suddenly feeling in control. *I'm doing it! I'm actually doing this!*

It was when the group of Navy boys caught her eye, some of them doubled over as they howled with laughter, that her new-found confidence faltered. She was going too fast, her mind suddenly blank as she tried to slow down, the grass slippery beneath the tyres, and that was all it took for her to lose her nerve. She wobbled and nearly fell off, managing to correct herself at the last moment, only in her confusion she accidentally accelerated, her fingers slipping when she tried to brake, the bike too fast beneath her.

And then everything began to happen too quickly, the wind whipping her face as she panicked about how to slow down, and before she knew it the fence was somehow coming towards her as she screamed. The impact of the front wheel on the wooden post was enough to send her flying through the air, plum over the fence to land with a thud on the grass on the other side.

Florence heard hoots of laughter and loud clapping, and she would have preferred to curl into a ball rather than sit up, but she couldn't exactly hide in plain sight like a child playing peek-a-boo with her hands over her eyes. Pain ricocheted up her hip and down her left leg, but she pushed herself up, not wanting to lie there.

'You all right there?' a voice said from behind her. She looked up at a frowning man wearing a Navy uniform, his blue eyes seeming to search her body. He was perhaps thirty years old, not handsome but not unattractive either. She imagined he'd perhaps be nicer-looking if he smiled. 'Is anything obviously broken?'

She wiggled her fingers and stretched out her legs, forcing herself to stand once she realised everything was still working. 'The only thing broken is my pride.' Florence gingerly touched her head, which had started to pound, wondering how on earth she was on the opposite side of the fence to the bike.

'This is exactly why women shouldn't be riding motorcycles,' he muttered, striding over to the wire fence and holding it down for her to climb over. She did so as modestly as she could in her skirt, trying desperately not to limp, and she nodded her thanks as they stood beside the motorcycle, joined within seconds by the commander and Theresa. She'd never felt so embarrassed in all her life.

'What a disaster!' Commander Mac exploded. 'To damage a motorcycle in less than a minute? Now that must be some sort of a bloody record!'

Florence was about to hang her head, but as she was beginning to look down, her eyes landed on a small van further away in the field. If only she'd been driving a vehicle instead of a motorcycle.

'I'm sorry, sir,' she said. 'I'm an excellent driver of vehicles, and I expected riding to be much the same.'

'I suggest you stop speaking,' he grumbled. 'Dismissed!'

She summoned all her bravery and faced him squarely, not following orders for the very first time in her life. She could not have her day end like this, as a complete and utter failure, an embarrassment that would almost certainly be reported to her superiors at Norfolk House. 'Sir, I'm sorry, but I would like a second chance to prove myself to you.'

His face had turned a deep red now, like he was about to explode, and Theresa was slowly shaking her head beside him, as if trying to warn her to stop talking. The other woman was looking at her as if she were crazy, but Florence felt far more confident now than she had sitting astride the motorcycle.

'Sir, I believe I can drive that van over there better than half the men watching.' She hooked her thumb at the men still gathered. 'If you just gave me the cha—'

'I'd say what you've just had was a chance,' he interrupted. 'And it wasn't successful, in case you've neglected to notice the state of the brand-new motorcycle you so elegantly dismounted from!'

Florence opened her mouth to speak again, but her words faltered. *What are you doing? Why can you not just admit that you've failed? Why can't you just walk away?*

Because I have something to prove. Because I have something to give. Because this can't be the end for me. Not today, not after everything I've been through, not after everything I've survived.

She caught movement from the corner of her eye and noticed Ava coming towards her, her eyes kind but her expression verging on pity, and it was all Florence needed to spur her into action. No one was taking pity on her. It was one thing to pity her for what had happened to her family – those looks she'd been able to accept – but she was not going to let anyone look at her that way again, not if she could help it. She was going to show everyone just how capable she was – that she wasn't just the poor girl who'd lost her family to the might of the Luftwaffe.

'I wholeheartedly suggest you stick with typing,' Commander Mac said, dismissing her for the second time as he turned to address Theresa. 'I'm not certain we should risk any more motorcycles after that spectacular failure.'

'Sir, with all due respect,' Theresa said, just loud enough for Florence to overhear. 'If we don't find some other riders to train soon, you'll have to withdraw men you were intending to send to the front. I'd say that would be more of a disaster than giving these other women a chance today.'

As he ran his fingers across his neatly trimmed moustache, clearly deep in thought, Florence decided to take matters into her own hands. She strode across the grass, refusing to limp even though her left hip was crying out at her to stop walking, and she didn't slow until she reached the small van that was parked on the concrete.

You can do this. You were driving from the moment you could see over the steering wheel. This is your last chance to prove that you're not just some useless woman!

Florence yanked open the driver's door, pleased to see keys in the ignition and hauled herself up into the driver's seat. She turned the key, relaxing somewhat when the engine fired and the van rumbled beneath her. It was then she looked up and saw some of the Navy boys running towards her, flapping their hands, and the commander throwing his hands in the air too, looking like he was about to erupt in anger. His red face was a stark contrast to his white hair.

But Florence was undeterred; she was going to show them all exactly what she was capable of.

First, she accelerated slowly to get a feel for the van, before going faster and driving between two power poles, swerving around a pile of wooden crates and then crossing the grass towards the small crowd. She didn't look at any faces, just focused on what she was doing, careful to slow on the grass so she didn't skid and lose control, before heading back out on to the concrete and doing another lap at speed, then reversing through the poles and finally coming to a stop.

Her breath came in big pants, as if she'd just run the course instead of driven it, and she forced her jelly-like legs out of the vehicle, taking the keys with her and shutting the door. She held her chin high as she marched, dropping the keys into the hands of Commander Mac when she reached him, refusing to think about the consequences of her little stunt.

'Sir, I might be terrible at riding a motorcycle, but I'm damn good at driving a van, so if you'd consider a different mode of transport for me to deliver memos in, I—'

He held out the keys, barking to the men huddled nearby to relieve him of them, before turning his attention to her, his face a blustering kind of red all over again.

'I suggest you make that the final time you disobey me, Wren . . .'

'Hughes,' she said, with an air of confidence that belied her nerves. 'Wren Florence Hughes.'

'You've demonstrated to me an outstanding ability to drive a van, far better than some of the men in my employ, you were right about that. However, the role I'm recruiting for is that of *motorcycle* rider. Motorcycles have been chosen for our dispatch riders because they are nimble and can weave through London despite the perils and unknowns, something no van or even car is able to do.'

She nodded, hanging her head. 'Of course, sir, I understand.' *You've made a big mistake, girl. You should have just accepted defeat.*

'However,' he continued, narrowing his gaze. 'I do know that there is a desperate shortage of competent, unflappable ambulance drivers at present. Do you have any first-aid training?'

'Ah, yes, sir, I do.' She'd been training to become a nurse early in the war, but after everything that had happened, she hadn't been able to continue.

'Shall I put your name forward, then?'

It took her only a moment to consider his question, even as memories swirled in her mind, threatening to fell her. *You can do this. You need to do this. Think of all the people you could help. You need to be brave. You can put everything you're good at to use.*

'Yes, sir, you may,' she said, her voice cracking as she tried not to sway on her feet.

'Dismissed,' he said, before chuckling and shaking his head, giving her an unexpected thump on the back that almost sent her flying. 'And some advice, Wren Hughes?'

She turned to face him again, her pulse racing.

'I'd like to think your motorcycle riding days are over. Please stick to driving vehicles.' He frowned. 'Actually, where *did* you learn to drive like that?'

'My father,' she said. 'He taught me to drive his delivery van when I was only a girl.'

She remembered sitting on the seat, her father's jacket folded beneath her so she could see over the steering wheel. His laugh had seemed to reverberate through the cab as he placed her hands on the wheel and told her to stop looking like a startled little rabbit.

'What will Mother say?' she'd said.

'You let me worry about your mother,' he'd said with a grin. 'If I can get you driving, then I'll be able to take you along with me every weekend. Heck, I'll be able to take a rest while you drive.'

She knew what he really wanted; to have a pint or two at the pub when he finished his deliveries, and for her to drive him home, but she dared not say it. She'd likely get a soda for keeping quiet, and besides, she liked spending time with him. At home he was always busy, but in his van, he talked to her like he had all the time in world. She shook her head to clear the memory and focused on what the man in front of her was saying.

'Well, I'd say he did a fine job. In fact, I'd say the Red Cross would like to thank him when they see how well you can drive. You'll be a real asset to them if you decide to take the position.'

She nodded and hurried off, her face burning hot as Ava stared at her with wide eyes and Olivia shook her head, biting her lip as if to stop herself from smiling.

'You're quite the surprise,' Ava murmured as she passed, touching her hand as she strode past to take her turn.

Florence stood next to Olivia, their shoulders almost brushing they were so close.

'Are you all right?' Olivia asked.

'I will be,' Florence replied, her chest rapidly rising and falling as the enormity of what she'd just done filtered through her. 'But right now, I can't stop shaking!'

You just showed blatant disrespect to a superior! You could have been stripped of your job as a Wren! What in heaven's name were you thinking?

'For what it's worth, I'm proud of you,' Olivia whispered.

'We're not going to be dispatch riders together though,' Florence whispered back, disappointed by the way the morning had turned out despite the fact she'd redeemed herself. So much for the three of them against the world.

'Maybe not, but it doesn't mean we can't still be friends.'

As they watched Ava receive her instructions, Florence couldn't help but smile. She'd been so caught up in her own grief these past few months – in simply surviving after her world had fallen apart – but today she'd felt alive again, despite her nerves at the prospect of driving an ambulance. She felt like the old Florence, the one who'd laughed with her father as a teenager as she'd driven around London behind the wheel of an oversized van, before everything about the country and the people she loved had changed. And despite the risk of what she'd done, she had the strangest notion that she'd do it all over again if she had to, that perhaps she was exactly where she was supposed to be because of her bravery.

I'd just try harder not to crash this time.

CHAPTER FOUR

AVA

Ava stepped forward when she was called, thinking how gutsy Florence had been as she digested her instructions and sat astride the motorcycle – a new one that Theresa had brought out, which had set poor old Commander Mac to blustering all over again. It felt different from what she'd expected, the seat firmer, the handle-bars more rigid. And she hadn't expected to be quite so nervous, either. All morning, she'd imagined herself mounting the bike and feeling instantly at home, but instead she felt completely out of her depth, and that wasn't something she was used to. Not to mention she couldn't stop thinking about her conversation with the general the evening before, when she'd dashed upstairs to see him before she left for the night, under the pretence of retrieving something from his office that she'd left behind.

'I hear you'll be at Camberley tomorrow.'

Ava nervously fiddled with a loose thread on her jacket as she faced him. Sometimes she didn't know quite how to take him; his tone was friendly but there was something about the way he was staring at her that made it impossible to know what he was thinking. 'I will be.'

He came closer, and she felt the familiar beat of wings in her stomach. 'I'm going to miss you, Ava.'

She still couldn't stop wondering about his wife, more so since Olivia had tried to caution her, but the way he was looking at her made her forget everything else. It was the way she'd waited her entire life for a man to stare at her, especially a man like him. She hesitantly reached out to touch his tie, running her fingers across the fabric just as she'd always wanted to do, emboldened by the fact that her time working for him had come to an end.

'Will you stay true to your word and come to visit me at night?'

He kissed her then. It wasn't gentle and romantic as she'd always imagined her first kiss with him to be, but it still sent a thrill through her.

'I'm worried about your wife,' she whispered. 'What if someone sees us?'

'My wife is in the country indefinitely, I've told you that,' he said, sounding impatient. 'How about you let me worry about my wife. Haven't you noticed the way I've been looking at you? I don't make my car available to just anyone.'

Ava smiled up at him, flattered that a man like him could be so attracted to her, even if she didn't like the way he was telling her what to do. She pushed thoughts of his wife from her mind as his eyes met hers.

'Would I risk everything if my wife was coming home to me?' he said, his tone changing. 'You're the one I want, Ava.'

Ava knew she'd always been a hopeless romantic – sometimes she felt like she'd been waiting her entire life to fall in love – but she'd imagined that her fantasies about the general would stay exactly that: fantasies. She nodded, liking the way he smiled down at her, how pleased he seemed with her, her heart soaring at how much he wanted her.

A noise behind them alerted her to the fact they were no longer alone on the Army floor, and she backed away, picking up her handbag.

'I look forward to seeing you again soon, sailor.'

She blew him a kiss and left, already imagining herself drinking Scotch with him at his townhouse, her misgivings about his wife

somehow forgotten as she indulged in the fantasy she'd always had about
him holding her in his arms and kissing the breath from her.

'Wren Williamson?'

'I'm sorry, what did you say?' Ava pushed her thoughts away and focused on the woman in front of her.

'Are you ready?' Theresa asked, as Commander Mac maintained his position some feet away and she rid her head of all thoughts. 'Have you ever ridden one of these before?'

Ava shook her head. 'Never, but I'm as ready as I'll ever be.'

'It's not going to go down well if you crash, not after the last one,' Theresa said quietly. 'If you feel things aren't going well, you're better just to stop and start again. *Please.*'

Ava understood; if she mucked this up then she'd be sitting behind a desk for the rest of the war, not to mention all the other girls would blame her for ruining it for them.

Theresa ran over some instructions with her and then stepped back, and Ava carefully went through each step in her mind, eventually managing to kick-start the bike after four goes, which required all of her weight to do it. Then she put it into gear and eased off the brake, gently accelerating. The bike skidded a little and she remembered Theresa's words, trying again but with less acceleration this time, and then suddenly she was rolling at a modest speed across the grass.

I'm doing this! I'm actually doing this!

Ava tried to keep calm as she accelerated a little more, not wanting to become overconfident even as she stopped wobbling, passing the fence that poor Florence had so spectacularly crashed into, not wanting to repeat her friend's error as she bit down on her lower lip and turned slightly. She wobbled again but managed to correct herself, determined not to fall as she turned a little again, maintaining a big circle and passing the spot from where she'd started. She saw Theresa nod to her as she went by, but she barely acknowledged her, and she dared not look at Commander Mac, not even for a second. And then, after riding round and round on the second circle, she slowed and then finally stopped. Her heart was racing and her jacket was hot and sticky against the back of her neck, but she'd never been so proud in all her life before. The only question was: had she ridden well enough to be given a chance?

'Well, at least the motorcycle is in one piece,' the commander called out. 'Next!'

Ava's legs were shaking as she passed Olivia, folding her arms over her chest as she stood back to watch her. She couldn't hear what Theresa was saying, although she guessed it was the same instructions she'd received minutes earlier.

Was anyone going to tell her if she'd done well enough?

'I think it's fair to say you passed,' Florence said.

Ava turned her head and smiled, taking a few steps backwards so they were standing together. 'I hope so. It was a lot more difficult than I'd expected.'

'You can say that again!'

They both laughed, although the moment the engine roared to life their attention turned firmly to Olivia. Ava was about to say something, but all thoughts left her mind as she watched the motorcycle speed effortlessly around the grass without so much as a wobble, going faster and faster, before slowing and then turning in the opposite direction and roaring off again. Olivia seemed to move with the bike, leaning low as she went into a tight corner of her own making and then coming to a fast stop beside Theresa. It had only lasted a few minutes, but even to Ava's untrained eyes it had been a success – Olivia looked as effortless on the bike as Theresa had when she'd given her demonstration.

'Do you think she's ridden one before?' Florence whispered.

'Oh, I'd say she's ridden one *many* times before,' Ava said tartly. 'That was . . .'

'Excellent,' Theresa cried, clapping as Olivia stepped off the bike and brushed escaped, windblown tendrils of hair from her face. 'Well done! You're an absolute natural!'

Olivia was smiling, but she looked almost embarrassed at how well she'd done when she looked over at them, and then mortified when the commander gave her a solid clap on the back which almost sent her flying. Ava thought she even saw him smile, which wasn't something she'd expected after the way he'd addressed them all earlier. Olivia beating her so convincingly definitely wasn't something she'd seen coming, either, although she was trying her best not to bristle.

Next it was one of the girls in dresses stepping forward, tying her skirt out of the way as she took her turn, which set some of the boys to whistling and clapping. But Ava was less interested in watching the stranger and more interested in finding out exactly how Olivia had managed to drive like that. Before she could open her mouth though, Florence beat her to it.

'I have a feeling one of us may have withheld some vital information today,' Florence said. '*Olivia?*'

Olivia's face turned a dark shade of pink as she faced them, her arms wrapping around her body. 'Honestly, it's been so long since I last rode, I didn't expect it to come back to me so quickly. I think I'm as surprised as anyone at how well I performed.'

'Who taught you to ride?' Ava asked.

'I'd very much like to know the answer, too,' Commander Mac said, walking towards them and clearly having overheard their conversation. 'I have a feeling I've just found my next Theresa Wallach, which means today hasn't been a total waste of time. Bravo young lady. Name?'

'Wren Oliva Blakely.'

He noted her name on his clipboard and walked off to watch the other girl, who was still trying to kick-start the bike, looking as if she was about to cry. When she finally managed it, she accelerated too hard and the front wheel left the ground, which made her promptly burst into tears.

Ava turned back to Olivia. 'Well?'

'I grew up the youngest of four, the only girl in the family,' Olivia explained. 'My oldest brother, Pete, he's the one who taught me. The others would have driven off and left me for the day, but not Pete.' She smiled, and it lit up her entire face. 'He's my favourite, in case that wasn't clear. He always said he wanted me to be able to do everything the boys could do, and motorcycle riding was one of them. My mother hated it, but she didn't have a hope of curtailing my fun, not with Pete taking me under his wing and sneaking me out of the house at every opportunity.'

'So, let me get this straight,' Ava said. 'You grew up riding motorcycles for fun, and yet you didn't think to mention it to us?'

'I didn't want to oversell myself! Or make you think I was bragging when I hadn't ridden in so long.' Olivia sighed. 'Sorry, it seems silly now, but I honestly just wanted you to like me, I suppose, and I didn't want you to think I'd be better than you.'

'Oh, I think we know that you're better than us. It's no contest, at least where I'm concerned!' Florence laughed, and her amusement was contagious because suddenly Ava couldn't stop smiling and Olivia was chuckling, too.

'Florence, stop!' Ava ordered. 'I'm trying to make her feel guilty here!'

'Honestly, I would have liked some pointers from you before I went and made a fool of myself, but . . .' Florence said, shaking her head. 'It was so embarrassing!'

'Sorry,' Olivia murmured. 'Although I don't know how I could have helped. It was as if you were hell-bent on going over that fence *without* the motorcycle if I'm completely honest.'

They all burst into laughter again, and Ava watched as Florence covered her face with her hands, clearly mortified. She would have been too, if it had happened to her – it had been a spectacular dismount, but at least they could laugh about it now.

'Ladies!' The bark caught their attention. Ava immediately stood ramrod-straight and she heard Olivia's quick, shallow breathing beside her as they waited for Commander Mac to address them.

But it was another man who commanded their attention now. They'd been so busy giggling and chatting that they'd completely missed the arrival of someone else.

'He's the one who helped me up earlier,' Florence whispered. 'I don't think he was very impressed that we were even here today.'

'I didn't even notice him,' Olivia murmured.

'Me neither,' Ava said, running her eyes over him and noticing a little scar on his face that ran through his top lip. He didn't smile, and she wondered why he looked so morose. 'Where was he standing? With those Navy boys?'

The girls didn't get a chance to reply before his eyes fell on them.

'Ladies, I'm afraid only three of you have made it through today. If I read your name, please stay and receive your instructions. Those of you who don't hear your name, you may leave and we thank you for your time.'

Ava held her breath as she waited, hearing first Olivia's name, along with a commendation, and then another, before finally hearing *Wren Williamson* fall from his lips. She gave him her most dazzling smile, surprised when she didn't receive a smile in return. It wasn't like he was her type, he was far too plain for her, but she wasn't used to men not finding her attractive.

'Wren Hughes, we see huge potential in your vehicle-driving abilities, so someone will be in touch with you about potential positions, most likely driving an ambulance with the volunteer brigade.

It will be a departure from your current employment as a Wren, and the choice is entirely yours, but we think it's worth considering, given your aptitude. They are desperately seeking competent drivers.'

'Thank you, sir,' Florence said. 'I'm prepared to be wherever the assistance is required.'

Ava glanced away from him to give Florence a quick wave, sad that her new friend was departing, but she was happy to at least have Olivia with her. She was also pleased that Florence had something to look forward to; she'd proven herself to be a spectacular driver, so today hadn't been a complete disaster for her.

'I'm Captain George Robinson, and for the next three weeks, beginning Monday, I'll be coordinating your training,' he said, nodding to the much older commander, who stepped forward and addressed them all again.

'Ladies, if you succeed in your training, you'll be partaking in one of the most dangerous activities in all of London and we need you to be able to ride fearlessly, no matter what the conditions. You must be prepared to risk your life to deliver each memo you're entrusted with.' He paused for a moment. 'I'm now going to leave you in the capable hands of Captain Robinson; however, I'll be keeping a close eye on your individual development. Good luck.'

Ava noticed that he seemed to look at Olivia the entire time he spoke, and she tried not to be jealous. But the truth was, *she* was used to being the one who commanded the attention of a roomful of men without so much as batting an eye. She shook the thought away, refusing to be anything other than happy for her new friend. This was not the time to be jealous.

'Over the course of the coming weeks,' Captain Robinson said, addressing them again, 'you'll be taught how to ride at high speeds and through difficult terrain, how to react fast to changes around you, how to camp out overnight if need be, and also how to maintain your motorcycles. There will be no mechanic waiting to work on your bike at the end of each day, or anyone coming to rescue you if you suddenly break down an hour or more from headquarters. *You* and only you will be expected to maintain and fix your motorcycle as required, to keep her running perfectly so that you're always ready for the next assignment. This is not a job for the faint-hearted, so if you don't think you can do it, then don't bother turning up on Monday.'

Ava glanced down at her nails. She kept them clipped fairly short, but she loved how manicured her hands looked and she cringed at the thought of her skin being stained with grease or her nails caked with grime. Surely she could find someone to do that work for her?

'For the record, I'm not a fan of women being in this role, but we are faced with a desperate shortage of riders. So, for the time being, you lot will have to do.'

Have to do? She bristled at his words, forgetting all about her manicure. Suddenly all she wanted to do was show this smug captain exactly what women were capable of. What was it with all the men in her life thinking women weren't capable of anything!

'You'll be issued uniforms on Monday, but I suggest you wear something appropriate that first morning. If you have trousers in your wardrobe, Monday is the day to wear them. Skirts are not appropriate attire for your training.'

Her parents would have a fit seeing her in trousers, but in all honesty, her father was going to have a fit either way, so perhaps trousers would be the least of her worries. Telling them she'd made it on to the training programme wasn't going to go well, not if her father's threats were anything to go by, so it might be better to simply get changed before training each day. If only she could live away from home, it would make being duplicitous about her work all the more easy. She fisted her hands, trying to push thoughts of her father from her mind. When he became angry, he was unpredictable, and she knew better than to underestimate how angry he'd be if he found out she'd disobeyed him.

'You,' Captain Robinson suddenly said, taking a step towards her.

Ava swallowed, forcing herself to look him in the eye. 'Sir?'

'I suggest wearing something heavy next week if you want to pass the physical during training,' he said. 'We don't generally take applicants of your stature; however, as you can see, it's slim pickings for new recruits, and you didn't embarrass yourself with your ability earlier, so I'm prepared to make an exception.'

'Yes, sir.'

She smiled, hoping it didn't look as false as it felt. Ava didn't need anyone to tell her she was too small; it was something her mother had always praised her for as one might praise the fattest goose ahead of Christmas – as something she should have been immensely proud of. But this past year, all her weight had done was threaten to hold her back from what she wanted to do. She'd barely made it into the WRNS, and heaven forbid she'd wanted to become a pilot – she wouldn't have stood a chance. Even with her bottom padded with cushions she'd never have been tall enough to see out of the cockpit window! It was the first time in her life she'd realised that her looks and her beautifully tailored clothes weren't enough, despite what her mother had always told her.

Captain Robinson slowly looked at each of them in turn, seeming to study them individually. 'Ladies, the memos you'll be delivering are of the utmost importance. I'm going to tell you the same thing I told the men who held these jobs before you, and that you've already heard from Commander Mac.' He cleared his throat, as if the words were difficult to get out. 'You deliver your documents, even if it kills you. You could be tasked with delivering a memo with sensitive information that could change the course of the war, which means that you have to be prepared to risk everything – to do anything within your power – to do your job.'

A shiver ran through Ava that left goose pimples forming across her skin, as she suddenly understood the enormity of what she was signing up for. In the beginning, all she'd seen was the freedom the position would give her, but now she could see that this job was truly her chance to prove how capable she was, to show everyone just how much she could achieve when given the chance.

'One last thing, ladies,' he said. 'You may call me George.'

George? 'Not Captain Robinson?' Ava asked, surprised.

'As far as I'm concerned, you might be Wrens but you're still women, not enlisted servicemen. George will do just fine.'

She watched him walk away, not sure if she liked him or hated him. She settled on the latter; his attitude was deplorable.

'What an arse,' she muttered.

'Ava!' Olivia looked horrified. 'You can't say things like that! Imagine if he'd heard you?'

Ava shrugged. She'd show *George* just how capable women were. She might not have impressed him today like Olivia had, but it was her first time on a motorcycle, so what could he expect? By the end of their three-week training, she was going to be the best damn woman he'd ever trained, and he'd have to take back everything he'd said, or thought, about her.

———— ⁀౦ఌ~ঌ ————

'Mother, please, if you could just listen to me—'

'Ava, no!' her mother cried, slamming her hands down on the table in a very rare show of anger, making the glasses rattle. 'I will not have my daughter risking her life. It's unacceptable. Absolutely *not*!'

'If this war doesn't end, what do you think will happen to us?' Ava asked, her nostrils flaring in anger as she stared at her mother, taking a few steps so she was standing at the other end of the table, her hands braced on the top. 'Do you think we'll be safe just because we're in London? Haven't you heard the news? The Germans occupy Norway, the Netherlands, Belgium and France now! Don't you listen to the wireless? We're next if we don't do everything we can, and it's a frightful lot better than just sitting around waiting for a bomb to fall!'

Tears filled her mother's eyes, but Ava didn't back down. She couldn't. She'd come home expecting to keep everything a secret, but then she'd blurted it out as soon as her mother had questioned her about why she was home earlier than usual.

'You can't keep this a secret from him.'

Ava bit down on her lip, steadying herself before she answered. 'You'd rather he know, so he can kick me out of this house as he threatened?'

Her mother shook her head. 'It's his house, Ava. We follow his rules, you know that.'

'It's *our* house, Mother!' she cried. 'Why does Father get to make up all the rules? Why do we have to follow so blindly? Can we not be trusted to make our own decisions or know our own minds?'

Her mother turned away from her then, leaving Ava to stand alone, her chest rising and falling as she breathed, fighting tears.

'I should have insisted you were married the day you turned eighteen. Perhaps it would have stifled your spirited nature.'

Ava laughed, hurling words at her mother like she never had before. 'Or perhaps you could allow Father to take his belt to me? You never did seem to mind how many times he whipped me as a girl, as if I were a disobedient horse!'

She shut her eyes a moment, wishing she'd held her tongue. She also wished she could pack a suitcase and march straight from the house, but she had nowhere to go. Not yet.

'I'll show them,' she muttered, knowing that her mother would be far too afraid to say anything when her father arrived home. But it was her mother who surprised her, walking silently towards her.

'When do you start?'

'On Monday,' Ava said in a low voice. 'We receive three weeks of training before we start the job. They urgently need us working so that they can send men to dispatch jobs at the front.'

There was silence once more, and Ava stood quietly, waiting for her mother to acknowledge what she'd said, hoping she understood what was at stake.

'And there's nothing I can do to change your mind?'

Ava shook her head. 'No. Nothing will change my mind. I'm doing this with or without your blessing.'

Her mother swallowed – Ava could see the movement in her throat – and then nodded brusquely. 'Very well then.'

Ava shut her eyes for a beat, wanting to squeal in excitement but knowing that the more restrained she was, the better the reaction from her mother.

'Thank you,' she said, kissing her mother's cheek, even though her mother was as stiff as a rod. But before she could step away, her mother caught her wrist, her fingers tight on her skin.

'I won't be the one to tell him, Ava, but if he finds out, there's nothing I can do to protect you.'

Ava swallowed. 'Thank you.'

Her mother dismissed her with a wave of her hand, beginning to fiddle with the table setting, which was already perfect. Ava knew it was her way of coping – that no matter what was going on outside the windows of their house, keeping order made her mother feel as though everything would be fine. So long as everything in her world *looked* perfect, all would *be* perfect, even if her husband might hurl one of her perfectly arranged glasses or plates at the wall in a fit of anger once he was home. Ava's father was like that; he was either the most gregarious, divine man in a room, or he was the most terrifying, and there was no way to know when he walked through a door which version one was going to receive.

Ava walked sedately to her room and quietly shut the door before falling on to her bed and clutching her pillow to her face as she screamed into it, excitement coursing through her. So long as her mother could keep her secret, in a few weeks' time she'd be racing around London on a motorcycle, and nothing had ever sounded so exhilarating in all her life. She also couldn't stop thinking about how many times she might be able to visit the general with her new-found freedom.

One day my father won't even have a say in what I do. She could already see herself at the general's side, her arm slipped through his as he showed off his second, much younger wife. The life she'd always dreamed of was within her grasp, and every time she thought about the general her heart skipped a beat.

She smiled smugly to herself. *What will you say then, Father?*

CHAPTER FIVE

FLORENCE

Florence stood outside the ambulance station, a few minutes early and taking a moment to catch her breath. It wasn't that the walk from the tube to the West End had been that taxing – she could barely catch her breath due to her nervousness. Her attempt to ride a motorcycle had crippled her confidence; she could still hardly believe she'd been so brazen in taking the van and driving it, and she could only hope that she had a better day today than she'd had then.

Heaven help me if I can't impress anyone here with my driving skills.

She glanced at her watch and saw there was only a minute to go before she was due to report for duty, so she squared her shoulders and forced her feet forwards. *You can do this. You're a great driver, they're going to love you.* But Florence knew that it wasn't her driving skills that were troubling her; it was the reality of what she was signing up for. She'd given up her dream of becoming a nurse after her family had perished; she could no longer stomach the idea of seeing pain and death on a daily basis, of having to confront others suffering as her own family had. It was why she'd become a Wren in the first place, because she'd be able to help without *seeing* the war. Something had changed in her, though, when she'd first seen that flyer for the motorcycle riders. She'd realised she had more to give, that she needed to go above and beyond to help the war effort, that what she was doing was no longer enough,. that she couldn't let what had happened to her continue to hold her back. Which was exactly why she needed to be brave and ignore her fears now – London needed as many ambulances on the road as possible, and if she could save even one family from the fate hers had suffered, then it would be worth every painful memory she had to endure.

'Florence?'

She was surprised to hear her name called. She looked up, not seeing anyone, before she noticed legs poking out from beneath an ambulance. The vehicle had been lifted up slightly, and she watched as a man slid out.

'Yes, that's me.' She cleared her throat. 'Reporting for duty.' Florence cringed as she heard the words come out of her mouth – if he knew her name, he certainly knew why she was there!

The man didn't reply as he stood and dusted himself off, and she couldn't help but notice how tall he was. He was broad-shoul-dered too, which made him appear a bear of a man as he took a few steps towards her, his eyebrows drawn together slightly as if he were studying her as much as she was studying him. And he had a pronounced limp, his body hefting to one side each time he took a step.

He held out a hand, and although she noticed the grease embedded into his skin, she didn't hesitate in holding out her own and clasping it. She was worried he was going to crush her fingers, but his shake was surprisingly light, despite her hand being lost in his.

'Jack,' he said. 'You're stuck with me for the next few weeks.'

Florence laughed, stopping herself when she saw he wasn't smil-ing. She clasped her fingers together for something to do, suddenly feeling even more out of her depth than before she'd walked in.

'There's no one else here?' Florence asked as she looked around, surprised by how quiet it was. 'I thought you must be training a group of new recruits, not just me?'

He grunted. 'It's just you. We're going to start today with working on that ambulance over there.' He hooked his thumb at the vehicle he'd been beneath when she'd walked in. 'Once you know how to look after her, then we'll get you out on the road.'

'I don't have to drive first? To prove myself to you?'

Her last question *almost* elicited a smile from him, but it was gone as soon as it appeared. 'We're not exactly being overrun with women volunteering to drive ambulances, although the ATS have recruited a fair few. The job is tough, we're in serious danger whenever we're called out, and it's damn hard work,' he said. 'I've heard you drive like a man, so that's all I need to know. My job is to get you on the tools and train you in mechanics.'

'Right, understood,' she said brusquely, looking around for somewhere to set her bag, and then glancing down at her WRN uniform and wondering what on earth she was going to do to protect it. Jack seemed to be one step ahead of her though, because he disappeared and came back a few minutes later, brandishing a pair of overalls. They looked enormous, but she thanked him and quickly took off her jacket, leaving her skirt on despite it being nearly impossible to put the overalls on over the top. She looked over her shoulder and saw that Jack was politely facing away, and she managed to hitch her skirt up a little higher before doing up the overalls. The legs needed to be folded up and the arms too, and despite it feeling like they would have been a better fit on him than her, she ignored how ridiculous she must look and bravely walked over to him. There was no time to worry about her appearance, not today.

She'd made the decision to volunteer, and she wasn't about to back out now.

'Let's get started then, shall we?'

Jack nodded and led the way. 'This is going to be your ambulance.'

Florence looked at the small van, wondering if it was some sort of a test. The sturdy vehicle had the words *Thackery Family Flowers* printed on the side in a sturdy, easy-to-read font. It wasn't the type of ambulance she'd seen the ATS women driving, but she wasn't about to complain.

'Outside London they're using buses for ambulances now,' Jack said. 'Truth is we're short on vehicles, and the owner of this one offered it to us. I don't think there are any Thackerys here in London to deliver flowers right now.'

She walked along one side, studying it. She supposed it was perfect for an ambulance, with plenty of room to fit patients inside. 'Do we repaint her?' Florence asked. 'Or does she just get a new interior fit-out?'

'Just the interior. No one cares what she looks like, so long as she can do the job.'

Even though it was nothing like the van her father had driven, it still made her feel nostalgic. Just as there were no Thackerys to deliver flowers any more, there were no Hugheses to deliver vegetables, either.

It's why you're here, Flo. Keep that chin up.

She watched Jack as he lifted the bonnet and turned to her. 'You ever changed the oil or checked the water in a vehicle before?' he asked.

She smiled. 'Yes, I have actually. My daddy didn't like his girls to be useless.'

Jack grunted, and she half expected a smile again although it never came. 'Good. I'll show you once where to look, and then you can do both. It's good practice.'

'I haven't done any of this for a while, so I apologise if I'm a little rusty,' she said, nudging her sleeves back up and standing on tiptoe to see what she was looking for. Jack pointed to the oil and then the water, and she took an old cloth he passed her and took out the oil dipstick, happy with the colour of the oil as she wiped the dipstick on the cloth then replaced it.

'The oil is fine,' she said, as much to fill the silence between them than anything. 'Now let's check that water.'

She unscrewed the radiator cap and peered in, turning to Jack when she realised how low it was. She could barely see any.

'Over there,' he said, inclining his head.

Florence looked around until she set eyes on a metal container with a spout, going to inspect it before picking it up. 'Is there a tap outside?'

He nodded and she went out, grateful for a second to herself to catch her breath. She had a feeling this was going to be harder than she'd expected.

Florence only let herself wallow a moment before filling up the container and going back inside, carefully pouring the water in until she was happy with the level.

'Are you an ambulance driver yourself?' she asked.

'No,' Jack replied.

She pursed her lips, wondering how on earth she was going to manage a one-sided conversation. She didn't find talking to people she didn't know difficult, but it helped when the other person gave more than one-word replies, and she didn't fancy spending the morning in silence.

He stretched out his leg then, and she glanced at it, the colour draining from her face as she recalled his limp. *Of course he can't drive an ambulance, you idiot! He has a damaged right leg!*

'So your role is primarily in training new drivers?' she asked, screwing the radiator cap back on.

'Sometimes.'

Oh good Lord, this man is impossible!

She set the water can down and turned to him, hoping she didn't look as flustered as she felt.

'We've been partnered together, for now. You and me,' he said, before gesturing at his leg. 'I can't pass the physical for driving myself.'

And this day is just getting better and better.

She stifled a sigh and forced a bright smile that belied her despair. 'Fantastic. Well, it's good to know who I'll be working with each day.' Gosh, she was going to have to get used to very long periods of silence if they were going to spend hours in a vehicle together.

'Nights,' he said. 'We'll be working nights, six till eight.'

'Right then.'

He dropped to his haunches then, and she noticed the tightening of his mouth when he lowered, the awkward angle he positioned his right leg at as he gestured to the tyre, his big hands steady on the rubber.

'You know how to change a tyre?'

She smiled, but this time it didn't feel forced. The poor man was clearly in pain and had been through some kind of terrible trauma, which meant she needed to perk up and keep the conversation going for both of them.

'I helped my father once, but I wouldn't say I know how to do it,' she replied. 'We were up to our ankles in mud, rain was pelting down and—'

'The less you talk, the faster we'll get through all this.'

Florence bristled. 'Sorry, I was just—'

'The tyre,' Jack said, grunting as he extended his leg out further, shifting his weight again. 'You need to be fast at taking it off and putting the spare on.'

'Righto,' she muttered, blinking away unexpected tears and hoping he hadn't noticed. She was furious at herself for getting emotional, but she couldn't help it, not used to such unfriendliness.

'When you're out at night, with bombs falling, a flat tyre could kill you if you can't change it quickly,' Jack said, his face softening as he looked at her. *So much for him not seeing her tears.* 'The most dangerous place you can be is out of your vehicle at night, so I need to know you can change it faster than anyone else out there. I may not always be with you, and you're the driver, so it'll be your responsibility.'

She nodded. 'Of course.'

'I'm not . . .' Jack made a noise in his throat that sounded half-grunt, half-sigh. He shook his head, as if he were frustrated with himself. 'Look, I used to be better with people.'

Florence quickly wiped at her eyes. 'War changes us. I do understand.'

Jack looked at her as if she couldn't possibly understand, or perhaps that was just him wondering how anyone could ever understand his personal pain – another feeling she knew well. There were so many times she looked at someone and wished they could see the pain inside her, the gaping loss that was almost impossible to live through. Wished they knew what she'd experienced, what the war had taken away from her, so they could understand her suffering.

'The tyre,' she said, trying to sound bright. 'Show me what to do.'

Jack leaned forward and began his demonstration, and as he did so his sleeve slipped back, showing skin that had healed red, the appearance almost twisted – as if the skin were struggling to stretch across the breadth of his forearm. *Burned flesh.* She wondered then what exactly he'd been through, whether he'd survived a fire or been burned while serving, and it was also then she noticed just how handsome he was. If he smiled, if his strong face wasn't marred by such sadness, she could imagine that he'd be the kind of man who could light up a room – the kind of man with a presence perhaps not only due to his size, but to a belly-deep laugh and a wicked grin that stretched his full lips wide.

But when Jack turned back to her, the sadness swimming in his eyes told her that even if he had been that kind of man once, his pain was too deep to ever let him be that man again.

CHAPTER SIX

OLIVIA

'Oh no, they can't be our new uniforms,' Ava cried.

'Shh,' Olivia hissed.

'Is there a problem over here?'

Olivia kept her head down as George walked over to them, watching the ground as his shiny boots came to a halt in front of Ava. Trust Ava to make a fuss.

'Not up to your standards?'

'They look like clothes for men,' Ava huffed. 'I was merely stating how unsuitable they appeared for *women*.'

'They look like they're for men, because they *are* for men,' George said, loudly enough for everyone to hear as he paced back and forth. There were four women gathered, Ava and Olivia, one of the other girls who'd been selected on the same day as them, and another woman who'd been chosen since. 'In case I haven't been clear, the positions you're filling are usually reserved for men, and as such, we are woefully unprepared for your arrival. So yes, these uniforms were made with men in mind, but I can assure you that they are perfectly suitable for motorcycle riders. Are there any more questions?'

Olivia shook her head, not at all concerned about the uniform in the first place. Why did Ava have to complain and draw attention to them? They were riding motorcycles, not working in a fancy office!

'I would like to point out, however, that these are to be your wet-weather uniforms. They are to be worn only in inclement weather, and you will also be fitted with a pair of wellies before you leave today,' George continued, walking back and forth before them. 'On all other occasions you will wear these uniforms,' he said, smiling at a woman who ran over with a folded pile of clothes. 'These will be suitable for riding in and also any mechanical work you find yourself undertaking. And I should add that sturdy leather boots will also be provided, and no other footwear, other than your wet-weather wellies, is ever permitted when riding.'

'Sir, will we be given helmets?' Olivia asked.

'You'll be issued with hats that will form part of your uniform. They have a solid brim at the front to keep the sun from your eyes.'

Ava leaned close to Olivia, her lips whispering against her ear, 'Would it kill him to crack a smile? He's so stern all the time.'

Olivia managed to keep her face straight, determined not to be lumped with Ava in George's bad books, and when he turned back she hoped the warm smile she gave him was convincing. He passed them all their dry-weather uniforms, and she resisted the urge to unfold hers and see how it looked. It turned out she needn't have been curious, as Ava held up the dull trousers and jacket immediately, not saying a word this time but with her eyebrows rising sky-high on her forehead.

'We can alter them,' Olivia whispered when George had his back to them. 'They might not be our Wren uniforms, but we can still make them look good if we cinch the waist.'

'Hmph,' Ava grumbled. 'I doubt *very* much we're going to look good in them.'

Olivia smiled. 'I don't know about you, but I'm here for the motorcycle riding. No, the uniforms aren't as fancy and stylish as our old ones, but how many other women can say they have a job riding *motorcycles*? I'd say that's enough on its own.'

Ava nudged her shoulder into Olivia's then, and Olivia nudged her straight back.

'I suppose you're right.'

'You suppose?' Olivia teased.

'Fine, you *are* right,' Ava whispered. 'But can you let me mourn my old uniform for just a little longer? I shall be hanging it on the back of my bedroom door so I can admire it. I can't help it if I like to look nice.'

George turned back to them then, and they both straightened, standing to attention and staying quiet. He certainly did seem very unimpressed with them all.

'Today you'll be taught how to maintain your own motorcycle,' George said. 'It's crucial that you keep your motorcycle running well, and that you don't find yourselves stranded on the roadside, unable to ride.' He nodded to a couple of men in overalls who'd been standing behind him, and they disappeared for a moment before returning, each pushing a shiny new motorcycle.

'Today is also the day you *receive* your motorcycle,' George said. 'No one else will drive your bike; for all intents and purposes they belong to you, so treat them as if they're your most prized possession.'

Olivia's eyes widened as she stared at one of the mechanics, realising he was coming directly towards her. She stepped forward, taking hold of the handlebars as she looked the motorcycle over. Ava was whispering something but she didn't even hear her; she was suddenly filled with so much pride, so much excitement about what they were doing.

Pete, you'd be so proud of me. I have my own motorcycle! I'm going to be riding it every day, delivering messages all over London! She wasn't certain when she'd see her brother and Leo again, but she couldn't wait. Actually, they'd both be so proud of her; Leo was as supportive of her as Pete was, they'd never told her there was anything she couldn't do, and it made her love them both all the more.

Olivia shut her eyes for a moment, squeezing the handlebars tightly now as she imagined how it would feel to be riding fast, the wind blowing through her hair, that intense feeling of freedom that she'd only ever had when she'd been riding a motorcycle. *The last time I felt like that was when Pete and I raced across the grass and around the apple tree, making our own little race circuit, squealing when he came so close he was able to nudge me with his elbow.*

'Olivia?'

She looked over at Ava.

'Stop drooling over your bike and hurry up.'

She realised everyone was already starting to turn and push their motorcycles to various stations that had been set up in the large workshop, and she hurried to catch up.

Olivia parked her motorcycle where she was told to and took the pair of overalls handed to her by one of the mechanics. She gratefully stepped into them and buttoned them up, laughing to herself about how comical she must look as she rolled the sleeves up to her elbows. And then she caught sight of Ava and couldn't keep her laughter to herself – her tiny friend was drowning in hers, not to mention pouting about the practical work.

'Nothing some good sewing can't fix,' Olivia assured her. 'I'm going to be busy on my sewing machine tonight, that's for sure.'

'You can sew?' Ava asked, looking surprised.

'Of course!' Olivia looked back at her, realising she wasn't joking. 'Can't you?'

'Ah, we usually have someone to do those things for us.'

'I'll do it for you – you can come home with me after training one day,' Olivia said, wondering just what kind of life Ava was used to leading. She'd grown up in a well-to-do type of family, but she'd still been expected to learn how to sew, and her mother was excellent at altering anything that no longer fitted.

'I wonder what Florence is doing right now?'

'Probably up to her elbows in grease, just like we're about to be.'

Before they could talk any further, George left them in the capable hands of the mechanics, and suddenly Olivia's fingers were stained with black grease that she doubted would ever come off her skin, no matter how hard she scrubbed. Although, when she glanced over at Ava, it appeared her friend was already using her charms to get a young mechanic to do the work for her.

Olivia had never felt so energised in all her life. They were training at the New Cross Speedway on Old Kent Road, a week after passing their mechanical course, and it was like nothing she'd ever experienced before.

'Excellent work, Olivia!' George called out.

She beamed, her heart racing as she took off her hat and ran her fingers through her hair, fluffing it off her forehead and the back of her neck to help alleviate how hot she was. Never in her life had she imagined riding at such speeds, but the more she did it, the more comfortable she felt, and even though she knew they wouldn't be riding that fast around the haphazard streets of London, it was reassuring to know what she was capable of.

'Next!'

She parked her bike out of the way and went to watch Ava. They'd developed a friendly kind of rivalry, competing to see who could change oil the fastest in their first week at Camberley, and now in their final week seeing who could beat the clock. But although Olivia liked to win, Ava seemed obsessed by it.

Olivia cringed as Ava appeared to take the first bend too fast, her motorcycle coming dangerously close to losing control, before she managed to correct it, the rear wheel wobbling as she raced even faster. It was terrifying to watch, and she dug her nails into her palm as Ava accelerated again, not seeming to have learned from her first near-miss as she leaned deeply into the bend.

'Christ almighty,' George muttered under his breath, just loud enough for Olivia to hear. She pretended not to, keeping her body angled slightly away from him as she grimaced, continuing to watch her friend.

When she finally finished, Ava let out a whoop as she pulled up beside them, seeming to miss the scowl on George's face.

'Time?' she asked, eagerly glancing at his stopwatch. 'Did I beat her?'

'One minute, fifteen seconds,' he said.

Ava's eyes flashed with what Olivia could only guess was pride, but she simply shook her head in return. Ava could have the win – she wasn't even going to try to compete with that speed.

'May I ask you something, Ava?' George's voice was surprisingly low.

Ava grinned, her eyebrows raised. 'You want to know my secrets for beating everyone?'

'I'd actually like to know whether or not you have a death wish.'

Olivia had to give her credit; Ava's smile never faltered, the brightness in her eyes barely betraying her surprise at his words – if she was surprised at all.

'I most certainly do not.'

'Overconfidence will get you killed in this job,' George said, moving closer to them, his eyes narrowing as he stared at Ava, before he glanced at Oliva and then the other two girls, who had walked closer as soon as Ava had finished her laps. 'I don't know if it's because you're used to everything coming easy to you in life.' He raised his voice, seemingly so they could all hear him even though he was speaking to Ava. 'Or perhaps you're just here for the adventure and think of this as a lark? Whatever it is, you need to keep your enthusiasm in check if you want to survive this job. It's dangerous enough without the reckless attitude.'

Olivia watched as Ava swallowed, the physical flutter in her throat the only thing that betrayed her otherwise confident demeanour, and then she saw a tear escape from the corner of her friend's eye. She hated seeing her upset, but George did have a point; this was serious work, not a game. Before Ava could reply, George stepped back to address them all.

'Girls, as of next week you'll all be reporting for your first shift,' he said. 'The hours are going to be long and you're expected to be available seven days a week, day and night. As I've said before, it's not a job for the faint-hearted.' He paused a moment. 'We're also looking to send some of our riders to Scotland in the coming weeks, so please let me know if you're open to being stationed there. If no one volunteers, we shall be making the orders based on suitability.'

'Will we have set shifts?' Olivia asked, realising she'd never actually asked before, and they hadn't been told. She didn't tell him that she absolutely did not want to be posted to Scotland, hoping someone else volunteered instead.

'Ideally, yes. But there will also be times where you're called in outside of those shifts. We're still desperately in need of more dispatch riders – our male riders are all being sent to the front over the next two weeks – so for now, the hours will be arduous at best.'

'You'll be recruiting more women?' Ava asked. 'Despite your obvious disdain for the fairer sex riding motorcycles?'

He laughed, and just the sight of him showing a sense of humour made Olivia smile. Or perhaps she liked the quip her friend had made, despite how bristly she must be feeling from his earlier rebuke.

'I actually have no problem with women riding motorcycles in their spare time,' George said. 'What I have a problem with is women serving and taking up dangerous roles that should only be filled by men, thereby putting their lives at unnecessary risk. What women choose to do in their leisure time is not for me to form an opinion on.'

Olivia touched Ava's back, hoping to calm her so she'd refrain from saying anything else inflammatory to George. She'd never seen two people rile each other up so much, and she was half expecting Ava to be fired before she even started on the job. George clearly disliked her.

'Are we clear?' George asked.

Olivia prodded her thumb into Ava's back, trying to prompt her into answering.

'Yes, sir, we're clear.'

When he finally walked away, consulting his clipboard and appearing to make some notes, Olivia steered Ava well away from him.

'What is it with you today?' Olivia asked, but what she really meant was *what is it with you every day?*

'He infuriates me, that's what,' Ava muttered.

'Oh, I can see that for myself!' she half laughed, half cried. Olivia was always a bundle of nerves just watching them spar from the sidelines, so she wasn't surprised when Ava started to pace back and forth.

'Don't you find him infuriating?' Ava asked. 'It can't just be me! He's an absolute beast.'

'Mildly irritating? Yes,' Olivia said. 'But not infuriating. I mean, some of his comments about our suitability for the job annoy me, but other than that I find him fair to learn from. He's been a good instructor to us.'

Ava's eyebrows shot up. '*Fair?* You actually find what he said to me *fair?*'

Olivia sighed. She could already tell this conversation wasn't going to end well, but it was about time someone stood up to Ava. 'You want me to answer that honestly?'

'Of course!' Ava folded her arms over her chest, looking defiant as she stared at her.

'I actually agree with him about what he said before. I think you are being reckless, I think you do need to pull your head in and listen to his instructions, because he's right. That overconfidence of yours could get you killed out there on the job, and this isn't a game. What we're doing is going to be dangerous and important work.'

Ava's bottom jaw went slack. 'You *agree* with him?'

'All I'm saying is that when it comes to safety, I think you should listen to him. If his goal is to keep us alive, then don't you think he might have a point?'

Ava stared at her a moment, a very long moment, before turning on her heel and marching off. When Olivia called out to her, she turned and glared at her, her face like thunder.

Olivia almost laughed, but it only took a moment for her humour to turn to anger. Perhaps being honest with her hadn't been the best course of action.

'Ava!' Olivia shouted, running after her and grabbing hold of her shoulder to force her to stop.

Ava spun around, her eyes flaring wide as she glared at her. 'What?'

'Don't you dare storm off on me like that again,' Olivia said, hands on her hips as she stared her down. 'Who exactly do you think you are? Treating a friend like that?'

Ava's mouth kicked up at the corners into a grin, but her smile quickly fell away when she saw how cross Olivia was. 'Sorry. It felt good at the time.'

'You're infuriating, you know that?' *How has she gotten away with behaving like such a child all her life!*

'So I'm told.'

Ava suddenly threw her arms around her and gave her a hug, which Olivia reluctantly returned. She was easy to be cross with, but somehow impossible not to love at the same time.

'I care about you, that's all. And I don't want you to be reckless and get yourself killed,' Olivia murmured. 'I want to see you taking this seriously.'

'Apology accepted,' Ava said, hugging her again.

Olivia pulled away. 'I wasn't apologising!'

Ava ran the last few steps back to her motorcycle, leaping on to the seat and expertly kicking it into life, sending fumes billowing into the air. 'Last one back to base is a rotten egg!'

Olivia wanted so badly not to take the bait, but as Ava accelerated off in a cloud of dust, she found herself getting caught up in the chase and revving her own engine, driving fast to catch up with her, although she did feel slightly guilty as she sped past the volunteer fire service women, who were making their way to the speedway on their second-hand, rusty-looking motorcycles that couldn't have been more different from the brand-new bikes the Wrens had been given.

Olivia flashed them a smile, knowing they'd probably think she and Ava were terrible show-offs.

It wasn't often she broke the rules, but Ava was right about one thing: going fast did make a girl feel kind of invincible, and right now, that was exactly the sort of feeling she needed.

'Flo!' Olivia cried as she saw Florence sitting at the bar, alone, though there was a man nearby clearly trying to catch her eye.

'Girls!' Flo's arms were wide as they approached her, all hugging and kissing cheeks after not seeing one another since before their training had begun almost a month ago.

'How did it all go? Are you a fully fledged ambulance driver now?' Olivia asked.

'Apparently, although all the other drivers said that I had to give my ambulance a name before it was official,' Flo said. 'I've been trying to think of something for days, but nothing sounds quite right.'

'Well, you could always call her Ava.'

They all laughed, including Ava as she shrugged and smiled, leaning across the bar and getting the bartender's attention. She ordered champagne, and before Olivia could protest Ava was sliding cash across the bar, not seeming to care about the high price tag.

'And you two?' Flo asked. 'I heard you're being called the Flying Wrens now?'

Olivia saw how Flo's face fell a little, and she resisted the urge to reach out a hand, wondering if she was still upset that she'd had to give up her WRN uniform to become a volunteer driver. But bless her, her smile barely wavered as she studied them.

'Apparently we go so fast we may as well be flying,' Olivia said. 'Although whoever came up with the title may have just seen Ava at the speedway. The rest of us travel at a more sedate pace.'

Ava snorted with laughter as she passed them their glasses of champagne, holding hers high and then gently clinking her glass against first Olivia's and then Flo's.

'To us,' Ava announced.

'To us,' Olivia repeated, chiming in at the exact same time as Florence.

'So, any ideas on what I can call her?' Flo asked. 'My ambulance?'

'Gertrude? Matilda?' Olivia suggested.

'Betsy?' Ava said. 'Ooh, what about Wendy?'

'She was a flower delivery van in her former life, would you believe? And now instead of brightly coloured petals being sent to brighten someone's day, she's being used to save lives.'

'How about Rose then?' Olivia said. 'Or Petal?'

'Petal!' Flo grinned. 'Thanks, Olivia, that's perfect.'

Olivia beamed, happy to have helped.

'So, tell me about your training. How did it go? When do you start work?' Flo asked.

'We start Monday, and the hours sound horrific,' Ava said. 'By the way, can you sew?'

'Sew? Why?' Flo asked.

'Our uniforms are terrible,' Olivia told her. 'I've already done some work on mine, but *someone* doesn't know how to sew. I haven't had time to do hers yet.'

'I'm all right at it, but my grandmother is the best, she'll help you. She made all my dresses for me as a child, and she even made my mother's wedding dress.' Florence's voice faded as she looked away, and Olivia spoke up, not sure what had made Flo go so quiet but wanting to take the focus off her.

'So this one here,' she said, dipping her head towards Ava. 'She's lucky to even be riding next week. She's managed to find herself on the wrong side of our captain. You know, the man who helped you when you fell off the motorcycle?'

As Ava protested loudly, Flo covered her face with her hand. 'Don't remind me about that day!'

'Come on, Ava, you must know how much you've infuriated him. I thought he was going to fire you before you even began!'

Flo giggled as Ava rolled her eyes. 'Don't be ridiculous. Someone has to keep him on his toes. And as far as him getting upset that I'm not doing my own mechanical work, I just don't see what the problem is! If I can talk someone else into doing something for me, why would I bother doing it myself?'

Olivia looked over at Florence in despair, which only made Flo laugh all the more as Ava continued to appear the picture of innocence.

'You know what?' Ava said, grinning as she expertly changed the subject. 'If you're going to name your ambulance, Flo, I'm going to do something to my bike. What do you think about a pink ribbon around one of the handlebars? Something to mark it as mine?'

'I think George will have something to say about that,' Olivia said. 'I wouldn't poke the bear any more than you already have if I were you.'

'Well, luckily you're *not* me, and honestly, George is the least of my worries right now,' Ava said with a sigh. 'My father told me he'd kick me out if I insisted on becoming a dispatch rider, and I don't particularly want to call his bluff. I'm not going to tell him, but the hours are going to make keeping it a secret a little bit difficult.'

'Do you want me to let you know if I hear of anyone with a spare room closer to headquarters? I can't say my parents are very happy about it all either, but it helps that they're not in the city. What they don't know won't hurt them, right?' Olivia said. 'To be honest, I don't think my father would care all that much if he didn't have to console my mother so often. She was hysterical when I told her what I was doing!'

'How about you, Flo?' Ava asked. 'What do your parents think about you driving an ambulance? You never did say.'

Flo went deathly pale again and Olivia cringed, wishing Ava had read the situation better. She clearly hadn't noticed the way

Flo had frozen before when she'd spoken about her mother and grandmother.

'Ah, well . . .' Olivia watched as Flo took a sip of her champagne, her hand shaking as she lifted it to her lips.

'Don't tell me, they're the complete opposite of mine and think it's fabulous!' Ava grinned and held up her glass to clink them all together again. 'Argh, you lucky thing.'

But Olivia kept her glass close to her body instead of joining in, watching the way Flo's shoulders inclined slightly, the tremble of her bottom lip as she looked up at Ava.

'I actually lost my parents earlier this year,' Flo said quietly.

Ava's smile dropped from her lips as Olivia glanced at her and then scooted around the table to be closer to Flo, reaching for her hand.

'I'm so sorry,' Olivia said. 'If I'd known I would never have talked about my own family so frivolously, I—'

'Don't be silly,' Flo said, dabbing at the corner of her eye with her free hand, her glass now set on the table. 'I don't ever want you to stop talking about your families because of me. I love hearing all the banter, it's what I miss the most about not having them.'

'What happened?' Ava asked, her voice softer than Olivia had ever heard it before.

'A bomb hit just near our house,' Flo said, as Olivia squeezed her fingers. 'We lived near a railway line that was targeted by the Luftwaffe, but they missed their target and hit the homes in our neighbourhood instead. I honestly don't remember much of it, other than hearing the sirens go off and hurrying to reach our shelter. And then I was waking up in a hospital with my head bandaged, and being told that my family . . .' Florence paused, and Olivia listened to her take a deep, shuddering breath. 'That my mother, father and sister had all perished. Somehow, I'd been dragged to safety, but none of them had made it.'

Olivia blinked away the tears in her eyes as she saw the pain in Florence's face. 'I'm so sorry. I don't even know what to say.'

'So you don't have *any*one?' Ava asked, her voice cracking as she too wiped at her eyes.

'My grandma,' Florence said, a faint smile touching her lips. 'She's everything to me. I moved to her house here in London as soon as I left hospital, and she's just amazing. Despite everything she refuses to wallow in grief, and I honestly don't know how I would have survived all this without her.'

Olivia and Ava looked at one another. What did you say to someone who'd lost everything? Olivia smiled at Florence, reaching for her hand again, holding her fingers tight.

'Flo, I wish I had the words, but . . .' Olivia sighed, hating that her eyes were filling with fresh tears when she was trying so hard to be strong. It was Flo who should be crying, not her, but somehow it was Florence who was maintaining her composure.

'You don't need to say anything,' Flo said, her smile bright. 'I'm just pleased I've told you, because when everyone talks about their families it's . . .' Her voice quavered. 'It's just easier when people know, that's all.'

'Well, I hope that one day you come to think of us as your family,' Ava said, and Olivia gave her a grateful look, thankful that one of them had managed to say the right thing. 'I want you to know that I'm here for you, whenever you need anything, even if it's just a shoulder to cry on.'

'Thank you,' Florence said. 'Honestly, I'm so thankful I've met you both. It's reminded me of what life felt like before the war. Before everything fell apart.'

They all sat, blinking away tears as Florence held out her other hand to Ava, and Ava in turn held her other hand out to Olivia. She wondered what anyone watching them would think, as they smiled through their tears, each taking strength from one another.

'We're going to make a difference,' Olivia said. 'We're going to help end this war with the work we're doing.'

'One motorcycle at a time,' Ava said, grinning.

'Hey, don't forget about Petal!' Florence said.

'To Petal!' Ava cried, letting go of them and raising her glass.

They all laughed, echoing Ava's toast.

'Actually, how about to us?' Ava said. 'To the London Girls.'

'To the London Girls!' Olivia and Florence both said at the same time, clinking glasses as a waiter hesitantly approached them.

'Ah, ladies, will you be ordering dinner?'

'What do you recommend?' Olivia asked.

'Unfortunately, our menu isn't as extensive as it once was, and the only item we have in oversupply each night is the Woolton pie.'

'Absolutely not,' Olivia made a face as she shook her head at him. 'I'd rather starve! I've eaten that enough at home.'

'We do have meatloaf with mashed potato, which is one of our most popular meals, but you'll want to order soon before it runs out.'

'What? No fillet steak?' Ava asked, in such a posh voice that Olivia had to put her hand over her mouth to hide her smile. 'Or lamb chops? Gosh, what I wouldn't do for a big juicy roast leg of lamb.'

'Anything would be better than fried spam,' Florence groaned. 'I feel like my grandmother has become obsessed with the stuff. She's actually convinced herself she can make it taste different if she cooks it in different ways.'

'The meatloaf it is then, for all of us,' Olivia said, smiling at the waiter. 'I'm sure it'll be delicious.' She hated to think what meat they might be using, but if it was tasty and covered in a nice sauce, she'd be happy.

She nursed her glass of champagne as she listened to Ava and Florence talk about all the food they missed, and what they wouldn't give for white flour, and a hearty plate of bacon and eggs.

'What about you, Livvy? What do you miss about before?'

A shiver ran down her spine when Ava called her Livvy. Her fiancé, Leo, was the only other person in the world who'd ever called her that, and strangely enough he was also the exact thing she was missing, although she wasn't going to admit that to the girls.

'Eggs,' she said. 'And sugar. I've a real sweet tooth so I can't wait to bake again.'

'Oh, sugar! How I would love sweet baking again!' Ava moaned.

'I lied,' Olivia said, changing her mind about opening up to them. 'I actually couldn't care less about eggs, I just want my fiancé to come home. I miss him so much, him and my brother.'

'Tell us about him,' Florence said, leaning forward. 'What's he like?'

Olivia sat back in her chair, seeing Leo in her mind from the day he'd left, his hat under his arm as he'd dramatically blown her kisses from the steps of the train, managing to make her laugh when all she'd wanted to do was cry.

'Leo's the man who can entertain everyone at a party with hilarious stories. He could arrive late and instead of everyone being cross with him for making them wait, he'd immediately light up the room,' she said. 'I miss dancing with him and getting home one minute before curfew, and sneaking out of my bedroom window late at night when he'd throw pebbles against the glass to wake me. He made life so much fun.'

'I think I need a Leo in my life,' Florence said with a sigh. 'I was just starting my nursing training before the war, and I expected to nurse for a few years and then meet a handsome doctor to marry.'

'You were nursing?' Ava asked.

'I was. But after what happened to my family, I just couldn't carry on with it.'

'I was training to be a teacher,' Olivia told them. 'Now I'd just be happy for Leo to come home so we can get married. All I've ever wanted was to have a family of my own.'

She and Florence both looked at Ava then.

'How about you, Ava?' Olivia asked.

'Honestly, I'd never thought about a career. I expected to find some dashing man to save me from my father, or go travelling around Europe, but the war began just after my debutante ball which ruined everything for me.'

Olivia watched Ava as she drained her glass of champagne.

'But none of that matters now, does it? Besides, you're not the only one with a man.'

Olivia almost choked on her drink. 'Please tell us that this is someone new and not your married man?'

Ava's smile was wicked as Florence's mouth hung open.

Olivia's heart sank for her friend. 'What about his wife?'

Ava shrugged. 'He's chosen me,' she said. 'He loves me.'

'You're going to get your heart broken, Ava, not to mention you'll break his wife's heart in the process if she finds out. Surely you can meet some gorgeous single man – look at you!'

Ava gave her the same defiant look she'd seen her give George at training. 'Not that it's any of your business, but he's going to leave his wife for me. He's barely seen her in months; she's living with family in the country. It's already over as far as he's concerned.'

Florence looked rather pale, and Olivia knew she needed to change the subject. She certainly didn't approve of Ava's behaviour, but what more could she say?

'And you trust him?' Florence asked. 'That he's going to end his marriage for you?'

'Of course I trust him!'

'Just be careful. I don't want to see you get hurt,' Olivia said.

'I'm a big girl,' Ava said dismissively. 'I'll be just fine.'

Olivia wasn't so certain Ava was going to be fine, but she knew it wasn't her place to say anything more, and as a band started to play, she closed her eyes for a second and wondered where Leo might be. It had been a month since his last letter, and she missed him terribly. *Don't you forget to come home to me, Leo. I've so much to tell you, and I can't wait for you to see me on a motorcycle. I'd give anything to see the look on that handsome face of yours when you come home!*

CHAPTER SEVEN

Ava

'Absolutely not!' George folded his arms across his chest. 'Take it off immediately.'

Ava smarted at his order, folding her own arms as she stood in front of him, not liking the way he was speaking to her. She had half a mind to ask him what his problem was.

'What's wrong with a little pink ribbon?' she asked. 'I just want to be able to glance over and recognise my bike. I don't see why you're so upset. Besides, it might even give me luck.'

'This is a Navy-issued dispatch motorcycle, not a little girl's toy,' he said. 'Your disobedience is unacceptable.'

'I'm sorry, but you've gone to great lengths to tell us that we're not real Navy personnel, hence your decision for us to call you George, and now—'

'You're treading a very fine line, Ava,' George muttered. 'I'm warning you, there's only so long I'll put up with your insolence. Our lack of dispatch riders doesn't mean I won't fire you.'

'Sir,' she said, trying not to smirk. '*George*, I mean. I only wanted to make it feel like mine. My intention wasn't to upset you, quite the opposite in fact. Perhaps if you just let me have it today, so as not to jinx this ride? I put it there for good luck and I can be quite superstitious.'

He threw his hands up in the air and muttered something she didn't hear, but Ava just continued to stand there and smile, eventually holding out her hand.

'Do you have my first message for me to deliver?' she asked sweetly.

George seemed to forget all about the pink ribbon then, picking up a satchel and walking closer to her. She stood still as he lifted it and put the strap over her head and on to her shoulder, the satchel fitting snugly to her body.

'You're to deliver this to the Naval Commander-in-Chief at the shipyards at Devonport, in Plymouth,' he said. 'This is a route you'll likely do often if you're successful. It's an important strategic outpost for us, so there are often messages to be ferried back and forth, but it's challenging because of the two-hundred-mile distance. The final stretch to Plymouth will see you cross peaty marsh that's often difficult to navigate, although I'm certain you've studied that on your map.'

She nodded. 'Understood.' Ava turned on her heel, trying to hide her smile from George, excited at the prospect of being given one of the toughest routes. *I'm really doing this! I'm actually going out on a motorcycle to deliver a message today!*

'Ava.' George said her name like a command.

She turned and looked back at him.

'Be careful. I want you back in one piece,' he said. 'If you need to camp out, then do it, but hopefully you'll be back in less than ten hours.'

That was when her excitement turned to nerves, seeing the worry etched on his face and facing the reality of how long it would take. This was a man who'd served at the front lines and was sending dispatch riders out every day, and the fact that he was worried about her told her just how dangerous he must think the trip was.

But she didn't for a second want him to see her sudden onset of nerves.

'*George*,' she said, flashing him a smile and wondering why he always seemed to be so grouchy. 'I'd almost think you were worried about me.'

He made a noise in his throat and waved her away. 'Just be careful. This is a big ride for you, but I have no one else on hand to do the job.'

Ava knew what everyone thought of her: that she was some sort of daredevil with a death wish. The truth was she did want to be the fastest – she had a growing desire to be the best damn rider out there, in actual fact – but she most certainly didn't want to die.

Just as she was sitting astride her motorcycle, she heard the familiar growl of an engine and looked up to see Olivia returning. Her face was flushed, and she pulled up right beside Ava. They'd been put on different shifts, so she hadn't expected to see her.

'What was it like out there?' Ava called over the noise of the engine.

'Exhilarating,' Olivia said, turning off her engine and taking her hat off. Her hair was flat and damp, and she shook it out as Ava watched. 'It was only a short trip though. Where are you headed?'

'Plymouth,' Ava said. 'It's going to be a long ride.'

'Get going now,' Olivia said as she stood. 'You want to get as much of the trip done before dark as you can.'

Ava nodded. She hadn't thought about the dark, other than sneaking around to her general's house under the cover of it, but she was prepared. But she knew the roads well; she'd studied the maps all weekend and she had a good feel for where she was going. Nothing was going to be easy about navigating the roads home come nightfall, and she didn't want to have to camp out unless she truly had no other option. She had a thermos of tea with her in case she needed it, as well as a sandwich her mother had given her that morning, but it wasn't a lot if she needed to stay the night. She sighed. So much for thinking she'd have plenty of time to see him at night once she took this job!

George appeared again then, smiling when he saw Olivia, and Ava gave them both a quick wave before turning her motorcycle around and heading out of the yard and on to the street. Her canvas satchel sat comfortably across her body, reminding her of the importance of her work, and she sat tall as she accelerated, determined to get to Plymouth as quickly as she could. She'd show George and everyone else who doubted her exactly what she was capable of.

—— ❧❧ ——

Ava's hands were sweating inside the leather gloves as she finally turned into the shipyards, the final stretch across the peaty marsh and granite uplands every bit as gruelling as George had warned her. Her back was sore from almost six hours straight sitting on the motorcycle, her head thumping from the stress of navigating her way. It should have taken her perhaps five hours, but she'd had to keep stopping to look at her map, and what she'd thought would be easy had suddenly seemed like the hardest job in the world. It was definitely harder than she'd expected, but she'd done it, and it was the very first time in her life that she'd felt such pride in herself.

She pulled up outside the gate just as the light was fading, and nodded to a man dressed in Navy uniform, standing outside the locked gate. In the past, she'd only ever commanded attention for her looks, and the feeling of holding such an important document, of being entrusted with something so crucial, sent a thrill of excitement down her spine.

'Name and purpose of your visit?' he called out, his hand resting on the gun slung across his shoulder, which made her unusually nervous. Who, exactly, did he think she could be?

'Ava Williamson,' she replied haughtily. 'I'm here to deliver a memo to the Commander-in-Chief.' She turned off her engine and patted the canvas satchel.

'You're the dispatch rider?' the young soldier laughed. 'You look different from the last one.'

'Well, thank goodness for that!' Ava rolled her eyes as she took the memo from the satchel and passed it to him. 'I'll need a receipt of delivery, and hurry, it's time-sensitive.'

The soldier reached for it, and as he left to get her a signature she stretched her arms out, trying to iron out the kinks in her back. She couldn't believe she had to turn around and go all the way back again; suddenly camping didn't seem like the worst option, although she hadn't exactly paid close attention to the lessons on sleeping rough.

'Should I be offering you a cup of tea or something?' the young man said when he returned, passing her the signed slip of paper.

She shrugged. 'Did the last delivery rider get tea?'

The soldier's face went a bright shade of red. 'Ah, no ma'am. But he wasn't a . . . a . . .'

'Woman?' Ava finished for him. 'I'm just teasing you. I'm fine, I have my own with me, but thank you for asking.'

'It's mighty dangerous on the roads at night, are you certain—'

'I'm fine,' she assured him, even as her hands started to become clammy again as she removed her gloves, her nerves making her sweat. Nerves were most definitely not something she was used to. 'But thank you for your concern.'

He gave her a quick nod, and after she'd poured herself a small cup of tea and eaten half her sandwich, she said goodbye and fired up the engine again, heading straight back to the road and praying she remembered the way. The motorcycle that had been so fun and easy to ride on the speedway was quite a different beast on the road for hours at a time, and after another fifteen minutes or so she felt like her teeth were rattling in her jaw, her fatigue building from having to navigate the roads in the fading light. When her eyes started to fail her, she was forced to slow down and then eventually she turned on her headlamp. Ava stayed focused, listening hard for the sound of approaching vehicles or planes overhead. George had made it very clear to them that the most dangerous moments were when they were stationary or riding in the dark, because it would be so easy for a lorry or even a car to hit them. Thanks to the blackout, they were encouraged to use their lights as little as possible, which made their job even more dangerous.

Ava was terrified of keeping the headlamp on for too long, but when she turned it off, she found it almost impossible to see and quickly turned it back on again. Her heart was racing as she accelerated, going nowhere near the seventy miles per hour the bike was capable of.

You can do this. You know this road, you've already travelled down it. You just need to make it home.

But within seconds of her turning her light back on, a boom sounded out like the loudest crack of thunder she'd ever heard. Ava glanced over her shoulder, fighting against the bike when it wobbled, and her breath caught in her throat as she saw what looked like a white cloud lifting towards the sky. She'd never been so terrified in her life.

We're being bombed. And I'm out in the open!

Ava knew then that she couldn't use the light at all; it would make her a target and put not only her but anything around her in danger. She jumped as there was another boom, but she didn't dare turn and look again. All she needed to focus on was getting back in one piece.

It was over eight hours later when Ava finally pulled back into the yard and parked her motorcycle in the workshop, and it was everything she could do to keep her composure when she saw George. The emotion of being safe and seeing a familiar face almost made her fall to pieces, despite how proud she was of what she'd achieved.

'I was expecting you back hours ago,' George said. 'What happened out there?'

She got off the motorcycle and her legs almost collapsed beneath her. If it hadn't been for George grabbing hold of her arm, she was certain she would have ended up on the ground, but she quickly righted herself and pulled away from him anyway.

'I'm fine, sorry,' she muttered. 'It was a long ride, that's all.'

'It's been one hell of a night,' George said, looking her up and down as if to convince himself she was actually still in one piece. 'I hate having riders out there when bombs are falling.'

'I'm fine,' she repeated, as much for herself as for him, gritting her teeth, not wanting him to see that she was anything other than fine. She glanced up at the light bulb hanging inside the building, trying to stop herself from crying as she stared at it. The last thing she wanted was for him to see how rattled she was, and she hadn't even expected him to still be there. Did the man never go home?

'The first time's always the hardest,' he said. 'How about I pour us a drink? It might help your nerves. Plymouth is a long ride for even our most experienced riders, so I'm sorry that had to be your first one.'

She nodded, following him on legs that felt ridiculously unsteady, her heart still pounding from the sheer adrenaline of her ride back.

'How many bombs?' she asked as they stood in George's office. He poured two nips of brandy into a glass and passed it to her, and she gratefully lifted it to her lips and took a small sip. It burned her throat and made her eyes water, but he was right, it did help her nerves. Or at least it seemed to numb them.

'A few,' he said, pouring another nip for each of them and drinking his down fast. 'We haven't had one for a bit though, so you'll be safe to head home soon. Once you've checked your tyres, oil and fuel.'

'I might wait until tomorrow,' she said with a yawn. 'It's been a long night.'

'No, you'll do it now,' he insisted. 'It's protocol. If an urgent memo comes in at the start of your shift tomorrow, you won't have time to go through your checks, and it's also a good way to decompress.'

Ava nodded, not having the strength to argue with him. She was only thankful she hadn't made plans to visit the general; she was exhausted and no doubt looked a mess.

'Would you like me to take you home, since it's still dark? Your parents must be quite worried about the hours you have to keep.'

Ava took another sip of her drink as she stood. 'I'll be fine, but thank you for your concern.' She cleared her throat. 'Actually, my father doesn't know; he didn't approve when I told him I'd be applying, so it's a matter of my sneaking back in tonight.'

'Well, perhaps I underestimated you,' George said with a chuckle. 'Good luck in keeping the secret.'

'Thanks.'

The truth was, she was terrified of making her way home alone, but she wasn't about to accept George's help. She studied him a moment while he shuffled some papers on his desk. She supposed he wasn't entirely unattractive, and when he wasn't yelling at her or telling them why women shouldn't be riding, he wasn't half bad.

She made her way over to her motorcycle, reluctantly crouching to run her hands over the tyres, her fingers brushing against the grooved rubber as she methodically inspected them. It was surprisingly therapeutic doing so, she'd give George that, and she found her heart rate decreasing as she worked, the tightness in her shoulders slowly disappearing.

'Oh, and Ava?' She looked up at George. 'You can keep the ribbon. I wouldn't want to give you bad luck after such a successful first night on the job.'

If she hadn't been so shaken up, she'd have laughed. But instead, she finished what she was doing, before beginning the long walk home as the sun slowly rose in the sky.

———— ⟋⟍⟋⟍ ————

'What are you still doing up?'

Ava walked into the kitchen an hour later, surprised to see a lamp on and even more surprised to see her mother sitting at the table. She had a book beside her, the spine splayed from being left open on a page, but her head drooped like she'd fallen asleep. She didn't remember her mother ever waiting up for her before, not even when she'd been out late at a party.

The moment she heard her daughter's voice though, her eyes opened and her head jolted back. 'Ava! I was sitting up waiting for you and then—'

'You fell asleep.' She smiled, despite how weary she was, crossing the room and slumping into one of the chairs. When she'd confided in her mother that she was going ahead with the dispatch job, a part of her had wondered if her mother would actually keep her secret. But so far, she'd kept to her word. 'You didn't need to stay up for me.'

Her mother rubbed her eyes before standing. 'Tea?'

Ava nodded. 'Yes please.' She wanted to drag herself to bed and sleep for a solid ten hours, but instead she sat across from her mother, too tired to move. The brandy she'd shared with George earlier hadn't done anything to alleviate her pounding headache.

'Have you eaten?'

Ava's stomach growled in response. 'Not for hours.'

She watched as her mother set the water to boiling and scooped two spoons of tea into the pot. Before the war, it had always been one scoop for each person and one for the pot, but they'd long since done away with that tradition. Ava smiled to herself as she watched her mother uncover a plate that had been sitting beside the cooker – the teapot wasn't the only thing that had changed. Before the war her mother had barely done anything domestic herself, but now they only had one woman who came in for a few hours each day, which meant her mother was having to learn to be a housewife all over again.

'I'd almost convinced myself that you weren't going to survive the night, Ava. We were down in the shelter as soon as the sirens started, but your father was fed up and came back inside after a few hours, and eventually I followed. He presumed you were working late at Norfolk House.'

She nodded. Trust her father – he didn't like being told what to do and he certainly didn't like being in a shelter. He'd had their small garden ripped up in order to build a shelter big enough for the three of them, which saved her mother from having to go to the closest tube station in an air raid.

Her mother set a steaming cup of tea and a piece of pie in front of her. 'I saved this from supper, sorry it's cold.'

Ava couldn't have cared less that it was cold – she was starving and grateful for anything – but when she picked up her fork, she suddenly couldn't take a mouthful and her hand began to shake.

'Ava? Is everything all right? I can warm it up, if it's not—'

Ava couldn't help it; she was trying so hard to hold it all in, but with her mother being so kind and the simple act of sitting safely at the table after the night she'd had, after the ordeal she'd been through . . . Tears slid down her cheeks then, big fat plops that fell straight on to her plate. She wasn't used to such kindness from anyone, let alone in her own home.

'I thought I was going to die tonight,' she whispered. 'I was so scared.'

Her mother's hand flew to her mouth and Ava immediately wished she hadn't said anything, although now she'd started, she couldn't stop.

'It was awful. I was so excited about it all at the start of my shift – it all seemed like such an adventure – but it was, it was . . .' A sob escaped from between her lips. 'It was *horrible*. It was so dark and I couldn't see anything, and when they said we had to deliver those memos even if it killed us, I—'

'Who said that!' her mother gasped. 'Ava, that's awful! You can't keep doing this!'

Ava cringed. She'd gone too far, she shouldn't have said it, but the enormity of what she'd signed up for, the reality of her new job . . . everything just seemed to be tumbling from her lips whether she wanted it to or not.

'I'm fine,' she said, taking a deep, shaky breath. 'Honestly, I'll be fine, it was just so different from what I expected. It seemed so exciting when we were training, but when there was no light left and I was in the dark, when the bombs started falling, I . . .' She sighed. 'I'll be fine.' It was almost as if she had to keep repeating the words to convince herself as much as her mother. Why was she even telling her all these things? 'If it hadn't been such a long trip, it wouldn't have been so terrifying.'

Her mother squeezed her hand, not letting go for a long moment.

'I'm so proud of you, Ava,' she said quietly. 'I sat up tonight to tell you that. I'm so proud of what you're doing, and I wanted you to know.'

Pride swelled inside her as she stared back at her mother, barely believing what she was hearing.

'I admire your courage, Ava. You're one of the bravest young women I know.'

'Thank you.' Her eyes swam with tears again, but this time it had nothing to do with how scared she was. Her mother very rarely dished out praise, which meant that Ava believed her without question when she did.

'You're so much braver than I've ever been – in life, with your father . . .' Her voice trailed off.

Ava swallowed, suddenly no longer hungry. She could feel a *but* coming.

'But as proud as I am of you, you can't keep doing this,' she said. 'How long do you think it will take before your father realises what you're doing? Before he realises you've defied him?'

Ava set down her fork. 'I'm not going to quit this job.'

'Ava, if he finds out, if he tells you to leave home, there's nothing I can do.' Her mother's eyes were brimming with tears. 'Can't you just get your old job back? Would it be so bad to admit defeat and—'

'Admit defeat?' Ava echoed.

So this was why she'd sat up – trying to make her feel like she actually cared about her when instead she wanted her to quit her new job. She was just scared of her husband's wrath, that was all.

'I'm sorry,' Ava said sadly. 'I'm sorry you married a man who's made you scared in your own home. I'm sorry that no one but us knows the monster he can be.'

'Ava—'

'No,' she said, standing and pushing out her chair. 'You are not going to tell me to quit just because of him. If he kicks me out, then so be it. Perhaps I'd be better off without him, anyway.'

Her mother sobbed but Ava chose not to comfort her, taking her cup and plate to the sink and quickly rinsing them. She felt sorry for her mother, she did, but she wasn't going to give up what she was doing simply because her mother was scared.

'This was supposed to be the most fabulous year for you, Ava. I expected you to be engaged last year after your debutante ball, with a society wedding like no other to plan this year. Everything I'd dreamed of for you was supposed to happen, and now the best years of your life are being stolen from you!'

Ava turned and shook her head. 'That's truly what you think? That my best years have been stolen from me?'

Her mother didn't reply, her head in her hands now.

'I'm riding motorcycles for a job, Mother! They're calling us the Flying Wrens, and in case you've forgotten, there's a war going on! People are losing their families.' She shook her head. 'It's not about me wanting to do something forbidden; I'm actually doing an important job, work that truly means something.' She thought of Florence losing her family, and of the people all over Great Britain who had someone who wasn't coming home. When she'd applied for the job, all she'd been able to think about was the freedom it would afford her, but now it already seemed like so much more than that.

'Tonight I had to drive for hours to find my way to a shipyard to deliver a message to the Commander-in-Chief of the Navy, and then I had to find my way back in the dark,' she said, excitement building inside her as she thought of the enormity of what she'd achieved. 'I've found something I might actually be good at, something that makes me feel so alive, so full of adrenaline.' She paused, seeing that her mother either wasn't listening or perhaps just didn't understand. 'I was so scared tonight, the responsibility on my shoulders and the danger finally hitting me, but I won't back down from this. I can't.'

'I'm going to bed,' her mother said, still dabbing at her eyes as she rose, but the shrill sound of their telephone ringing made them both jump. Ava glanced at the clock and saw it was barely five a.m., and she ran to answer it, hoping it hadn't woken her father. Who on earth would be calling at this time?

'Hello?'

'Ava, it's George. I need you back here for an urgent dispatch.'

She smiled to her mother, seeing the worried look on her face. She placed her hand over the receiver for a moment. 'Everything's fine.' Her mother was clearly thinking that a call at that hour had to be bad news.

'Do you need me *right* now? I was just heading to bed.'

'You're one of the only girls with a telephone at home,' George said. 'I need a message delivered urgently, and everyone else is either at home or already dispatched.'

'All right. I'll be there as soon as I can.'

Ava hung up the phone and sighed, her eyelids so heavy she wondered how she was possibly going to stay awake. When George had told them it was a twenty-four-hour-a-day job, he clearly hadn't been exaggerating.

'Ava? Please tell me you're not leaving again already?'

'Duty calls,' she said, bending and dropping a kiss to her mother's cheek.

'What will I tell your father? The phone will have woken him.'

'Tell him the truth or make something up; it's your decision, but you know mine.' With that she picked up her coat in the hallway where she'd left it and walked outside, thankful it was still dark. Because as scary as night was, sometimes the morning was the most terrifying of all. Because morning was when they'd see what damage the city had suffered and wonder how they could keep surviving night after bomb-filled night.

Ava hurried down the street, the smell of smoke filling her nostrils, refusing to give in to her fears as she prepared to go and face them all over again. And as she walked, she thought of Florence and wondered just how she and Petal had got on during their first night on the job, and if it had been as horrendous as her first experience out on her bike.

I hope I have a home to come back to after this ride. Heaven help me if my father has all my belongings packed and waiting at the door.

CHAPTER EIGHT

FLORENCE

'You don't have to go out in this,' Jack said, his brows drawn tightly together as he stared down at her. 'We can wait until it's safer. No one's forcing you to head straight out.'

'No, we should go now,' Florence said. 'If we wait, people will die. They need us out there.'

'You're no use to them if you die.'

He didn't need to tell her that; she well and truly knew the risks of being out there, but who would she be if she waited until it was safe? Florence looked over her shoulder, seeing the other drivers all hunched over in the cellar, waiting until the bombing abated. She turned back to face Jack.

'People will be trapped and waiting for us to help them,' she said. 'I honestly don't see that we have a choice in the matter.'

He nodded. 'Fair enough. But it's your call, you're the driver.'

She straightened, still surprised that there was only one other driver preparing to go out immediately. Of course they could be hurt or even killed, but if they waited it out, so many more people could die. So many more families could be torn apart, and that wasn't something she wanted on her conscience. Every single mother, father, sister or brother she could help save was worth the risk. It had to be. Otherwise, what was she even doing?

'We're heading out,' she said, sounding far more confident than she felt. 'Every second after a bomb is dropped is critical, and I don't want to be sitting here waiting when we have a job to do.'

Jack didn't say anything, he just turned and started walking towards her ambulance, and she hurried after him.

It was now or never – and if she overthought it all? It could firmly end up being never.

———— ❧ ————

Thirty minutes later, Florence was worried she might damage the steering wheel she was holding it so tight. It was her first proper night on the job, and despite the Luftwaffe going easy on them for the past few weeks, they were certainly making up for it now.

She kept her head ducked low, eyes strained from focusing on the other ambulance ahead of her. They were travelling in a convoy from the West End with fire engines leading the way, and she was starting to wonder if she had been too quick to volunteer to go out.

A reverberation sent the vehicle moving sideways beneath her, and she yanked the steering wheel to keep it straight on the road. Jack was silent beside her, but his shoulder bumped hers when the vehicle lurched again, his big body filling the passenger side as they continued in the dark. She was grateful to have him with her, despite his quiet demeanour; he was a steady presence in a night that was anything other than predictable, although she couldn't read him tonight. Was he cross with her for insisting they go out, or pleased?

'You still think this was a good idea?' Jack asked, his voice gruff and impossible to read.

She turned with the convoy, disorientated by the dark and the smoke, but knowing that all she needed to do was follow. For now.

'I didn't see that we had a choice,' she replied, as much to convince herself as to answer him.

Part of her wanted to tell Jack what had happened to her – what was motivating her to go out when almost everyone else thought they were crazy – but another part of her didn't want to share her life with him. Not yet. Sometimes it was nice to just be Florence, to not be the girl who'd lost her parents and her sister, to not be the one everyone felt sorry for. She knew he'd look at her differently if he knew; everyone always did.

'Look out!'

Florence slammed on the brakes, narrowly avoiding hitting the ambulance in front of her. Her heart was thumping, her hands still glued to the steering wheel as she stared at the back of the other ambulance, the only other one who'd chosen to brave the night.

She dared not look at Jack beside her, even though she could feel his eyes on her.

'Let's go,' he said, opening his door and getting out when she finally pulled over.

Florence took a few seconds to compose herself, furious that she'd been so easily distracted on her first night out. She needed to do better next time; she needed to stay focused and not get pulled back into her memories. What must he think of her for almost crashing?

But as she stepped out into the night, as the acrid smell of smoke filled her nostrils and then her lungs, making her cough as it curled in her throat, everything came violently rushing back. An air-raid warden ran past, blowing her whistle and using her light to show them the way; a fire engine was parked nearby, perhaps the one that had led the convoy, positioned to get wayward flames under control. Suddenly she was back in the house, trapped as she screamed for help, listening for her family, trying to figure out where they were and why they weren't calling out too.

Hands reached for her, big burly hands that wrapped around her arms and hauled her from beneath the debris that had fallen on her, moving a piece of furniture or maybe it was part of her house that had pinned her. She blinked through the grit in her eyes, hazily making out the rubble around her as lights flashed, as someone with a torch searched.

'Help them,' she croaked. 'Please, help them first.'

She couldn't hear anything, even though she could see lips moving. The person nearby, and then the person hauling her, they were speaking but she couldn't hear a thing as she blinked, seeing flashes of their faces and moving mouths.

And then she saw them. Her mother covered in ash, her eyes wide open, someone walking away from her, leaving her.

'Help her!' Florence screamed, even though she couldn't even hear her own voice. 'Please!'

It was then that it dawned on her – why people were rushing past, tripping over her mother's body as if she were nothing, as if she weren't precious and loved and capable of saving.

Her mother was gone. And as everyone rushed to the next house – as they departed what was left of her family's home, of her family – she knew.

There was no one else to save. She was the only one who'd survived.

'Florence!'

Jack's call spurred her into action, and she ignored the choke in her throat as she hurried forward, pulling her scarf up over her mouth and nose.

'Are you ready for this?' he asked as a sharp whistle sounded nearby, telling them where to go.

'I'm ready,' she replied, coughing again as they rushed after the firemen. She tripped on the rubble as she shone her light on a doormat that had miraculously survived, untouched, still lying there on the ground with its *Welcome* stitching visible to all who crossed over it.

The ground rattled then as another bomb fell elsewhere in the city, and a siren wailed all over again, piercing the night as Londoners continued to hide in underground shelters, desperate to stay alive as homes and buildings were destroyed throughout the city. Most would spend the night underground if they could, if they had somewhere safe to go, if they'd had enough warning and could leave their homes in time.

A steely determination ran through her as she held her scarf more tightly to her mouth.

I can do this. This is what I was supposed to be doing; this is my calling.

Florence had never felt so certain about anything before in her life. She'd also never been so grateful to have Jack beside her, when so many other drivers were doing it on their own.

By the time Florence took her final trip to the hospital at the end of their shift, it was almost eight in the morning. She and Jack had worked tirelessly all night: following the urgent blow of whistles, driving quickly in the convoy after fire engines and other ambulances, ambulances that had finally joined them once the bombs had subsided. They'd managed to transport countless injured men, women and children to hospital, and she'd seen death first-hand, something she'd coped with far more competently than she'd expected, because it was the people who were trapped, the people who were still alive and who were desperately waiting to be saved that she focused on, thinking only of them and what she could do for them.

'You know, you were right about going out tonight.'

She glanced at Jack, yawning as she turned back down the road. She slowed as she approached the corner, relaxed in her driving now that it was morning and she wasn't navigating the streets in the dark. Daylight had never felt so reassuring.

'About what?' Florence realised they'd barely spoken to one another for an hour, maybe more. They'd been so focused on their work, and she had to admit they'd made a good team.

'You have to go out as soon as the bomb drops,' he said, his body angled away from hers as he stared out of the window. 'That's when people need you – not later, when it's safe.'

She nodded, even though he wasn't looking at her. 'So why did you seem unsure at the time?'

Jack grunted as he moved, repositioning himself in the seat. She'd noticed that his limp had become more pronounced when they were leaving the hospital after their last trip and wondered how much pain he was in, although she dared not ask.

'So many people join us and think they can stay safe in the cellar until it's all over,' he said. 'They won't take their ambulance out until the smoke clears, so to speak, and half the time they're the ones with all the training.'

'That's not me, Jack, and it will never be me, I can assure you of that,' Florence said, hearing the quiet determination in her own voice. 'That's not why I'm here.'

There was a long pause as she turned down Tottenham Court Road and then took a left, into their headquarters.

'Then why *are* you here, Florence?'

Florence fixed a smile on her face, not about to tell him what had drawn her to the ambulance service – what would make her take Petal out even if no one else was heading out. She smiled because if she didn't smile, she would cry, and that wasn't something she'd ever do in front of Jack, or anyone else she worked with.

'I could ask the same of you,' she said. 'But I have a feeling both of us want to keep our reasons to ourselves.'

He grunted. 'Fair enough.'

They sat for a moment as she stopped Petal and turned off the ignition, her chest rising and falling with her breath as he stared straight ahead, like he was lost in thought – another feeling she knew well, from when the memories became too much.

'You'd better check her over. Make sure she's ready for tonight,' he finally said.

'Will do,' Florence said.

As Jack opened his door and walked away, she cursed herself for not opening up a little to him. Perhaps if she had, he might have told her something about himself, and she had to admit she was curious. He was different from the others, and from what she could gather he was a volunteer just like her rather than an ATS trained recruit. Not to mention he clearly had advanced medical training, which made her wonder if he'd been an Army medic earlier in the war, perhaps before sustaining the injuries he suffered from.

He clearly had a story, and she hoped that one day he would trust her enough to tell it.

———— ✦ ————

Florence wiped her forehead with the back of her hand, sweat trickling down her skin as she faced the fire. The previous nights she'd worked hard, but nothing had compared to what they were facing now. It was as if her first week had merely been preparation for tonight.

'We're not going in there, it's too dangerous.'

The commotion around them was loud; whistles were blowing, people were screaming, firemen were yelling. But the one sight Florence could barely tear her eyes from was a man standing in the street, turning slowly in circles, as if he couldn't comprehend what was happening to him. He was dressed in a striped nightgown, and she'd never seen anyone appear so bewildered in all her life. If she'd had time, she would have gone to comfort him, led him safely to a neighbour's house or *somewhere*, anywhere other than leaving him in the middle of the road. But there was no time to provide comfort to the able-bodied – their job was to save those who would otherwise perish. Which was exactly what she was going to do.

'I'm going in, Jack,' she said, defiantly staring back at him. 'There are people in there, we can't just leave them.'

'And I'm not letting you,' he said, moving to stand in front of her.

'We don't have time to argue! Get out of my way!'

Jack's fingers curled tightly around her wrist as she attempted to pass him, but she yanked hard, not caring how much it hurt. She wasn't going to waste time fighting with him when they had a job to do.

'Can we go in?' she yelled to the closest fireman.

'We're doing our best to dampen the flames,' he yelled back. 'If you think you can get in there, you can. But that roof could fall in at any moment.'

Florence didn't waste time thinking about it. She leapt forward, intent on getting in and seeing if there were any survivors. The warden hadn't attempted to go near the house and the firemen were too busy dousing flames to look for people, which only made Flo all the more determined to enter.

If not me, then who? She looked back at Jack, knowing that without him she had no hope of dragging anyone out. She needed his strength, and he knew it.

'Are you coming or not?' she called out to him.

'Damn you, woman!' he cursed, lumbering forward like a bear charging towards her.

Florence pressed on, covering her mouth with her arm to stop from choking on the smoke. If there was anyone in there alive, they weren't going to survive much longer.

'Hello!' she yelled, muffled as she kept her arm held high. 'Hello!' She coughed and kept moving forward over the unsteady debris beneath her that had once formed a house, trying to tie her scarf even tighter.

'Here!' came a weak call back. 'Help!'

'I'm coming!' she shouted, dropping her arm as she frantically picked her way through what was left of the room. She used her light, flashing it around as she tried to find where the call had come from. The inside of the house looked like a wrecking ball had demolished it – that anyone had managed to survive was a miracle.

'Help!' came another cry, just as the house creaked, making Florence stop moving as she shone her light towards what was left of the ceiling.

'We'll die in here if we don't get out soon!' Jack yelled. 'Florence, we need to hurry!'

'Go and get help,' she said. 'Please, Jack, we can't leave them in here.'

'Christ almighty!' he swore as he backtracked, leaving her in the remnants of the house alone. 'You stay safe, you hear me! Stay safe and get out if you hear the roof cracking!'

But when her light caught a waving hand, raised just high enough for her to see, she knew it had been worth the risk. She dropped, digging through the wreckage, her nails bleeding as she frantically tried to save the person. It turned out to be a girl, perhaps twelve or thirteen, and as Florence found a strength she hadn't even known she possessed, she freed her and in doing so uncovered the girl's brother, too.

'Can you walk?' Florence asked.

The girl tested her leg and let out a loud yelp, but big hands caught her as she fell, Jack appearing beside her at just the right moment. Despite his own physical limitations, somehow Jack hefted her over his shoulder and began to carry her out, and Florence helped the boy up, prepared to carry him herself if she needed to.

'Can you walk?' she asked. 'We just need to follow him out of here, but we have to hurry.'

The boy nodded, tears making wet lines through the filth covering his face as she shone the light on him.

'Go, follow that man. He'll take you to safety.'

The boy scrambled away, half walking, half crawling through what was left of his home. She knew there had to be at least one parent buried somewhere too, and she didn't want two orphans on her conscience.

'You have to get out of here! It's about to fall!'

The call of a fireman sent a shiver through her as the framing around her creaked more loudly this time, water spraying the side of her face as they valiantly fought to put out the fire on the side of the house.

'Get out of there!' Jack was yelling at her now, but she wasn't listening to him. Instead, her head was cocked as she heard a faint tapping.

'There's someone else in here!' She tripped over all sorts of things as she hurried forward, knowing they only had minutes, possibly even seconds, before they lost their own lives, too.

Two firemen appeared beside her as she pinpointed where the sound was coming from.

'Quickly, they're here!' she screamed. 'There's tapping right here.'

Florence dropped down low as the firemen pulled rubble away, her heart almost skipping a beat when she saw an arm emerge, the men heroically lifting something, *someone*, from beneath a large piece of broken furniture.

'The roof's about to collapse!' someone yelled. 'Get out of there! There's no more time!'

Jack pulled her, his grip unrelenting as he yanked her backwards, out of the falling house. She wanted to fight him, but she knew there was nothing else she could do. If there was anyone else inside, they were gone now.

It felt like the longest moment of her life as they stood waiting for the firemen to emerge, and when they did the relief hit her so hard she almost dropped to her knees. The woman was limp, but they wouldn't have been carrying her if she wasn't alive.

'Get them loaded in!' Jack called, and she ran with him to the ambulance, holding the doors open as they put the woman in the back.

Jack was bent low, his fingers to the woman's throat as he felt for a pulse. He didn't need to tell Florence that she needed to drive quickly; if they were going to save this mother, she was going to have to get her to the hospital faster than she'd ever gotten there before.

'Florence?'

She paused, holding open the door that she'd been about to close.

'Don't you *ever* pull a stunt like that again.'

Florence didn't reply. She shut the door and ran around to the driver's side, hands shaking violently as she fumbled for the keys.

And just as she started the engine, there was a loud cracking sound as the remnants of the house they'd been in moments earlier crashed to the ground, the roof giving way completely, crushing everything beneath it. Tears pricked her eyes as she thought of the family in the back, and as she drove through the broken street, past the man still standing in his striped nightgown doing circles as he looked around, bewildered.

If I had to do it all over again, if I had to make that choice to go in, I'd do it in a heartbeat.

'What the hell was that about?' Jack's voice was a thundercloud as he growled out the words.

Florence didn't answer. Or more like, she couldn't answer. The words choked in her throat like the smoke in the night air.

'I asked what the hell that was about!' Jack thundered beside her.

'Perhaps you don't have the right to ask me that,' she smarted, her hold on the steering wheel tight as she accelerated down a small part of the road that was untouched by the chaos of the night of bombing. The West End had been fortunate so far.

'I'd say I have every damn right to ask you,' he said. 'You don't ever put your life in danger like that again. It was reckless and stupid and—'

'I'm an orphan,' Florence said, hurling the words at him as if it were all his fault. 'I lay there in my home, pinned to the ground with my family dead around me after a bomb hit just near our house, all because no one came to save us until it was too late. I'm the only one who survived, Jack, and I'm not going to have that happen to another family, not on my watch.' Her breath shuddered out of her as she fought to get her words out. 'Not if there's something within my power that I can do.'

Her breath was coming in rapid pants now, tears hiccupping in her throat as Jack's silence deafened her. She cleared her throat and used one hand to quickly wipe her cheeks, hating that she'd let her emotion get the better of her. She was usually so good at hiding her emotions from others.

'So, when I tell you that I'm going in, that nothing will stop me?' She shook her head. 'I damn well mean it, all right?'

'All right,' Jack replied quickly, and she caught his nod when she glanced sideways at him.

'All right then,' she muttered in reply.

After a beat of silence that felt hours long, Jack said, 'You know, you should have told me.'

Florence almost laughed. Most people would have consoled her or given her some form of pity, but not Jack. 'I don't see that it was any of your business, and besides, I don't like talking about it.'

Jack didn't say anything else; he sat in silence as she drove the rest of the way, wrestling with the voices in her head, the memories of her parents and her sister: their laughter, their smiles, their hugs. She was never going to see them again, but that family they'd saved tonight – they had a fighting chance of being together again, of all surviving to see another day. That was something she'd done, something she could feel proud of, knowing those children still had their mother, despite the fact that their home had been lost.

When she stopped the ambulance in the garage, she got out quickly, intending on doing a quick check over the vehicle before going home and crawling into bed. But when she walked around the back, she saw that Jack had moved to stand in her way, his big frame making it impossible to get around him.

'I'm sorry,' he said, his shoulders slightly stooped as he looked down at her. 'I'm truly sorry for your loss, Florence.'

She nodded, moving forward a step to make it clear that she wanted to get around him and that she didn't want to talk, but he still didn't move.

'Any house you want to go into, anyone you want to save, I won't ever question you again. That's a promise.'

Florence stared up at him, finally meeting his gaze. She could have sworn she saw tears in his eyes, but if she had, they were gone by the time he blinked.

'Thank you,' she said.

He shifted from one foot to the other, and she wasn't sure if he was in pain or simply uncomfortable talking to her.

'It's fair to say I've got my own demons. I know what it's like to lie awake at night, I know . . .' His voice trailed off.

Florence instinctively reached for him, placing her hand on his upper arm. She was at a loss for words herself, but she wanted him to know that she was there for him. What surprised her was how he jumped, clearly taken aback by her palm against him, and his arm tensed beneath her. But instead of pulling back she left her hand there, even though it would have been so much easier to back away.

'I suppose what I'm trying to say is that I know what it's like to lose those closest to you,' he said.

'Well, that makes two of us then, doesn't it?'

They stood and stared at one another a long moment as she finally retrieved her hand, folding her arms in front of her.

'You have someone at home?' he asked. 'I mean, are you, do you—'

'I have my grandmother,' she said, when she realised he didn't know what to say, just as she had been. 'I live with her now; it's just been the two of us since my parents and my sister died.'

'Oh, well, that's good,' he mumbled. 'I just . . . well, I didn't like the thought of you being alone, that's all.'

Voices interrupted them then, and Florence took her chance to move past Jack, deciding to come in early to check over the van before her next shift instead. She was too tired to do it now – and talking about her family, it always took something from her, drained all her energy even at the best of times.

She patted Jack's arm as she passed, collecting the bag she'd left in the office before beginning her long walk home, knowing she'd never sleep, despite her exhaustion, if she didn't clear her head first.

'Do we really have to go to the shelter? The bombs aren't going to hit houses.'

Flo smiled at her little sister before she caught her father's frown over the top of his newspaper.

'Of course we have to go to the shelter, girls. When Wailing Willy sounds, we all go, that's what we've been told to do. The Luftwaffe haven't been entirely accurate with their bombing, so we need to be careful.'

They both giggled, still finding the term Wailing Willy hilarious, especially when their father said it in his proper voice, peering over his glasses as they slid down his nose.

'Come on, girls, off we go.'

They all hurried to grab their coats, and Florence took the basket her mother had prepared. She had food and jars of water packed for them, in case they had to spend hours underground waiting out a bombing. There had been so much talk of bombings, of what to do, and her father hurried them all up, gesturing at the door.

'I can't find Mittens!' her sister suddenly called.

Florence paused, turning in the doorway. 'He'll be fine, come on!'

'Flo's right, he'll be fine. Animals always find their way to safety. We need to go!'

She wasn't entirely certain she agreed with her mother, but she was certain about getting her sister out of the house as the siren continued its wail, nervousness building inside her.

'I'm not leaving without him!'

Her sister had declared that Mittens would be carted down to their little shelter in the garden if the family had to go, and Florence could already imagine his meows of indignation and his clawing of her sister's shoulder as she manhandled him to safety.

'Clare!' Florence yelled. 'Just leave him!'

Her father sighed and let go of the door, which banged her as it closed. Florence marched off after him as they called for Mittens, who was apparently smarter than all of them. She bet he was hiding so he didn't have to go with them.

'Mittens!' she called. 'Here, puss, puss.'

And that's when it happened.

When she was on her hands and knees, peering beneath the sofa and snapping at her sister to go upstairs and look on the beds, as she muttered how they were wasting time looking for the stupid cat when a bomb could fall at any moment, not caring that she made her sister cry.

Before the bomb fell, everything seemed to go silent. One second Florence was on the floor looking for the cat, and the next she was moving to stand, wondering why her father was making a strange whistling sound as he looked for the cat. Only it wasn't her father whistling. And then the bomb had fallen.

She knew she'd never forget that whistle for as long as she lived. Even after, as she lay on the stretcher, when everything else was silent around her, when the ringing in her ears was the same pitch as the bomb whistle.

The whistle that had changed her life forever.

And the very next day, after she begged her grandmother to let her go to the house, to search through the rubble with the whistle still sharp in her mind, she saw something that she'd never, ever forget. As firemen pulled aside rubble, doing one final search, she saw her sister, recognised a tuft of her pretty blonde hair.

It was an image she knew she'd never be able to get out of her head.

When Florence finally walked through the door to the home she shared with her grandmother, battling her memories all the way, she ran straight out to their makeshift shelter to check on her. She threw back the heavy wooden door, squinting as she looked in. Her grandmother wasn't there. Florence's heart rate picked up as she ran back into the house, glancing around for any sign of her. She darted upstairs. *Please let her be here. Please let her be safe.*

'Flo? Is that you?'

Her grandmother's voice was as creaky as the stairs Florence ran up, taking them two at a time, rushing into the bedroom and throwing her arms around her. She burst into tears, the emotion she'd so carefully held in check suddenly flowing from her as her grandmother held her, shushing her as she might have when Florence was just a girl, her lips to the top of her head as she curled against her.

'Let it all out,' her grandmother murmured. 'It's been a long time coming.'

'I miss them so much,' she cried. 'I just, tonight, I . . .'

'Before you ask, I was in the shelter all night. I only crawled into bed at daybreak to get some sleep.'

Florence tried to slow her breathing, still curled against her grandmother, grateful for her arms around her and her fingers gently raking through her hair.

Tonight had been a success, she'd saved people who would have otherwise perished, but opening up to Jack hadn't been something she'd planned on. Just like she hadn't planned on her memories being so hard to combat that she sometimes felt as if they were swallowing her whole.

CHAPTER NINE

OLIVIA

Olivia parked her motorcycle and stood for a moment, so tired that she could have curled up right there on the ground beside it and gone to sleep. She'd never experienced fatigue like it, but going out day after day – or this past week, night after night – was starting to take its toll. The night before she'd been so jealous of her flatmates, curled up listening to an old episode of *It's That Man Again* with Tommy Handley on the wireless, their hair in rollers as they sipped their tea. The shift work was the only part of her new job that was making her mourn her old one.

'Tea?'

She turned to find Ava behind her, holding out a steaming-hot mug. She took her gloves off and tucked them into her pocket, reaching for the drink and wrapping her hands around it.

'How did you know when I'd be back?'

Ava grinned. 'I didn't. I made that for myself actually, but you look like you need it more than I do!'

Olivia took a sip. Sometimes Ava seemed to think of no one other than herself, and other times she managed to take Olivia completely by surprise. 'Thanks. I owe you one.'

'It's brutal, isn't it?' Ava said. 'I don't think I'd ever have believed how hard it would be, even if someone had told me. My old job is seeming rather easy in hindsight.'

'*Brutal* is an understatement,' Olivia said. 'Thinking of going back to a desk job?'

'Wash your mouth out! I would never do that!'

Olivia laughed, despite her exhaustion. Ava was nothing if not entertaining, although Olivia wondered if they were doing the job for different reasons. Olivia felt a deep connection to motorcycle riding and wanted to make a difference, whereas she wondered if Ava simply thrived on the adventure aspect of what they were doing.

She suddenly needed to sit, her legs tired as she lowered herself to the ground, leaning against the concrete wall of the garage. Ava did the same, their shoulders touching, heads tipped back as they shut their eyes for a moment.

'I'd make myself another cup of tea, but I don't think I'll ever be able to get up.'

'Here, share this with me,' Olivia said, passing the mug over. 'I feel bad having it all anyway.'

Ava took it gratefully, sipping before handing it back, and Olivia wrapped her fingers around it again, thankful for the warmth. Despite wearing gloves while she was riding, her hands still turned to ice sometimes when she rode at night.

'Are you going home to bed?' Ava asked.

'Actually, I'm heading back to my parents' country house as soon as I check over the bike. It's my mother's birthday, and I know I'll never hear the end of it if I don't turn up today.'

'How are you getting there?'

'Would you believe that George is letting me take the motorcycle? It'll take me about forty minutes to get there so long as there's no damage to the roads between here and there.' She sighed. 'Just my luck there'll be some obstruction and it'll end up taking me hours.'

They sat a while longer, eyes shut, too tired to talk.

'I know it sounds silly because we haven't known each other very long, but I kind of miss Florence,' Ava said. 'How do you think she's getting on?'

'I don't think it's silly, I miss her too. I so wish we'd all been able to stay together.'

'What do you say if, when you're back, we organise a get-together? Even just a picnic lunch in the park would be nice, or maybe we could come over to your flat?'

'Sounds great. How about you find out when she's available?'

'You girls all right out here?'

Olivia opened her eyes to see George watching them from a few paces away. At the beginning of the week, she'd have jumped to her feet for fear he might think she was slacking off, but now she simply didn't have the energy. And surely by now he knew how hard she was prepared to work.

'Just two girls taking a rest,' Ava answered for both of them. 'You've worked us to the bone.'

'Enjoy your day of leave, Olivia,' he said. 'See you back on deck for your night shift.'

'Thanks.' She smiled and eventually pulled her legs in, groaning as she hauled herself up and then reached down a hand for Ava. 'I really need to get going. If I don't go now, they'll think I'm not coming, and I don't think my mother is coping very well with the children she's taken in. It sounds like her little evacuees are quite the handful, so I promised I'd help since it's her birthday!'

Ava took the mug from her, downing the dregs at the bottom. 'Have fun. I hope you have a fast trip back home and a gloriously long sleep tonight.'

So did she. Ava blew her a kiss and disappeared, and as Olivia started looking over her motorcycle, checking the wheels and the fuel, she noticed that someone else was looking over Ava's for her. *Typical. The rest of us are up to our elbows in grease and she manages to find a man to do it for her.*

'Make her do it herself!' she called over to the young mechanic, who gave her a guilty look in response.

Olivia shook her head and finished what she was doing, before mounting her bike again. If she didn't hurry, she'd never be able to keep her eyes open long enough to make the journey.

———— ◦⃝◦ ————

'I'm home!'

Olivia called out from the hallway, taking off her hat. She put it down and ran her fingers over her scalp, fluffing her hair so that her mother didn't despair the moment she saw her. She glanced down at her trousers and waterproof jacket and suddenly wondered if perhaps she should have changed before walking in, but it was too late now. Dowdy trousers weren't exactly clothing that her mother would approve of; she'd never come to terms with the fact her daughter was a tomboy, and her current occupation wasn't of any help.

'Dad?' she called. 'Mum?'

She took off her boots, not wanting to trample mud through the house, and slowly padded across the floorboards towards the kitchen. She was about to call out again to announce her presence, but as she walked into the room she found her mother bent low over the table, quietly sobbing, and her father with his head in his hands. He looked up when she walked in, his eyes glassy, reaching out a hand to her and beckoning her to join them.

'What's happened?' she whispered, looking between them and wondering what on earth was going on. 'Please tell me it's not—'

'Pete,' her father choked out her brother's name, tears starting to roll silently down his cheeks as her mother let out a loud sob beside him. 'It's our Pete.'

'No.' *No!* It couldn't be Pete. Not her darling eldest brother. *Not Petey.*

Her body started to shake as she stared at her father.

'Are you certain? How do you know? When did you find out?' She gasped out the words, falling into the seat beside her mother and immediately opening her arms to her.

She followed her father's gaze to a discarded letter on the table. Olivia let go of her mother temporarily to reach for it, hand shaking as she held it and traced her eyes over the words, taking a moment to focus her gaze. Surely there'd been some kind of mistake!

I very much regret to inform you that your son is reported missing as a result of an air operation last night, and I wish to convey to you the sympathy of all members of this Squadron, and myself, in your anxiety while awaiting news. Whilst the classification 'missing in action' means exactly that, that your son's whereabouts are currently unknown, it is unfortunately likely that he has perished.

Olivia dropped the letter, pushing it away, not wanting to read any more. Her brother was missing, presumed dead? Her brave, strong, capable, *fun* brother was gone? She could barely comprehend the news, the contents of the letter so unbelievable – something she simply hadn't prepared for even though she knew she should have.

'When did it arrive?' she asked, her voice raspy. *And on my poor mother's birthday, of all days.* 'How long has he been . . .' She couldn't say the word. *Gone.*

Her father glanced up at her, his eyes red-rimmed, looking like he was about to say something. Then he reached for her mother, who had also, finally, lifted her gaze. It was like looking at a house without the lights on; her mother's usual lively nature that could fill a room, extinguished as if it had never existed in the first place.

Olivia was about to repeat her question when a voice from behind her made her freeze.

'Hello, Olivia.'

It couldn't be.

Leo? She turned, not believing her eyes when she saw a man standing there, wearing a plaid shirt that she recognised as belonging to one of her brothers, his hair wet and freshly combed. His hair was longer than she remembered, his skin more golden and his cheeks hollow, but there was no mistaking it was he.

'Leo!' She almost fell over her chair in her haste to reach him, running across the room and into his open arms, throwing herself against him. He held her as tightly as she held him, his cheeks freshly razored and soft against hers, his body warm and very much alive. Even then she kept tightening her hold, as if to convince herself she wasn't dreaming. She'd spent so many hours fretting over whether or not Leo would make it home, and yet it was he standing before her and her brother who hadn't returned.

'I'm so sorry about Pete,' he murmured, holding her at arm's length as his eyes seemed to trace every inch of her face. 'I wasn't due leave, but when all this happened, when . . .'

His happiness at seeing her was as short-lived as hers, and her eyes swam with tears as she folded her arms around him again, needing to be held. She knew this would be every bit as difficult for him as it was for her.

'I had to deliver the news personally. I couldn't . . .' He faltered before clearing his throat and beginning again. She could see it was taking all his strength not to break down in front of her – it was the first time in all the years she'd known him that she'd seen him cry. 'I needed to be the one to give your parents the letter. It's the least I could do for your family – to be the one to break the news.'

Olivia wiped her tears and took Leo's hand in hers, steering him back towards the table with her. Her parents were still sitting quietly, her father staring into the distance as if he wasn't even present, lost in his thoughts or perhaps his pain.

'Tea,' her mother announced, abruptly standing. 'We all need tea. Tea fixes everything.'

Olivia glanced at Leo, who looked as perplexed as she felt. But, seeing her mother wringing her hands and marching off to find the teapot, she supposed that making tea would at least give her something to do.

'He's gone, isn't he?' Olivia whispered, still clutching Leo's hand, terrified that if she let go he might be taken from her, too. 'They tell the family that missing doesn't mean dead, to give us hope, but . . .' She swallowed. 'You think he's gone, don't you?'

Leo only looked at her. He didn't need to say anything, his sad gaze told her everything she needed to know, and when he squeezed her fingers in his, it was all she could do to hold herself together. Her beautiful big brother was gone; she was never, ever going to see him again.

'Olivia, love, when did you get here?' Her mother returned from the kitchen, staring at her and giving her the most quizzical gaze, as if she genuinely hadn't realised she was there. 'And what on earth are you wearing? You look ridiculous!'

Olivia looked down at her oversized jacket and trousers. What she was wearing didn't seem relevant given the circumstances, but she could imagine it wasn't exactly the kind of outfit her mother expected her to wear for her birthday.

'It's my uniform,' she said. 'I came straight from work.'

'Well, you look quite frightful. Go and get changed, would you? Your Leo is here, and he hardly wants to come home after all these months and find you looking like that. What a disappointment that would be, hmm?'

Had she seriously not seen her embracing Leo, or sitting beside him at the table? She was speaking as if Olivia had no idea he was even present!

Leo grinned at her, arching an eyebrow as he looked her up and down and leaned in closer. 'You look quite fetching, actually,' he whispered.

She smiled, despite the sadness of the occasion, feeling a familiar spark inside when he grinned at her. 'Thank you,' she mouthed.

'It's ridiculous, you risking your life like that each day. They're death traps! We've had enough, haven't we, Roger?' her mother said, looking at her father, who didn't even appear to be listening. 'I shouldn't have to worry about my daughter as well as my sons. It's just not suitable for women, that kind of work.'

Olivia pursed her lips, not about to argue with her, given the circumstances. She wasn't going to stop her work for anyone, and certainly not because her mother didn't think it was ladylike enough. The news about Pete only made her want to help more, made her more determined to do whatever it took.

'Shortbread,' her mother suddenly announced. 'The boy needs shortbread. And perhaps a roast. Would you like a roast, Leo? How about I see what I can rustle up for dinner?' She sounded almost hysterical now, swinging between deep grief and fussing over Leo and what he might need. 'We don't have much meat these days, but I'll find something.'

Olivia glanced at her father, who was still staring at nothing in particular, and then back at her mother again as she fluttered around the kitchen, her face so drawn and white, her mouth so tightly pinched, that she barely recognised her. A small cake was sitting there, forgotten about after the news they'd received, the birthday celebrations no longer relevant. And all the while Leo just quietly held her hand as if he'd never left her side in the first place, keeping her steady, reminding her so much of her brother as he sat there in Pete's shirt that it made her heart bleed. She could almost see Pete walking through the door, taking the seat beside Leo and slapping him on the back as he teased them about being engaged, about how lovey-dovey they were in front of him.

'Mother, why don't you come and sit down,' Olivia said, finally letting go of Leo and reaching for the teapot her mother was holding. 'Let me do all this. I'm happy to help.'

'I can't, I have to . . . Leo, I mean Pete, I—'

'Shhh.' Olivia gently steered her mother to the table and sat her down again. 'Just sit a minute, and I'll bring you the tea.' It took all her strength not to break down in tears at the sight of her mother, but she somehow kept her composure. She hated seeing her mother like this, and she would have done anything to ease her pain.

'Not Petey,' her mother whispered, as if only just admitting the news they'd received. 'Heavens no, not my Petey.'

Her father seemed to come back then too, his face crumpling in a way she'd never imagined possible before. Her stoic father, with his perfectly groomed moustache and his broad shoulders that she'd never even seen droop, now looked like a hunched old man, the life within him as good as extinguished. She set the teapot down and poured her mother a cup.

'How long are you here for?' Olivia whispered, reaching for Leo's hand beneath the table as she sat down beside him, trying to draw on his strength even though she knew he'd be grieving almost as deeply as she was. Leo and Pete had been best friends since school, and she'd never imagined when they'd set out together for war that one might come home without the other – that anything could stop her big brother from finding his way back to his family. It just hadn't truly occurred to her that she could lose him; he'd always seemed somehow indestructible, which seemed ridiculously naïve in hindsight.

'A few days. It was all I could get, unfortunately,' he murmured back.

She nodded as a fresh wave of tears rose within her, choking her as she stared at her mother and father and wondered how they would all survive such a loss – how they would even continue on. How could they feel like a family ever again without Pete's cheeky smile and belly-deep laugh, without him at their dinner table after the war, without him in their lives?

It was as if her mother was having the very same thought, her face crumpling all over again as her body started to shake and a low moan escaped her lips, a sound Olivia hadn't even known her mother was capable of making. Olivia hurried back to her, enveloping her in her arms as they both cried.

I have two other brothers over there, too. What if neither of them makes it home? What if we have to go through this again with them, as well? What if I'm the only one left?

A shuffling sound made her look up then, and she saw two little faces peering around the door, wide-eyed. She rose, leaving Leo to console her parents. She'd been so caught up in the news of her brother that she'd forgotten about the two children they'd taken in since she'd been gone.

'Hello,' she said, bending to their level as they blinked back at her. 'I'm Olivia.'

They shuffled closer together, but neither of the children spoke. It seemed like a lifetime ago that she'd dreamed of becoming a teacher; she'd always loved children and had liked the idea of teaching before having her own family, but the war had scuppered her plans.

'Tell me, do you like cake?' she whispered, leaning forward with her hand half cupping her mouth, as if she were telling them a secret.

They both nodded.

'Well, how about you go up to your room and I'll bring you each a piece.' It seemed a shame to waste the cake when there were two scared children in the house.

They both smiled and she watched them run up the stairs, waiting until they'd disappeared before going to cut them a slice. They were no doubt heartbroken about being sent away from their parents to live with strangers, and scared about what they'd been listening to from their spot in the hall, but while she was there, she'd do everything she could to make them smile.

As far as she was concerned, it was the least she could do.

—— ⌒⌒ ——

'It all just seems like a bad dream.' Olivia sat on the large wooden seat in the garden with Leo, tucked against him, his arm looped protectively around her waist. They'd come outside after it had become almost unbearable to be around her parents at the table any longer, and once the children were tucked up in bed. She'd needed some time with Leo and for her own thoughts, and after cleaning up the dinner dishes, they'd decided to go outside for some air.

'Nothing about losing Pete seems real.'

She'd never seen Leo cry before; like her brother, he always seemed perpetually upbeat, always smiling, always happy no matter what the day. He was always the last to leave a dance, the first to suggest playing games or to strip off his clothes to swim in the river on a hot summer's day. But there was a seriousness about Leo now that hadn't been there when he'd left for the war; he seemed more mature somehow, and his red-rimmed eyes told her that he'd shed just as many tears as her family had. She hated to think what he'd seen, what he'd been through in the months since he'd left home.

'I wish you could stay for longer,' she said. 'I don't know how I'm going to say goodbye to you all over again.' She sucked back a breath as fresh tears threatened to fall. 'If I'm honest, I don't think I know how to live without him.'

Leo's lips brushed her forehead, his arm tightening around her. 'You and me both, Liv,' he whispered. 'You and me both.'

She tucked even closer against him, trying to convince herself that he was real, but as much as she didn't want Leo to be a dream, she wanted the news he'd brought with him to be one. Because every time she caught herself thinking how lucky she was to have him home, she was reminded why he was here. And then emotion would catch in her throat all over again and she'd find herself swallowing enormous gulps of sadness.

'I'm so happy you're here, but—' She choked on the words.

'It's bittersweet, isn't it?' His fingers thrummed against her waist, a gentle reminder that he was in fact real, that he was indeed sitting beside her, holding her, comforting her.

'It is.' She stared out into the night. 'I imagined Pete being there at our wedding, toasting us and laughing, sharing stories about how his best friend somehow fell in love with his sister. I can't imagine him not being there for everything.'

Leo's laugh was low, and she tipped her head to his shoulder. 'Do you remember how nervous I was, asking him for permission to take you to a dance that first time? I genuinely thought he was going to kill me.'

137

She laughed. 'Yes! I remember watching you from the staircase, leaning out to listen to what you were going to say to him, and you could barely get the words out!'

'I'll never forget the way he grinned,' Leo said. 'Telling me that I'd better do right by you, because he couldn't think of anything better than having me as a brother-in-law. All those weeks of wanting to ask you out, worried that he'd hate me for it, when in fact he couldn't have been happier for us.'

Olivia absently fingered the ring hanging around her neck, and Leo seemed to notice because he leaned back a little and reached out to touch it, too.

'I was able to wear it until I took this new job, but now I keep it around my neck, just to make sure it's safe.'

He nodded, a half-smile making his mouth appear crooked. 'You can wear it any way you like, Olivia.'

She grinned. 'Leo—'

'Liv—'

They both smiled. 'You go first,' she said.

'I know it's terrible timing, what with Pete and everything, but I don't know when I'll next be home, or what might even happen between now and then, and I just, well . . .'

She sat patiently, taking his hand as she waited for him to find the words. But instead of holding her hand he abruptly stood and paced a few steps away, before turning back around to her. His frown scared her.

'You don't want to end our engagement, do you?' She tried to stop the crack in her voice, but it was impossible. *Please God, not more bad news in one night!*

'Liv, no, of course not.' He moved closer, looking down at her with a look that was somehow half sad, half happy. 'I just, well, I want to know if you'll marry me, before I leave. I don't want to wait any more.'

She blinked up at him, barely believing what she was hearing.

'I know we'd only have a couple of days to organise it, and it won't be the wedding we'd planned, but after—'

'Yes!' she gasped, jumping up and throwing her arms around him, almost knocking him over with her enthusiasm. 'Oh Leo, of course I'll marry you!'

Her eyes filled with tears all over again, overwhelmed from the day and everything that had happened, but also because she wanted to be Leo's wife. It was all she'd ever wanted, and after what had happened and the lengths he'd gone to to come home, nothing had ever felt so right.

She pressed her cheek to his chest, tired beyond words as she wrapped her arms around him and listened to the steady thud of his heart.

'I'm so proud of you, Liv,' he murmured. 'The work you're doing, the way you've coped with everything while I've been away. I just want you to know that, whatever happens, I couldn't be prouder of you.' His lips touched her hair. 'Even if you do have to wear trousers.'

She pulled back and looked up at him, loving his smile. 'Don't you dare tease me about the trousers!'

He laughed. 'I wasn't kidding when I said you looked fetching in them.'

Leo dipped his head then, his eyes flickering from her eyes to her mouth, and she lifted her chin as he brought his lips to hers, nervous in a way she hadn't been since they'd first started courting. The kiss was tender, lips softly brushing lips, and when he finally pulled back, she couldn't help but smile up at him. She had nothing to be nervous about.

'How did I ever get so lucky?' he whispered.

Olivia let Leo pull her back down to the seat, nestling her body into his again, his warm arms circling her as she leaned against his chest.

How was it that today was one of the happiest of her life, as well as the saddest? She heard a noise inside and knew it was her mother crying, and as much as she wanted to go to her, she just needed a moment with Leo, to have him comforting her, his fingers gently rubbing up and down her arm. Leo would be gone in days, whereas her mother would have her care forever.

And there was something comforting about mourning her brother with Leo, because she and Leo knew the same Pete, not the restrained version he had so often presented to their parents, but the fun-loving, quick-to-laugh, daredevil Pete. The Pete who was always so much fun to be around, who'd welcome anyone no matter who they were. It was because of that, that she knew Leo would understand her grief in a way no one else possibly could.

'He'll be there with us, in spirit,' Leo whispered into her ear as he drew her even closer. 'We have to believe that he's looking down on us from somewhere.'

'I know,' she whispered back.

'We can just have your parents and mine there to see us say our vows,' he said, keeping his voice low. 'Perhaps we'll be able to have dinner somewhere, and a night away, just the two of us?'

Olivia could barely imagine a wedding, however intimate, that didn't involve Pete standing by her side, but she nodded, pushing the thought away. If she wanted to marry Leo, this was the only way. 'I'd like to invite two friends, if I can,' she said. 'Two girls that have come to mean a lot to me in a short time. It wouldn't feel right not having them there.'

'Of course.' He kissed the top of her head. 'I'll leave it all up to you.'

She shut her eyes as Leo continued to thrum his fingers across her arm, suddenly close to sleep she was so exhausted.

'One day we'll have our own home, filled with our own children,' he said, holding her close. 'Can't you just imagine?'

She sighed. 'All I have to do is close my eyes,' she said. 'When you're gone, and I can't sleep, I just lie there and see us with our children around us, visualising the kind of home we'll live in.'

'Do you still think about teaching?' he asked. 'I know how much you were looking forward to being a teacher before you become a mother yourself.'

Olivia smiled. He was the one person in her life she'd always confided all her hopes and dreams in, and she loved how seriously he took her aspirations. 'I don't often think about it now, there's just so much other work to be done and so little time.'

'Leo, Olivia!' Her father's call made her jump to her feet, ending their conversation, and Leo was right behind her as she ran inside.

Her mother was still slumped at the table, but the wireless was on and her father was sitting close to it, waving for them to join him. Winston Churchill's clear, steady voice drew her closer, and she sat beside her father on an armchair as they listened.

'The gratitude of every home in our island, in our Empire, and indeed throughout the world except in the abodes of the guilty, goes out to the British airmen who, undaunted by odds, unwearied in their constant challenge and mortal danger, are turning the tide of the world war by their prowess and their devotion. Never in the field of human conflict was so much owed by so many to so few. All hearts go out to the fighter pilots, whose brilliant actions we see with our own eyes day after day, but we must never forget that all the time, night after night, month after month, our bomber squadrons travel far into Germany, find their targets in the darkness by the highest navigational skill, aim their attacks, often under the heaviest fire, often with serious loss, with

141

deliberate, careful discrimination, and inflict shattering blows upon the whole of the technical and war-making structure of the Nazi power.'

Olivia took a deep breath as she continued listening, looking over at the blackout curtains so tightly sealed, thinking about the children upstairs, about her brother who could be alive but was most likely gone, about the pilots so bravely protecting their skies. And then she glanced over at Leo.

Marrying him is the only thing that feels right in a world that feels so very, very wrong.

CHAPTER TEN

AVA

Ava couldn't stop smiling as she rode. *Married!* Olivia's news before she'd started her shift had taken her completely by surprise, although from the way her friend's hands had been trembling when she'd told her, Olivia hadn't exactly been expecting it either. The poor thing had swung from smiles to tears as she'd explained what had happened, but after consoling her about her brother as best she could and reminding her that missing didn't *always* mean dead, Ava had flung her arms around her and promised to help her with the wedding plans. Although she wasn't exactly certain when she was planning on helping her, not with George keeping her so busy.

Ava accelerated, loving the wind against her face, wishing she had her hair streaming out behind her instead of being tucked beneath her hat. She liked to moan about the hours she worked, but truth be told, she wouldn't trade it for any other job. Working at Norfolk House had given her a taste of what it felt like to work, to actually do something with her life, and delivering memos was the most exhilarating thing she'd ever done. The first few days had been nothing short of terrifying, but now that she'd settled into it, there was nothing she'd rather be doing.

She tipped her head back just a little, grateful to be riding during the day for once instead of at night, to feel the sunshine on her face and be able to see the streets and landmarks around her. Someone else had taken over her night shift for a while – George was adamant that they all take turns so they had experience at both – and she was eternally grateful to get a reprieve for even one night. She'd almost forgotten how liberating it was to ride during the day instead of being on tenterhooks at dusk and into the dark. She straightened her back and focused on the road despite how distracting the sunshine was.

Her mind shifted back to the wedding then. *What to wear? My navy dress, or is that too dark a colour for a wedding?* She smiled, imagining her mother's excitement when she told her she needed help choosing an outfit. It wasn't often they had an occasion to dress up these days, and she couldn't wait. *Perhaps the lavender one that I wore to that last dance before the war?*

If only the general could come with me. She sighed, wishing she could spend more time with him. He'd asked her to keep their time together a secret when she'd last seen him, and she hated that she couldn't tell anyone about him yet.

'It's best we keep this between the two of us for now,' he said, as she curled up against him in bed.

His fingers traced down her back, and she kissed his bare chest.

'If only we could wake up together every morning,' she whispered, pushing herself up on her elbow to look down at him.

The general looked at her like he wanted to devour her, and she loved the effect she had on him. For as long as she could remember, his eyes had seemed to smoulder whenever she walked into a room at work, but now they only ever met at his townhouse and he didn't waste any time in taking her straight to his bedroom.

'I haven't told my wife yet, but it's only a matter of time,' he said, reaching for her and pressing a firm kiss to her lips.

Ava pouted down at him. 'If she's not coming back, then why can't I just live here with you? Wouldn't you love to wake up to me every morning?' she purred.

He pulled her closer, and she knew exactly what he wanted from her. 'Just be patient, there's no need to rush. We have a war to win, Ava, and my wife is not your concern. You don't need to worry about her.'

She surrendered to his kisses, easily distracted, but as she rolled around in his sheets she could already see herself as his wife, showing off her ring and being the mistress of the beautiful townhouse.

'Christ!' Ava swore as she realised, a moment too late, that she was approaching the bend in the road too fast.

In a second that felt like the slowest minute of her life, the motorcycle started to slide out from beneath her, her body falling away from the corner instead of expertly leaning into it as she'd been taught, and she fought to correct her mistake even though she knew there was no way to change what was happening. She hit the ground fast, her trousers tearing on impact as she fell, the bike falling and sliding across the ground.

Ava was stunned for the longest moment, lying prone, before her brain suddenly remembered her training and she leapt to her feet, stumbling as she surveyed the road around her. She looked down at the big rip in her trousers and the slash through her leg, blood slowly dripping from her knee. Her shoulder hurt too, the pain making her grimace as she tried to lift her arm, patting at the satchel as if to convince herself that it was still there, that she hadn't lost it.

You have to deliver the memo. Protect the memo above all else!

She ran then to her motorcycle, hauling it up as her shoulder screamed to her to stop, righting it and quickly pushing it to the side of the road in case an unexpected car or lorry came around the bend and didn't see her.

The light is broken. It'll fall off if I leave it like that. It was only midday but she still needed to secure the light, just in case she needed it later. *Think of something, come on, you need to improvise here!*

She grabbed the headlamp, frantically trying to think what she could use to secure it. *My pink ribbon!* Thank goodness she'd left it on there. She quickly untied it and then did her best to secure the light on the front. She wasn't convinced it would hold for the entire journey, but it was all she had right now, and she just had to hope she hadn't damaged either of the tyres in her unexpected crash. If she had to patch the tyre, it could be disastrous.

Ava did her best to ignore her throbbing leg as she tried desperately to start the engine, cringing as it spluttered and then died. *Why didn't I pay more attention during mechanics!*

'No!' she yelled. 'You are *not* dying on me now. Come on!'

She tried again, thrusting her heel down in a desperate attempt to kick-start the bike. When it spluttered again, she almost lost hope, but as she gave it one last go, it suddenly fired up and she gripped the handlebars tight as she accelerated and started to move forward again. It could stall at any moment, and she wasn't wasting a second.

'Thank you, God!' she cried and, despite the blood steadily dripping from her knee, she took off without a second thought for her injuries. She just needed to keep the bike going long enough to deliver her memo; after that, she'd figure out what to do about herself.

The motorcycle stuttered and she held her breath, half expecting it to stop right then and there, but somehow it kept going as she cursed her stupidity, hating her amateur wobble as she fought against the cotton-wool feeling inside her head. *This is on me. If I'd been concentrating, this would never have happened.*

She glanced down at her bag. The memo she was entrusted with was the only thing she should be thinking about, and she knew she'd never forgive herself if she failed – one mistake, one message not delivered to the right person . . . She pushed the thought away.

And all because I was too busy thinking about getting all dolled up for a wedding. She refused to admit she'd also been thinking about a man.

––––– ⠪⠕⠥⠙ –––––

An hour later, with perhaps two miles to go until she reached headquarters on her return, Ava's luck ran out. She heard the change in the engine, the way it stuttered and spluttered, before it came to a complete stop. The silence was deafening.

'Bloody hell,' she swore, trying valiantly to start it even though she knew it was well and truly dead. 'Ugh!'

She dismounted and took a breath, looking down at her knee and not liking what she saw. If she'd thought her shoulder hurt before, it was almost unbearable now, and just looking at her exposed flesh made her stomach turn.

'It's not so far,' she said out loud, as if to convince herself. 'Come on, you can do it, girl.' Everything George had said suddenly made sense. All the times he'd insisted she do her own repairs, scolding her for not paying attention and insisting she listen. *He was being hard on me because he didn't ever want me to be in this position, because he wanted me to be capable, and I ignored him.*

She pushed hard to get the motorcycle rolling, grunting with the effort until she got it moving, her eyes stoically trained forward as she focused on her destination. *I've delivered my message. So long as I make it back in one piece, it doesn't matter how long it takes.*

After almost an hour of pushing and stopping, desperately catching her breath in a throat that felt like sandpaper, she eventually limped back into the garage, her back slick with sweat beneath her thick jacket. Ava was fighting fatigue like she'd never known before, but she propped her motorcycle up with the stand, knowing she had to do everything in her power to get it running again before George saw it. He'd be furious with her, and she couldn't lie to him; she'd have to admit that the error was hers alone. Perhaps this was all penance for how easily she'd dismissed his concerns about her overconfidence. Hadn't he said that it would get her killed one day? The worst thing was that it hadn't even been speed that had tipped her up.

Ava glanced down at her hands, wishing they'd stop shaking as she turned her gaze to her bike. Suddenly she didn't even know where to start, her head feeling woolly as she held out a hand to prop herself up against the wall. The concrete was cool, and she shut her eyes for a moment, desperately needing a drink of water.

'Ava?' A loud voice echoed in the concrete garage. 'Christ, I thought something had happened to you! You should have returned hours ago!'

She let her hand fall from the wall as she turned, and it was the worst thing she could have done. Her legs immediately gave way beneath her, the ground rushing up to meet her well before George could catch her.

'Ava!' She heard his call as her legs buckled, hands flying out to break her fall.

'Sorry, I . . .' she mumbled, barely about to get her words out.

'You're bleeding. Your leg, what happened out there?'

George helped her up to a sitting position so she was leaning back against the wall, and he stayed on his haunches as he examined her knee. She wanted to tell him she was fine and pull away, but she simply didn't have the strength.

'This doesn't look good.'

'You should see the bike,' she whispered.

His eyes moved from her knee to her face. 'I'll deal with the bike later. How badly does it hurt? Are you feeling dizzy?'

'Not as bad as my shoulder hurts.' She grimaced as she tried to move it, but when she glanced down at her knee, she could see why he was worried about it. The blood had dried in parts, but the main wound was still bleeding and her trousers were badly ripped. 'And I'm feeling woozy, but not because I hit my head. I'm actually not great with blood.' That was a gross understatement. She looked down again and wished she hadn't, her stomach lurching at the sight.

'What happened out there?' he asked, as he stood and crossed the garage, going into the first-aid cupboard and pulling some things out.

'Ahh, well—' she started.

'You'll have to take your jacket off so I can look at your shoulder. I'll do my best to treat you here, but if you'd rather go to the hospital—'

'No,' she said firmly, closing her eyes as the room began to spin. 'No, I'll be fine, I just, I think I need some water.'

She heard George drop what he was carrying as he swore, his heavy footfalls indicating that he was going to get the water for her. She tipped her head back, enjoying the cool of the concrete, wishing she could just lie all the way down . . . *Did I hit my head?* She couldn't remember, everything suddenly feeling like a blur.

'Ava? Here, sit up.'

It wasn't until George took hold of her arm and righted her that she realised she was all slumped over.

'Drink,' he ordered, holding a glass to her lips as she greedily gulped it down, not stopping until she'd drained it.

'Thank you,' she managed. 'I feel better already.' Ava went to stand, but George's hand came down on her shoulder.

'No. You just stay sitting there. I don't need you fainting on me.'

She went to scoff at him, about to tell him that she'd never fainted in her life and she wasn't about to start now, but the way the ceiling appeared to be moving told her that he might just be right. Perhaps her fear of blood had amplified now that she'd had to confront so much of her own.

George went to collect the first-aid supplies he'd dropped earlier, before coming back to her and lowering himself in front of her. He was gentle as he turned her leg from side to side, examining the wound before taking out gauze and some iodine in a small bottle, and she realised that despite his often gruff exterior, he certainly had a kind side.

'This is going to hurt a little,' he said, 'but I want to make sure it's clean.'

She nodded, bracing herself for the sting. It hurt, but she gritted her teeth and stayed silent until he was done, his face a picture of deep concentration as he eventually covered the wound with gauze and wrapped it.

'Was there something on the road?' he asked.

'Hmm?'

He looked up at her, his eyebrows drawn together as he stared at her. 'To make you fall off,' he said. 'Was something obstructing the road?'

Ava cleared her throat, breaking eye contact with him and shrugging properly out of her jacket for something to do. He swore under his breath as he looked at her shoulder, and it was only then she noticed that even the shirt she wore beneath her jacket was torn. She'd really done a number on herself.

'I, ah – well, I think I was going slightly too fast,' she said quickly. 'I tried to brake but I overcorrected and . . .' Ava gulped, glancing back at him. 'I'm sorry, I know you must be furious with me. It was a stupid mistake and I was distracted and . . .'

'Did you perform a full mechanical roadside check on the bike? You had your tools with you?'

It wasn't often she blushed, but she felt a deep pink heat spread across her face as he watched her.

'No,' she admitted.

'Because you've spent the past weeks batting your eyelids and convincing someone else to do your mechanical work for you, and you didn't know how?'

She couldn't see the point in lying. 'Yes.'

'Christ, Ava! You have the opportunity to keep yourself safe, you've been given all the training possible, and yet you've chosen to let yourself be helpless out there!'

She bristled, pulling away from him and slipping her jacket back over her shoulder. 'I am *not* helpless, thank you very much.'

'Only when there's no one around to convince to do the work for you. Don't try telling me I'm wrong.'

Ava let go of a breath she hadn't even been aware she was holding, hating how angry he was with her and wishing he'd stop raising his voice. 'Look, I'm sorry about the motorcycle. It won't happen again.'

'I don't give a damn about the bike, Ava,' George muttered as he rose. 'Motorcycles can be replaced, humans can't.'

Ava watched him go, surprised when he spun back around.

'You know what, Ava?' George said. 'One of my riders is in hospital tonight; she's not expected to make it. So if you wonder why I'm so hard on you? That's why.'

She went still. 'Not Olivia?' *Please God, don't let it be Olivia!*

'No, not Olivia. It's Jenny.'

George turned on his heel then and Ava blinked away tears. She wanted to hate him so much, but he was right. She should have studied harder and done the work herself. When her bike had broken down, she'd been scared and felt completely hopeless, and she'd hated it. And poor Jenny; it broke her heart thinking one of their own was so badly injured.

She hissed out a breath as she took her jacket off again, looking at her shoulder and wishing she'd kept her mouth shut long enough for him to finish bandaging it. Ava stood and picked up the first-aid supplies, deciding she'd convince her mother to help her when she got home instead.

Ava unlocked her front door and stepped gingerly inside, taking her coat off. She was surprised how much her body hurt, how stiff her shoulder was and how achy her leg had become with each step. But it was finding her mother standing in the hallway, wringing her hands together, that made her stop walking.

'Ava.' Her mother's voice was barely a whisper.

'I fell off my bike,' she said, starting to take her coat off. 'I need help with—'

Her father strode with such speed from his study that she didn't notice the panicked look on her mother's face until it was too late. His face was red, and when he stopped barely an inch from her face, she could smell the alcohol on his breath.

'How dare you set foot in this house after disobeying me!'

She shrugged her coat back on properly and went to open her mouth, to say something in her defence, but the moment she did that, she knew it was the wrong thing to do. Her father's open palm connected with her cheek so fast that she didn't have time to move. She was so tired, so sore, that she'd let her guard down, and his hand slapped hard against her skin, stinging her cheek and making her teeth rattle in her jaw.

'I'm sorry,' she stammered, nursing her face as he stood over her, his anger palpable as she cowered.

'Your mother has packed your things,' he said, smoothing his hands down his waistcoat, as if to banish imaginary wrinkles. 'This is no longer your home.'

'Daddy, please!' Ava begged, crying now as he turned and walked away from her. 'You can't do this to me! I've been in an accident, you can't just kick me out!'

'You brought this upon yourself,' he muttered.

His study door shut with a bang and she was left standing in the hallway with her mother, speechless, and there was a pain in her chest she'd never experienced before.

'Please,' she said, holding out her hands as she walked towards her mother. 'You can't let him do this to me. Mother, you can't kick me out, this is my home!'

'Ava, I'm sorry, but I told you I couldn't protect you from him if he found out.'

Ava stared at her for a long moment, waiting for her to change her mind, but all her mother did was glance at the bag and suitcase she'd packed – items Ava hadn't noticed sitting in the hall when she'd arrived.

'Mother?'

Her mother just looked at her feet, and as much as Ava wanted to hate her, she still stepped forward and opened her arms, giving her a quick hug. She was surprised to feel her mother return it.

'I'm sorry,' she whispered into Ava's ear.

'I'm sorry, too,' Ava whispered back. 'That you chose to marry such a monster.'

She gathered her things, grimacing when her shoulder screamed in pain at the weight of her bag, but she intended on walking out with her pride intact, and that meant ensuring her father could see her walking with squared shoulders when he looked out of the window of his study. She certainly wasn't going to let him know she was injured, either, and with her coat covering her shoulder – and thankfully long enough to hide her torn trousers – he wouldn't even know she'd been hurt.

'Where will you go?' her mother called out.

'I have somewhere, don't you worry,' she replied, as she thought about the general and the look on his face when she arrived at his door. At least he'd be happy to see her; she only wished she'd had time to arrange it so she could have had his car collect her.

———— ❧～❧ ————

It had taken Ava the better part of an hour to make her way to the general's townhouse. It involved a walk so long she'd been on the verge of collapse, but she'd managed to get a taxi the rest of the way. They were far and few between in London now, with all the young drivers sent off to war, but she was grateful for the old, grey-haired driver who'd stopped for her.

In the taxi she'd managed to fix her hair and found her make-up in the smaller of the two bags her mother had packed for her, so she'd applied some lipstick and powdered her face, but there was little she could do about the uniform she was wearing.

Ava stood outside for a long moment before deciding to stride up to the door and knock. Chances are he'd still be at work and she'd have to wait – with the hours he worked she certainly doubted he'd be there – but she didn't mind resting against his door. Although, if his housekeeper was there, perhaps she'd be kind enough to let her in?

She raised her hand and knocked three times, standing back and wondering if she should unbutton her shirt a little, but the door swung open just as she was lifting her fingers to do it.

'Can I help you?'

154

A beautiful blonde woman stood on the other side, perhaps in her forties, with a pearl necklace resting over what appeared to be a cream cashmere jumper, her hair elegantly swept up off her face. This was most definitely *not* the housekeeper.

'Can I help you?' the woman asked again.

'I'm, ah, well, I'm looking for the general.' Did she have the wrong house?

The woman's eyes seemed to dance over Ava's luggage and then traced the length of her body as Ava stepped back to check the number on the door.

'He's not here,' she said. 'I'm sorry, but how do you know my husband, and what exactly are you doing here?'

Ava swallowed. It wasn't like her to cry so easily, but after the day she'd had, tears suddenly burned her eyes. 'You're his wife?' she croaked.

'I'm the general's wife, yes,' she said, folding her arms and looking impatient.

'I thought you were in the country. I thought . . .'

'I've recently returned from visiting my mother. I'm sorry, what did you say your name was?'

Ava wished the ground would open up and swallow her. What was his wife doing back in London?

'Wren Williamson?' the deep, booming voice of the general made her jump. She spun around, her heart singing as she saw him stepping from his black shiny car and walking towards her. He was here now; he'd be able to clear up whatever was going on. His wife must have returned unexpectedly; perhaps he'd asked her to come to London to discuss divorce? Or maybe he didn't even know she was back, and it would be as big a surprise to him as it had been to her!

But as she smiled and held out her hand to him, he walked purposely around her and greeted his wife with a kiss, his arm slipping around her waist, the picture of a perfect couple as they stood together, watching her from just inside the house.

'What in God's name are you doing at my home, Wren Williamson?' he asked, his eyes darkening as he stared at her, angry just like her father had been. 'And why do you have bags with you?'

His stare was almost a challenge, and as much as she wanted to blurt out exactly why she was there, she lifted her chin and forced a smile. 'I was only wanting to ensure you'd received a message,' she lied, her voice quavering. 'I couldn't find you before I left work, to tell you that the Chief of Staff's meeting time had been changed for tomorrow.'

Her hands were shaking and she reached for the bags she'd dropped at her feet, wanting to get as far away from him as she could, as quickly as possible.

'One of my most dedicated Wrens, although perhaps a little overeager,' he boasted to his wife, his arm still around her waist. 'It'll be dark soon, would you like Fred to drive you home? I do appreciate you coming all this way, although it was entirely unnecessary.'

Ava wanted to say no, that she didn't want anything else from him, but she was so tired and sore, she decided to forfeit her pride and just say yes. What did it matter if she took the ride? It wouldn't make her humiliation any less, or lessen the sting of seeing his wife in the flesh. *How could I have fallen for his lies?*

'That would be very much appreciated,' she managed, before forcing a smile at his wife, despite her humiliation. 'Nice to meet you.'

'Let me walk you to the car, and I'll let Fred know.'

The general picked up her suitcase, snatching it from her hand, and she felt that at any second he might grab hold of her ear and march her the rest of the way, as if she'd behaved like an insolent child and deserved punishment. But he didn't need to touch her to break her heart.

'Don't you *ever* come here without being invited *ever* again,' he hissed.

She blinked at him, wondering how she'd never seen this side of him before. Is this how her mother had felt about her father, when after so much kindness she'd discovered he was actually a beast?

'But you said you were leaving her?' she whispered. 'You said you loved me. I don't understand!'

'I thought *you* understood what our relationship was,' he muttered. 'Now get in the car before you embarrass both of us.'

He opened the door for her and as good as shoved her in the car, as tears began to stream down her cheeks, as she opened her mouth to speak but couldn't find the words. *He was never going to leave his wife. He just played me for the fool to get me in his bed.*

He slammed the door before giving Fred instructions through the front window, as Ava fought against her tears and let only one escape.

That was the last time a man was ever going to make a fool of her. From now on, she was going to learn to look after herself, and no man was ever going to control her life or tell her what to do.

Thankfully Olivia had given her the address for her flat, and Ava recited it to Fred, relieved when he finally pulled up outside. She carried her own bags, walking up two flights of stairs before knocking, her knees trembling as she waited.

When this door opened, it was Olivia who answered, her face breaking into a smile when she saw who it was, which made Ava promptly burst into tears. Music was playing from inside, and as Vera Lynn sung 'A Nightingale Sang in Berkley Square', it only made her sob all the more.

'Sweetheart, what's wrong?'

'My father kicked me out and the general isn't leaving his wife for me!' she cried. 'Everything was a lie, our entire relationship.'

'Come here,' Olivia said, giving her a big hug.

'Please don't say you told me so. I know what a fool I've made of myself.'

'I wasn't going to,' Olivia said kindly. 'Now, let's dry those tears and get you inside.'

There were two other girls in the living room, lying on the sofa smoking, and another girl walked out of a bedroom, her hair in rollers. But bless them, none of them said a thing at her bedraggled appearance and tear-streaked face, other than to offer her a cup of tea and make room for her on the sofa.

'I'm going in for my shift soon, so you can sleep in my bed until I'm home, all right?'

Ava nodded, her hand shaking when the kind girl brought her tea.

'Everyone, this is Ava,' Olivia said. 'Ava, this is Cathy, Lizzy and Charlotte.'

She nodded to everyone, setting her tea down to take off her coat. It felt like it was stuck to her shoulder now, and Olivia didn't miss her grimace.

'What on earth?' she gasped when Ava showed her.

'I fell off my bike,' she whispered, as more tears gathered in her eyes.

Olivia gave her the kindest smile and waved one of the other girls over, as Ava sat back and shut her eyes, so exhausted she barely knew how she'd even make it to bed. But best of all, Olivia didn't ask her to explain herself, and for that she was eternally grateful.

CHAPTER ELEVEN

OLIVIA

'Ava, why didn't you tell me!' They were at Florence's for the dress fitting, and Florence's hands hovered over Ava's shoulder as they both stood and stared at the deep cut and grazes that spiralled down her upper arm. She thought she'd done a good job of patching her up the night before, but clearly Florence disagreed. But it was her puffy red eyes that Olivia was worried about; she'd never seen Ava upset over anything before, but it was obvious she'd cried a great deal during the night.

'You're so lucky to walk away from a crash like that,' Florence said. 'Honestly, you're like a cat with nine lives.'

Florence had a small dish of warm water that she was dipping a cloth into, carefully cleaning the wound as Ava sat silently, barely a grimace marking her face even when Florence gestured to Olivia to spread some cream across her wounds.

'Ava, you could have stayed in bed, you know. I wouldn't have minded,' Olivia said. 'You can have my bed for as long as you need.'

'Wait, *your* bed?' Florence asked. 'What am I missing here?'

Olivia glanced at Ava, seeing how uncomfortable she was. Tears clung to her lashes, and Olivia knew her usually bold friend was on the verge of crying again.

'Ava stayed at my place last night,' Olivia said gently.

'My father kicked me out, and it seems you were both right about my married man.' Tears streamed down her cheeks as Olivia reached for her, using the backs of her knuckles to dry her skin for her. 'It seems he doesn't want me any more than my father does, and his *wife* was there.' Ava's voice cracked. 'It was the most humiliating night of my life.'

Olivia took a deep breath and swapped glances with Florence, who looked as worried as she felt.

'Ava, please, why don't you let me tuck you into bed for a bit?' Florence asked. 'You've been through so much, and we'd all understand if you wanted—'

'It's just a scrape, I'm absolutely fine, or at least I will be,' Ava said, braving a smile and quickly wiping away fresh tears. 'See, all patched up, I'll be good as new before you know it.'

'You're certain?' Olivia asked.

'I wouldn't miss this for the world,' Ava replied, her attempt at sounding bright not fooling Olivia.

She held out her arm as if to convince them both that she *was* in fact fine, but when Florence dropped low and took off the bandage, exposing Ava's knee, she almost hit the roof.

'Ava!' Olivia cried. 'How bad was this crash? Does George know?' *Why didn't she show this to me last night?*

'Oh, he knows all right.' Ava hissed this time as Florence dabbed at the wound, and Olivia quickly sat beside her and took her hand.

'What did he say? Was he furious?' She'd bet he was absolutely livid! She'd had to go to work almost immediately after Ava had arrived the night before, leaving her in the care of one of her flatmates, and she wished now that she'd stayed longer with her.

'Well, he wasn't as angry as I thought he'd be,' Ava said. 'He seemed more concerned about my injuries than the damage to the

160

motorcycle, which was surprising. And these wounds have already been cleaned, so I'm finding this all a bit unnecessary.'

'He didn't yell at you? Scream bloody murder? Demand that all women be banned from riding motorcycles for ever more?'

Ava shook her head. 'Actually, he was the only man last night who treated me with respect and dignity.'

Before Olivia had time to question her further, Florence's grandmother walked in and stole the attention away from Ava's wounds. She was holding the ivory lace fabric in her hands that Olivia had brought with her, and the older woman's eyes were twinkling as she came towards them.

'Mrs Hughes, I—'

'Ivy,' Flo's grandmother said, swatting at the air with her hand as if to dismiss the use of *Mrs*. 'You can both call me Ivy. No need for formalities here.'

'Can't I just call you Grandma?' Ava asked. 'I really need a grandma right now.'

Olivia smiled at Ava, knowing she was trying to make them all laugh, but she could still see how upset she was. But she had to hand it to her; even heartbroken, she was capable of charming a stranger, and an old lady at that.

'Flo told me all about you,' Ivy said, making a tutting noise with her tongue.

'All good things I hope?' Ava asked.

'Well, she didn't mention you had a shoulder that looked like a hunk of meat, that's for sure.' Ivy sighed. 'But I'll figure out a way to hide it, don't you worry.'

Olivia hid her smile behind her hand, loving Ivy already. Anyone who could put Ava in her place so effortlessly rated highly in her books, and she'd done it with a gentleness that told her Ivy had seen the pain behind Ava's bravado.

'So, what do you think?' Olivia asked, eyeing the fabric. 'Can you make it work?'

Ivy came towards her, her walk steadier than she'd have expected in an elderly lady, the fabric of the dress outstretched. She draped part of it over Olivia's shoulder, the rest hanging, and Olivia couldn't help but smile as she looked at the lace.

'A wedding dress would usually take weeks to finish, but we'll make something work,' she said. 'I suppose I'm lucky you didn't bring me a silk parachute and ask me to fashion that into a dress at short notice.'

'I honestly don't want to trouble you, I—'

'Nonsense, this is no trouble at all. Who would have thought I'd come out of retirement in the middle of the war?' Ivy's smile was as warm as her touch, her hand finding its way to Olivia's shoulder. 'You've made this old lady's day, and it's so good to finally meet you girls. Florence has told me so much about you both. This dress is going to be perfect, just you wait and see.'

'You truly think so?' Olivia asked, fretting. 'It all feels so rushed.'

It was Florence who spoke then, crossing the room and directing Olivia towards the full-length mirror, her hands on Olivia's shoulders as she stood behind her while Ivy held up the dress again and draped the fabric against her body so she could see it.

'If anyone can make you a beautiful dress this quickly, it's my grandma,' Flo said. 'I promise you can trust her. If she says it's going to be perfect, then it'll be perfect.'

Olivia blinked away tears as she looked at the lace and imagined herself in her wedding dress, standing in front of Leo. It didn't seem right to feel so happy given what had happened, each burst of happiness short-lived when she remembered why Leo was home.

'Hey, no crying!' Florence gently wiped Olivia's cheeks with her thumb. 'You deserve this, Liv. You're going to make the most beautiful bride.'

She nodded, trying to swallow the lump in her throat. 'I just wish Pete were here. I keep thinking about him, wondering if he's truly dead, or if he's injured or being held captive. I can't get him out of my mind; I just can't believe he's gone.'

Florence hugged her then, wrapping her arms tightly around her. 'I know,' she whispered. 'Trust me, I know the pain.'

Ava flung her arms around them, joining in on the hug, and Olivia noticed Ava hung on just that little bit longer than necessary, and she tightened her arms, hoping she knew how much she cared.

'How do you keep going each day?' Olivia asked when they finally stepped back, looking over at Florence. 'How can you keep living knowing that they're . . .'

Florence's eyes met hers. 'Because you have to. Because we have to keep living for them. It's what they would want for us.'

Olivia dabbed at her eyes and took a breath, nodding at Florence as her friend smiled back at her.

'Girls, we have dresses to organise and barely a day to do it!' Ivy said, throwing her hands up in the air in despair as they all turned. 'Now, when can I get you back for another fitting? You'll need to try it on again.'

'I'm on night shift tonight, but I could come back in the morning?' Olivia suggested.

'Come here then, girl,' Ivy said, setting the lace down and fumbling about for something. When she turned her mouth was full of pins, carefully positioned between her lips as she mumbled. 'You stand here in front of the mirror and let's see what we can do.'

Olivia stood, staring at her face, at her body, wondering when was the last time she'd actually looked at herself. She barely recognised the woman looking back at her – how slender she was, how strong she looked, how much pain filled her eyes. The past year had changed her, but the past few weeks seemed to have defined her.

'How long did you get off for the wedding, love?' Ivy asked, as she helped her strip out of her skirt and jumper, before assisting her to step into the lace dress. It had already been picked apart on one side, and Ivy started to pin it again, making it cling to Olivia's figure.

'Just a twenty-four-hour leave pass,' she said. 'I wish it could be longer, but it is what it is. They don't have enough dispatch riders, so I was lucky to even get that long.'

'So, no honeymoon, then?' Florence asked. 'What a shame.'

'Hey, they only need one night to consummate the wedding!' Ava teased, with a hint of her usual spark.

A shoe flew through the air and Olivia laughed as she saw Ava duck, and a look back the other way showed a very unimpressed Florence scowling at her.

'Do you have any plans?' Ivy asked, her voice low as she continued to position the pins in her mouth on to the dress. 'Perhaps a night somewhere? Even a little time alone would be nice for you both, before your man heads off again.'

Olivia knew she was blushing, but she couldn't help it. She cleared her throat, hating that she was embarrassed. 'Honestly, I haven't even thought about it.' Would Leo think of it? Would he organise something? Or was that something she should do?

Worry fluttered inside her as she thought about their wedding night, about what would be expected of her, about where they might be. She certainly didn't want to stay at her parents' house for their first night as husband and wife, although she supposed they could go to the flat if no one else was going to be there.

'No need to worry, love,' Ivy said. 'That husband-to-be of yours will probably have it all figured out. That's the one part they usually get right; they're so desperate to get their new bride alone.' She

164

patted her hand. 'If you have any questions, things you don't want to ask your mother, well, just ask away. There's nothing I won't give you an answer to.'

'Thanks, Ivy. When Flo said you weren't like other grandmothers, she wasn't joking.'

There were things she wanted to know, like what it would be like on her wedding night and what her husband would expect, but they were questions that lodged in her throat. No matter how kind Ivy was, Olivia doubted she'd ever be able to ask them, no matter how much she'd have liked the answer.

'You're going to make a beautiful bride, Olivia,' Ivy said, standing back with her hand over her heart. 'Your Leo is a lucky boy.'

Olivia kept staring at herself, seeing what Ivy saw. But as much as her heart skipped a beat when she looked at her reflection and imagined her wedding day, imagined the way Leo might look at her when he saw her walking towards him, another part of her kept breaking down, wondering how or why she'd ever consented to a wedding, however small, with Pete missing.

And presumed dead.

'Grandma Ivy,' Ava suddenly said, in a voice much smaller than usual. 'May I ask you a favour?'

Olivia turned to Ava, and realised she still hadn't asked her whether she needed to stay another night.

'Don't tell me, you need a wedding dress too!' Ivy cried.

They all laughed, except Ava.

'I was actually wondering if I might be able to stay here for a few days, just until I find somewhere else,' Ava said quietly. 'My beastly father kicked me out and it turns out I've nowhere else to go.'

Olivia reached for Ava's hand and held it tight. She could see how heartbroken her friend was, even though she'd been doing a brilliant job of hiding her pain.

'A friend of my Flo's is a friend of mine. You can stay with us as long as you need.'

'I'll make up the spare bed,' Florence said. 'It'll be lovely having you here.'

Ava started to cry again as Olivia kept hold of her hand, but this time she was smiling through her tears. 'I'm a terrible cook and I can't do housework, but I promise to make up for it with my incredible personality.'

Olivia had never laughed so hard in all her life.

———— ⌾⌾⌾ ————

The very next day Olivia stood, barely able to breathe, after she turned in a little circle in front of Ivy. Florence hadn't been lying when she'd said how capable her grandmother was; she'd worked a miracle to get her dress finished in time.

'Ivy, I don't know what to say,' she whispered, as Ivy set her hands on her hips to stop her from moving.

'Your smile is reward enough,' Ivy said. 'Now, stand still while I make a few adjustments.'

She wished the other girls were with her, but Florence was sound asleep and Ava had promised to meet them later. For once, Olivia wasn't exhausted, although she did wonder if perhaps she was running on adrenaline. It had been a fairly quiet night, with not one bomb falling. They'd had so many days straight of bombings in London, it was a welcome reprieve – and she only hoped that the reprieve lasted for at least a few days longer.

'Ivy,' Olivia started, chewing on her bottom lip.

'Yes, love?' Ivy looked up expectantly at her.

She wanted to ask her how she'd coped with losing her family, how she stopped herself from drowning in her grief, because her own mother wasn't coping. She knew it was only natural for her family to be in mourning – she felt the same deep grief at the loss of her brother – but she also needed her mother, more than she'd ever needed her before.

'It's nothing,' Olivia murmured, suddenly not even sure what she was going to ask.

'What did I miss?' Ava burst through the door then, but she stopped in her tracks the moment she saw Olivia. 'Oh, Liv, *look at you!*'

Ivy patted her hand, as if to say that they could pick up their conversation later, and as Ava came towards her, arms outstretched, Olivia couldn't help but smile. 'You like it?'

'I *love* it. Truly, it's absolutely stunning. You're the most beautiful bride I've ever seen.'

'I feel amazing,' Olivia said, smoothing her hands down the lace. 'My mother thought the dress would never work, but Ivy's certainly worked a miracle.'

'Is your mother coming here to get ready with us?' Ava asked gently. 'You haven't said a lot about her.'

Olivia shook her head. 'My dad said he'd make sure she was there on time to see us get married. She's in a bit of a fog at the moment; I honestly don't know how to comfort her.'

'Well, we'll get you ready for the big day, won't we, Grandma?'

Ivy chuckled to herself. 'Yes, Ava, we will. Now, make yourself useful and wake Flo up, would you? I'll get some tea brewing.'

Olivia hugged her arms around herself, closing her eyes for a moment as she felt the weight of the lace on her body, and imagined seeing Leo standing in his uniform.

'Stop daydreaming about that fella of yours and come on down for some tea,' Ava whispered in her ear. 'You've got all night to be seeing his handsome face.'

Olivia laughed, opening her eyes and seeing her friend's infectious smile, happy that her eyes weren't as puffy as they'd been the day before. 'Help me out of this, would you?'

Ava moved behind her and carefully unbuttoned the dress, helping her to step out of it and giving her an impromptu hug once she'd put her regular clothes on.

'What is it?' Olivia asked, seeing tears in Ava's eyes.

'Nothing! I'm just so happy for you.'

Olivia narrowed her gaze, not believing Ava's words or her smile. 'Ava, tell me. What is it?' She studied her friend's face. 'Is this about what happened to you the other night, or . . .'

Ava gave a quick sniff and wiped quickly at her eyes. 'Let's talk about it tomorrow,' she said. 'I just want today to be about celebrating you and Leo. Would you like to come and see my room? Grandma Ivy outdid herself making me feel at home.'

'Ava!' she demanded. 'For goodness' sake, just tell me.'

Florence walked in then, rubbing her eyes, her hair messy from bed. 'I think I slept for nine hours,' she mumbled. 'And yet somehow I feel even more tired than I did yesterday.'

Olivia was still staring at Ava, both of them silent, and Florence suddenly seemed to notice what she'd walked in to.

'Ava?' Olivia asked again.

'It's Jenny,' Ava whispered.

Olivia studied Ava's face. 'What's happened to her?'

'Jenny was hit by a lorry, the night of my crash,' Ava whispered. 'I stopped by to see George this morning, to let him know I had a change of home address, and he told me that she didn't make it.'

Olivia's eyes shut. It could have been her. She and Jenny often worked the same shift.

'Did you know she was injured?'

Ava nodded. 'I did. George told me when I came back all bruised and bleeding, but he didn't want me to say anything. Not until he knew more about what had happened and what her condition was.'

Olivia hated that Ava had kept the news from her, but she understood. If George had given her an order, she would have obeyed and respected his wishes, too.

'Was Jenny the other girl who was chosen that day?' Florence asked. 'The day we were all there?'

Olivia slowly nodded, taking a deep breath as she looked at her friends.

'I didn't want to tell you, not today,' Ava said. 'George was hopeful she was going to recover from her injuries, but in the end, they were just too severe. There's going to be a little service for her tomorrow, so we can pay our respects.'

'Should I still have the wedding? It seems wrong, I just—'

'Olivia, this is *your* day,' Florence said. 'We're in the middle of a war, terrible things are happening all around us, but it doesn't mean you can't have a wonderful few hours this afternoon, all right? We all need this.'

Olivia straightened her shoulders and held her chin high. 'Of course, you're right. I just need a moment.'

'Come on, let's go downstairs and have tea and something to eat,' Florence said gently, looping their arms together and leaning her head on Olivia's shoulder. 'No matter what, we're going to make this day special. You hear me?'

'Flo's right,' Ava said. 'You deserve this, Liv. You deserve to marry your man and be happy, no matter what. And I don't think I'm the only one who needs to be part of something joyful right now.'

Olivia nodded and smiled, letting herself be guided downstairs. They were right, she knew in her heart they were, but being happy amidst so much pain was much easier said than done. And it also reminded her that it wasn't only Leo's safety she had to worry about once he left; they'd been warned how dangerous their dispatch jobs were, but it wasn't until today that she'd truly understood just how easily they could lose their lives.

She glanced at Ava, who was already standing beside Ivy and helping to fill the teacups. But it was her shoulder that Olivia was looking at – heavily bandaged, a reminder of how quickly her friends could be taken from her.

Ava looked up then, meeting her gaze, and her smile was a blend of warmth and sadness.

'Grandma Ivy, are you sure you don't have something stronger?' Ava asked. 'I think we need to toast our beautiful bride, and maybe help her nerves!'

Olivia laughed. Despite everything, she couldn't help but have a giggle. Ava was nothing if not entertaining, a perpetually cheerful friend who somehow always saw the best in every situation and did everything to make others smile. And it couldn't have been so easy for her to be upbeat either; whatever had led to her being kicked out of home must have been awful, and she'd clearly been let down terribly by her lover, too.

'You just stick to your tea, Ava,' Ivy said. 'I'll rustle something up before it's time to leave though, to calm the bride.'

Olivia took the tea passed to her, taking a sip. She actually wasn't nervous about getting married; she loved Leo and nothing could ever change the way she felt about him. She only wished things could have been different.

'To Jenny,' she suddenly said, deciding that it was better to acknowledge their joint loss rather than keep it buried just because it was her wedding day.

'To Jenny,' Ava and Florence repeated, holding their teacups high.

'And to our bride,' Ava said. 'Today, *my darling*, is all about you.'

'To our bride!' Florence cried enthusiastically.

Olivia took a sip of her tea as her stomach started to dance a little, and she started to get more than a touch excited about seeing Leo. Perhaps she was more nervous than she'd realised?

'Have something to eat, beautiful bride,' Florence said, passing her a slice of bread. 'I'm giving you the last of Grandma's marmalade as your wedding present. And trust me, you'll thank me when you've tasted it.'

Her mother might not be there, but as she looked around the room, at her friends smiling at her and Florence's grandma busy making food for them, she realised that she had all the support and love she needed right there in that little kitchen.

Olivia felt like she'd been waiting all day to see Leo, having not seen him since he returned to his parents' home the day before, and the moment she saw him, she had to fight not to run into his arms. He was walking into the little church, beside the vicar who'd christened her as a baby, looking as dashing as could be in his uniform, his hands clasped behind his back. But it was the sight of her mother inside the church that stopped her in her tracks – she was sitting clutching a handkerchief, but when she saw Olivia, a smile transformed her face.

'Oh, darling, look at you.'

Olivia took her mother's hands in hers as she rose. 'If this is too insensitive, if you don't think we should be doing this, if—'

'This is exactly what we should be doing,' her mother said, even as tears filled her eyes. 'I'm only sorry I was too wrapped up in my grief to help you today.'

She hugged her mother, holding her tight and trying to stop from crying. 'I just wish he were here. I would do anything to have him here.'

'Pete would love nothing more than to know you two were getting married.' Her mother gently dabbed her face, drying her tears. 'Now off you go and marry that dashing young man.'

Olivia kissed her mum's cheek as her father leaned in, proffering his arm to her.

'It's time,' he murmured, patting her hand when she looped it through.

Olivia turned her focus back to Leo, who was patiently waiting for her. The pews were empty, other than his parents who were seated by her mother. Florence and Ava had entered through the side door, and as she started to walk she heard the door behind them close. She glanced back, surprised to see George standing there in full dress uniform. He gave her a nod, and when she turned back around, she met Ava's gaze and raised her brows in question, receiving a shrug in reply. She certainly hadn't expected to see him today, and she hadn't invited anyone else due to how quickly they'd had to organise everything. It hadn't felt right to invite old friends or even extended family given the circumstances – she hadn't even asked her flatmates.

She quickly forgot about George as they walked towards Leo, nervously biting her lip when her father let go of her arm and kissed her cheek before he shook hands with her husband-to-be. And then she was lifting her hands, with Leo catching her fingers and smiling at her in a way that she knew she'd never forget in all her life.

'You look so beautiful,' he whispered, stepping closer to her and receiving a frown from the vicar, which made Olivia grin.

'Thank you,' she whispered back, admiring him in his uniform, which somehow made him look even more handsome than when he was in civilian clothes.

They said their vows, she in a shaky voice that slowly found its confidence, and it felt like only moments later he was tenderly lifting his palm to her cheek as he leaned in to kiss her, once they'd been pronounced man and wife. Olivia tilted her face to meet his, forgetting anyone was watching him as she gently parted her lips.

'Hello, wife,' he whispered.

She grinned, wishing she could kiss him again. 'Hello, husband.'

Leo held her hand and they turned together, smiling as their parents beamed at them, both mothers dabbing at their eyes. He pressed his lips to her hand before slowly letting go of her so that their families could congratulate them, and it wasn't until after Olivia had hugged Ava and Florence that she remembered George. She looked around, seeing him still standing near the entrance to the church.

She waved him over, and when Leo whispered in her ear asking who their mysterious guest was, she just smiled and took his hand.

'George, what a lovely surprise,' she said. 'George, this is Leo, my husband. Leo, this is Captain George Robinson, my boss.'

'Great of you to come,' Leo said, heartily shaking George's hand. 'Tell me, she's not too reckless on that motorcycle, is she? We rode together before the war and I thought she was a bit of a madwoman!'

George laughed. 'Olivia is one of our most capable and dependable riders,' he said. 'You have nothing to worry about there.' She could almost hear him thinking: *Now her friend Ava, she's the one I have to worry about.*

Leo put his arm around her and she leaned into him, already thinking about how little time they had together before he had to leave. Her heart felt full to bursting just knowing they were finally husband and wife.

'Will you join us for dinner?' Leo asked. 'It'd be an honour to have you with us.'

'I need to get back, unfortunately,' George said. 'I'm pleased I had the chance to congratulate you both in person, though.'

Leo nodded. 'Well, if you change your mind, the invitation is open.'

Leo squeezed her hand and turned back to their parents, but Olivia didn't move. She could sense that George wanted to speak to her. 'He's right, we'd love you to stay, and I really do appreciate you coming today, it does mean a lot,' she said. 'You're certain you have to leave so soon?'

'Unfortunately, I do,' he said. 'I'd hoped to come along and tell you not to come back for a couple of days, but I'm afraid we're going to need you first thing tomorrow morning instead of the afternoon.'

'Oh, right, of course.' She hoped she didn't sound too disappointed. She'd been so looking forward to her night with Leo and a leisurely morning before reporting for work in the afternoon.

'You heard about what happened?' he asked. 'To Jenny?'

She nodded. 'Yes. I'm so sorry.'

'We're desperately understaffed, and with Ava needing time off too . . .' He cleared his throat.

'It's fine, I understand,' she said, braving a smile as she digested what he'd come to tell her. It wasn't George's fault he was the bearer of bad news. 'War isn't going to wait for me to have a honeymoon, is it now?'

Ava and Florence joined them then, and she couldn't miss the change in George as Ava approached. He straightened his shoulders and his gaze turned from friendly to . . . She couldn't quite put her finger on it.

'Ava, good to see you,' George said, looking decidedly uncomfortable, the complete opposite to the man who'd been standing talking to Olivia. 'You all look lovely.'

'If you ignore the bandages, you mean?' Ava rolled her eyes. 'I look *ridiculous*.'

'You most certainly do not look ridiculous,' George spluttered.

Olivia felt like she should give them a moment, but before she could step away George was clearing his throat and making an apology about having to go, and she ended up standing there as he said an awkward goodbye before turning on his heel and leaving.

'Well, wasn't that nice of him to come,' Ava said brightly. 'Perhaps he isn't such an arse after all.'

'Somehow I don't think he came to see the bride,' Florence said.

'What does that mean?' Ava asked, looking between them.

Olivia laughed. 'Oh, sweetheart, didn't you see the way he looked at you? He definitely wasn't here to see me, and I certainly don't think he's an *arse*. The man is lovely!'

Ava looked perplexed, which made the entire situation even more entertaining.

'Don't be ridiculous!' Ava scoffed. 'That man can't stand the sight of me! He's always on my case about going too fast or not listening to him. He was probably thinking how ridiculous I looked with my bandaged shoulder, all trussed up in a dress.' She huffed. 'And I take it back. He *is* still an arse. In fact, *all* men are arses, with the exception of your lovely Leo.'

'Silly us, of *course* that's what he was thinking! I'm sure he couldn't stand the sight of you!' Olivia teased as Florence laughed so hard she had to clap her hand over her mouth.

'You two have rocks in your head,' Ava muttered. 'Honestly, I don't know what you're going on about. George is not interested in me, and I'm most definitely *not* interested in him, or any other man for that matter!'

Olivia laughed along with Florence, giving both girls a quick, impromptu hug, even though Ava was stiff as a board and clearly not happy to be the butt of their joke. 'All teasing aside, thank you both for being here today. It means so much to me.'

'We wouldn't have missed it for the world, would we, Ava?'

Ava shook her head. 'She's right. After everything, being part of something so happy is exactly what we all needed. Even if you are both deluded over this George business. Anyway, I'm sworn off men for good.'

As much as she would have loved to stand and talk to her friends all day, Olivia left them to find Leo, leaning into him, her arm wrapped around his waist as he dropped a kiss into her hair. It certainly wasn't the wedding she'd imagined, but when she looked around she knew she was surrounded by people who genuinely cared about their happiness, and that meant the world to her.

She looked up at Leo and into his blue eyes. They had dinner with their family, then a night just the two of them, but in only twenty-four hours he was going to be gone.

'I don't want you to leave,' she whispered, unable to help herself. 'Another day isn't long enough.'

He pressed his lips to her forehead. 'I'll be gone less than a week, and then I have another two days with you before I ship out. And what's a few more months away when we have the rest of our lives together?' he whispered back. 'One day when we're old and grey, we'll laugh about how we couldn't stand the thought of being parted for just a little bit longer.'

Olivia hugged him tightly, her cheek to his chest.

She certainly hoped he was right.

CHAPTER TWELVE

FLORENCE

'So, tell me all about this wedding.'

Florence smiled, seeing that Jack was clearly trying to make an effort and strike up a conversation with her as they sat together at the start of their shift. 'It was beautiful,' she said. 'Sad at times because of her brother, but we had a wonderful time.' She sighed, thinking about the way Leo had looked at Olivia and wondering if anyone would ever look at her like that. It had been a few days since the wedding; Jack had taken some leave so she'd been on her own the past few nights, and she was grateful to have him back.

The silence that stretched between her and Jack wasn't unwelcome; the night was quiet, there hadn't been a bomb for a few days now, and she'd become so used to being near him without talking that it seemed to come easily. Even if the Luftwaffe did decide to resume their nightly bombing routine, they had at least an hour before the sirens would go off. It was only nine o'clock, and they'd never had an air raid before ten.

'Jack, I hope you don't mind me asking . . .' she started.

'I'm sure I will,' he said. 'Mind, I mean.'

Florence laughed, shaking her head as she stared at him. 'Honestly, sometimes I don't know whether you're just being sarcastic or you're actually just a grump.' His voice was so deadpan it *was* impossible to tell.

His eyes crinkled at the sides, softening in a way she hadn't seen before. 'Look, I wasn't always like this. Before the war, I was . . .' He looked down at his hands, seeming to study them before slowly looking up. 'Things were different then. Sometimes I barely recognise the man I am these days.'

'Your medical training,' she said softly. 'I'm just curious. You seem so capable and I was wondering—'

The words had barely left her mouth when the wailing sound of a siren coincided with a boom that made the ground shake beneath their feet, reverberating through them, plaster dust falling from the ceiling above.

'Here we go again,' he muttered, rising and holding out a hand to her.

She clasped it and stood, almost knocked off her feet when another explosion rocked the room. She shut her eyes, willing the thoughts to go away, hating the way her mind took her straight back to that night.

'You all right?' Jack asked. It was then that she realised she was still holding his hand.

She let it go, smoothing her palms down her trousers. 'We'd better go,' she said, folding her arms to hide the shake of her hands. 'It sounded close.'

'And far too early,' he muttered. 'If they've started already, I hate to think what the night holds.'

As they started to hurry out of the room, which was tucked away at the back of the large building where the ambulances were kept, one of the volunteer firefighters she'd gotten to know came running towards them.

'It's bad out there,' he said. 'Really bad.'

'How close?' Jack asked.

'Can't be more than a street or two away. How many drivers do you have tonight?'

'Not enough,' Jack said, grimly. 'I'll go and get everyone moving. We need to get out there as soon as possible.'

A tremor ran through Florence as she walked quickly over to Petal, the ceiling shaking above her again and sending more plaster dust falling around her. She'd already checked Petal over, knew that she had a full tank of fuel and that she was running well, but as she waited for Jack she still went over everything again, running through the checklist in her mind.

A thudding of uneven footsteps made her turn and she saw Jack lumbering faster than she'd ever seen across the concrete floor, the look on his face showing his agony.

'What is—'

'One of the bombs has hit the theatre,' he said, and she felt her face drain of all colour as she stared back at him. 'It will have been full of people at this time of night.'

'Oh Lord,' she whispered, knowing what that meant – how many lives could have been lost. It also explained why they'd felt the explosion so strongly; they were only a few streets away.

There was another boom that made the floor reverberate beneath her feet, and suddenly there was more noise around them as other ambulance drivers made their way in. The fire engines were already moving, and she caught Jack's eye one last time before she found her way to the driver's seat and carefully turned Petal around, hating to think what they were about to encounter as she tucked into the convoy of fire engines heading to the theatre. It was a route she knew like the back of her hand, and one that was only minutes long, but as they edged closer, it felt like the longest drive of her life.

It was then she felt Jack's leg nudge hers, and although she daren't look down, her eyes fixed on the truck in front of her, she did appreciate the touch. He projected a tough, burly-bear image that had almost sent her running scared that first day, but she'd glimpsed a different side of him enough times now to know that there was more to him. That he had his own reasons for doing this job, that he'd suffered something traumatic, just like she had.

But the brush of his thigh against hers was long forgotten when she stopped abruptly, the scene facing them like nothing she could have ever imagined, even after everything she'd seen.

'What on earth . . .' she started, as she carefully stepped out on to the road. But her question died on her lips as she digested the carnage that confronted them, and she stood rooted to the spot, staring. The noise was deafening, as whistles were sharply blown, men yelled, as people screamed in agony, and then another bomb fell, shuddering through the ground, almost knocking her over.

Florence had thought she'd seen it all, had thought she'd hardened herself to what they were faced with night after night, but nothing could ever have prepared her for this.

'There were so many soldiers here tonight,' Jack said beside her, raising his voice to be heard. 'A few nights home on leave, and this is what happens to them. It's like that first night the Luftwaffe bombed all over again.'

Florence was speechless, staring at the bodies, at the men thrown like toy soldiers across the concrete. She supposed they'd been leaving, or perhaps waiting outside and smoking a cigarette, or maybe their night was only just beginning; whatever they'd *been* doing, it was their final moment alive before they'd been caught unawares.

'What do we do?' she asked, as two firemen ran past her and almost knocked her over.

Jack reached out to steady her and she found herself clasping his hand, as an air-raid warden bustled up to them, flicking on her light.

'Don't try to enter what's left of the theatre, just check the bodies. Some were hit out here, others have been carried out,' the woman said. 'Use your lights sparingly, Lord knows we don't want another direct hit.'

Florence let go of Jack's hand then. 'Come on, let's start at this end.'

He followed her and they both dropped low, using their lights to quickly check each face before feeling in the dark for pulses, ignoring the sticky sensation of blood covering so much of the skin they touched. Florence could hear moans coming from somewhere, but so far she hadn't found a live soldier yet. And every single one was a soldier – all young men who'd deserved a night of fun after what they'd been through.

'Flo!' Jack's call sent her scrambling, and she used her light to check the man he was crouched over.

'He's alive?' she asked.

'Barely, but there's a pulse.'

She stuck her light back in her pocket. 'You go and get the stretcher. I'll stay with him.'

Florence began to sing a little song, filling the silence as she held the man's hand and prayed that he'd make it long enough for them to get him to hospital. She would have preferred moaning or crying out to his silence, and when she touched her palm to his forehead, she hated how cold he felt.

'Florence?'

'Here!' she called back, reaching for her light and flashing it once so Jack could find her. He put the stretcher down beside the man. 'You take his shoulders, I'll take his legs.' Florence bent, bracing herself to lift and reaching down, but she only connected with one leg. 'Hang on a minute, I just . . .'

Florence turned her light on again, wondering why she was finding it so hard to do her job, when bile suddenly rose in her throat and she doubled over, vomiting on to the pavement.

'What's—'

'He doesn't have a leg,' she gasped. 'His, his, his leg is gone!'

No wonder he'd felt so clammy, his lips pursed from the pain. The poor man's leg had been blown off from the knee down!

'He's not going to make it, is he?' she asked.

'Our job is to get anyone with a pulse to the hospital,' Jack said quietly, tying off the leg to stop the blood flow. 'Can we lift him now?'

'Yes,' she said, dropping down low again, refusing to think about what she'd just seen, about what she was so nearly touching. Florence hefted his good leg with all her strength, and within seconds they were carrying him to their ambulance.

They loaded him in and hurried back for another. It was a hard choice, when he was so close to death, but they couldn't drive all that way for one man.

'Here's another!' Jack called out.

As they dropped to check this one, their stretcher already placed beside him, something touched Florence around the wrist, and she startled, instinctively pulling away.

'Help me,' the man whispered.

'One moment, let us just get this soldier on to the stretcher,' she said, before flicking on her light.

The man was clutching his arm, which was bleeding profusely. 'Help me,' he whispered again.

'Sir, can you walk?' she asked, yelling to be heard over the fresh commotion of fire engines and raised voices.

'I think so.' He stumbled to his feet and she steadied him before lifting her end of the stretcher. 'If you can follow us, we can take you straight to hospital,' she promised.

The man did his best to keep up with them, and Florence found herself panting with the exertion of carrying a grown man on a stretcher, struggling to keep up with Jack's long, loping stride. But she kept reminding herself that he was likely in pain and just pushing through, which she had to do, too.

Florence gritted her teeth, her arms burning, but she managed to push everything out of her mind as she focused on what they had to do. She ignored the screams and cries for help; she refused to look down as she tripped and stumbled, as bodies started to line the street, as lights flashed and as the unmistakable boom of another bomb falling made the ground move beneath their feet.

She coughed through the smoke as they finally reached their ambulance, manhandling the stretcher in and, once he was secured, turning around and frantically searching for the other soldier who'd been following them. Only she couldn't see him.

'Jack, we've lost him!' Florence took a few more steps, spinning around, using her light to search for him. In despair, she dropped low and started to shine the torch on the faces of men lying there, most of them dead.

'We need to load some others in,' Jack said. 'And fast, before we lose this one.'

Florence put her light between her teeth when she reached another soldier, using all her strength to turn him over. She groaned from the exertion as she pushed him, taking her torch from her mouth and using it to look at his face.

No. No, it can't be!

She dropped her light, fumbling for it then scrambling backwards, bending over, palms on the road as she vomited over and over again.

'He's here, I've found him!' Jack shouted.

Florence couldn't call back to him as she quickly stood and hurried away from the body, needing to get away from it. Olivia had told her he was home for two days, that he hadn't shipped out yet, that she was so looking forward to seeing him again.

'Flo, help me get this one in,' Jack said as she neared him.

She bent and did her best to help haul the man inside, as a fireman yelled at them and came hurrying over with a young woman in his arms, her body limp as he begged them to take her, their ambulance already overloaded. But Florence could barely hear what was being said to her as she stepped away from the ambulance and doubled over again, unable to keep down the burning-hot bile as it rose in her throat.

'Let's go!' Jack yelled.

She took a deep breath and forced herself to stand, closing the back doors and hurrying around to the driver's side. But as she slipped into her seat and started the engine, she was almost paralysed by sadness.

The soldier she'd seen, the soldier whose pale, ghoulish face would haunt her forever, was Leo, and she was the one who was going to have to break the news to Olivia.

Poor, darling Leo, who'd survived war only to die at home on leave.

Tears streamed down her cheeks as she carefully drove them towards the hospital, remembering the people in the back who still had a chance at living, who she could still save.

Olivia is a widow. My friend who's been married less than a week is going to have to bury the man she loves.

The night stretched on into the early hours, the most deadly and horrific night of bombings that Florence could remember, and now that the sun was rising, the carnage of the evening before was chaotic at best. They picked their way down the street, systematically turning bodies over, checking for pulses amongst the young men still littering the street. It was impossible for anyone to leave when there could still be survivors.

She'd stayed clear of the area closest to the theatre, not wanting to see Leo's body again. Even though she'd seen countless men dead over the past few hours, something about seeing his body had affected her terribly, and she couldn't bear to look at his face again.

'There's no one else here to check,' Jack said as he walked slowly towards her. There was something comforting about his odd gait now, the way he lumbered along seeming so familiar.

They stood together, looking out at the bodies, surveying the mess the Luftwaffe had left behind. The brutal reality of what had happened, of the lives lost and the buildings destroyed, of how many bodies now lined the street, was almost impossible to comprehend, even though she was seeing it with her own eyes.

'It seems wrong, doesn't it,' Jack said, shifting slightly beside her. 'Leaving all these bodies here.'

She nodded, wrapping her arms more tightly around herself. They weren't allowed to take the bodies with them in the ambulance; their job was strictly to transport patients to the hospital, not the morgue. But Jack was right, it did seem wrong to leave them. Especially Leo.

Tears welled in her eyes, and she tried to blink them away, but this time it didn't work. Now that everything was over, now that their job was done, all the sadness she'd been keeping down suddenly came bubbling up in a way she'd never experienced before.

A sob that sounded more animal than human erupted from deep inside her, and she lurched forward, clutching her stomach as the pain took hold of her all over again.

'Florence?'

She'd tried so hard to hold it all in, to stop the tears, but when Jack's arms came around her, holding her and cradling her to his chest, she stopped trying and gave in.

'Shh,' he murmured, rubbing big circles on her back. 'It's been an awful night, but we did everything we could. There was nothing more we could have done.'

Florence clung to Jack and cried until his shirt was wet and she had no tears left to shed. Since she'd lost her parents, she'd tried to stay strong for her grandmother – had forced herself to carry on even though most days she wished she'd perished with them. But seeing Leo had been the last straw for her, the ultimate act of cruelty in a world that had done little but take from her over the past few months.

Her sobs had finally eased, turning into hiccups of air that were gently shuddering from her lips, and she pressed her cheek to Jack's chest, listening to the steady beat of his heart.

'Earlier tonight,' she started, taking a deep breath, 'I saw a man I knew.'

Jack's hand stopped tracing circles on her back. 'Why didn't you say something?'

She should have, but at the time she'd thought that if she told him then she'd break down and not be able to do her job – would have been useless to him when he'd needed her the most. 'I couldn't. I just . . .' She *should* have told him. 'It was Leo.'

'Leo?' Jack repeated, but as his hands ran down her arms, he suddenly stopped. 'Your friend's husband?'

Florence hadn't thought she had any tears left, but just hearing him say the word *husband* brought it all back to her, her eyes damp again as they started to slip down her cheeks.

'Let me take you home,' he said, turning her slightly but keeping her firmly at his side. She let him walk her back to the ambulance, trying not to look at the bodies they passed, trying not to see their faces, eyes open and faces smudged with dirt. She didn't complain when he put her in the passenger seat, and she tucked her knees up tightly to her chest, shivering violently as he got into the driver's side.

It seemed like they were in Petal for hours. Jack asked her if she was cold and what her address was, but otherwise they drove in silence until he pulled up outside her grandmother's house. Florence lifted her head, staring out of the window as rain began to fall, blurring the glass as she listened to Jack get out, registering the fact that he was opening her door.

Florence didn't resist when he scooped her into his arms, carrying her from the ambulance as if she weighed no more than a child. She wanted to tell him she could walk, that he didn't need to look after her, but she couldn't seem to utter a word.

Somehow he knocked on the door without putting her down, and she leaned into his chest even as she heard her grandmother speaking and Ava come running.

'Is she all right? Oh, good lord, what happened?'

'My guess is she's in shock. Upstairs or down?'

'Upstairs. Her room is on the right.'

Florence listened, not protesting when he carried her into her room and placed her gently on the bed, as he carefully removed her shoes and pulled a blanket over her, his hands lingering as he tucked it around her shoulders. As Ava called out that she was just down the hall if anyone needed her.

But instead of leaving her, of hearing his footsteps cross the room and the door shut behind him, she heard Jack settling into the chair that was barely large enough to hold him. She could sense him there even though she kept her eyes tightly shut, wanting to block the world out for as long as she could, knowing that when she finally admitted what had happened, she would have to be the one to go and break the news to Olivia. *I can't do this job any longer, I can't go out there another night. I can't get in that ambulance ever again.*

'Florence, I need to tell you something,' Jack said.

She curled into an even tighter ball, her eyes still shut, but she was listening. He pulled the chair closer, the legs dragging on the wooden floor.

'I know you've noticed the way I walk,' he started, clearing his throat. 'Most people assume I was injured serving, but the truth is I didn't get a mark on me on the front lines, because I was never able to go. My injuries happened just before the war began.'

Florence wanted to sit up and listen to him, to show him that she cared, but for some reason she couldn't seem to move.

'I had a wife and a daughter, and I loved them both more than I could ever tell you. But one night, when I was working late, I didn't get home in time.' He cleared his throat, as if it was hard to get the words out. 'I was hurrying back, I heard sirens, and I just had this terrible feeling that it was my house. I started to run, and when I turned into my street, when I saw the fire engines outside my home . . .'

Jack was silent a long while, and even with her head tucked into the pillow she could still hear the whoosh of his breath, in and out. She heard movement and guessed he'd dropped his head into his hands, or perhaps pressed his palms into his knees.

'The closer I got, I just knew that my life was over.'

Florence forced herself up then, clutching the covers to her as she stared at Jack, into eyes that were full of such sadness they almost made her forget her own grief.

'I was too late, but I refused to admit it,' he said. 'I ran into the house – what was left of it – and started digging, screaming for my family as the fire spread. I found my baby. I found her and I carried her out, and when the firemen came across me I was holding her body in my arms and I didn't even know how badly burned I was.'

She blinked, staring at him, her voice catching in her throat when she tried to tell him how sorry she was.

'It's why I limp so badly now. I was so badly burned I almost lost my leg. They kept telling me what a miracle it was that I was able to keep it. But I couldn't have given a damn about my leg; it wasn't the miracle I'd been praying for.'

Florence pushed the covers down and swung her legs over the side of the bed, staring at Jack a long moment before going to him and folding herself into his lap, her arms circling his neck as his seemed to instinctively wrap around her waist. It was only now she realised she hadn't even thought about him driving her, and how difficult that must have been for him.

'I was partway through studying to be a doctor before the war broke out, before the fire, and I couldn't pass the physical to join the Army, so I decided to work with the volunteer ambulance service. We'd always planned to live in Central London when I graduated, to have more children, to grow old together. Instead, she was gone before our fifth wedding anniversary, and life almost seemed too hard to live any more.'

'I'm sorry,' Florence whispered. 'For all of it.'

Jack didn't say anything for a long moment, his chin settling on top of her head.

'We're not so different, you and I,' he whispered. 'Sometimes it feels like it would have been easier to die with the ones we loved, but what's happened to us, it's what makes us go out every night to save lives. It's what makes us more determined when others are too scared. It's what makes us good at what we do.'

'Because we have nothing left to lose.'

When she heard the muffled sound of Jack crying, Florence didn't say a word. Instead, she let him hold her, wondering if somehow they'd been brought into each other's lives for a reason.

Florence knew she needed to pull herself together, to deal with what she'd seen and go and tell Olivia the news. But she also needed to be held, even for a moment, for someone to comfort her and whisper to *her* that everything would be all right. She knew in her heart that it wasn't true, that nothing was ever going to be right again for any of them, but just for a moment, she wanted to pretend. *That this isn't the last time I'll be seeing Jack, that I'm not a complete failure.*

Her nights of driving an ambulance were over. *Once I tell Olivia, I'm done. I have to tell Jack that I'm not going out again.*

CHAPTER THIRTEEN

OLIVIA

'I'm coming, I'm coming!'

Olivia tied her dressing gown around her waist as she hurried towards the door, expecting to find Leo on the other side, looking sheepish for forgetting his key. She'd only finished work a few hours earlier; it had been a long night, and with all the bombings she'd had to wait and take cover before riding back to headquarters after delivering a memo, and she was exhausted.

She glanced around the flat, not used to being home alone. Her flatmates had made themselves scarce, promising to stay elsewhere for the one night her Leo was home, and she'd only seen him for a couple of hours before she'd had to leave for work. After that he'd gone to see some old friends, wanting to celebrate the amazing news they'd had by telegram only hours earlier – that her darling brother was alive – and she was guessing he'd gotten a little carried away with the celebrations. She could barely be cross with him though. Leo loved nothing more than to be out with friends; he was the perpetual life of the party, and he'd certainly had something to celebrate.

The knock sounded again, and she unlocked the door and pulled it open, ready to admonish him for losing his key before wrapping her arms around him and dragging him to bed. Tired or not, she intended to enjoy every single hour she had left with him.

Oh.

'What are you girls doing here so early?' Olivia looked between Ava and Florence, beckoning them in. 'Were you not working the night shift? Gosh, it was a horrible one last night, wasn't it? The absolute worst!'

'Olivia—'

'You won't believe it, but we've had the best of news!' she said, dropping into the plush chair by the window and waving at them to sit on the sofa. 'My brother has been found alive! He's badly injured but somehow he managed to survive. We received the news yesterday but I didn't get a chance to tell either of you before I had to report for work, but it appears that Leo is still out celebrating the good news. I expected it to be him arriving home when you knocked.'

She sat back, curling her legs up beneath her. It was only then she realised how quiet Ava and Florence were. Florence in particular looked almost green, as if she were about to be sick.

'Why are you both here, anyway?' she asked. 'When I heard the knock, I thought Leo must have lost his key, and I was about to give him a right telling-off.'

'Olivia,' Ava said, and as Olivia looked at her friend and then glanced at Florence, she realised just how ashen Flo's face was.

'Is everything all right? Flo, would you like a cup of tea, you look awfully pale?' Olivia went to rise, but it was when she saw tears shining in Ava's eyes that she knew something was wrong. Very wrong. 'Has something happened?'

'Olivia, I'm not sure if you know, but a theatre was bombed last night, amongst other places,' Ava said. 'There were a large number of soldier casualties.'

'It's terrible, isn't it? When is this ever going to end!'

'Florence was working last night,' Ava continued. 'She was there.'

'Oh Flo, is that why you look so terrible! Why aren't you catching up on some sleep instead of being here? It must be so hard to get all those images out of your head – of what you saw.'

Florence let out a gasp then, and Olivia went to her, putting an arm around her as she tucked in tight to her on the sofa.

'It's Leo,' Florence whispered, her eyes like saucers as she pushed back and lifted her gaze and met Olivia's stare.

'Leo?' Olivia asked, frowning. 'What about Leo?'

'Olivia, I'm so sorry, but Leo was at the theatre last night,' Ava whispered, her voice only just audible. 'He was . . .' She hesitated and Olivia's blood ran cold. 'Olivia, he was amongst the dead.'

'No,' she gasped, looking between them as Florence reached for her hand on one side and Ava on the other. 'No, you've made a mistake. It can't have been him, it—'

'I was the one to find him,' Florence said, her voice low as she squeezed Olivia's hand. 'If there was anything I could have done, if there was even a chance of saving him . . .'

Olivia looked into Florence's eyes.

'He was already gone when I found him.' Flo's voice was painfully quiet. 'There was nothing I could do, I'm so sorry.'

'No,' Olivia said, standing and pacing across the room, digging her fingers into her palms as she fisted her hands. 'No, Leo wasn't there. You must be mistaken, you must have . . .' She stared out of the window and took a deep, shuddering breath. When she turned, she shook her head. 'No, Leo wasn't there, he can't have been!'

Come home to me, Leo! Walk through that door. What happened to growing old together!

'Liv, I'm so, so sorry.' Ava was standing beside her now, her arms open, her face falling as she nodded her head as if to convince Olivia that it truly was Leo who'd been found.

Florence was crying now, and Olivia knew. She started to nod too, shaking, her heart racing and her legs wobbling beneath her as she digested the news.

'We've arranged a car to take you home to your family,' Ava told her as she eased her down on to the sofa, her arm still around her even when Olivia was sitting. 'If you want one of us to come with you, we can. Anything you need, we're here for you, all right? There's nothing Florence and I wouldn't do for you, and we'll tell your flatmates so you don't have to.'

Olivia looked down at her hand, at the simple band on her finger, her engagement ring back to hanging around her neck. An hour ago, she'd been waiting for her husband to walk through the door. A few minutes ago, she'd thought she'd be wrapping her arms around his neck and dragging him to her bed. She lifted her gaze and stared at the door, knowing that he was never going to come walking through it ever again.

'I love you,' Leo whispered, his lips in her hair as she lay, tangled in his arms.

'I love you, too,' she whispered back in the dark, her body curled against his.

'Goodnight, wife,' he murmured. 'I'll never tire of saying that.'

'Goodnight, husband.'

Olivia pulled herself from her memories, not wanting to go back, not wanting to remember, not now.

'Do you know where his body is?' she heard herself ask, as if she were listening to someone else.

'They were all being taken to the morgue,' Florence whispered. 'If I could have taken him in my ambulance, I would have.'

Olivia shut her eyes as a wave of emotion crashed through her, as Ava curled even closer to her and Florence curled up at her feet, her cheek against her knees.

Leo wasn't coming home, but Pete was.

A day ago, she'd have traded anything to get her brother back. Today, she'd have done the same for the life of her husband.

'I need to tell his parents,' she murmured through her tears. 'I'll have to go there on my way home. They need to know. I have to be the one to tell them.'

'How about I come with you, then?' Ava said, gently, as if she were talking to a child. 'You don't have to do any of this alone.'

'And George, I'll need to tell George. He'll have to make arrangements if I can't make it into work tomorrow, if—'

'Olivia, we'll take care of everything,' Ava said. 'Now, let's go and pack you a bag so we can get you home, hmm?'

Ava rose with her, holding her hand, guiding her, but Olivia noticed that Florence stayed put, quietly crying as she hugged her body. Ava led her away, keeping hold of her as she took her into her room. She stared at the bed Leo would never lie in with her at night, imagining what the bed in their home would have looked like after the war, the bed they'd have snuggled up in one day with their children tucked beneath the sheets for a cuddle, where they'd spend lazy Sunday mornings drinking tea and reading the newspaper.

She turned and numbly reached for a bag, letting Ava fold her clothes for her as her legs gave way and she dropped to the bed, watching her.

I'm a widow now.

I'm a widow and my Leo is never, ever coming home.

PART TWO

CHAPTER FOURTEEN

Christmas Eve, 1940

FLORENCE

'Do you think she'll come?'

Florence had been asking herself the same question all morning, and now she couldn't help but say it out aloud to her grandmother. The past month had been difficult – so difficult that she'd found it almost impossible to go to work or drag herself from bed; what had happened with Leo had taken her right back to the night she'd lost her parents.

'The girl's been through a lot,' her grandmother replied, as she mixed the pudding. 'As have you. If she doesn't come today, then all you can do is ask her again another time. You, more than anyone, know what she's going through, so just be patient.'

She was right, her grandmother was always right, but it didn't make the waiting any easier. The truth was, she missed Olivia terribly, and she hadn't seen her since the service held for Leo immediately after his passing. Instead of going to visit, she'd written to ask if she'd like to join them for an early Christmas dinner, and although Olivia had written back and said she'd be there if she felt up to it on the day, Florence hadn't heard anything since. Part of her had the most horrible feeling that Olivia blamed her for seeing

Leo that night and leaving his body there in the street. It was a decision that she'd regretted ever since, even though all she'd done that night was follow the rules.

She opened the oven and checked the mutton and vegetables they had cooking, receiving a flick of a tea towel from her grandmother.

'Shoo! Stop looking at that food; it's not going to cook any quicker from looking at it.'

Florence sighed and walked into the dining room, checking the table for the umpteenth time and trailing her hand across the back of the chair. *It's not just Olivia that I'm all in a knot about.* As much as she wanted to see her friend, her restlessness was more about the fact she'd asked Jack to join them too, and she'd been criticising her decision ever since she'd invited him.

Things had been different between them since the bombing of the theatre. She closed her eyes a moment, holding the back of the chair as she remembered what it had felt like to be curled on his lap, waking with her head on his shoulder and her arm still looped around his neck. It must have been terribly uncomfortable for him but he'd never moved that night, both of them so tired from what had happened, and in the end it had been her grandmother's gentle knock on the door that had woken her. Bless her, she'd never said a word about finding Florence asleep with Jack; perhaps she'd sensed that they were as broken as each other and had needed the contact.

The problem was that, since then, although she felt enormously close to him after what they'd shared, she hadn't been able to return to work. And although he'd told her repeatedly the next day that he understood, and had encouraged her to take some time off, the few times she'd seen him since had been awkward.

She'd gone to see him before his shift once, and had offered to assist with maintenance on the ambulances, but even seeing Petal had brought back so many emotions, and instead of explaining it all to Jack, her words had caught in her throat. Perhaps she was embarrassed, too; he'd seen her at her lowest and opened himself up to her, although he'd been able to find the strength to continue and she hadn't.

But despite all that, her grandmother had insisted Florence ask him to join them for Christmas since he didn't have a family, and much to her surprise, he'd immediately said yes.

'Are you fiddling with the table again?'

Florence laughed when her grandmother called out. She knew her too well. But before she could call back to her, there was a knock on the door.

'I'll get it!'

She smoothed her hands down the front of her dress, hating how nervous she was. *For goodness' sake, it's probably just Ava. Stop making such a fuss.* But as she pulled the door open and a cold blast of wintry air came rushing towards her, she discovered that it was most definitely *not* just Ava. And, silly her, Ava wouldn't have knocked in the first place; she was still staying with them and treated their house like her own.

'Jack,' she said, staring for a moment at the man standing before her, his breath creating puffs of white in the cold. *Gosh, I've missed him.*

'Florence, you look . . .' he said, shaking his head slightly before meeting her gaze and smiling at her. 'You look beautiful.'

She glanced down, her cheeks flushed as she realised he'd never seen her wearing a dress before. For two people who'd been used to seeing one another on a nightly basis, it was ridiculous how awkward they were as civilians.

'Ah, it's terribly cold out here, so if we could come in . . .'

'Oh, of course! I'm so sorry, I don't know what I was thinking.' She moved aside, beckoning him in, and saw that he wasn't alone at the same time she realised he'd said *we*.

'Flo, there's something I should have told you,' Jack said, looking uncomfortable as he reached for the small boy's hand. 'This is . . .'

She waited expectantly, smiling at the child and wondering from where Jack had managed to pick up a stray child on the way to dinner. Although the child didn't exactly look hard done by; he was very well dressed.

'Florence, this is my . . . ah, this is my son. William.'

His son? Florence knew her mouth was hanging open, her manners forgotten. 'I'm sorry, your . . . your *son?*'

He has a son!

Jack nodded, looking decidedly uncomfortable. The little boy was wearing mittens and holding his father's hand, blinking up at her and appearing as uncertain as she felt.

'Jack, you told me . . . that night when you opened up to me, you never mentioned . . .' She lost her words. He'd told her he'd lost his entire family! Why would he have kept a secret like this from her?

Jack's gaze was fixed on hers, and she looked from him to the boy. It took her a moment to regain her composure, to get past the shock, but she knew it was a conversation for another time, *not* one to have in front of the child.

'Florence,' he said gently.

'William!' she said, realising she was speaking in a very high-pitched voice as she tried to calm herself. She immediately started to fret whether they'd have enough food or not. With rations it was hard to invite others over, and it certainly wasn't going to be a feast for so many people, even though they'd been able to secure the piece of mutton. But this was Jack's son; she needed to pull herself together, secret or no secret. 'It's so lovely to meet you, William. Where are my manners. Please come in and shut that door behind—'

'Move aside, let a girl in out of the cold, would you?'

Ava. Thank goodness for her confident, forthright friend arriving home. She was exactly what they all needed to make things less awkward. She'd get a handle on the situation.

'Merry Christmas!' Ava said. 'You must be Jack?'

'Yes, this is Jack and his . . . ah, well, this is his son, William.'

Florence watched as Jack held out his hand to shake Ava's, but he turned back to her straight after, when Ava dropped down to speak to William, something Florence would have done herself if she weren't so shocked.

'Florence, this is for you,' Jack said, passing her a bottle of brandy.

'Thank you,' she managed, still finding it hard not to stare at the child.

'I would have rather given you flowers, but none of the gardens we passed, well . . .'

'Wintertime, huh?' Ava said with a shrug as she stood, once again defusing the awkwardness.

'Florence, I should have told you, but until yesterday I didn't even know he'd be with me, and we haven't exactly seen much of one another lately,' Jack said quietly, moving closer to her as Ava chatted away with William, taking the boy's hand as they started to walk towards the kitchen. 'I . . . he's . . . I don't know where to begin.'

'I thought you'd told me everything,' she whispered. 'But instead you've kept this secret all this time? You had so many opportunities to tell me!'

Anger pulsed through her. She'd thought she and Jack had told one another their deepest darkest secrets! She'd thought they knew everything there was to know about what the other had been through.

'Florence, this isn't easy for me,' he said, stepping closer as he lowered his voice. 'It's complicated.'

She wrapped her arms around herself, not sure what to think. 'Where has he been all this time?'

'With my sister,' he said, looking uncomfortable. 'In the countryside.'

'I honestly don't know what to say,' she said. 'Other than I wish you'd trusted me enough to tell me.'

'He's the only thing I have left,' Jack said, running his hand through his hair as he stared down at her. 'For months after the fire, I could barely look at him. I felt such guilt that he was having to grow up without his mother, and every time I saw him, all I could see was the child I'd lost.'

'So you sent him to live with your sister?' she asked quietly.

'I told myself I was sending him for his own safety, but really it was because I couldn't stand to see him without his mother and sister.'

Florence blinked away tears, taking Jack's hand without even thinking about it as she saw the pain in his gaze. It also struck her just how much she'd missed being with Jack each night in the ambulance. 'Well, I'm pleased you brought him with you,' she said. 'It was a shock, that's all, but I'll get over it.'

Jack opened his mouth, as if he were about to say something, when a gentle knock at the door interrupted the moment.

'I should answer that,' she said, stepping back and letting go of his hand as she turned to the door. When she opened it, she found Olivia standing there, wrapped in a wool coat and holding a plate. 'Olivia!' Florence forgot all about Jack then, other than to quickly pass him the plate as she ushered Olivia in, closing the door behind her before giving her a hug. She wrapped her arms around her friend and held her, not letting her go for a long moment. It put everything with Jack into perspective; his secret had shocked her, but Olivia was here, and that was all that mattered.

'It's so good to see you,' she said, finally releasing her. 'I didn't know if you'd come, if it was too soon after . . .' She sighed. 'After everything.'

Olivia looked pale, and Florence gently touched her shoulder, keeping her hand there.

'I almost didn't come,' Olivia said.

'Well, I'm so glad you're here. You've made Christmas for me.'

When Olivia smiled, Florence sighed with relief, realising she'd most definitely done the right thing in inviting her.

'I suppose I don't need to tell you how strange it is, to have your life turned upside down but have everything else continue as normal around you,' Olivia said, unbuttoning her coat.

'That's a feeling I know very well,' Florence replied. 'How is your family? Your parents?'

'They're well, and thrilled about my brother coming home,' Olivia said. 'But my mother has been fretting about me constantly; it all became a bit much to be honest, so I've been spending most of my time with the two children she took in. They're so inquisitive and lively, despite everything they've been through, so I'm really going to miss them.'

'You're not going back there?' Florence asked, surprised. 'You're staying in London?'

'I gave up my place in the flat after what happened, but I was actually wondering if Grandma Ivy might let me share Ava's room,' Olivia said with a nervous smile. 'Wallowing at home isn't going to do me any good, I'd rather keep busy; and I did pack a bag just in case she said yes.'

'Olivia, of course she'll say yes! We would love to have you here.'

'You're certain?' she asked, looking hopeful.

'I've been worried all these weeks that you might somehow blame me,' Florence blurted out. 'That night, what happened . . .'

Olivia gave her another hug, and Florence was happy to see the colour come back into her friend's cheeks. 'That couldn't be further from the truth. Please don't ever think that again.'

They both sighed, and a weight lifted from Florence's shoulders that she hadn't even known was there.

'That man, is that—'

'Jack!' Florence whispered. 'We're just friends, so don't go making a fuss, but—'

'Flo, would you really invite someone who was just a friend over for Christmas dinner?' Olivia whispered back, linking their arms and leaning into her.

'I invited you and Ava, didn't I?'

Olivia laughed, dropping her head to Florence's shoulder as they walked. 'I've missed you so much. You and Ava both.'

'And we've missed you, too,' Florence said. 'It just hasn't been the same without you.'

'So, you and Jack, you're certain there's nothing romantic between you?' Olivia murmured.

Florence leaned in close, about to answer and tell Olivia about his son, but then Jack caught her eye. He was standing beside her grandmother, saying something that had her grandma laughing like a woman half her age.

'Because from where I'm standing, your Jack isn't looking at you like he wants to be just your friend.'

Florence let go of Olivia as Ava greeted and embraced her, and she turned to Jack and found herself wondering if Olivia just had an overactive imagination or whether maybe, just maybe, she might be right. But it didn't change the fact that he'd kept a rather large secret from her. If he'd been able to keep that from her, what else could he be hiding?

She took a deep breath and decided the mutton needed to be checked. At least it gave her an excuse to bolt from the room, instead of trying to make awkward small talk with Jack.

—— ⌒⊙⌒ ——

'I can't tell you how good it is to see you, Liv,' Florence said, as they sat at the dinner table long after they'd finished eating. Jack and William were sitting playing a board game with her grandmother, which meant the three of them were able to have a few moments alone together before they dished up their Blitzmas pudding. Her grandmother had declared the making of plum pudding with carrots instead of their usual sweet, fat plums a travesty, but Florence had insisted it was better than nothing, and now she was pleased they at least had something to serve. She found herself observing Jack, seeing the way he was with his son. It was obvious they hadn't spent much time together; there was something stilted between them even though William smiled frequently up at his dad.

'When I first got your letter,' Olivia said, pulling her from her thoughts, 'I honestly didn't know whether I'd be able to come or not. But now I'm here, I'm so pleased I did.'

Florence noticed the tears in her eyes but she pretended otherwise, knowing that it was kinder not to acknowledge them since she was clearly trying hard to keep her composure.

'Well, you certainly made Christmas for me. Having you here is better than any gift I could wish for. And my grandma's face when you asked if you could stay? I don't think you could have given her a better Christmas if you'd tried.'

She patted Olivia's leg, so grateful to have her friends with her. Worrying about Olivia had taken her mind off her own memories, but when she glanced over at her grandmother, laughing once again at something one of the boys had said, it all came back to her in a flash.

Mother singing in the kitchen, her father smoking his pipe and reading a book as she and her sister scurried back and forth to set the table and serve the food. Her grandmother arriving with pudding and gifts and joining her mother in the kitchen.

She found herself blinking away her tears, and this time she saw it was Olivia noticing *her* emotion but being kind enough not to say anything.

'Have you thought about when you might return to work?' Ava asked Olivia. 'It's just not the same without you there.'

Florence shifted uncomfortably in her seat. She was anxious about anyone asking her the same question, and she was grateful the attention was firmly on Olivia.

'I think I'll start soon,' Olivia replied. 'I actually went to see George on my way here, and I convinced him that the best thing for me was to be keeping busy. He said he wanted to make sure I was ready, because if I was distracted I could be a danger to myself, so he said to come back next week and he'd let me know his decision then.'

'We're desperately in need of more dispatch riders,' Ava told her. 'The last two nights have been just horrendous, but let's hope we get a reprieve tonight. The last thing I want is to be stuck in a shelter when I'm full to popping with food!'

'It is good to see you smiling, Liv,' Florence said. 'I know how hard life can be after trauma.'

'Actually, girls, if I'm honest, I've had this feeling as if life has just started to pass me by. I know it's only been a short time, but I know I need to start living again,' Olivia said. 'It's the strangest thing, but I don't want to give up just because Leo is gone. I can't keep questioning why it happened, why he was in the wrong place at the wrong time; all I know is that there's nothing I can do to change it.'

Florence nodded, placing a hand on her arm as she watched Olivia brush her cheeks dry.

'You're so brave, you both are,' Ava said. 'Especially so soon after what happened.'

'Actually, a letter arrived for me,' Olivia said. 'Leo sent it, sometime between when we were married and when he returned. It's what made me realise I couldn't hide in my parents' house and cry forever.'

'What did it say?' Ava asked, as Florence gave her an exasperated look. *The poor girl might not want to share the contents!*

'One day I'll share it with you, but for now – well, he pointed me in the right direction. He made me remember what I wanted before the war, and who I was before everything changed. Why I have to keep going, even when I doubt myself.'

Florence nodded. Sometimes she felt like she needed a reminder of what she was like before the war too; what she'd dreamed of and what she'd wanted to do.

'Anyway, what's the news? Surely you girls have some gossip for me?'

'Well, I'd like to know what's really going on between Florence and Jack,' Ava said. 'Flo, you can't honestly tell us that the two of you are *just friends.*'

Florence glanced over at him, studying Jack's features as he leaned forward in the chair and rolled the dice. For a man who'd taken so long to smile in her company, he was certainly making up for it now, despite the rather large secret he'd arrived with. Perhaps it was her grandmother, or maybe it was simply that he felt he could be himself in her home. Whatever it was, she liked seeing him so relaxed, the polar opposite of the man she'd met her first day on the job.

'He's been through a lot,' she heard herself saying. 'You could say we have a shared understanding, although he certainly took me by surprise tonight.'

'A shared understanding that you're falling in love?' Ava teased, which made Olivia giggle.

'Oh, ha ha, very funny,' Florence said, rolling her eyes. 'But I'll take it if it means hearing Olivia laugh.'

Olivia gave her an impromptu hug, and Ava elbowed her in the side.

'I thought you said he was a burly man of few words?' Olivia asked, as she appeared to watch him. 'What changed?'

Florence quickly glanced away when Jack caught her looking at him, studying her hands instead. 'It seems his gruff demeanour was just his way of protecting himself. He's been through a lot, just like I have. But I'd be lying if I said I wasn't hurt that he kept his son a secret. I honestly thought he'd opened up to me about everything.'

'Flo, one thing I've learned is that life is too short,' Olivia told her. 'If you have feelings for the man,' she whispered, 'take a chance, have some fun. Lord knows you deserve it. And don't forget that sometimes people keep secrets to protect themselves from getting hurt. The fact that he brought his son here tonight . . . well, maybe that was his way of showing you how much he trusts you?'

'I agree,' Ava murmured, as she and Olivia both stood. 'I'm going with the *life's too short* part. All the men I've met were bastards, so I highly approve of this one!'

'Ava!' Florence scolded.

'What? They have been.'

'George isn't a bastard,' Oliva said. 'And neither was Leo.'

'Well, I'll give you Leo, but George doesn't count. He's hardly my type.'

'Your previous type was married,' Florence said bluntly. 'I'd say it should have been clear what type of man he was.'

Ava sighed. 'Fair point. But it doesn't matter anyway. I'm not going near another man, not for a very long time.'

Florence took a moment, watching as her friends went to join whatever game the others were playing. They were right – of course they were right – but she had so little experience with men, and so *much* experience with heartbreak, that it made her overly cautious.

The rest of the evening passed quickly and Florence marvelled at how well everyone was getting along. Olivia had been quiet in the beginning but had really come out of her shell, seeming to find comfort in talking to William, and Ava was as animated as ever, keeping both her grandmother and Jack entertained. It was nice seeing her grandmother's face light up with so much joy so often throughout the night, and to hear Jack's deep laugh that she'd rarely heard before. As for her, she liked keeping watch, smiling whenever anyone turned to her, and dipping in and out of conversations, but mostly just content to watch everyone else. And she'd become expert at staying just far enough away from Jack that she didn't have to strike up a conversation with him.

'Well, it's time I went to bed,' Ava announced with a yawn. 'It's not often I'm the first to leave a party, but I have to be at work early and I'm already exhausted.'

Olivia looked like she was about to fall over her own feet from exhaustion, too.

'I don't think you're the only one in need of bed,' Florence said. 'Ava, could you show Liv where the spare sheets are? She's sharing with you.'

Olivia came closer and Florence embraced her, holding her tight. 'You're amazing, Liv. I'm so proud of you for coming tonight, after everything you've been through.'

'I knew you'd understand if I burst into tears over dinner, and besides, I've missed you so much,' Olivia said, holding her tightly. 'We've all been through a lot, haven't we?'

211

'You can say that again.' Florence paused. 'Liv, there's actually something I need to tell you.'

Olivia reached for her hand. 'Is it about you not driving this past month?'

'You knew?'

'Ava wrote and told me,' she said gently. 'It's one of the reasons I knew I had to come tonight.'

'I was too embarrassed to say anything, after everything you'd been through, the loss you suffered . . .'

'I think it's fair to say we've both had our share of loss, Flo,' Olivia said. 'But if you'd let me, I'd like to spend some time with you tomorrow, to take you somewhere.'

Florence embraced her again and kissed her cheek. 'Of course, that sounds lovely. It really has been so good seeing you again.'

Olivia hugged her back. 'Things will get easier, Flo, I promise. Just remember what I said before about life being too short, because I think there is a very nice distraction waiting for you, if I'm not mistaken.'

Florence nodded, realising that Olivia was looking past her at Jack. 'I'll remember. Now, up to bed, young lady, you need your beauty sleep.' She watched Olivia go, relieved she'd finally told her about her job, or lack of one.

'I, ah, I think I'll help to clear up,' Jack said from behind her, running his fingers through his hair. Florence blushed when he glanced at her, and she quickly looked away. Perhaps Olivia was right, after all!

'Oh, don't be silly, you don't need to do that,' Florence said.

But then Jack hooked a thumb towards the armchair, and she saw that William was curled up, sound asleep.

'Well, this old lady needs to rest her feet,' Grandma said. 'Jack, would you mind terribly if I took you up on that offer of helping to clear up? I'd love to have some sleep before those blasted sirens go off.'

Florence stared at her grandmother, who didn't make eye contact with her as she patted Jack on the shoulder and headed for the stairs. Something was amiss; her grandma never went to bed without having a cup of tea first, and she certainly wouldn't ever let a guest clear the dishes. Everyone had deserted her and left her with Jack!

'Grandma, are you feeling all right?' Florence asked, hurrying after her and touching her elbow before she could start up the stairs.

Her grandmother had a twinkle in her eye when she turned. 'I'm absolutely fine, love. I only thought perhaps you might like some time alone with the young man. You've done an exceptionally good job of avoiding him all night.'

Florence's cheeks burned like they were on fire as she let her grandmother go and slowly turned to Jack, who had his hands in his pockets and appeared to be taking a great interest in the light hanging in their hallway.

'Well, let's get tidying, shall we?' she announced briskly, deciding it was better to pretend he couldn't possibly have heard their conversation.

He nodded and started to collect plates and glasses with her, the pair of them not saying a word until there was nothing left to clear and she was in the kitchen standing at the sink.

'I hope you know how much I appreciate you asking me here today,' Jack said, leaning against the door as he watched her. 'I thought bringing William would be easier than trying to tell you, but I can see that hasn't been the case.'

Florence didn't know what to say, but as she opened her mouth she started to laugh. She couldn't help it.

'Now it's funny?' Jack asked, as dry as ever. 'It's funny that I have a son?'

'Jack, you're impossible!' she cried. 'You keep a secret like that and then you just show up and charm my grandmother like nothing at all? I didn't even get a chance to be angry with you!'

He was smiling now, too. 'I figured it was better to beg for forgiveness.'

'He's gorgeous,' she said with a sigh, glancing over her shoulder. 'I can't even imagine what the two of you have been through. How long is he here?'

'Just one more day,' Jack said. 'I brought him tonight because I wanted him to meet the other person in my life who means something to me.' He cleared his throat. 'I also needed a reason to see you. It turns out I rather miss being in an ambulance with you every night.'

She felt her cheeks heating up, and she quickly turned, reaching for the tap to fill the sink.

Florence heard Jack move closer, and she busied herself with making sure the water was soapy enough, not sure what to do with him being so near to her and suddenly losing all her words.

'You know, you didn't have to stay. You could have woken William up,' she said. 'It's not like you get many nights off, and the last two must have been . . .' Florence shook her head. She shut her eyes for a moment, feeling such a coward for hiding in a bomb shelter when she should have been out with him, driving her ambulance.

'I know you feel guilty about not coming back to work, but you don't have to,' Jack replied, standing so close now that, when she took a deep breath, she could feel his shoulder touch hers. 'You've been through so much.'

There were so many things she could have said, but for some reason she couldn't utter a word.

214

'Florence.' He said her name as if it were a question, but she couldn't bring herself to look up at him.

'Mmm,' she murmured, reaching for a plate and soaping it up before rinsing it, her pulse starting to race.

She instinctively passed it to him, as she would her grandmother if they were washing dishes together, but although he took the plate, Jack also took her hand.

'Florence,' he said again, more quietly this time, his fingers slipping slightly on hers thanks to all the soap suds.

This time she did look up, turning slightly and seeing a warmth in his eyes that terrified her as much as it pulled her in.

'I'm sorry I kept William a secret from you. Talking isn't my strong suit, in case you hadn't noticed.'

'Oh, I'd noticed,' she whispered back.

Jack's hand lifted, cupping her cheek as he gazed down at her. And then, without another thought, she stepped into him as his other arm curled gently around her waist, pulling her in as his lips met hers. Their kiss was slow and warm, so unhurried that it made her relax against him, his lips brushing against hers then stopping for a moment, his breath ragged against her mouth before he kissed her all over again.

When it was finally over, instead of turning back to the sink or backing away, she clutched the front of his shirt in one hand and pressed her cheek to his chest, letting him hold her as if they were slow-dancing in one another's arms.

This time, his lips found the top of her head instead of her mouth, and they stood there together until the water went cold, until Jack took her hand and led her to the sofa and they both sat down. His arm stretched along the back of the sofa, and even though her instinct was to still be shy around him, she moved closer. When his fingers brushed her shoulder, she kicked off her shoes and curled her feet up, wriggling until she was leaning against him, as if it were the most natural thing in the world to do.

'We really should get some sleep,' he said, his lips finding her hair again as she nestled even closer. 'The sirens will be going off before we know it.'

'I'm so tired, but somehow not remotely sleepy either,' she said.

'I know the feeling.' Jack chuckled and she could hear the sound through his chest, against her ear.

'I can't stop thinking about William losing his mother. How old was he when she died?' she whispered, almost too scared to ask but wanting to know everything about him.

'William was four, and our daughter had just turned two.' She felt his body tense as he spoke about them.

'That must have been so hard for him, and for you.' She took a deep breath. 'My sister, she was sixteen. There were only four years between us, but she'd always been the baby of the family. Had us all wrapped around her little finger.'

Jack started to stroke her arm, and she lay there, listening to the steady beat of his heart, talking in a way he hadn't to anyone since the night he'd lost them.

'Do you ever just want to scream at people – people just living their lives?' he asked. 'Those first few months when I got out of hospital, I hated seeing people doing normal things when my Andrea and Cindy had been taken from me like that. I wanted everyone to see my pain, but then when I left the hospital, I suddenly couldn't bear to see William. It hurt too much, knowing I couldn't save the rest of our family, knowing he was going to grow up without his mother, and that I should have been able to save her.' He cleared his throat. 'The only thing that helped was rum, and I wouldn't let him see me like that.'

Florence nodded against his chest. 'Everyone says the pain will get easier with time, but it's a lie. It never does.'

'I miss you,' he whispered into her hair. 'Every night, I miss being in the ambulance with you.'

Tears filled her eyes. 'I miss you, too.'

Jack continued to stroke her skin, and she found herself absently trailing her fingers over his hand, the one he had resting on his thigh. And they talked about everything and anything, even as the sky started to lighten outside, before she finally fell asleep in his arms.

It seemed only a minute had passed since she'd closed her eyes when she woke to the creak of the stairs.

'What happened to the dishes?'

Florence blinked and sat up a little as her grandmother threw her hands into the air before turning to see them curled up on the sofa, Jack still fast asleep. Florence looked over and saw that William was still sound asleep in the chair as well.

Their eyes met, and she knew her grandmother understood when she smiled at her.

Jack happened, Grandma.

And despite Florence not uttering a word, her grandmother nodded and turned, draining the water and filling the sink with hot water, as Florence carefully extricated herself from the man she'd been tucked up beside all night. She doubted he usually slept so peacefully, and the last thing she wanted was to wake him, not when they'd miraculously had a night with no bombs.

She went and picked up the tea towel from where Jack had dropped it the night before, taking the first plate her grandmother passed her and being rewarded with a little smile.

'He's a good man, that Jack. And that William is a dear little boy.'

'I know, Grandma,' Florence said, glancing over her shoulder and watching Jack sleep for a moment. 'Trust me, I know.'

CHAPTER FIFTEEN

*A*VA

Ava tugged the blanket up a little higher, waiting to hear the King's speech on the wireless. It was Christmas Day and she still had an hour before she had to leave for her shift, and Olivia and Florence had come in to listen, too. Florence sat at the foot of her armchair, and Grandma Ivy came in with a pot of tea on a tray.

'If I'd known how good it was here, I'd have left home sooner!'

Ivy just chuckled and Ava beamed back at her. She wasn't joking. All her life she'd been on tenterhooks around her father; one day he'd adore her and she'd lap up his attention, and the next she'd somehow look at him the wrong way and he'd fly into a rage. Her mother had done her best, she could see that now, but being in a home like Ivy's was fast showing her what a loving home really looked like.

'Ava, did you ever rekindle your romance with the man you were seeing?' Grandma Ivy said. 'I haven't heard you talk about him since before the wedding.'

Ava made a fuss of taking her tea and choosing a biscuit, doing her best to ignore the question. Her cheeks burned whenever she thought of that day; she'd never been so embarrassed in all her life.

'Ava?' Ivy asked gently.

'No,' she huffed. 'It turns out he just told me what I wanted to hear to get me in his bed while his wife was away.'

Florence dropped her head to Ava's lap and hugged Ava's knees. 'He was married?' Ivy asked.

Ava cleared her throat. 'I can't lie to you, Grandma. He was.'

'And did you know this before your romance began?'

Ava glanced up at Olivia, not wanting Grandma Ivy to think less of her. 'Yes, I did. But in my defence, he told me all along that she was living in the country, that their marriage was over, and I bought all his lies. And before you ask, I'll never make that mistake again. I've learned my lesson.'

'You're right, a man will say anything to get a pretty young thing in his bed,' Ivy said. 'But he's the one who's married, Ava; he's the one who broke his marriage vows, and don't you forget it. He's the one to blame, not you.'

Ava sipped her tea, not wanting to acknowledge Grandma Ivy's kind words, lest she suddenly burst into tears. She didn't want anyone to know how much he'd truly hurt her.

'Ava, do you hear me? When an older man behaves like that, they're taking advantage of you. It's not your fault.'

Ava couldn't hold her tears at bay then, and she frantically blinked, trying to clear them. 'Thank you. I needed to hear that.'

'Did you love him?' Florence asked, still hugging her legs.

Ava nodded. 'Yes.' She quickly wiped her cheeks. 'Or maybe I didn't. Maybe I've always just been in love with the idea of love.'

Grandma Ivy left the room, and Ava panicked for a moment that she was going to kick her out after her confession, but instead she returned with an extra biscuit and passed it to Ava, before pressing a warm kiss to the top of her head.

'Don't stop believing in love because of one broken heart,' Ivy said, as the wireless crackled to life with the introductory anthem before the King was to speak. 'Just promise me you won't take up with a married man again. It never ends well, no matter what they say.'

'I promise,' Ava whispered, as Olivia turned the radio up and they settled to listen to the King shuffle his papers before his voice travelled across the airwaves.

There hadn't been an awful lot of news from the front, not since France had been occupied, other than whispers of England being next. So hearing their King's Christmas message after a blessed night with no bombings was exactly what they all needed.

'*In days of peace the feast of Christmas is a time when we all gather together in our homes, young and old, to enjoy the happy festivity and good will which the Christmas message brings. It is, above all, children's day, and I am sure that we shall all do our best to make it a happy one for them wherever they may be.*

'*War brings, among other sorrows, the sadness of separation. There are many in the Forces away from their homes today because they must stand ready and alert to resist the invader should he dare to come, or because they are guarding the dark seas or pursuing the beaten foe in the Libyan Desert.*

'*Many family circles are broken. Children from English homes are today in Canada, Australia, New Zealand, and South Africa. For not only has the manhood of the whole British Commonwealth rallied once more to the aid of the Mother Country in her hour of need, but the peoples of the Empire have eagerly thrown open the doors of their homes to our children so that they may be spared from the strain and danger of modern war.*'

As Ava listened to the rest of his speech, tears glistened in her eyes. And when Grandma Ivy looked over at her, her smile so kind, her eyes so non-judgemental, she wished she could have grown up in a house that wasn't filled with fear. She also realised that it was time for her to grow up.

In her entire life she'd relied on her looks and her social standing, expecting life to be easy, expecting to have everything she'd ever wanted. She looked at Olivia and Florence, two women who'd become her closest friends in such a short time, and she knew she wanted to be more like them.

From now on, she was going to pull her weight, at home and at work. No more getting others to do things for her; it was time to stand on her own two feet and show the world exactly what Wren Ava Williamson was capable of.

_____ ❧ _____

'Merry belated Christmas, Ava.'

Ava looked up and found George standing there, his arms folded over his chest as he watched her. She wiped her hands on a rag, not even caring that her skin was stained with oil, and stood. He looked surprised.

'Merry *Blitzmas*, George,' she replied with a grin as he raised his brows. 'Although it hardly felt like Christmas this year, did it? Despite everyone trying their best to be festive.'

He shook his head. 'You're right about that. There's something strange about not having Christmas carols in the street.' It was one of the main things she'd noticed this year, and although she'd never thought much about it before, she'd suddenly have done anything to hear someone singing 'Silent Night'. 'There's also something strange about this picture. I don't recall you being so at ease with having a tool in your hand.'

'You've been away a few days. Things have changed.'

'I can see that.'

Ava studied him a moment, before picking up her rag and the tools she'd been using and putting them back where they belonged. She'd actually missed him over the past few days; he'd been on a period of leave to return to his family in the country, and she was surprised how happy she was to have him back.

'Did you hear that some of the bigger shelters were decorated so people could have their Christmas celebrations?' she asked. 'Apparently, there were all types of shows being organised underground, and there still are.'

'So I've heard,' he said, before clearing his throat. 'Ava, I'm sorry to do this to you, but it's going to be a long shift for you. I hope you're up for it.'

'Of course I'm up for it.' She crossed back to her motorcycle. 'Has something happened?'

He unfolded his arms and stepped towards her. 'Actually, I'm expecting an urgent message tonight, but I don't know whether it'll be within ten minutes or a few hours. It'll need to be taken immediately to the shipyards in Plymouth, and you know that route like the back of your hand. There's no one I trust more than you to get this message there quickly.'

She placed her hand on her heart. 'Why George, I'm flattered. I'm not used to such praise from you.'

He gave her what could only be described as a withering look, and she laughed, playing the role she always seemed to perform in front of him. Part of her wished she could admit how scared she was some nights, but it always seemed easier to paint on a smile and pretend that she'd never felt fear before.

'Have you had dinner?' he asked. 'My sister packed me roast vegetables and beef, and I'm more than happy to share.'

'Are you certain this staying-late business isn't a ploy to get me to have dinner with you?' she asked.

George didn't reply, but she did hear him groan. 'Don't make me regret this, Ava. I could easily eat alone.'

'Now where would be the fun in that?' she replied, surprising herself at how easily she was chatting to him. George had always managed to irritate her more than anything else, although she was starting to see just how much she may have irritated him with her earlier behaviour, too.

When she stepped into the back room that he used as an office, she waited as George cleared part of his desk and then produced the bundles of carefully wrapped food.

'Thank you,' she said, as she sat across from him. 'I know I joke around a lot and make fun of everything, but I really do appreciate you sharing this with me.'

'You're most welcome, but it's my sister you have to thank for the food. She hated the thought of me coming back to work so soon, so she put this little post-Christmas feast together. Only, I knew it was far too much food to ever consume on my own.'

'Well,' Ava said, 'I certainly appreciate it. Make sure to thank her for me.'

The phone was beside them, and Ava noticed the way George glanced at it often, as if he was expecting it to ring at any moment. She turned her back to it slightly, her attention on him as he put some food first on her plate, and then his.

'So, tell me, what made you want to do this job, other than your obvious appreciation of fast motorcycles?' George asked.

Ava sat back, her stomach growling at the sight of food. She hadn't eaten since breakfast.

'You want my honest answer?' Ava took a mouthful, eyelids shutting momentarily as she swallowed the food. It was exactly what she needed after a long day.

'I read your intake form. I know what you said on the record, but I have a feeling there's more to you than that.'

Ava looked up at him. 'I signed up for all the wrong reasons, and I'm embarrassed to say that it was more about the independence and adventure it afforded than the actual job itself.'

George leaned forward in his seat. 'I probably should berate you and explain to you the seriousness of war, but if I'm not mistaken, you've seen that for yourself now.'

She nodded. 'I have. Recently more than ever, if I'm completely honest.' She smiled at him. 'I've also realised how much I love riding a motorcycle and how much I respect the enormity of our job, the role we're playing in the grand scheme of things. I'm so grateful to be here, truly I am.'

'Well, I suppose that if we're making confessions, I have one of my own,' he said.

Ava watched him, surprised that he was being so candid with her. 'And what would that be?'

'I think that perhaps my feelings on women assisting with the war effort were unfounded.'

She opened her mouth, ready to admonish him for *ever* feeling that way, when the telephone rang and almost sent her leaping through the ceiling in fright.

'Captain George Robinson.'

She quietly took another mouthful of food, not wanting it to go to waste if she had to leave in a hurry.

'Yes, sir, I understand.'

Ava swallowed. She was certain his sister was a wonderful cook, but the cuts of meat available this Christmas certainly hadn't been the best, and she could have done with a drink to help wash it down.

'Ava, I'm terribly sorry, but we're going to have to cut our dinner short,' George said when he hung up the telephone.

'It's fine. It's not like the war waits for mealtimes to be over.'

'Right then,' he said, gathering his jacket and hurrying out the door, calling over his shoulder as he spoke. 'Have that motorcycle ready to go, I'll be back as soon as I can.'

Ava watched him leave before eating the rest of her meal. When she'd finished she put the plates away, hoping he'd have time to eat his leftovers later.

She smiled as she thought of George then, surprising herself by even thinking about him. *Pity I'm sworn off men, because there's something about that man that's actually not so bad.* He wasn't suave and devastatingly handsome, or full of bravado or dripping in money – all things she'd been attracted to in the past. But after tonight, she was starting to wonder if perhaps she'd been missing what was right in front of her.

She smiled to herself as she went out to her bike, checking her pink ribbon was tied tightly and thinking back to how horrified George had been when he'd discovered it that first time.

The rumble of another motorcycle made her turn, and she went to open the heavy door to let the driver in. She looked out at the dark night sky, wondering if they'd have another evening without bombs falling, or whether all those people would indeed be spending another night post-Christmas underground. It was then she noticed a piece of holly hanging from the doorway opposite her, clearly supposed to look like mistletoe, and she wondered what she'd do if she found herself beneath it with George. The thought quickly put another smile on her face, and it was still there a few minutes later when another rider arrived back, and she called out hello and shut the door behind her, going back to tinker with her motorcycle until George returned.

He immediately strode towards her, but just as he opened his mouth to speak, a loud boom rang out and Ava shuddered, knowing exactly what that noise meant. It truly was Blitzmas.

'You were fast,' she said when George stayed silent, his face twisting as he seemed to wrestle with his thoughts, or perhaps what to say.

She held out her satchel, surprised when he hesitated before taking it from her. She watched as he put a document inside and then closed it, securing the buckle and handing it back to her.

But when she went to take it, he didn't let go.

Ava looked up at him, and saw a softness around his eyes that she hadn't ever seen before. There was a look there that took her completely by surprise.

'I can find someone else to do this,' George said, quietly.

She blinked. 'I'm sorry, what did you say?'

'Ava, it doesn't have to be you. I should never have asked you to stay late after an already long shift.'

Her hand started to tremble then, and she tugged at the satchel, furious that he'd even suggest such a thing.

'Give me the bag,' she said, glaring at him.

'Ava, please—'

'Who would you send in my place, George?' she hissed, her anger rising. 'Olivia? Or perhaps one of the less experienced riders? What on earth is wrong with you?'

He didn't say anything straight away as she stood her ground, her breath coming in rapid pants.

'You told me yourself that I know that route better than anyone else. I've been riding it for months now and I'm not putting anyone else at risk just because you're suddenly worried about me.'

'It's dangerous out there tonight,' he said. 'I know you'll hate me saying this, but I don't want anything to happen to you.'

'And I don't want any special treatment,' she snapped. 'I'm good at my job, and I don't want you protecting me. Not when it means putting someone else in danger instead of me.'

'There's no one else I trust more with the Devonport deliveries, I just . . .' His voice trailed off.

'Why have you changed your mind, George? About women?' she asked, impatient to hear what he'd begun to tell her earlier.

'Because when I was away fighting, the only thing that kept me going was knowing that the women in my life were safe at home. I needed to imagine my mother, my sisters, my nieces all safe, to believe I'd have them to come home to. It wasn't because I didn't see them as capable, it was because I needed to know they'd be there, that it wasn't all for nothing.'

George held her gaze for the longest of moments, before he stepped closer to her. She was about to fight him, thinking he wanted to take the satchel from her, when she saw the way his eyes had dropped to her mouth.

He wants to kiss me.

She quickly stood back, holding the satchel close to her body. She knew better than to become entangled with a man at work; if her liaison with the general had taught her anything, it was to be careful whom she fancied.

'Ride safely then,' he murmured.

'Always.'

With that, she strode away from him, collecting her hat and gloves and mounting her bike, before starting her engine and rolling backwards, giving him one final look before riding out of the garage and into the night.

———— ⚬⚬ ————

Ava shifted her weight slightly, her bottom starting to feel numb after sitting for so long. The trip to the shipyards took hours, but she was well used to it and she was also proud of the fact it was her route. George had told her on countless occasions that it was one of the most important outposts, due to its proximity to the coast, which meant she was entrusted with some of the most highly classified, highly important, war documents.

The night was almost too quiet, the houses and buildings she'd passed all blacked out so no one could see them from the sky, and she had her headlamp on to show the way. Some nights, if there was enough light from the moon, she left her light off completely. She hated the thought of being a target to a hidden plane lurking in the airspace above, but most often there was simply no way to ride without having it on. They were all told to ride as fast and efficiently as they could; the hope was that their speed would make them an impossible target, or at least that's what they were told.

A loud noise made Ava jump, and she glanced over her shoulder, not sure where it had come from. It almost sounded like a lorry crashing, but she just kept riding, accelerating a little more as her nerves started to rattle.

You're fine, just stay focused on the road and keep riding.

Another noise, a much louder boom this time, and just like that she knew how bad the night was going to be.

The road ahead was straight and Ava went even faster. She couldn't get caught in whatever devastation was happening behind her; she had to get to the shipyards as fast as she could. She leaned into a slight bend, breathing slowly as she did her best to keep her mind calm, her focus absolute. But she suddenly couldn't stop thinking about the look on George's face as he'd kept hold of her satchel, as if he'd known something she didn't. Why had he been so concerned about tonight when he'd returned? Why was tonight any different from the other nights she was dispatched with a memo? Or was it that he suddenly felt differently towards her after the moment they'd shared dinner in his office?

Stop overthinking everything, you know this route like the back of your hand. You just ride like you always ride, there's nothing to worry about. He was probably just feeling protective of you, after spending some time with you.

Ava sat up a little straighter, taking comfort from the weight of her satchel at her side, her eyes trained on the road, carefully keeping a lookout for any dangers.

Only, no amount of focus could have prepared her for what was to come.

The blast was so sudden, so intense, that she didn't even know what had hit her. Her motorcycle jerked abruptly, making it impossible for her to stay in control, her ears feeling like they were bleeding. She hung on to the handlebars for as long as she could, her body falling as she collided with something, as the ringing in her ears made her scream from the pain.

It was like being slammed into a concrete wall, her fingers losing grip as the motorcycle went one way and her body flew through the air and hit the road.

———— ∞◦◦∞ ————

Smoke curled through the air, threatening to choke Ava as she slowly opened her eyes. She reached out a hand, fumbling in the dark, clawing at the ground as she tried to drag her body from the hard road beneath her.

Where am I?

She blinked, the black skyline in the far distance punctuated by large, rising clouds of white smoke that she knew could only mean one thing. *Bombs are falling on London.*

The ringing in her ears was so loud she could barely think; a high-pitched scream that made it almost impossible for her to piece together what had happened.

Ava finally hauled herself up, frantic now as she realised she'd come off her motorcycle on the road and could be hit by a vehicle at any moment. The blackout meant that the roads were the most dangerous place to be as night fell, with most vehicles forced to drive without lights. She couldn't remember what had happened, how she'd ended up on the ground, her body flung so far from her bike. Had she hit something? Had a bomb been dropped near her?

I was riding straight and then . . . Her mind felt like a sieve, unable to piece together the moments that had left her on the ground.

She searched for her torch, barely able to see as she shuffled across the road. Eventually her foot connected with something hard and she bent to collect it, grateful to discover it was what she'd been looking for. She turned it on, banging it against her leg when it didn't immediately work, and then suddenly there was a pool of light around her, illuminating the crash. *There was a tree.* It all came rushing back to her then: the explosion that had sent her careering sideways, the fallen tree trunk she'd seen too late; swerving across the road, her front wheel clipping the trunk and sending both her and the motorcycle flying up into the air.

Ava's breath caught in her throat, rasping as she hurried to inspect her bike. She wiped at her face, eyes stinging as she hauled her motorcycle up, her light positioned between her teeth now, and desperately tried to start it. But it was a waste of time; the front wheel was pushed back into the frame, and even if she could have started the engine, she never could have ridden it. It was a mangled mess.

She hauled the motorcycle off the road, arms screaming in pain as she used all her strength to move it, hoping it would look salvageable come morning, and she checked the satchel across her body, sliding her hand inside to make sure the document was still there. Her head was spinning and she lifted her hand to it, wondering if perhaps she'd hit it. When her hand came away sticky with blood, she realised there was a good reason for how woozy she felt. Her head had started to pound and she was finding it difficult to balance, let alone walk, her ears still ringing and making it almost impossible to think. She stood in the dark, her light turned off now for fear of being seen from the sky as more booms echoed out, more than she'd ever heard before, and she tried to ground herself, tried to keep her feet steady as she focused on breathing in and out.

You deliver those documents, even if it kills you.

Ava had never forgotten the words relayed to them during their training, and as she set off down the road on foot, her canvas satchel firmly across her body, bombs falling behind her and wreaking havoc on the city she loved, she wondered if it was to be her last dispatch. Every time she was sent out with a memo, she knew she was carrying an order or piece of information considered crucial to the war that was highly time-sensitive; they all knew they were risking their lives every single time they set out. She'd just been lucky up until now.

She forced her legs into a run, like a newborn foal trying to gain its balance as she stumbled along, determined to do her job even if it took her all night. How much time had passed? She wracked her brain, trying to remember where she'd been, how long she'd been riding for before the crash.

Devonport. You were trying to get to the shipyards at Devonport, in Plymouth. You know the route like the back of your own hand. You can do this.

She stopped a moment, turning her light on to get her bearings again. She was a long way from her destination, but so long as she could walk, if she could just keep moving, she could still make it before morning. *I'm not going to let anyone down. I can do this. I'll hitch a ride with a passing vehicle as soon as one comes along.*

Another boom sounded out so loudly that she felt it reverberate through her feet, the ground shuddering with the force of it as she propelled herself forward again, as she refused to accept defeat. But in that moment there was something scaring her more than the bombs; she could smell smoke, and it was becoming thick in the air, filling her nostrils, sending a shiver down her spine as she realised what was happening.

London wasn't just being bombed. It was on fire.

If ever there was a night she was in danger of losing her life, it was tonight.

CHAPTER SIXTEEN

FLORENCE

SIX HOURS EARLIER

'So, what is it you wanted to show me?' Florence asked Olivia as they walked along an unfamiliar street just outside London. She glanced at her watch, worried they wouldn't make it back in time.

'It's easier to show you than try to explain,' Olivia said. 'We're just about there.'

They kept walking, and Florence kept wondering, and when they finally stopped outside a large house, it was the sound of children squealing and laughing that she noticed first. 'I'd forgotten what it was like to hear children,' she said. 'It's been such a long time.'

She remembered now how quiet it had seemed when large numbers of children were sent to the countryside for safekeeping, but after so long she no longer noticed it. Until now.

'Where are we?'

'We're somewhere special,' Olivia said as she opened the door with a key. 'This place saved me after Leo's passing, and if I'm not wrong, you need some help getting back to your life, just like I did.' She paused. 'Leo would hate to know that he was the cause of you giving up when you were so good at your job, and if I'm honest, it breaks my heart knowing you haven't been back since that night. I only hope that, in coming here, you might change your mind and realise just how needed you are.'

Florence wanted to reply, but the words stuck in her throat, so instead she quietly stepped inside after Olivia. She stood, surprised to see children sitting down, drawing and playing, some in wheelchairs, and others she could see through the window playing and running outside. *Is this an orphanage?*

'I haven't been entirely honest with you, Flo,' Olivia said as she waved to some of the children. 'I haven't been with my parents all this time. I actually spent a week here helping out before I came to your place for dinner.'

Florence didn't know what to say, other than to assure Olivia that she didn't have to explain herself. What was it with people in her life keeping secrets from her?

'Is it an orphanage?' she asked, looking around.

'Of sorts,' Olivia said. 'But all of these kids hopefully have a parent or family member who will come for them, eventually. Some of the parents are still in the hospital recovering, some they haven't been able to locate yet, so their kids are sent here to be cared for and to receive schooling. These are children who stayed behind in London instead of evacuating to the countryside.'

Florence smiled. 'You said to me once that before the war you wanted to be a teacher.'

Olivia grinned back. 'I did. I also thought I'd be a mother, but with what happened to Leo . . .' Her smile was tinged with sadness now. 'Anyway, I want to be surrounded by children, and this feels like the best way to honour my own dreams and my marriage. I can't be a mother, but I can make a difference in the lives of these children.'

A girl of about seven came racing up when she saw Olivia, holding on to her leg and then twirling around in excitement.

It was then that Florence noticed the girl's arm was heavily bandaged.

'What happened to her?' she asked.

Olivia had dropped low to give the child a hug. 'Flo, these children are survivors. It's why I wanted to bring you here. They're only alive because of people like you and Jack who risk their lives every night. This is where they come when they're discharged from hospital, if they have nowhere else to go; you may have even saved some of these children that you see here.'

Florence burst into tears then, she couldn't help it. The children continued to laugh and play, their little voices lifting around her as Olivia's arms found her and held her tight. *This is where those children go.* She thought of the family she'd saved in her first week on the job, the mother with the two children; could they be here somewhere, waiting for their mum to recover?

'They're alive because of you and others like you, Flo,' Olivia whispered. 'I needed you to see them, because I knew it would give you the strength to go back to work. I had a feeling that you were struggling more than you've let on, more than you've wanted to tell me.'

Florence nodded, not trusting that she wouldn't cry again if she spoke.

'This is the reason you can't give up, Flo,' Olivia said. 'And when you return to work, every time it's hard, every time you think you can't keep going? You need to shut your eyes and think of these children.'

As a little hand found hers, tugging at her to come and see something, Florence felt something shift inside her. Olivia was right. She'd been so caught up in the pain of her memories, in her fear of something terrible happening again to someone she loved, that she'd forgotten what good she'd already done. What good they'd done night after night through the bombings.

She stepped out of Olivia's embrace, mouthing 'thank you' before following the child whose hand had slipped so easily into hers.

Olivia had suffered so much pain, and yet somehow she'd turned her darkness into light. Florence already loved her, but this made her love her friend all the more.

'I'm so lucky to have you in my life, Liv,' she said, turning back to glance at her friend.

Olivia's smile was as warm as sunshine. 'It goes both ways.'

——— ⚯ ———

Six hours later, Florence was numb. When she'd turned up before the night shift started, the surprise and then relief in Jack's eyes had told her she'd done the right thing in returning. She'd been filled with so much hope, so much determination, but it had fast become the most heart-wrenching, desperate night of her life, and she had the strangest feeling that she wasn't even in her body any more; the day she'd spent with Olivia seeming like a lifetime ago. Jack was silent beside her, the toll of what they'd seen too much for any one person to deal with, let alone a person who'd lost his own family in the same way.

She wanted to shut her eyes to block out the terror, but Florence knew that, just like the memories of her own family, she would never be able to erase them, even if she tried to follow Olivia's advice and think of the children. The smell of burned flesh, the sound of people screaming, the sight of the thick smoke that had seemed to engulf all of London, swirling and threatening to choke everyone in its path.

London had been on fire, the incendiary bombs starting a firestorm like nothing she could have ever imagined, and it still wasn't all extinguished. The saddest part of her night had been, without a doubt, taking two firemen to the hospital, covered in burns and screaming out in pain. One of the men hadn't made it, losing consciousness on the way, and she'd wondered if his friend had prayed for the same fate. She hated to think what he'd go through if he did live beyond the night.

They still had a long way to drive to get back to headquarters, having broken protocol to take another injured firefighter home to his family at the end of their shift, and Florence was grateful she could see the road. The smoke had been so thick in parts that it had completely obscured the road like fog, and it didn't matter how tightly they had the windows wound up, the smoke had still seeped in and made them cough.

She blinked through her tears as she drove, her knuckles visibly white as she clutched the steering wheel.

Florence slowed as she passed something on the side of the road, the glint of metal catching her eye. The sky was already light now, the horrendous night of bombing over, but it took a second to realise what she was looking at.

Oh my god, it's a motorcycle!

She pulled over, her hands starting to shake as she turned off the engine.

'What are you doing?' Jack asked, but she didn't have time to answer him.

Florence leapt out of her seat, running across the road to check the motorcycle. She heard Jack limping behind her, and she called back to him, unable to take her eyes from the wreckage before her.

'Check for a survivor,' she cried.

It was then that her heart almost stopped beating. *No. No, no, no, it can't be.*

Florence forced her feet to keep moving, dropping to her haunches as she reached her trembling fingers out to the soft pink ribbon. It was smudged with grease, or perhaps it was dirt, but there was no mistaking that it was the ribbon Ava had told her about.

'There's no one here,' Jack said, coming up behind her. 'I've had a good look around the area.'

She tried to open her mouth but no words came out. Florence's hands dropped to the ground in front of her as she tried to steady herself. After everything she'd been through, this was the moment that finally broke her.

'Florence, what is it?' Jack asked, lowering himself down beside her. 'Tell me what's wrong!'

She lifted her hand, opening her palm with the ribbon she'd tugged from the handlebars.

'This is Ava's motorcycle, Jack,' she whispered. 'It's hers.'

Jack's eyes met hers for a moment before he stood, holding out his hand. And it was then she saw the blood on the road.

'We'll find her. I promise you, Flo, we'll find her.'

'Ava!' she screamed. '*Ava!*'

'If she was here, I'd have seen her,' he said. 'Come on, let's go and see what we can find out.'

Florence clung to him as they walked back to the ambulance and she frantically looked around, half expecting to discover her friend's body on the road. But there was nothing, no sign of her. Jack put her in the passenger side and got behind the wheel; she pressed her nose to the window, forgetting how difficult it was for him to drive.

Ava, where are you?

———— ◦❦◦ ————

Florence recognised the way she was feeling, because it was the same as when she'd lain in bed in hospital, waiting for news about her family. She'd known they were dead, but there was still that glimmer of hope – that maybe she was wrong, that maybe they had been rescued and at least one of them had made it.

They'd gone to see George, but he wasn't there, and so she'd left a note for him and then returned home. It was the last thing Olivia needed to deal with after everything she'd been through, and she also hated how worried her grandmother was, too.

'Florence?'

She looked up from where she was sitting as Jack bent low. She'd almost forgotten he was there.

'I'm going to go and see what I can find out,' he said. 'The hospitals are full to overflowing, but someone has to know something.'

She nodded. 'Thank you.'

'You stay here with Olivia, so I know where to find you.'

Florence reached out to him, and Jack took her hand, bending even lower this time as he pressed a slow, gentle kiss to her forehead before leaving.

'Here, have this,' her grandma said, sitting across from her and passing her one of the two cups she was holding. 'I wish I had some sugar for you – you look like you need it.'

'Last night,' Florence started, as she wrapped her fingers around the mug, grateful for the warmth.

'Last night was horrible,' Olivia said for her, shaking her head. 'I mean, look at it out there.'

Florence followed her gaze out of the window. London wasn't burning any more, but she was certainly still smoking. The firefighters had worked valiantly to control it – to stop the fires from spreading any further – but it was still horrendous to see their city so broken.

'Sometimes I wonder if it will ever end,' Olivia said. 'All the news from the front seems so morose, too. It's like everyone expects that England will fall next, unless the Americans come to our aid.'

'We'd lost a great deal more men by now in the Great War. So, unlike you young ones, I'm still feeling mighty optimistic that we'll be victorious.'

They all sat for a long while after that, sipping their tea and lost in their thoughts about the war, until eventually Olivia stood up and went to boil more water for another pot.

'You know, if anyone can survive a crash, it's Ava,' Olivia said. 'Honestly, if you could have seen her during our training, she was just crazy. Poor George actually looked like he was going to have kittens most of the time!'

Florence smiled; she couldn't not. It definitely didn't surprise her to hear how reckless Ava had been.

'I wish I could believe you, but if you'd seen the motorcycle, what was left of it, I just . . .' She let out a breath. 'I suppose I can't see how anyone could survive it.'

They moved their chairs slightly so they could stare out of the window, and the minutes passed slowly as they sat, both lost in thought. But a loud thump sent Florence jumping and her teacup rattling.

'What was that?' Olivia asked, setting her cup down and standing.

'I don't know, but after all those bombs, the slightest sound has me on edge.'

There was another thump, and Olivia ran to the door with her grandma hot on her heels. 'It's something outside, at the door.'

Florence looked around for a weapon, convinced something terrible was on the other side of the door, and she was just about to tell her grandmother what she thought when the door opened and Ava fell inside, slumped over and bleeding heavily.

'Oh my god!' Olivia screamed.

Florence ran forward, dropping to her knees as she quickly supported Ava's head, panicking when she felt her fingers instantly moisten with sticky, warm blood. It was then she noticed a man standing there, a lorry parked outside her grandmother's house that must have belonged to him.

'She insisted I bring her here,' the man said, clutching his cap so tightly it looked like he was wringing it dry. 'She wouldn't let me take her to the hospital, I didn't know what to do.'

'Thank you, we'll take it from here,' she said, as they struggled to get her into the house.

'Ava, can you hear me?' Florence asked, looking over her body for other injuries. 'Ava!'

'Too loud,' Ava croaked.

Florence looked up and traded glances with a horrified-looking Olivia.

'What do we do? Should we take her to a hospital?' Grandma asked.

'We need to clean her up, do what we can here first,' Florence said. 'If you help me move her to the sofa or even your bed, I can tend to her while you call for help. The neighbours four houses down have a telephone.'

Olivia and Grandma dropped down beside her, and together they carefully lifted Ava and carried her to the sofa. There was a blanket draped over the back of it, and Florence tucked it around her, worried about how cold she was.

'I need towels, a bowl of warm water and any bandages you have,' Florence said, wishing Jack hadn't left. He was the one who was good at this sort of thing; her training was much more basic. 'Ava? I need you to stay with me, all right? I need to clean your wounds and figure out what happened to you.'

Ava made a moaning sound, but she did open her eyes. Her lips were cracked and dry, and Florence sent her grandmother after Olivia to fill a glass of water, helping Ava to lift her head and take a sip when she returned with it.

She noticed there was now blood all over her grandmother's cushions, and it worried her how much was coming from Ava's head. When Olivia came back into the room, Florence got her to help prop Ava up a bit more, so she could inspect it.

'Can you go and find a way to contact George? He needs to know where Ava is. And we need transport to take her to hospital.'

'No hospital,' Ava murmured.

'She's going to hospital,' Florence said, ignoring her. 'Come back as quickly as you can.'

Olivia touched a hand to her shoulder briefly, before hurrying off to call for help, and Florence set to work cleaning Ava's head as best she could. But it was one of her ears she was most worried about, as it was bleeding profusely now and she had no idea how to treat it. In the end, she wound a bandage around Ava's head, covering her ear, before moving on to the rest of her body.

'How bad is the pain?' she asked.

Ava had moaned a little while she'd cleaned her head, but she seemed to be slipping in and out of consciousness now. 'Bad,' she whispered.

'Florence!' Jack's voice was unmistakable on the other side of the door as he knocked.

'Come in!' she yelled back.

Jack rushed inside, his eyes wide when he saw Ava on the sofa.

'Do you still have Petal?'

He frowned. '*Petal?*'

'The ambulance. Where is she?'

'Yes. Supplies?' Jack said, clearly realising why she was asking. 'Do you need morphine?'

'Yes. And more bandages,' Florence said. 'I haven't even made it past her head yet.'

Jack came closer instead of walking away, and she watched as he crouched down to look at Ava's head. Blood had already seeped through part of the bandage. 'I think we should just bundle her up and take her to hospital,' he said.

'No,' Ava murmured. 'I don't want,' she grunted, 'family to know.'

'Florence, we're taking her,' Jack said, scooping Ava up into his arms before either she or Ava could protest. 'This is our decision to make, not hers.'

'We're your family now, Ava. No one else needs to know but us,' Florence told her.

She watched as Jack limped through the room, and she glanced at the mess she'd left, knowing her grandmother would understand. Florence picked up her jacket and shrugged into it, hurrying after Jack and almost walking straight into Olivia as she stepped on to the street.

'We're taking her to hospital,' she said. 'I'll contact you as soon as I know anything. Tell George she's alive, but her injuries are too bad for us to treat at home.'

Olivia gave her an impromptu hug and she returned it.

'She's going to be all right,' Olivia whispered. 'She's tougher than all of us put together.'

'I hope you're right,' Florence said, letting go and hurrying after Jack so she could open the back of the ambulance.

Sometimes, being tough wasn't enough. She knew that better than anyone.

It had been a long day, made even longer by the fact Florence had worked a twelve-hour shift through the night before finding her friend and still hadn't made it to bed. She was also due to report for work in the early evening, which meant that even if she managed to fall asleep, she'd barely get a few hours.

'Come on, let's get you inside.'

Ava had been allowed to leave hospital since they were full to overflowing, so long as she had someone to take care of her, and in her morphine-induced muddle she'd become agitated that someone might try to take her to her actual home.

Bless her, Florence's grandmother didn't even bat an eyelid when they arrived back, she just patted Flo's shoulder and looked into her eyes with that all-seeing, all-knowing look that only she seemed to possess.

'She needs somewhere to recuperate,' Flo said. 'I'm so sorry, but—'

'Of course. You let me care for her; it's time you got some sleep I'd say,' her grandmother said. 'She's been living with us for months, I'm hardly going to kick her out now.'

'Thank you.' Florence could barely croak the words out, but she did lift her arms to give her grandmother a long, warm hug.

She turned to see Jack walking down the stairs, and when his eyes lifted to hers, she knew he had something he wanted to say. She waited as he said goodbye to her grandmother, watched as his face changed when he spoke to her, softening around the eyes as he smiled. But the usual serious look that bracketed his face returned as he walked towards the door, to Florence, and she followed him outside.

'What a day,' she said, leaning against the door after she closed it.

'You can say that again. I can't believe she walked most of the way on foot to deliver her message. Talk about doing whatever it takes.'

'Not to mention making it all the way home.' Florence shook her head, still in shock over the events of the past few hours. 'I can't believe she convinced someone to drive her, but refused to go straight to hospital. Whatever happened with her parents, it must have been bad; she was just so determined to keep it from them.'

Jack was staring out towards the road, towards where Petal was parked, and she mistakenly thought he must be thinking about the ambulance.

'Do you think we need to take her back?' she asked. 'Petal, I mean. We're breaking protocol by not returning her to the—'

'Florence, I don't give a damn about the ambulance.'

She crossed her arms, suddenly feeling the cold as she stared, wide-eyed, back at Jack. 'It's been a long day,' she said. 'I think we both need sleep.'

'Florence, there's something I've been wanting to ask you, something I want to say, but I'm not good with my words.'

She wrapped her arms even tighter around herself as she watched him, wishing he'd turn around so she could see his face properly, but he'd paced a few more steps away and he couldn't seem to bring himself to look at her.

'Jack, whatever it is, you can talk to me,' she said, letting go of her arms and taking a step towards him. 'No secrets any more. Remember?'

Jack's eyes caught hers when he finally turned, and she had the most unusual sensation, as if her breath had been stolen from her. 'Florence, I . . .' He took a step towards her, and then another, as she waited, her feet locked in place where she stood. 'I was wondering, when we finally have a night off, whether we could see one another? What I'm trying to say is—'

'I'd love that,' she interrupted, wanting to put him out of his misery as he fumbled for the right words. Florence couldn't help the smile that crossed her face. She'd been braced for him to say something terrible, and all he'd wanted was to ask her out.

When Jack closed the distance between them, his palm gently cupping her cheek and his lips so carefully brushing hers, she managed to forget about everything else. The night they'd had, how tired she was, the loss they shared between them. All she could feel were his lips on hers and the overwhelming sensation that her legs were going to give way beneath her.

'I'll see you tonight,' Jack whispered, his mouth barely an inch from hers.

'I'll see you tonight,' she replied.

Jack walked backwards a few steps before turning, and with her fingers pressed to her lips she watched him go, wondering how she'd ever manage to sleep now that he'd gone and kissed her again.

CHAPTER SEVENTEEN

OLIVIA

Olivia sat beside Ava, still finding it hard to accept that her usually larger-than-life friend had been so badly injured. They'd only lost one rider they both knew well so far, but they all knew the realities of their job – there were already a handful of women who'd died dispatching messages.

'Tell me something interesting,' Ava said, reaching for the cup of tea beside her. Her head was bandaged and Olivia found herself constantly looking at it. 'I'm going crazy sitting inside all day.'

'You've only been doing it for two days!' Olivia laughed. 'Have you told your parents yet?'

Ava shook her head, then cringed, clearly regretting the movement. 'My parents? Not a chance. My father made it very clear that I wasn't to set foot in their house again.'

'What about your mother though? Would you like me to visit and tell her at least?'

Ava shut her eyes. 'Thank you, but no.'

Olivia sighed. 'I know families can be difficult, and whatever happened with your father sounds horrid, but she's your mother after all. Perhaps this will make them change their minds?'

'My mother chose my father,' Ava said firmly. 'As far as I'm concerned, Grandma Ivy is my new mother. She treats me like a daughter should be treated.'

'While we're talking about telling people,' Olivia said, leaning forward a little and deciding to change the subject. 'George has been asking after you. I think he'd like to come and visit.'

'Visit me?' Ava's eyes widened. 'Are you certain?'

'I am,' Olivia replied. 'After your accident I went to see him again. I told him I was ready to come back, and although he wanted me to wait a while longer, he's desperately short of riders and he's agreed that I can come back tomorrow.'

'And you're certain you're ready?' Ava asked.

'I am.' Olivia smiled. 'Nothing is going to bring my Leo back, I've accepted that. Life has continued without him, and now more than ever I want to do everything I can to help end this damn war. I'm going to live a life of duty now.'

Ava's smile was kind. 'I knew you wouldn't be able to stay away for long.'

Olivia laughed, more freely than she had in a long while. 'That's why I love you so much, Ava. Everyone else keeps asking if I'm all right and telling me I should be taking it easy and not even thinking about work, but not you. You treat me just the same as always.'

'Pleased to be of service,' Ava said, but this time when she smiled, it came with a groan.

Olivia jumped to her feet. 'What can I do? Where does it hurt?'

'Everywhere,' Ava said through gritted teeth. 'I'll be all right, it was probably all that laughing. My head is pounding.'

'How about I leave you to rest,' Olivia said. 'Perhaps you should get some sleep?'

Ava gave a little nod, but just as Olivia was about to leave, she heard her murmur.

'Tell George I'm going to be fine,' Ava whispered. 'If he wants to visit me, he can.'

Olivia was more than surprised, but she just smiled. 'Of course.'

'He's not so bad, you know. I mean, he acts like he has a stick up his arse sometimes, but I'm actually coming around to liking him,' Ava said.

Olivia kissed Ava's cheek and squeezed her hand. 'I'll tell him. About the being able to visit part, not the stick. Get some rest.'

Ava's eyes had already fluttered closed, and Olivia quietly shut the door and left, wondering what on earth had happened to make Ava soften so much towards George. She'd been so clear about him not being her type, but then perhaps Ava's type hadn't worked out so well for her so far.

———— ❧ ————

Olivia loved watching Florence as she sat at the table, drawing and colouring with a group of young children. Just as she'd expected, her friend had fitted in seamlessly, her kindness of spirit and genuine warmth drawing the children to her.

'Liv, I don't know how to thank you,' Florence said when she pulled up a chair at the table. 'This is like homemade soup for the soul.'

Olivia grinned. That was *exactly* what this place was. 'There's nothing quite like spending time with children. I feel like they make me see the world differently.'

'You couldn't be more right,' Florence said. 'It's given me such perspective. You bringing me here has shown me just how important our work is. These children are all the inspiration I need.'

'Talking about children, has Jack opened up to you more about his son? He seemed like a delightful little boy.'

She met Florence's gaze when she looked at her. 'Not really, he's a man of few words. But I feel like I finally know all his secrets now. Or at least I hope so!'

The children commandeered their attention then, and it wasn't until they rose to leave an hour later that they had a chance to talk again.

'Florence, I have to confess that I had an ulterior motive in bringing you here.'

Florence linked arms with her as they walked out on to the street. The day was gloomy, but their moods were anything but. 'And what is that? If you're looking for donations to keep this place running, I'm afraid to say I don't have any money.'

Olivia slowed her walk. 'It's not your money I want, Flo. It's your time.'

'Oh, that's a given! I'll volunteer here as much as I can,' Florence said.

Olivia stopped walking and let go of her. 'I want you to open a school with me, or perhaps even a home for children who've lost their parents or been displaced during the war,' she said. 'I need someone with compassion and love to work alongside me – once the war is over of course – and I can see how happy this kind of work makes you.'

Florence was smiling, but she looked surprised. 'I don't know how good I'd be as a teacher, but I do love children.'

'Just promise me you'll think about it,' Olivia said, linking their arms again as they continued to walk.

'I will,' Florence said.

'Think about it?' Olivia asked.

'No, I mean I'll do it. Once the war is over, once all this is behind us, I'm in, boots and all. I don't need to think about it.'

'Truly?'

Florence held her arm and leaned into her. 'Truly.'

Olivia smiled to herself as they walked. Her life had changed in ways she never could have imagined, but being with her friends, doing work that truly meant something to her, it was all making her realise that she did have a future; just not the one she'd expected. She'd mourned Leo with all her heart and she couldn't ever imagine being with another man, but she had a life to live, and she knew now that she could live it while still honouring his memory every single day.

———— ❦ ————

'Good to see you back,' George boomed from across the garage as Olivia walked in.

'It's good to *be* back,' she said, surprised that he'd heard her enter.

'You're feeling up to the task?' he asked. 'I'm grateful to have you here, but I don't want you back if you're not ready.'

She nodded. 'I wouldn't be here if I wasn't. Where to today?'

George took her satchel from where it was resting on her motorcycle and placed a memo inside, securing the buckle and passing it to her.

'You'll be delivering this to Norfolk House, your old place of work. It's a good short ride for your first dispatch.'

'Thank you. I appreciate it,' she said. 'I'll be fine once I get out there.'

He looked like he was about to say something else, so before it became awkward she spoke instead.

'I thought you'd like to know that Ava is recovering well, and she said she'd happily receive you, if you still want to visit, that is?' She watched him closely but he didn't give anything away. Part of her had always wondered if perhaps George and Ava would be the perfect fit; there weren't many men who could handle her friend, but George seemed more than capable of the task.

'Thank you, I appreciate you checking with her,' George said. 'Now ride safely, I can't go losing one of my best dispatchers again. I'll be seeing you soon.'

'See you soon,' she replied.

With a smile she turned and sat astride her motorcycle, rolling backwards and then firing up her engine and driving out of the garage.

As she eased into her first ride back, accelerating slowly to begin with, she had the most overwhelming feeling of being free. Olivia went faster, finding the speed she was most comfortable travelling at, eyes on the road as she leaned into bends and turned corners, as she passed blackened, broken buildings and houses with the sides ripped off, like doll's houses that were waiting for a giant arm to reach in and move all the furniture around. But despite the devastation around her, Olivia felt the happiest she'd felt in . . . She sighed, wishing she could tip her face up to the sun.

This is the happiest I've been since the day I was married. Since Leo held me in his arms and made me his wife, since we lay together in bed, in the hotel, our heads sharing the same pillow as we looked into each other's eyes.

Olivia blinked away tears, but they didn't steal her smile. Nothing could steal her smile, not now that she was back on her motorcycle, with a classified message against her hip in her satchel, ready to do the work she felt she was born to do.

She glanced sideways, imagining her brother beside her, remembering when it had just been the two of them, racing over the grass, leaving the others for dead as she tried her hardest to keep up with him.

'Come on, Liv, go faster!' he yelled into the wind. 'Don't let them catch you.'

252

She dared not look over her shoulder for fear of wobbling and falling off, but Pete had said the one thing he knew would make her accelerate. She didn't want to be second to anyone but him; she wanted to do everything as well as he could, be better than her other brothers.

It was her and Pete against the world.

She leaned down lower as he pulled ahead of her, her heart pounding as she fought against her fear and went faster still, not caring about the wind whipping her hair from her face or the mud flying up from below and splattering her trousers. She didn't care that her mother was going to scream like someone had been murdered when they arrived home, or that she'd forbid her from joining her brothers again.

Pete looked back at her, his smile stretching his face wide as she almost caught up with him again, as they left the other two in the dirt behind them.

It was the best day of her life.

Olivia smiled as she relived her memories. Pete was coming home soon, and no matter how bad his injuries, no matter what he'd been through, there was nothing she wouldn't do for him. Just like there'd been nothing he wouldn't do for his tomboy sister who'd spent her entire life trailing one step behind him.

She turned one of the final corners and accelerated, the wind whipping harder against her face and leaving her with a smile that had been absent for too long.

CHAPTER EIGHTEEN

*A*VA

'Hello, stranger.'

Ava leaned in the doorway to George's office, pleased to see the surprised look on his face when he looked up. She'd toyed with the idea of coming all morning, almost changing her mind even on the walk here, but she was pleased she'd followed through.

'Ava!' George stood, his eyes darting over her face. 'I can't believe you're here. Please tell me you didn't walk all this way in your condition?'

'Well, I was actually waiting for you to come and visit me, but when you never did I figured I'd come and see you instead.' When his cheeks turned visibly pinker, she smiled. She was used to men admiring her and fawning over her, but George was different. George had seemed permanently immune to her charms, and she certainly hadn't ever seen him in a romantic light, but there was something about how stable he was, how dependable, that she was starting to appreciate. She only hoped she hadn't irritated him so much that he couldn't see past her flaws now.

'I'm sorry, Ava, it's been impossible to get away from work for even a moment.' He sighed and folded his arms. 'But it's great to see you today, even if I'm not convinced you should be out of bed yet after barely a week of rest.'

'It's fine. I didn't exactly look my best with my head all bandaged, so it was probably good you didn't see me.'

George nodded, taking a few steps closer to her and slowly lifting his hand. 'Your face,' he said, hesitating before skimming her temple with his fingertips. 'Even after all these days.'

'Nothing but scrapes and bruises,' she said, but her voice caught in her throat and came out much more quietly that she would have liked. *George? I'm getting giddy over George?*

He pulled his hand back and stuck it in his pocket, but she could tell he was still studying her face. No matter how hard she tried to disguise it, she was missing hair around her ear where it had been shaved off to deal with her wound, and there was a large scab on her bottom lip and scrapes on her cheek and above her eye. Suddenly she was conscious of how terrible she looked, wishing she hadn't come to see him while she was looking such a fright.

'If something had happened to you . . .'

'Something *did* happen to me,' she quipped.

'Ava! I'm serious. If the crash had been worse or if you'd lost your life, I never would have forgiven myself for sending you out that night.'

She sighed. This time it was she searching George's face. 'I was doing my job, George. You couldn't have stopped me if you'd tried – and actually, from my recollection, you *did* try!'

'Would you join me for a walk?' he asked, surprising her. 'I could do with some fresh air and I'm not expecting anything urgent to arise in the next fifteen or so minutes.'

She nodded. 'Of course.'

The weather was chilly, but she was wearing a warm coat and scarf, and she had gloves on to help stave off the cold. Thankfully the sun was doing its best to peek through the clouds, which made it less grim than it had been earlier.

George held out his arm and she took it without thinking, looping hers through as they strolled. It suddenly felt like the most natural thing in the world to be spending time with him.

'How are you, really?' he asked. 'You can tell me, Ava. You must be in terrible discomfort still.'

'Actually, that's why I wanted to talk to you,' Ava said.

George was silent a moment, and when he didn't say anything she decided to carry on.

'George, I know it's only been a week since the crash, but I'd like to return to work as soon as possible.'

'Return?' He stopped walking and let go of her arm, facing her, his face like thunder. 'Ava, I thought you'd come to tell me you wouldn't be returning at all, and instead you want to come back a week after almost losing your life? You're unbelievable!'

'Clearly you don't know me at all if you think I'd give up so easily,' she said. 'Haven't you noticed how dedicated I've been lately? How I've been trying to do all my own mechanical work? I'm not going to give this up, I couldn't. It means far too much to me.'

'Of course I've noticed, but I almost lost you, Ava,' he said, shaking his head. 'I've never been so worried about another human being in my life.'

She digested his words, trying to stop her jaw from hanging open. *He's been worried about me?* 'Truly? You were that worried about me?'

'Christ, Ava, you're the most infuriating woman I've ever encountered. How can you not know how I feel about you?'

Ava gave him a coy smile. 'Does that mean I can come back to work on Monday?'

George swore under his breath as he stepped closer, and before she had time to say anything else he kissed her. Ava shut her eyes, tipping her head back as his mouth moved against hers, and a different kind of butterflies fluttered in her stomach. These butterflies were unexpected; they beat their wings inside her in a way she'd never felt before; because she felt safe with George in a way she'd never felt before with a man. *This* was what a kiss was supposed to feel like – lovely and warm and toe-curlingly exciting, all at the same time.

So much for not getting involved with another man again.

'I have to get back to work,' George murmured. 'I suggest we resume this conversation another time.'

Ava stood on tiptoe and stole another kiss, before whispering against his cheek: 'Or you could just say yes.'

George chuckled in response, but his smile disappeared as he gently stroked her lower lip with his thumb, and then her temple, his eyes travelling over her physical injuries.

'When the doctor clears you – and only then – I'll consider your return.'

Ava pouted, but she could see that he was immovable in his decision. 'I can't watch from the sidelines for long, George. That's not me and you know it.'

'Then take the time to rest and recover, and when you have it, bring me the letter from your doctor. I won't stop you once you have that.' He gave her a warm, long smile before he stepped away. 'It was good to see you, Ava. I've missed you.'

She stood and watched him go, surprised by the flush of her cheeks and the flutter inside her. 'I've missed you, too.'

But it wasn't only George she'd missed. She hadn't been lying when she'd said she couldn't stand being on the sidelines; recuperating was torture. But what she hadn't been honest about were the headaches she was having, the pain rippling from her ear through her head for no apparent reason.

She watched him until he disappeared, before turning to start the long walk back home. Seeing George had lifted her spirits and made her wonder how she hadn't seen what was right in front of her all this time, but it had also reminded her of what she'd lost, of the job she was no longer doing.

She fixed her smile again – the Ava she wanted the world to see back in place. Deep down, she was still traumatised from what had happened, the memories of that night making it almost impossible for her to sleep. Which was why she was so desperate to return to work, because if she didn't get back on a motorcycle soon, she knew she might very well lose her nerve entirely. And that wasn't something she wanted to admit to anyone, even herself.

———— ∞⁓⌆ ————

'Ava?' Florence called out, appearing in the kitchen doorway as Ava tried to step quietly through the house.

She groaned, knowing that she was about to be told off for leaving her bed. If only she hadn't taken so long, she'd have been tucked up again before Florence had even noticed she was gone. Florence always worked the night shift when the ambulances were needed during the bombing raids, so usually she slept most of the day.

'I didn't expect you to be up so early,' Ava said, smiling as she walked into the kitchen. 'I'd love a cuppa if you're making one.'

Florence's eyes narrowed, and Ava knew her attempt at smiling her way out of trouble wasn't working.

'I've been so worried about you,' Florence said, her entire face drawn into a frown. 'Where did you go? Why would you get up against doctor's orders?'

Ava sighed, moving past her friend and setting the water to boil for something to do. Her head was starting to spin and she regretted going for such a long walk, but she wasn't about to admit that to Florence, not with her standing there all righteous.

'I went to see George, actually,' she said, turning and leaning against the counter, her palms braced against it and keeping her steady. 'I was feeling better when I woke up, and I couldn't face another day of lying in bed, doing nothing. I figured the walk would do me good.'

'You're not doing nothing, you're healing,' Florence said. 'Rest is what you need right now, not walking!'

'That is doing nothing,' Ava replied.

'So what were you off seeing George about?' Florence asked. 'Was Olivia right in guessing there is something romantic developing between the two of you?'

Ava hoped her cheeks didn't flush and give her away. 'She said that to you?'

'She did.'

'Actually, if you must know, I went to talk to him about returning to work.'

She may as well have dropped a bomb in the kitchen. Florence's face looked like it was about to explode.

'Return to *work*?' she repeated.

'Mmm-hmm.'

'Ava, are you crazy? You could have died, and instead of taking your recovery seriously, you're trying to figure out when you can *return*?'

'It seems you and George are on the same page where I'm concerned, so there's nothing for you to worry about.'

She turned her back to Florence, not wanting to argue with her. Her hands shook as she scooped tea into the pot, not trusting her voice to ask if Florence wanted a cup, so making extra anyway.

'Ava,' Florence said. 'Please can you—'

She spun around, her eyes burning as she lost the battle against her emotions. 'Stop telling me what to do! I know I've been injured,

I know I need to be grateful that I survived and to look after myself, but I also can't stand the thought of another week in bed!'

Florence looked like she'd been punched in the stomach, and Ava immediately regretted hurling words at her like that.

'Flo, I'm sorry, I shouldn't have spoken to you like that.' She quickly wiped her cheeks with her knuckles. 'I'm just frustrated and my head hurts and—'

'Have you ever, just once, thought about how I felt finding your motorcycle that morning? The terror I felt? The pain in my heart when I thought you were dead?' Florence shook her head, madder than Ava had ever seen her before. 'I lost my family last year, Ava. I lost the people I love. I lost them because there was *nothing* I could do to save them, and I thought I was about to go through that all over again with you. But somehow, by some miracle, you survived, and I *was* able to save you.'

'And I'm so grateful that you did,' Ava whispered.

'Then why don't you show me and your body some damn respect and stay in your damn bed!'

Ava had never heard Florence yell at anyone before, and the anger flashing in her eyes took her by surprise.

'You want to know why I went to see George today? Why I want to go back out there again?' she asked.

'Please, enlighten me,' Florence muttered.

'It's because I can't stop thinking about the crash either. It's because every time I shut my eyes, I see it happening; I see myself trying to drag myself up, managing to make it all that way to deliver the memo with my head bleeding,' she whispered. 'I thought I was going to die, and I'm so terrified of getting back on a motorcycle, Flo. I'm worried that if I don't do it soon, I'll lose my nerve completely and I'll never be able to do it again.' She shut her eyes and took a deep breath. 'That's why I went to see George today, all right? Because at least getting out of bed and walking stopped the memories, even for just a few hours.'

Florence nodded. 'I wish you'd just told me that in the beginning,' she said. 'Because I know all about trying to outrun memories.'

Ava turned back to her tea-making, needing something to do with her hands, her head pounding even more after arguing with Florence.

When she turned back, teapot in hand, Florence was gone, but Grandma Ivy was walking into the kitchen.

'What are you doing out of bed, dear?'

'Just stretching my legs,' Ava replied. 'Fancy a cup of tea?'

The old lady's eyes sparkled. 'I've always got time for a cuppa.'

So Ava sat at the table, pouring them both a cup and listening to the latest neighbourhood gossip, hearing the front door shut with a bang as Florence left for her shift without bothering to say goodbye.

———— ⁌⁍ ————

Later that day, Ava did something she'd been avoiding for months. She stood outside the door to her family's townhouse, breathing deeply before taking out her key to unlock it. She had the strangest sensation that she should knock, but she knew that was stupid. It was her home, and despite being kicked out, she wasn't going to behave like a stranger.

'Ava?' her mother called out the moment she stepped into the hallway. 'Ava, is that you?'

'Hello, Mother,' she called back.

She saw the look on her mother's face the moment she walked into the room, because it was one she was familiar with: panic.

'Ava, your father is home, you can't be here,' her mother whispered. 'Oh my goodness, what happened to your face? To your hair?'

Ava stood still, wishing her mother would open her arms and hug her, tell her that she was welcome back and that she'd kick out her monstrous husband before letting him kick his daughter out of the house again. But of course she didn't, because that would require standing up for herself.

She heard the heavy tread of her father's footsteps before she saw him, but the difference today was that she wasn't wondering what version of her father would appear. Today she knew which one she'd get, and surprisingly she wasn't scared.

I've survived too much to be scared of him now.

'Hello, Father,' she said evenly.

'I thought I was perfectly clear when—'

'I'm here to collect some things, and to thank you for asking me to leave,' she said.

His face turned red and her mother seemed to shrink before her, but Ava continued, needing to say what she'd practised in her mind on the way over.

'Leaving here has shown me that I don't need to live my life in fear of my father's temper,' she said. 'It's shown me how loving a home can be, and what I've missed out on all these years.' It had also shown her that she'd always fallen for men just like him – men who wanted power over her, men who thought of her as their possession instead of their equal.

'You ungrateful little cow,' he muttered, striding towards her.

But she didn't cower before him like she would have once done. 'Do you see my face, Father?' She turned her head and lifted her hair to show her ear. 'These bruises weren't given to me by a man. I was injured doing my job, a job that you tried to stop me from doing. I've found something I love, something I'm good at,

262

something that makes me feel like I'm flying every single day. But if you want to add to these bruises then do your worst, because I'm not scared of you any more.'

Tears formed in her eyes then, but it wasn't because of her father. It was because she believed in what she was saying. Motorcycle riding had given her a confidence in herself that had nothing to do with her looks or status; it had to do with her being good at something.

'I'm going to be riding motorcycles until the day I die, and I wanted to come here one last time so you could see the woman I've become.'

'Get out of my house!' her father screamed.

But Ava didn't leave. She walked to her old room and started to pack a bag, taking things that belonged to her, things she didn't want to leave behind. But when her mother appeared, taking another bag down and helping her, that was when she started to cry.

'Ava,' her mother whispered.

She turned, surprised by the softness of her mother's gaze and the way she opened her arms and hugged Ava.

'I'm so proud of you,' she whispered. 'I wish I could be as brave.'

Ava hugged her back, and after she finally let go, she found a pen and scribbled down Florence's address.

'You can always come and find me,' Ava said, before picking up the two bags.

Her mother nodded and Ava walked out of the house, hearing her father throw something that sounded like glass and wishing her mother had been brave enough to leave with her.

CHAPTER NINETEEN

OLIVIA

'Hi Petey.'

All morning Olivia had been waiting for her brother to look into her eyes, and when he did, she couldn't stop grinning. He'd been asleep when she arrived at the hospital, and so she'd sat patiently, waiting for him to wake up.

'Liv,' he croaked, as she reached for his water and held it for him, cupping the back of his head to help him lean forward and sip from the straw. His eyes were bright, but she had to mask her surprise at how hollow his cheeks were. Even his neck seemed skinny compared to that of the man she'd waved goodbye to at the very beginning of the war.

'I can't believe you're back,' she said. 'Look at you!'

'Look at you,' he replied, his entire face breaking out into a smile. 'You look as fresh as a daisy compared to how I feel.'

'Well, you could do with a shower, but other than that you look great to me,' she said, taking his hand and shifting to sit on the bed beside him. She wasn't lying either; he might be thin but he was still Pete, still her gorgeous brother, and she couldn't have cared less how he looked so long as he was there. 'I mean, Petey, you're alive, so what else could possibly matter? It's just so good to have you home, especially after we were told to expect the worst.'

He grimaced and she moved a little, hoping she wasn't hurting him.

'It's my leg,' he said, and he shifted the sheet, still grimacing as he adjusted his position. 'I was sent home to see if they could save it, but it's not looking good.'

She blinked at him, trying not to react. He was alive. That was all she needed to focus on, the fact that he was there. 'I see. Well, I hear we have the best of the best surgeons here, so—'

'It's not looking good, Liv. No amount of positive thinking is going to help me with this one.' He sighed. 'I've come to terms with it, I'll accept what has to be done, but I just want a chance to save it. If there's even a slim chance, I just . . .' She watched as he swallowed, clearing his throat. 'All I want to know is that I've done everything I can to keep it first.'

Olivia stayed silent a moment, clearing her own throat and refusing to let her emotions get the better of her. Seeing her strong, strapping big brother reduced to a shell of his former self, in a narrow hospital bed and fighting back tears, it was almost too much to bear. 'Well, I'll tell you what is going to help you, and that's hearing about my job.'

'Oh yeah? My little sister the Wren, huh?'

She grinned. 'Your little sister the *motorcycle dispatch rider*, actually.'

'I don't believe you!' he laughed.

'Well, you'd better believe me,' she said, loving that she'd made him smile. 'I told everyone that you taught me how to ride, and when I'm out there sometimes, it's like it's you and me again, racing as kids. I can actually see you beside me.'

'Can you also still hear Mother shouting bloody murder from the front door? I thought she was going to have my hide for taking you out there with me, but it was worth it. It was always worth it.'

They both erupted into laughter then, and she squeezed his hand. 'It's so good to have you home, Petey. I don't know how I could have survived if you hadn't made it.'

He nodded, but the loss they both shared stretched between them, unspoken but unmistakably there. He'd made it home, against all odds, and somehow Leo had died on home soil. It just didn't seem fair, but then nothing about war seemed just or fair.

'You just focus on getting back on a motorcycle, you hear me?' she said. 'I want to see if I can finally beat you now that I'm riding every day.'

'You're already back at work?' he asked. 'After, well, you know.'

'Only just,' she said. 'But I couldn't start my shift today without seeing you first.'

Pete smiled up at her. 'Anyone ever tell you you're the world's best sister?'

She laughed. 'Only you, Petey. I don't think our brothers share that feeling.'

'The two of us against the world,' he said, and she saw unshed tears clinging to his lashes. 'It was always just the two of us, wasn't it?'

'The two of us against the world,' she repeated, dropping a kiss to his forehead and hugging him.

'I'll be back to see you again tomorrow,' she whispered. 'I promise.'

'Ava, is that you?'

Olivia walked closer and saw that it was indeed Ava, sitting on her haunches, wearing overalls and working on a motorcycle.

'I decided that if I can't ride,' Ava said, grunting as she used a spanner to tighten a bolt, 'I can help you all out with mechanical problems and take some of the workload.'

'Well, you do make a very pretty mechanic,' Olivia teased. 'Although I have to say, I think it's the first time I've seen you with tools in your hand. Should we trust you?'

'You most certainly can trust me,' Ava said, standing and wiping her hands on her overalls. 'I have a bit of catching up to do, but I'm actually liking the manual work. I also appreciate the fact that you didn't tell me I should be home in bed the moment you saw me.'

'Should you be?' Olivia asked.

Ava just raised her eyebrows in reply.

'You're a big girl, Ava. If you choose to be here, then that's up to you,' Olivia said. 'Trust me, I know what it's like to not want to be at home, and you were the one who encouraged me instead of telling me what was best for me.'

Olivia put her bag away and sat down on the concrete floor, telling Ava all about her reunion with her brother, happy to see unexpected late-afternoon sunlight make a pool of brightness on the ground nearby. The garage door was open for riders to come and go during the day, and there was something about seeing the sun that made her feel positive about the future, about what was yet to come, rather than dwelling on what she'd lost or left behind.

She sat for an hour or more, until Ava had no more repairs to do and came to sit beside her on the ground. She had sandwiches she'd made earlier in the day, and she shared them with Ava, the pair of them content to sit and eat as the sky turned dark.

'Olivia!' George's bark made her jump. She looked over her shoulder and saw him walking quickly towards them, which made her get up and dust herself off.

'You have a message for me?' she asked.

'This one is urgent,' he said. 'And top secret.'

'Aren't they all?' Ava asked, and Olivia gave her what she hoped was a withering look.

George ignored her, and Olivia hid her smile. 'I need you to leave immediately and deliver this to the shipyards at Plymouth.'

'Of course,' she said, at the same time as Ava leapt to her feet.

'George, you know that's my route! I know it like the back of my hand, it's—'

'The route that almost killed you,' George ground out. 'And in case you've forgotten, you haven't been cleared by a doctor to return to work. It's only because of my good grace that you're here at all.'

Ava pouted, but bless her, she kept her mouth shut after that.

'I've studied the route before, I'll be fine,' Olivia said, looking between the two of them. 'Ava, it'll be all yours again as soon as you're back on deck.'

She retrieved her satchel and held it out to George, looping the strap over her neck and setting it on her hip when he passed it back to her.

'Girls, while you're both here, I want you to know that I'm recruiting for a new role,' George said. 'I've been asked to appoint the most well-suited rider to train new recruits, and I'll be deciding between the pair of you. Truth be told I'm reluctant to put either of you out of service, so I'm still working through the logistics.'

Olivia grinned at Ava, who gave her a smug look back.

'Let the best woman win then,' Ava said.

Olivia nodded. 'Let the best woman win.' With that she was on her bike, revving the engine for Ava's benefit before riding out of the garage and out into the night air.

As she rode, taking care navigating the dark streets, she thought about the letter in her pocket, the one Leo had sent her from somewhere in England before he'd come home on leave again. Before he'd died. It hadn't felt right leaving it at home, so she'd decided to take it with her, to keep him close, and she liked knowing it was there, as if he was somehow still with her.

A familiar boom sounded out then, a bomb far enough away that it didn't terrify her, but close enough to make her cautious. She slowed slightly, listening for danger, knowing she should turn her light off to avoid being seen. The moonlight was just bright enough to illuminate the path ahead, so she turned the headlamp off and leaned down lower, her eyes focused on the road as her thoughts switched back to the letter, and then to her brother.

You'll be riding beside me again in no time, Pete, just you wait.

CHAPTER TWENTY

FLORENCE

'You look like someone just killed your dog.'

'I don't have a dog,' she replied.

Florence looked up and saw Jack leaning against the open door of the ambulance. She'd decided to clean Petal for something to do, but now she was sitting in the passenger side with the door open, cloth in hand.

'Something on your mind?' he asked.

'You could say that,' she said with a sigh.

Jack folded his arms, clearly waiting for her to tell him.

'It's Ava,' she said with a sigh. 'She's being so pig-headed about going back to work, and we've barely spoken since an argument we had the other night. I just don't understand why she can't take her recovery more seriously. It's too soon for her to go back.'

'I see,' Jack said.

'Now you're giving me that look like you don't agree with me. You were there that night, you saw how badly injured she was with your own eyes. Tell me you agree with me.'

He groaned. 'Florence, it's not about me agreeing with you or not.'

'So you think I'm wrong? That she *should* be back?'

He unfolded his arms and looked at her, long and steady. 'That's not what I'm saying at all. But if Ava wants to be back at work, there's nothing you can do to stop her, and it's not up to us to say whether it's too soon or not.'

'I thought you of all people would understand,' she huffed. 'She almost died, Jack!'

He crossed his arms again, no longer leaning against the door. 'Someone might have said the same about you working and becoming a Wren so soon after your family were killed,' he said, his voice low. 'We cope with grief and pain in different ways, so all I'm saying is that she probably has her reasons, just like we do.'

Florence threw her oil-stained cloth at Jack's chest and pushed past him, anger firing inside her. She'd genuinely thought he'd understand, that he'd remember how close she'd been to losing her friend that night and support her on this. She hated the way she was behaving, especially towards him, but she just couldn't stop thinking about seeing Ava's motorcycle that morning, thinking she'd lost her. She already felt like she'd lost enough to last a lifetime.

She walked to the door of the garage and pulled it open, needing the fresh air. They'd had a quiet night so far, which was why she'd decided to stay busy by cleaning Petal; she should have taken the time to rest, but staying busy somehow always seemed like the better option.

The sky was surprisingly clear, and there was something peaceful about staring up at the moon as the clouds gently moved across it. When she heard Jack come up behind her, she softened, waiting for him to come close, wishing she could lean back into him and feel his arms encircle her body. But he stayed just far enough away that they didn't touch.

'I'm sorry,' she said. 'I didn't mean to lash out at you like that.'

'It's fine, I'm sorry too. I—'

He never got the rest of his sentence out, as an explosion like nothing she'd ever heard before sounded, too close for comfort. She reached for him then, and the distance immediately closed between them as she took a moment to hold his hand, to pull strength from him for just a second.

So much for a quiet night.

The boom of another bomb landing had her bracing against the wall, before turning and running back to Petal. It reminded her of that fateful night when the West End had been bombed.

The Luftwaffe have arrived. Again.

She only prayed that tonight wouldn't be as bad as the rest of the nights they'd had over the past week.

Florence knew her prayers hadn't been answered within thirty minutes of joining the convoy, following tightly behind fire engines as they picked their way to the worst-hit streets. Every time, her stomach clenched like someone had hold of her insides, but it was the terror that kept her moving, refusing to stop no matter what the danger.

'I think we need to hold back,' Jack said, as they inched forward.

Flames had engulfed a row of homes around them, and somehow they'd ended up being the only ambulance accompanying the many fire engines that were already in position.

'You think we should reverse and come in on foot?' she asked.

Jack didn't say anything for a moment, and she glanced across at him.

'I'm saying that I think we should stay put,' he said.

Florence digested his words. Since that very first disagreement they'd had, Jack had never once told her they shouldn't do something, which was why she was inclined to listen to him this time.

Just as she was about to try to get them out of the convoy, Jack slammed his hand down on his thigh. 'Don't listen to me,' he said. 'Keep going.'

She breathed a sigh of relief. She'd been torn about what to do, but hearing him say that gave her confidence. 'If not us then who, right?'

She inched forward, blocking out the noise of the siren and the air-raid wardens blowing whistles as they waited for orders. Within minutes there was a bang on the window, frightening the life out of Florence, and she quickly wound the glass down.

'We have reports of people being stuck ahead, a few more houses down. We're trying to dampen the flames so we can get to them.'

'We'll be right behind you, waiting to take them,' Florence said, winding up her window the moment he left.

She heard Jack let out a breath beside her and imagined he felt as relieved as she did that they'd stayed.

'I'm going to keep going, get us nice and close,' she said, moving around the fire engine and driving up on the pavement slightly to get past, biting down on her lower lip as she manoeuvred them.

One moment Florence was driving, steady as could be, and the next a strange sound swept around them, like a severe gust of wind had caught them and wasn't letting go. Only this wasn't wind.

They were on fire.

'Jack!' Florence screamed.

'Stop the vehicle!' he yelled, leaning past her to press his hand on the horn, frantically beeping it.

Florence froze as she watched the flames engulf them. *I'm going to die. I'm going to be burned alive!*

'No one's coming!' she cried.

Jack kept beeping, but at that moment Florence sprang back into life, pushing her foot hard on the accelerator. She was not going to let them be burned alive. They had people to save!

'What the hell are you doing?'

'Getting someone's attention!' she cried, her hands sliding on the steering wheel, slick with sweat. *Am I imagining it, or is it getting hot in here?* Her hair was stuck to the back of her neck, her pulse racing as she leaned on the horn, not letting anyone ignore them.

She let out a gasp as water suddenly rained down outside the ambulance, the heat hissing as it was tamed, firemen yelling at them. Florence slumped forward, giving herself a second to catch her breath before turning to Jack.

'We have people to save,' she murmured. 'This is not our night to die.'

Jack started to laugh, and she joined him, their humour fast turning to something that felt far more sober as they stared at one another long and hard, before hauling themselves out of the vehicle, thankful to be alive and knowing that someone had been there to help them.

Florence glanced back at Petal, shining her light over the ambulance and taking in the blackened, charred paintwork that was closer in resemblance to an overcooked piece of meat than a shiny flower-delivery vehicle. She was unrecognisable.

'You've done us proud, girl,' Florence muttered, as she turned and hurried away beside Jack. *Even if you never get to deliver flowers again, Petal, you've most definitely done us proud.*

But she didn't want to think about the fact they'd almost been burned alive ever, ever again. She'd almost joined her family – likely been minutes or even seconds from death if they hadn't been hosed down – and for the first time she no longer wished she'd perished alongside them.

For the first few weeks and then months, she'd only wanted to live for her grandmother, to save her from more pain. But now, with her work, with Jack, with her friends, she *wanted* to live, for herself. And in that moment, she'd thought of Olivia too, of the children she was so focused on helping. She wanted to live for them as well.

They stopped as the smoke became even denser, making her cough even as she pulled up her scarf to cover her mouth and nose, waiting to hear the call that it was safe to enter or that there was a survivor.

As soon as I'm home, I'm apologising to Ava. She doesn't deserve my anger.

'We've got a woman being pulled out from the rubble!' Jack yelled, his light shining ahead of them.

Hope filled her heart. This was the moment she lived for, the moment of knowing she'd made a difference, and they stood side by side, eyes burning from the smoke as it persistently curled around them.

'Tonight's a good night to save lives,' Jack said, putting an arm around her and holding her close.

She tipped her head to his shoulder, finding peace in a moment that should have been anything but peaceful.

'Tonight's a good night to save lives,' she whispered back to him.

A sickening crash made her jump, and they both watched, helpless, as one of the houses being hosed down collapsed before them. And just like that, she wondered if they would end up saving anyone at all that night.

Florence had experienced many nights that had felt like they were never going to end. Ones that stretched for so many hours they felt like many evenings merged together instead of just the one. Tonight was one of those nights, and she and Jack had worked tirelessly to transport the wounded. Most importantly, they hadn't had anyone die on them, which was a miracle in itself.

She was sitting on a patch of grass with Jack, the pair of them leaning back against a tree, too tired to move. There were a handful of firefighters doing the same, except they were lying stretched out on the grass. These nights took a toll on them all, and not just because of the physical work or the hours they had to keep. It was the fear of not being able to save people that hit hardest, that kept adrenaline pulsing through each one of them, night after night. But as soon as it was over, the adrenaline always turned to sheer exhaustion.

This morning though, a mobile canteen had pulled up nearby, serving hot tea and buns to all the night volunteers and workers. She'd never been so grateful in all her life, and from the look of the contented men and women around her, they all felt the same. It had certainly lifted morale.

'Are you two still working?'

Florence opened her eyes and looked up, seeing a fireman standing over them, still holding his cup. She sat up, nudging Jack.

'We can be,' she said. 'Does someone need an ambulance?'

'There's word of a crash about an hour from here. Road's blocked and we've been called to help.'

Florence stood, brushing her trousers. 'Do you know anything else?'

The fireman shrugged, calling over his shoulder as he ran back to his vehicle. 'Only that there was a motorcycle involved.'

Her blood ran cold. 'A motorcycle?' she called back. But he was already gone.

Jack's hand was steady on her shoulder. 'It doesn't mean anything,' he said. 'It could be anyone on a motorcycle, it could be—'

'I hope Ava didn't do anything stupid,' she said, as they hurried back to Petal, who was almost unrecognisable with her newly charred exterior. Jack was slow, his legs always stiff after sitting down for too long, and she had the engine running by the time he got in.

'There's no way she would be allowed on a motorcycle without being cleared,' Jack said, as he pulled his door shut and she took off.

Florence sighed. 'Then you don't know Ava. That girl could talk her way out of murder if she needed to.'

Jack chuckled and she glanced at him as he settled into the seat. 'Eyes on the road,' he said.

She tried to release her grip on the steering wheel a little, relaxing her body back into the seat slightly, but it didn't work. Within seconds she was gripping it tightly and leaning forward, accelerating as they hit a straight stretch of road.

If it was Ava, she was going to kill her with her own bare hands for being so irresponsible. But at the same time her heart was pounding. *Please Lord, don't let it be her.*

——— ⁌～～⁍ ———

'Oh, good lord,' Florence whispered as she slowed, approaching the scene. Her heart skipped a beat as she saw a motorcycle wedged beneath a large overturned lorry, and she found her eyes searching for a familiar pink ribbon. She couldn't see it, but it did little to allay her fears.

'Pull over there,' Jack said, his voice gruffer than usual as he directed her.

She pulled Petal to the side of the road and they both got out, the fire engine parked just in front of them and a small group of firemen crowding around the overturned lorry.

'What are we dealing with here?' Jack called out.

'Lorry driver died on impact, but the motorcycle rider—'

'Olivia!' Florence's scream cut through the otherwise silent morning air, and all the men turned to stare at her as she ran forward, dropping to her knees and reaching for her friend.

'We don't know the best way to get her out, to avoid . . .' The firemen continued talking, but she blocked everything else out, gently touching her friend's face, stroking her hair as beautiful, big blue eyes blinked back at her. The skin on her face was smudged dark, and she was bleeding from her nose, but it was, unmistakably, Olivia.

'We're going to get you out of here, sweetheart,' she said, not trusting her voice but knowing she had to say something to comfort her. 'Everything's going to be absolutely fine.'

Olivia's lips parted and her mouth moved, but Florence couldn't work out what she was trying to say. Tears fell from her eyes on to Olivia's face, and she quickly, gently, wiped them away with her fingertips, leaving a streak on her cheeks.

'Jack,' Florence said in her calmest voice, not taking her hands off Olivia as she looked back. 'Jack, we need to get her out from under here.'

Jack was beside her now, so close she could feel his breath on her shoulder as he peered under the lorry.

'They're waiting for a tractor to try to move it,' he said quietly. 'They want to try to clear it before—'

'We don't have that long!' she said. 'We need to try to move her now.'

'If we move her now—'

'If we don't move her, we lose her,' she interjected. 'We're doing this now. I'm taking charge of this situation.'

Florence looked at the mangled motorcycle half wedged beneath the truck and wondered how on earth Olivia was even breathing still, it was so badly damaged, but she pushed all that out of her mind as she placed her hands gently on her friend's shoulders.

Olivia murmured something again, but Florence still couldn't work out what she was saying. She wished she could ask her where it hurt the most, what had happened, but Olivia wasn't capable of communicating and they didn't have time. Every second of not getting her medical treatment could be the difference between losing her and saving her life.

Jack stood and indicated that she do the same, and although she didn't want to leave Olivia for so much as a moment, she did what he asked.

'If I hold her shoulders and gently pull her out, can you crawl under there and make sure there's no part of her body impaled or stuck on anything first?' Jack asked.

Florence looked at the lorry and the small space she'd have to navigate. There was only a narrow gap because it was wedged against a tree.

'I'll do it,' she said. 'Of course I'll do it.'

'I just don't want to go pulling her and losing half her body on the way out.'

Florence launched forward and retched at Jack's words, unable to help the bile that rose inside her just thinking about her friend that way. It was the first time one of the people they'd fought to save wasn't a stranger.

Florence dropped low and wriggled forward, past Olivia, the space so small that her cheek was pressed hard to the road, scraping her skin. Her hands and elbows felt like they were bleeding as she dragged herself, the smell of fuel becoming overwhelming the further she got under the lorry.

But she was certain there was no part of Olivia impaled, although the space was so tight over her friend's hips and lower legs, she wondered how they'd ever move her. As she wiggled back, trying not to panic about how tight the space was as she fought to get out, Jack called out to her.

'You all right?'

'Coming out now!' she called, finally emerging to find the group of firemen all positioned around the lorry.

'We're going to try lifting, and even if we can move it just half an inch, it'll be better than nothing.'

Florence waited, tears streaming down her cheeks as she listened to them heave, ready to cradle Olivia in her arms once they pulled her out. But when Jack did pull, the cry that emanated from Olivia was so primal that Florence knew it was worse than she'd imagined.

Florence leapt up to help carry Olivia a few paces away, well clear of the lorry and the road, and she sat with her in her arms as Jack stood, staring down at her friend's beautiful face, her lips parted now as if every breath was an ordeal. Florence pushed open Olivia's torn jacket slightly to see whether she had any obvious injuries and gasped at what she saw, at the blood seeping out of her middle region.

'Jack, we need morphine,' she said, glancing up at him and indicating for him to look.

When he did, his eyes said it all.

Olivia was dying, and it wouldn't matter how fast they drove or what they did, Florence was almost certain there was nothing they could do.

She clenched her teeth together so hard she felt they were going to break, the pain inside her overwhelming, but she refused to cry.

Her friend was dying, and that meant she had to be strong for her in these last moments, to show her compassion and love as selflessly as she was able.

Olivia's lips were still moving, trying to say something, and Florence bent low over her, ear close to her mouth.

'Take,' she gurgled. '*Message.*'

Florence sat up straight, suddenly understanding the word her friend had been saying over and over again.

'The memo!' she said, and Olivia blinked slowly up at her, as if trying to tell her she was right.

Of course, she needed Olivia's bag; it would have the memo in it that she was supposed to deliver, and Florence knew from what little she'd been told at the training day that the dispatch riders were told to protect their satchels with their lives. Olivia obviously hadn't made the delivery yet.

'I'll find it, don't you worry. I'll make sure to get your satchel for you. I'll get your memo.'

Jack came lumbering back then, with a blanket that he carefully wrapped around Olivia and a vial of morphine, which he passed to Florence to administer.

'I know it doesn't look good, but I don't think you'll ever forgive yourself if we don't at least try to get her to hospital,' Jack said, looking as terrible as she felt, dark smudges under his eyes showing how tired he was.

Florence nodded. 'You're right,' she said. 'Let's get her loaded into the ambulance. Can you drive?' She didn't want to leave Olivia for so much as a second.

She watched as Jack glanced down at his leg, but he nodded anyway. 'I'll drive.'

'That morphine should start working soon, Liv,' she whispered to her friend, brushing a kiss across her forehead before helping Jack to lift her.

She steeled herself against Olivia's cry, but once they had her settled, she never made another sound, which was even worse.

'I have to find her bag, just give me a second,' Florence said to Jack, running as fast as she could back to the lorry and peering under it, ignoring the firemen telling her it was too dangerous. 'There you are,' she muttered when she finally saw it, reaching out and tugging it free. The strap was broken but it was still safely buckled up, and she ran back to the ambulance and got in beside Olivia, seeing that Jack had bandaged around her friend's middle in her absence.

She tucked the blanket around her, feeling for a pulse, reassuring herself that Olivia was still alive. It was a long drive to the hospital, but Jack was right; if they didn't try, she'd always wonder if there was something she could have done to save her.

'Everything's going to be fine,' she whispered. 'We're going to set up that school, Liv, we're going to care for those children. Don't you give up on me.'

But even as she said the words, she knew she was lying. They'd need nothing short of a miracle for Olivia to survive the night.

———— ⚬⚬ ————

The drive to the hospital seemed to take all day, but the moment they got there it was a blur of nurses and doctors, stretchers and calls for help. Within minutes of Jack hurrying inside and begging for assistance, Olivia was being taken away from them and hurried into surgery, and Florence was left clutching her friend's satchel, which was stained with Olivia's blood.

And now, when she could finally collapse and cry, her eyes were dry.

'What do you want to do?' Jack asked, coming up beside her.

He opened his arms and she walked gratefully into them, shutting her eyes for a moment and just breathing, trying to comprehend what had happened. But she knew she couldn't fall apart, not yet, not before she'd followed through on her promise.

'Can you stay here?' she asked. 'I don't want to leave her, but I have to get this bag to someone who can deliver the message.'

'I can do it,' Jack said, stroking her hand as he gently held it. 'You don't have to go.'

'No, I need to do it myself. I promised her that I'd do it.'

Jack lifted her hand and pressed a kiss to her knuckles. 'Then go. I'll be here waiting.'

She was about to turn when she noticed Olivia's jacket, discarded on the ground. The nurses had cut it off her the moment they arrived, and she bent to pick it up, surprised to see something fall from the pocket. She collected it and realised it was a letter, folded carefully, perhaps having been tucked into her breast pocket.

Florence opened it, her eyes quickly scanning the words to see whether it was important correspondence that she needed to do something with.

Only, it wasn't anything official. It was a love letter, and soon Florence's tears stained the page as she was unable to look away.

Dearest Olivia,

I know I'm going to see you again in only a few short days, but I still couldn't stop myself from writing to you. Our wedding day was the happiest day of my life, and you were the most beautiful bride I could have imagined. If I didn't have something to fight for before, then I certainly do now.

We have our whole lives ahead of us, but it doesn't stop me wishing that I could have stayed at home for longer. I told you on our wedding night that a few months mean nothing when we have the rest of our lives to grow old together, but I was lying. I even considered shooting my own leg so that I would have a reason to stay home with you, to hold my beautiful bride in my arms, to make more memories that I could hold close for when I had to leave you, but of course I would never turn my back on my duty. I only wish that in doing so, I didn't have to walk away from you.

Florence took a deep, shuddering breath as she stopped reading and tucked the letter into her pocket, then she left the hospital behind, forcing her feet to keep moving. It was a private letter that she should never even be holding, let alone reading, the words supposed to be for one woman and one woman only. Olivia had told her about Leo's final letter, told her that one day she'd share it with her, and now here she was reading it alone while her friend fought for her life.

I'm going to have that memo delivered, Olivia. If you've died for this, it won't be for nothing, I promise.

CHAPTER TWENTY-ONE

AVA

Ava whistled as she worked, a cloth tucked into her overalls as she admired her efforts. She might not be able to ride, but she'd polished all the motorcycles and checked everyone's fuel, and she was feeling good about doing *something*. It felt good to be capable, to know what she was doing and not have to rely on anyone else to help her, and she had to admit she liked having her own money. It had contributed to her confidence in leaving home, and it also meant she was able to pay Grandma Ivy for her room and board, which meant a lot to her, as well as build up her own little nest egg for after the war. She might never be able to afford fancy dresses and the glittering social life she'd once enjoyed, but she would be able to remain independent, and more importantly stay away from her father's house.

She glanced up at the clock, and then looked over to where Olivia's motorcycle should be. It was strange, but she wasn't worried, not yet. She knew first-hand what a long ride it could be – once it had taken her twelve hours to get there and back – and she'd kept wondering if perhaps Olivia had gone straight to visit her brother instead of returning to base. She'd been so excited about having him home, and the hospital visiting hours were likely rather strict.

A noise made her turn, and when she saw it was George, she left the motorcycle she'd been working on and followed him into his office, receiving a groan in reply.

'Ava, please,' he said, before she'd even had time to say anything. 'This is not something we should even be discussing yet, not until you have clearance from your doctor.'

'I only wanted to remind you what an *excellent* dispatch rider I am,' she said, smiling her sweetest smile as she moved to stand in front of him. 'I mean, Olivia is good, don't get me wrong, but I have the passion, the—'

'Ava,' George said.

'Please hear me out,' she said, before she realised that he wasn't looking at her.

George's face had gone pale, his lips parted as if he were about to say something, and Ava slowly turned to see what he was looking at – what had caused such sadness to bracket his face.

'Florence?' she gasped, seeing her friend standing there, her eyes filled with tears. But it was when she held out a blood-splattered satchel, her equally bloodstained hands shaking as she did so, that Ava felt the floor fall from beneath her. 'Florence!' she gasped, louder this time, moving forward to hold her.

Florence fell into her arms, and Ava stroked her hair and then her back as she hugged her. But Florence only let herself be held a moment before she straightened, holding the satchel out again.

'What . . .' Ava started, before she backed away a step, realising what it was. 'That's . . . that's . . .' She stared at the blood, not able to get the words out.

'Olivia's,' Florence whispered.

'Why . . . why do you have this,' Ava whispered. 'What—'

'I promised her I'd make sure it was delivered. I promised, I—'

It was George who stepped forward to take the satchel swiftly in one hand before putting his other arm around Florence and guiding her to a chair. Ava was frozen, still staring at the bag.

'Where's Olivia?' she finally managed. 'Florence, where is she!'

Florence's face was ashen white as she looked up and met Ava's gaze, her eyes like saucers. 'There was an accident. She's at the hospital. Jack's with her.'

'She's alive?' Ava asked, the words sticking in her throat.

Florence nodded. 'Barely.'

Ava looked away, biting down hard on her lower lip, trying to keep her tears at bay.

'I promised her that I'd get this delivered. I promised her she hadn't given her life for nothing,' Florence said.

'Her life?' Ava asked, hearing how hysterical she sounded. 'You think she's going to die?'

Florence didn't say anything, she just nodded and then looked away, as George took out the memo and discarded the bloody satchel. Ava's stomach turned at the sight of it, knowing the blood belonged to her friend.

'This message needs to be delivered,' George said, starting to pace. 'Damn it! It should have been delivered hours ago!'

Ava felt like she'd just been punched in the stomach, George's words hurting her like nothing in her life before. 'My friend might be dead and you're worried about the undelivered message?' she cried.

'Olivia, you – *all of you* – are like family to me, so don't you dare think for a second that I won't be grieving her like everyone else,' George said. 'But this memo? The message she was carrying? It was marked top secret, which means it's of the utmost importance, and the fact that it was going to that particular outpost makes it even more important that it gets there. Florence is right; if she loses her life it can't be for nothing.'

Ava's heart was racing as she stood there, as she forced herself to comprehend what was happening.

'She knew that?' Ava asked. 'That it was top secret?'

'Yes,' George said. 'It's why I gave it to her. Because the two of you are my best riders, and it had to be one of you.'

Ava listened to the sound of her own breath, clenching her fists as she shut her eyes for a beat. 'Let me do it, George,' she finally said. 'Let me deliver the memo.'

'You're not ready to be back at work,' he said, shaking his head. 'You're not ready to be riding again, we've already discussed this.'

'George, please, you know I'll be able to get there, and fast. I don't see that you have a choice,' she said, standing tall, refusing to buckle despite the sadness inside her. 'How long will it take to call someone in? All your riders on this shift are already out; you'd have to wait for someone to return.'

'I also know this route is where I could have lost you,' George said, his voice gravelly, his eyes searching hers.

She stepped forward and took his hands, reaching for him for the very first time, as if touching him were the most natural thing in the world. 'I can do this. Please let me do this, for Olivia.'

George didn't say anything, but he did give her a brief nod, his eyes pulling away from hers as if he couldn't believe that he'd given his blessing. But she didn't let the moment pass, rising on her tiptoes and pressing a kiss to his cheek.

'You deliver this to the Naval Commander-in-Chief,' he said. 'No one else has eyes on this, Ava, no one.'

'I'll get it to him as quickly as I can.'

She turned to Florence then, dropping to her knees as she reached for her hands, hands that were folded tightly in her lap.

'I'm going to do this, for Olivia,' Ava whispered. 'This is not going to be for nothing, whatever happens. I need her to know that.'

Florence's eyes met hers and they stared at one another a long moment before Ava stood, letting go of her hands even though her instinct was to stay and comfort her. Whatever she'd been through, whatever she'd seen, Ava knew it would leave scars on Florence forever.

'Go to the hospital,' she said. 'I'll meet you there when I'm finished.'

'I can't lose you too,' Florence whispered.

Ava took a deep breath. 'I'll see you soon. I promise.'

She turned to take a clean satchel from George with the memo inside, and somehow, as she approached the spare motorcycle that was parked where hers had always been, she felt as though she had a piece of Olivia with her. Ava fixed her hat and settled on to the seat, starting her engine and rolling backwards before putting the bike in gear and heading for the door, which George had opened for her. She wobbled for a second then corrected herself, her fear like a knot inside her stomach that was slowly rising up to her throat and threatening to choke her.

She'd been so worried she might not be able to ride again, that her fear would take over and stop her from doing her job. It was one of the reasons she'd decided to come back and work on the bikes, simply to be around them again, and it was also why she'd been so desperate to get back out there. Her plan had been to ride at the speedway a few times, to ease back into it again, and instead she was going to ride the same route that had almost cost her her life.

And possibly the life of her friend.

You're going to make it, Liv. Just like I'm going to deliver this message. There's no you without me, there can't be.

As she roared down the street, she only hoped she was right on both counts.

CHAPTER TWENTY-TWO

FLORENCE

Florence sat with Jack's arm around her. She'd barely moved in hours, the busyness of the hospital passing her by as she waited for news, barely doing more than blinking and breathing.

At one point, Jack had asked her if she wanted anything, a drink, a change of clothes, a blanket so she could curl up and get some sleep. But she'd just squeezed his fingers and stayed firmly at his side, not wanting to move, not wanting *him* to move, not wanting anything unless it was a surgeon coming towards them to tell them news.

Until she saw Ava walking towards her, and then she realised there was something else she wanted. She rose, and they stood in one another's arms for the longest of moments, neither of them attempting to let go of the other.

'I came straight from delivering the memo,' Ava said, her voice low. 'Has there been any news?'

Florence started to shake then, and Ava eased her down into the seat. She held out her hands, feeling the most overwhelming, desperate desire to scrub them clean again, even though she'd already washed them thoroughly.

'I feel like I still have her blood on me,' she said, hating how manic she sounded. 'I've washed my hands over and over, but I can still feel it.'

'You don't,' Ava said, her arm still around Florence's shoulders. 'I promise you, there's no blood, your hands are clean.'

Florence dropped her head to Ava's shoulder then, and Ava tilted her own head so it was resting on Florence's.

'Thank you for delivering it,' Florence said. 'It would mean, it *will* mean, so much to her.'

Ava didn't say anything, and Florence wished they'd never fought about her going back to work. She couldn't stop thinking how unkind she'd been, how she hadn't taken the time to see how much Ava was struggling with being home, worrying that she might not have the same confidence if she wasn't allowed back sooner rather than later.

'It's all my fault,' Ava suddenly said, as Florence grasped her hand and held it tight. 'If I hadn't crashed that night, if that bomb hadn't hit me, if I'd just gone faster, then it would have been me delivering that message last night.'

Ava sat up and they stared at one another, tears running erratically down Ava's cheeks.

'*It should have been me.*'

'Shh, don't say that,' Florence said, starting to cry as she saw her friend break down. 'It's not your fault. None of this is your fault, Ava!'

'It should have been me,' Ava whispered again as she sat ramrod-straight, staring ahead, a ghost of the confident, vibrant woman Florence was used to.

It wasn't until Jack cleared his throat that Florence even remembered he was there. He'd sat so quietly, but now he was pulling his chair out a little so that he was closer to Ava.

'When my family were taken from me, I blamed myself for as long as I can remember,' Jack said, his eyes downcast, voice gruff. 'I couldn't stop wondering, if I'd only got home sooner, if I hadn't stayed at the hospital talking to a patient so long, if I'd only walked faster.' He looked up then, and Florence watched the way he stared at Ava, truly seeing how strong he was. 'There are so many *if onlys*, but the truth is, it wasn't my fault, just like none of this is your fault. But what *is* my fault? It's that I blamed myself so much for what happened that I couldn't see my son, because I thought he would blame me too. I couldn't see how much I still had to live for.'

Florence kept holding Ava's hand, smiling at Jack. He'd told her once that he never shared his story to anyone, that he didn't like reliving it because it was just too painful, so she knew how hard it must have been for him to open up to Ava now. And the way he spoke about his son, about the guilt he felt, suddenly him keeping William a secret from her for so long made sense.

'The war is to blame, Ava,' Jack said. 'Nothing else. There is nothing you could have done differently, there is nothing you did wrong. The war did this to your friend, and you need to accept that, or this pain, this guilt, will eat you alive.'

Ava nodded and Florence squeezed her hand.

'War is brutal. It takes everything from us, and it makes us do things and see things we should never have to be witness to.' Jack rubbed his hands over his forehead, and as she saw the visceral pain in his face, the torture in his eyes from revisiting those memories, she knew that she was in love with him. He was the bravest, strongest, most *broken* man she'd ever known, and she loved him for what he'd survived, and what he'd become.

'Jack's right, none of this is your fault,' Florence said. 'If Olivia were here right now, she'd be horrified to hear you say such a thing.'

Jack tapped her knee then and she followed his gaze to a doctor walking towards them. His eyes were fixed on them, and she knew, in that moment, that they were finally going to hear Olivia's fate.

'You're the family of the young dispatch rider brought in earlier?'

Florence was about to explain that they were friends, but Jack stood and spoke for them before she had the chance.

'Yes, we are,' Jack said. 'You have news?'

'There's no easy way to say this, but unfortunately the young lady succumbed to her injuries. She made it through the initial surgery, but we had to operate a second time and in the end her injuries were too severe, and she just lost too much blood to survive.'

Florence felt as if the ground were opening up to swallow her whole. Even though she'd known, when they'd found Olivia, that saving her would be impossible, she'd started to hope when they'd made it to the hospital and she'd still been alive. When Jack had told her there was always a chance. When they'd taken her into surgery.

She turned to Ava, who had her eyes shut, her body shuddering as she sobbed.

Florence could hear Jack thanking the doctor, but all she could see was Ava as her friend slowly opened her eyes.

'She's gone?' Ava cried. 'Our beautiful Liv is gone?'

'She's gone.' Florence cried with her, hugging her tightly until they couldn't hold each other any longer.

When they finally parted, Florence reached into her jacket and pulled out the letter she'd tucked there earlier, the letter she'd forced herself to stop reading. But now she wanted to read it, to keep Olivia's memory alive – to keep Leo's love for her alive.

'I found this, when I picked up her jacket,' Florence said. 'It's the letter she told us about, the letter Leo sent her that arrived after his death.'

Ava took it, whispering the words aloud as she held it, making Florence remember the way Leo had looked at Olivia, remembering how much hope their union had given her for the future when she'd stood in the church and watched as they'd recited their vows.

My dream is to come home and find a big house in the country somewhere, to fill it with children and let their laughter drown out the memories of war. I know you want that too, Liv. I know you can't wait to hold our firstborn in your arms, and to have daughters racing around and climbing trees with their brothers, just as you did as a girl. But if I don't make it home, if something should happen to me, don't let my death stop you from living your dreams.

Remember you always used to tell me that you wanted to open a little school of your own one day? And I teased that we'd have enough children for you to open a school just for them? Keep hold of that dream for me, because when I'm away that's how I want to imagine our future. My beautiful wife surrounded by children, laughing, smiling and singing.

You're all I ever wanted from this life, Olivia. Should I die, at least I'll die a happy man, but I hope that instead we can grow old together.

With all my love, your faithful husband, Leo.

Neither of them had dry eyes when Ava finished reading.

'Did she ever speak of this to you? This school she wanted to start?' Ava asked quietly. 'I knew she wanted to be a mother, but it sounds like she wanted to be a teacher, too.'

Florence nodded. 'She did. But only a few days ago. It seems that her desire to become a teacher, or to look after displaced children, was the one thing keeping her going after she lost him.' She would tell Ava more, when the time was right.

'Should we ask to see her?' Ava murmured.

'I don't think you want to see her,' Florence said. 'I can't *stop* seeing her, the way I found her, how broken she was . . .'

Ava nodded, her breath a gasp as she clutched Florence's hand.

It was Jack who gathered them up and ushered them out, steering them outside. It was Jack who kept an arm around each of them as they stood on the street, staring at one another in disbelief. And it was Jack who held Florence's hand when it was time to part ways with Ava.

'I wish we could go together now,' Florence said.

'I'll come home as soon as I've taken my motorcycle back,' Ava said.

If she noticed the blackened state of Petal she never said, and Florence watched as Ava started her motorcycle and rode away, standing on the street until she couldn't see her any longer. When Jack tucked her protectively under his arm, she let him lead her away, as memories of Olivia swirled in her mind and threatened to engulf her.

'You did everything you could today, Flo,' Jack said when they reached the ambulance. 'I want you to know that there's nothing you could have done to change this.'

She looked up at Jack, reaching for him, pressing against his chest as everything she'd held in earlier came bubbling up inside her, as her tears flowed and her breath hiccupped in her chest.

Olivia was gone. She'd never see her bright smile again, never hear her laugh, never look back on what they'd done during the war with her. Never work side by side with her with the children at the special house.

Jack guided her into the ambulance and she curled up in the passenger seat, her eyes dry as she stared out of the window at the city she loved, the city that had been bombed to oblivion yet was somehow still standing. And she thought about Olivia and the dreams she'd had – dreams that Florence would never let be forgotten, for as long as she lived.

CHAPTER TWENTY-THREE

*A*VA

Ava stood and waited, trying her hardest not to fidget. She didn't want to be there; every part of what was happening felt wrong, especially without Olivia. She would have traded everything, every success, every accolade, to have her friend by her side.

'I don't deserve this,' she whispered to herself, digging her nails into her palms. *This isn't right. It's not I who should be standing here.*

'Wren Ava Williamson, you are hereby awarded the British Empire Medal for bravery, for displaying great gallantry and complete disregard for danger on the night of the twenty-ninth of December, when you delivered on foot a message to me personally at Admiralty House, as bombs continued to fall around you, on a journey that took you a great many hours. And for courageously volunteering to travel that same route to deliver a message of great importance, despite not having yet recovered from your injuries.'

Ava smiled and nodded politely, knowing what was expected of her and understanding what a great privilege it was to receive such an award. Only it didn't feel like she deserved it. What was it for? All she'd done was her job. She was standing there and Olivia wasn't, and that alone told her exactly who deserved the medal.

'Thank you, sir,' Ava said, as the Naval Commander-in-Chief shook her hand and presented her with the award. She was dressed in her formal WRN uniform for the occasion, and she looked down at the medal as it was pinned to her lapel, wishing she felt something other than guilt at seeing it there.

The Ava who'd started out as a Wren would have done anything to receive such an award, but after everything that had happened since, she barely recognised the Ava of the past any more.

As if sensing her discomfort, George stepped forward once the ceremony was over, and she clasped his outstretched hand when he offered it, taking the chance to move closer to him.

'You deserve this, Ava. I can almost see the cogs working in your brain, telling you that somehow this shouldn't be yours. But you're wrong.'

She smiled, despite her glum thoughts. 'I didn't realise I was so easy to read.'

George pulled her a little closer, still holding her hand as he whispered to her. 'You'll be pleased to know that I've made an official recommendation for Olivia to receive a medal posthumously.'

Her eyebrows peaked in surprise. 'You have?'

'I have. But that doesn't take away from what you've received here today, Ava. No matter how you feel right now, you deserve this. You can hold your head high and know that, no matter what, you've displayed great bravery and delivered messages that could very well change the course of the war, and for that you deserve to be recognised.'

'Thank you,' she said, finally letting go of his hand. 'That means a lot.'

George looked at her a long moment before speaking again. 'Ava, I know the past weeks have been difficult, but I'd like you to take over training the new recruits, if you're willing. When you're ready, of course.'

She swallowed. Weeks ago, she'd have done anything to beat Olivia to the job, but now, hearing the news was bittersweet.

'I'm sorry you have to give it to me,' she said, looking down at her shoes. 'I know she was the better candidate, and for that I'm truly sorry.'

George's fingers touched beneath her chin, slowly lifting her face up.

'Ava, the job belongs to you,' he said, softly. 'Olivia was one of our best riders, she was conscientious and incredibly capable, but the rider you've become, the woman you've become in this role, it's perfect for you. Your enthusiasm is exactly what our new recruits need.'

Ava couldn't help but smile. 'You mean that?'

'Yes, Ava, I most certainly do.'

'Thank you,' she said. 'Your praise means more to me than anyone else's.'

'No need to thank me,' George said, smiling as he reached out and touched her medal with his fingertips. 'Just promise me that you'll wear this with pride, and remember how much your actions will inspire another generation of women.'

She blinked away tears. 'I'm not that same girl you trained all those months ago,' she said.

'I know.' His fingers brushed her cheek then, as he stared into her eyes. 'You're now a woman who knows how to balance her speed and enthusiasm with a sense of duty and respect. I liked that girl, but it just so happens that I love this one.'

Ava stood for a long moment after George walked away, wondering if Olivia was looking down on them from above, as George's words continued to play in her mind.

She touched her medal and smiled, seeing her friend beside her, feeling the warm embrace she would have given her, hearing the laughter they would have shared.

I'll never forget you, Liv. Not for a second.

Life would never feel the same without her, but she had no choice; the work she was doing was the most meaningful thing she'd ever done, and it was a responsibility that she cherished. She owed it to Olivia to live every day to the fullest, and although it was Olivia who'd been the true motorcycle enthusiast in the beginning, Ava had come to understand that her own life would be forever connected to motorcycles, too. Truth be told, she couldn't imagine a life that didn't involve riding them, even long after the war.

When Ava's eyes met George's across the room, she knew that part of living every day to the fullest was embracing whatever it was that was happening between her and George, too. Grandma Ivy had been on at her non-stop to invite him over for dinner, and maybe one of these days she might just say yes.

———— ⚭⚬ ————

'Today you will have the opportunity to ride a motorcycle, and show me if you have what it takes to become a motorcycle dispatch rider,' Ava said, walking up and down in front of the six women gathered. 'If you succeed, this job will be like nothing you've ever experienced before.'

She paused, looking at the young women, feeling so much older than them but knowing she was barely a few years their senior.

'We've lost many brave women in this job – women who were braver than any of you standing here today. Some of them were also more capable riders than you will likely ever be, so skill and bravery are not always enough to keep you alive.'

One of the women looked like she was about to be sick, and Ava nodded to George, who was standing behind them. He was smiling, his arms folded as he watched her, but it was the photo of Olivia hanging in the open doorway that stole her attention. Ava cleared her throat, refusing to allow emotion to enter her voice.

'There was one thing I was told on the very first day I became a dispatch rider that I will never forget, and it's something I learned first-hand to be true, so I'm going to repeat it to you all today.' She moved closer to the women, lowering her voice as she slowly looked from face to terrified face. She fixed her gaze on the one girl who looked unfazed, who was smiling as if this were exactly the challenge she'd been looking for.

'You must be prepared to die for the memo in your satchel,' she said. 'You do anything, and I mean *anything*, to deliver your message, even if it means crawling the rest of the way on your knees to do so.'

Ava pointed to the girl, who was still looking as confident as could be.

'You,' she said. 'Name?'

'Wren Oakbridge.'

'You're up first,' Ava said, indicating the motorcycle behind her and beckoning the young Wren to follow. She ran through the basic instructions and gestured for her to sit astride the bike. 'Accelerate slow and steady, and make a couple of full circles for me.'

The girl nodded and Ava stepped back, feeling George beside her before she heard him.

'Remind you of anyone?' he murmured.

Ava laughed. 'She certainly does.'

They stood and watched as the Wren confidently rode the motorcycle around them, side by side, their shoulders almost touching.

'You're good at this job, Ava. It suits you,' George said.

'Olivia would have been better,' she replied. 'She would have had a level of patience I'm not certain I'll ever have.'

'Olivia would have been good at this job, I agree,' he said. 'But she wouldn't have been better than you.'

Ava nodded when the girl returned, taking hold of the bike and climbing astride herself as she revved the engine.

'And why's that?' Ava asked.

'Because your students are going to be equal parts in awe of you and terrified!'

Ava took off then, skidding the back wheel as she raced off, showing the watching recruits exactly what she was capable of – what she expected *they'd* be capable of when they finished their training with her.

Keep me safe, Olivia. God knows I need someone looking out for me.

EPILOGUE

June 1944

FLORENCE

Florence stood at the graveside, looking down at the bunch of flowers in her hand that she'd bought for Olivia's birthday and wishing she'd bought something bigger. Flowers hadn't been easy to come by, but still, what she'd brought didn't feel substantial enough for the occasion.

'Hello, stranger.' The husky, warm voice was impossible not to recognise, and Florence turned to see Ava walking towards her across the grass, looking as elegant as could be in her Wren uniform, her hair swept off her face.

'It's so good to see you,' Florence said, her face breaking into a smile that mirrored Ava's as they hugged.

'Sometimes it only feels like yesterday that we lost her, don't you think?' Ava said, slipping her arm around Florence's waist as they stood and stared at Olivia's gravestone. She'd been buried beside Leo, the two of them passing within weeks of one another. 'It's almost impossible to believe it's been so long.'

'I keep thinking about their wedding day,' Florence said. 'The way Leo looked at her, it just made me feel, for a day at least, that perhaps there was something to hope for. That there was life after the war.'

'And yet here we are,' Ava said with a sigh. 'Still in the thick of it.'

Florence placed her flowers and took a step back so Ava could do the same. It took her a moment to realise what Ava was putting down, but then she saw it was a piece of paper. Ava obviously noticed the quizzical look on her face.

'It's the letter we found in her pocket,' she said. 'I've kept it ever since you gave it to me to read at the hospital that day, and I wanted Olivia to finally have it. Does that seem silly?'

'No,' Florence said, 'it doesn't seem silly at all.'

'It's hard to believe how many dispatch riders we've lost since Olivia passed,' Ava said, as they started to walk away from the graveside and into a patch of sunlight, where there was a break in the trees that had been shading them. 'We're up to almost ninety women across England. Ninety families who've lost a daughter, sister or wife. It's almost impossible to fathom.'

Florence turned the number over in her mind. It *was* hard to fathom, Ava was right.

'Do you think it will be over soon? What have you been hearing lately?' Florence asked. 'I mean, it feels like things are changing, that the tide is turning somewhat in the Allies' favour, but who knows what to believe?'

'I hope so,' Ava replied. 'But then if you'd asked me a year ago, I'd have thought it would be over by now, so perhaps it's simply wishful thinking on my behalf.'

'Are you still riding often?' Florence asked as they sat on the grass. She tucked her legs to the side and absently plucked at a stalk of grass. Now that Ava didn't live with her, they didn't see one another as often, and she missed her terribly sometimes. It had been like having a sister again when she'd had Ava and then Olivia living with her.

'I still ride the route to Plymouth – it's become a standing joke that no one else can ride it as efficiently as I can – but I'm spending most days training our new recruits and keeping everyone on their toes.'

'I'm sure you're keeping George on his toes, too,' Florence teased.

'George,' Ava said with a sigh. 'Who'd have thought the man I needed in my life was right there beneath my nose all that time. I laugh sometimes at how often I told you both he was most definitely *not* my type.'

They both laughed.

'You know, Olivia always suspected he was the one for you.'

'She did.' Ava smiled. 'She was so good for me. Without her, I don't think I'd have become half the woman I am today.'

'Do you often think of her?' Florence asked. 'When you're riding that route?'

'Every time,' Ava whispered, and Florence saw tears glistening in her eyes. 'Sometimes I talk to her, sometimes I just think about her and wish we could have one last night together, just the three of us. Or one more Christmas all together at your grandmother's house. Other times, I'm just too sad to think about her at all.'

Florence nodded. 'I can still see it in my head like it was yesterday, and I hate that I keep seeing her like that.'

'I'm sorry,' Ava said, shaking her head and reaching for Florence's hand. 'I'm so sorry you can't see her like I can. You were right not to let me see her that day, I only wish you weren't carrying that burden alone.'

Florence inhaled and looked up at the sky. 'Talking to you, it's helping bring back some other memories. Nicer memories, the ones I should be trying harder to remember.'

'How's your grandmother?' Ava asked.

'She's actually not very well,' Florence said. 'She won't admit it but her health isn't the best, and to be honest I don't know how much longer I'll have her.'

'She might surprise you; she's tough as nails,' Ava said, smiling. 'Can I come and see her? I feel terrible, it's been weeks now since I've been to visit.'

'She'd love that. Truly she would.' Florence smiled. 'According to her, all she needs is a few days' rest and she'll be as good as new. Ever the optimist, my grandmother.'

Ava laughed, but Florence could tell there was something on her mind, especially when she reached for her hand again.

'And the children's house?' Ava asked, her eyes bright. 'How is that coming along?'

'It's wonderful,' Florence said. 'I wish I had more time to spend there, but after the war I'm going to follow through with Olivia's wishes and try my hand at teaching. It feels like the right thing to do, especially when it helped me through such a difficult time myself.'

'You'll make a wonderful teacher,' Ava said.

'Well, I love children, so let's hope that's a good start.'

'Flo, while we're talking about children, there's something I need to tell you.'

'Let me guess, you're giving up motorcycle riding to become a teacher, too?' she teased.

'Actually, I'm pregnant,' Ava replied, her face blooming into a smile.

Florence dropped her hand and then grabbed for it again. 'Pregnant? You're *pregnant*?'

Ava nodded. 'I am.'

Florence leaned forward and flung her arms around her. 'Oh, Ava, I'm so happy for you! I can't believe it!'

She let her go and reached out a hand, gently touching it to her friend's stomach.

'George must be thrilled?'

Ava looked guilty. 'Well, actually, you're the very first person I've told.'

Florence knew her mouth was hanging open, but she couldn't help it. 'Ava! How can you not have told him?' She was secretly thrilled to be the first, but there was something wrong about her knowing before the baby's father. 'Do you not think he'll be happy?'

'Oh, I know he'll be happy,' Ava said. 'I suppose I just haven't found the right moment to tell him. Yet.'

Florence sighed. 'It's because you know he'll take you off the roster, isn't it? He won't let you ride again as soon as he knows.'

A guilty smile twisted Ava's mouth.

'Ava, you know how much I love you, and I'm so proud of the work you do, but I can't lose another friend,' she said. 'If I lost you and your unborn baby, I don't know how I'd survive, not after Olivia.' *Not after my family.*

Ava sighed. 'I know. And I promise, tonight will be my last ride. I just couldn't bear the thought of giving it up, not after everything this job has given me, but I can't stand the thought of risking my baby, either.'

They sat a moment, as the clouds drifted away from the sun again, and Florence looked across at her friend. She hadn't realised quite how much she'd missed Ava until today. Life had become so busy, and with so many hours spent working there was barely time to do anything during the day other than sleep and volunteer with the children, but she wished she'd made the effort to see her more. It must have been a month at least since they'd last spent time together.

'Think of it as a break,' Florence told Ava. 'You can ride motorcycles until you're old and grey if you want, but you just need some time away to grow your beautiful baby.'

'I know, you're absolutely right. And I will, I promise. I just can't stand the thought of sitting idle.'

'I'm sure you'll find something to keep you busy,' Florence said. 'I can't imagine you doing nothing until the baby is born, you just need to do something less dangerous.'

Ava grinned.

'Well, I'd better be going,' Florence finally said. 'I'd much prefer to spend the day with you, but I have so much to do before my shift.'

She stood and held out a hand to Ava.

'Promise we won't leave it so long next time?' Ava asked.

Florence placed her hand on Ava's stomach again. 'And miss this little cherub growing? Not a chance.'

'I'll see you soon, then,' Ava said.

'See you soon,' Florence repeated. She kissed her friend on the cheek and walked away, barely able to wipe the smile from her face as she thought about Ava having a baby.

'The London Girls forever, right?' she heard Ava call.

Florence laughed. 'The London Girls forever.'

There were times she wondered if there was any kindness or hope left in the world, but news like Ava's reminded her what they were fighting for.

Florence drove the ambulance slowly through the streets of London in the early hours, the sun just starting to rise in the sky. She was driving a different ambulance now; Petal had been a workhorse for years, but the fire damage she'd received, as well as being hit by a fire engine some months later, had meant she'd needed significant repairs, which meant Florence had a new ambulance to drive for the time being.

She hadn't named the new one; it just hadn't seemed right the second time, not when Olivia had been the one to help her name Petal.

'I saw Ava today,' Florence said.

'Oh? How was she?'

She glanced at Jack as he turned in his seat slightly to face her. 'She was great. I mean, it was sad remembering Olivia today, but Ava is always great. I only wish I could see her more often; it was so wonderful when she used to live with us.'

Florence turned the ambulance towards their headquarters and the remnants of the theatre they passed each day, but instead of driving on, she pulled over.

'Is something wrong?' Jack asked, sitting up and looking out of the window.

Florence smiled, turning in her seat to face him. 'No, nothing's wrong,' she said, trying to decide if she was going crazy, or just overtired, or possibly both. Or maybe it was simply that it was Olivia's birthday, and it had made her realise all over again just how short life was.

'Then what are we doing here?' Jack asked.

Florence took a breath and reached for his hand. 'Jack, once this war is over, would you like to get married?'

Jack made a noise in his throat that made her laugh, and she watched him expectantly, her heart racing as she prayed she hadn't made a mistake in asking him.

'Yes,' he finally said. 'I'd actually like that very much.'

Florence cupped his cheek, brushing her thumb across the roughness of his stubble, gently pressing her lips to his. Jack felt

309

like home to her; he felt like safety and warmth and love, and she knew that she didn't ever want to let that go.

'It has to be for something, doesn't it?' she whispered. 'It can't be for nothing.'

Jack kissed her again, his fingers warm against her wrist. She could see the tears in his eyes, and knew her eyes would reflect the same pain, the same combination of loss and hope that she felt battling inside her every day.

'We'd best make a trip to see your grandmother on the way home then,' Jack murmured. 'Ivy would hate for us to be keeping a secret like that from her.'

Florence laughed. He was right. If her grandmother wasn't the first to know, she'd never forgive them.

When Florence pulled the ambulance back on to the road, she couldn't stop smiling. Because suddenly there was hope, and before then, since Olivia had gone, there'd only been sadness. And she knew her friend would have wanted more for them. If she were here, she'd have been the first to celebrate their engagement, which made what Florence had done seem like the perfect way to honour her death and remember her by.

I'll never forget you, Liv. Never.

AVA

Ava pulled into the dispatch headquarters, enjoying the rumble of her engine, moving her hands over the handlebars and wondering when she'd next be sitting astride a bike again. Motorcycles had become more than a job to her; they'd become her life.

It had been a long night, but a successful one, and in some ways she hadn't wanted it to end. She'd savoured every moment of her ride; the wind in her face, the rumble of the engine, even the ache in her back from sitting astride the motorcycle for so long, it all felt so familiar to her.

But end it had, and now she could see her husband pacing, his face lighting up when he saw her parking.

'Ava! I was starting to worry.'

She dismounted. 'I took it a little slower coming home,' she said.

'Were there obstructions on the road? Did something happen?'

'George, stop,' she said, taking off her gloves and shaking her head at the worried expression on his face.

His eyebrows were drawn together as he looked at her, and as she always did, she counted her lucky stars that she'd found him. Or, more importantly, that he'd been patient enough to give her a chance.

'I took it slow because I've decided to retire,' she said. 'Tonight was my very last dispatch.'

George looked like he was about to choke. 'I'm sorry, your *last* dispatch? Are you injured? Has something happened that I'm not aware of?'

Ava placed her palm over her stomach, smiling so hard it was almost impossible for her to get the words out. Poor George, he looked so worried. 'Darling, I'm pregnant.'

He stared at her as if he hadn't heard what she'd said. '*Pregnant?*' he finally repeated.

'Pregnant,' she said with a grin. 'I – well, I didn't think you'd want me riding one of these *death traps* with our baby on board.'

George was still staring at her with the most comical look on his face, and she walked over to him, looping her arms around his neck since there was no one else around. 'Darling, please say something. I thought you'd be ecstatic.'

He finally seemed to digest the news, but instead of his face breaking out into a smile, he looked like he was about to explode.

311

'You've been delivering dispatches when you knew you were *pregnant*?' he blustered.

'Well, when you say it like that . . .'

'Ava, of all the irresponsible, reckless things you've done, this, *this*—'

'George,' she interrupted, taking his hand and holding it to her stomach. 'Darling, I'm pregnant. We're going to have a baby. Surely we don't have to be theatrical about what I have or haven't done up until this moment?'

Just like she'd known it would, the instant his hand covered her belly, his face softened, all traces of anger disappearing.

'We're going to have a baby?' he whispered.

'Yes, George, we're going to have a baby.' She laughed. 'So can we forget all about the reckless behaviour part and just celebrate the fact I've voluntarily given up work? I feel like it's quite an accomplishment for me to be so mature.'

George laughed then, too. 'I suppose it is a miracle.'

'You *know* it's a miracle,' she murmured against his mouth, before planting a kiss on his lips. 'We're going to be parents, George. Can you believe it?'

He took her into his arms, kissing her back, and she knew then that he'd most definitely forgotten all about how cross he was with her.

'Heaven help me if we have a daughter,' he muttered. 'How in God's name would I deal with another girl like you?'

'Easily,' she said, tilting her head back as she looked up at him. 'You've dealt with me just fine up until now.'

He raised an eyebrow, clearly not convinced, before wrapping her in his arms and lifting her clean off her feet.

'What are you doing?' she squealed. 'George, put me down!'

But George carried her straight out to the street and didn't stop.

'George!'

'This is no place for the mother of my child. I'm taking you home.'

'I can walk!' she protested, unsuccessfully wriggling against his hold. 'George, please! I'm pregnant, not sick!'

But he completely ignored her, taking her to the little flat they'd shared ever since they'd married, and kissing her on the head once he deposited her outside the front door.

'Rest,' he said. 'I'll be home soon.'

And, for the first time in her life, once she'd waved goodbye, Ava followed his orders without hesitation and curled up in bed, ready to sleep the day away until George came home.

The next evening, Ava lay on her back, propped up slightly with pillows and looking down at George. His hand was placed protectively over her stomach, and she laughed when he bent to kiss it. There was a gentle curve there now, whereas before it had been flat, and she sighed as he moved up the bed to kiss her lips. She was half surprised he hadn't noticed the change before she'd told him, although she well knew that men were often hopeless when it came to things like that.

'I'm sorry you had to spend last night alone,' he said.

'I'm fine,' she replied. '*We're* fine.'

His hand moved back to her stomach. 'Ava, about your last dispatch—'

'Stop,' she said, wriggling back and holding up her hand. 'Before you say anything, I know I should have stopped riding sooner. I'm sorry, but you know how difficult it is for me to—'

'Ava.' George's voice was firm as he interrupted her. 'I'm not angry with you.'

'Oh.' She studied his face, trying to understand why he looked so happy. She was certain he'd be furious with her for putting their baby at risk the way she had. They'd lost so many dispatch riders since the beginning of the war; what she'd done wasn't even a calculated risk, it was just an outright risk.

'Ava, the last memo you delivered, it contained orders that may very well end the war.'

She blinked back at him, her eyes still searching his face. 'Truly?'

'Truly.' He stroked her bare shoulder as he smiled at her. 'I understand that the Allies have landed early this morning in Normandy, and that you delivered the message confirming those orders.'

She laughed as George pulled her closer, and she nestled against his chest, listening to the steady beat of his heart. *I did that. I delivered those orders.* Ava closed her eyes, thinking about the child growing inside her and about the feat of her final dispatch.

'I'm going to be able to tell our child that he or she was with me when I delivered that message,' Ava whispered. 'If this war ever ends, if this invasion is a success, I'll have one hell of a story to share.'

'Yes, Ava, you certainly will.' George pressed a kiss into her hair as she settled even closer to him.

She'd never imagined when she'd begged for permission to become a dispatch rider that her job could become so important, that she could be responsible for delivering messages that had the power to change the course of the war. Being in love with a married man, her time working at Norfolk House, it all felt like a lifetime ago. As did taking the job of dispatch rider simply so she could sneak out at night – it was as if she'd been a silly girl then, and her job had helped her to become a woman. She'd never been so proud of anything as she was of her work.

'George, if we have a daughter, I'd like to name her Olivia.' Ava didn't know where the thought had suddenly come from, all she knew was that she needed to find a way to honour her friend's memory – for the role she'd played in the war and in Ava's life.

'It's a beautiful name,' he said. 'A *brave* name.'

Ava shut her eyes, exhausted from a long night and ready to finally fall asleep in the arms of her husband.

The war is almost over. I can feel it in my bones.

'Darling, how would you feel about me coming back to work for just a *little* bit longer?' she asked, still with her eyes closed as she fought sleep. 'This news about Normandy is all so very exciting.'

'Don't push me, Ava. I'll have you locked up in this flat if I have to.'

'Purely for training or overseeing purposes, of course. Surely that would be permissible? Surely it would be helpful to have me there assisting?'

He groaned. 'As if I could say no.'

She smiled. *Your daddy is going to dote on you, little one. Your mother is the reckless one, but your father? He's the one who'll always keep you safe.*

'Goodnight, Ava,' George mumbled, clearly as exhausted as she was.

'Goodnight,' she whispered back.

As sleep found her, she found Olivia, on a motorcycle beside her as they raced around the speedway, both laughing as they fought to be first, grinning as the sun touched their skin, the roar of their engines all Ava could hear as she smiled at her friend.

AUTHOR'S NOTE

As always, I'd like to make a note that this book, although inspired by history, is very much a work of fiction. For those of you who have a deep knowledge of World War II history, especially in London throughout this period, you will notice that I reference the West End being bombed in 1940 during The Blitz. The West End was in fact bombed in April of the following year; however, I wanted to mention this catastrophic event within my novel, due to the close location of Florence's ambulance headquarters, and I was bound by some other constraints! Namely, I wanted my depiction of the recruitment of the dispatch riders from the WRNS to be factually correct in 1940, and I needed them to be doing their job during the most dangerous period – the Blitz. That meant much of my story had to take place in late 1940. I also want to make a note that Winston Churchill's famous speech that I had Olivia and her family listening to was in fact broadcast in August 1940, whereas in the timeline of my story I have this happening slightly later that year. I felt it was too important not to include though!

The deadly night of 29 December, when the devastating German bombing attack targeted the city of London, creating an inferno and resulting in the Second Great Fire of London, was also something I was determined to include from the outset. You'll know by now that this is the night Ava has her accident, and it's also the night Jack and

Florence rescue people from a collapsed shelter on Keyworth Street. There was, in fact, a shelter on this street that collapsed after taking a direct hit, and it was actually a former telegraph linesman named Signalman Robert Tinto who helped with the rescue of the trapped civilians there, crawling through a small hole and digging with his bare hands to get to those trapped below. I know I only mentioned the collapsed shelter briefly, but I did want to mention the man who saved those London residents, for he was the one who made it possible for them to be taken by ambulance to hospital.

By 1940, all of the Navy's dispatch riders were women, which allowed men who had previously undertaken the job to go to the front. These women, who were recruited from the Women's Royal Navy Service (WRNS) were nicknamed Wrens, and they worked eight-hour shifts day and night, although they were often expected to be available at all times. I would also like to make special mention of the route Ava takes from London to the shipyards at Plymouth, as this was a long and dangerous ride by night, but some of the most important war memos were dispatched by female riders to Plymouth during this time, due to its proximity to France's Normandy coast. The orders to invade Normandy were in fact delivered by a woman on motorcycle to those very shipyards, which I chose to reveal at the end of the story. Would the dispatch rider have ever found out what orders the memo contained? I highly doubt it. But I wanted the reader to understand just how vitally important women like Ava were during the war, so I chose to have George reveal that information to her at the very end.

In terms of Ava's big crash in the novel, that was inspired by the true story of Wren Pamela McGeorge, who was caught in a bombing raid and crashed after being blown off her motorcycle by a bomb! Despite the significant crash that left her bike in pieces, she ran the remaining distance on foot to deliver her dispatch, and for that she was awarded the British Empire Medal for her 'great gallantry and complete disregard for danger'. Once again, an important moment that showed just how brave these women were!

Of the almost 100,000 British women who served during WWII, 303 lost their lives during active duty, and 100 of those women were motorcycle dispatch riders. When I read this statistic, I became even more determined to share a glimpse into the lives of these women – to honour their memories and to shed light on the incredible work they did. It also meant that Olivia's death had to happen, and trust me, there were many conversations back and forth between my editors and me over whether we could save her! Deep down, we all wanted her to survive, but we also knew that it was important to show how truly dangerous and fatal the job could be.

Post-war, most of these women resumed their usual lives with little mention of the incredible bravery they displayed, so I hope that this novel goes some way to recognise the contributions they made to the war effort.

In writing this novel, I initially found it hard to uncover large amounts of information about the Wrens, but what I did discover was absolutely fascinating. These women were incredibly brave and came from all walks of life, but what they had in common was their unwavering desire to assist in the war effort. Oh, and their love of their gorgeous Navy Wren uniforms! I actually couldn't believe that after so many years researching this time period that I'd never heard of female motorcycle dispatch riders, so I hope this is something new and interesting to my readers as well.

With each novel I write that is set during WWII, my desire is to give a voice to women, and to explore the war from the female perspective. It's an incredible privilege to tell stories based on fact, and which are inspired by the extraordinary women of this time period. My hope is that in creating fictional stories inspired by historical events, we can keep the memories and true stories of these women alive.

ACKNOWLEDGEMENTS

As I write these acknowledgements, I'm at home in isolation with my family – I'm the only one in my family without Covid right now! It's been a challenging time, but I know how fortunate I am to have a job that allows me to work from home. The past two years have brought many challenges, but I've still been able to escape to my keyboard every day and continue writing the books of my heart, for which I am eternally grateful.

I'm so fortunate to have a wonderful support team, from my family to my colleagues. My acknowledgements are always rather repetitive, but I do have to thank the same core group of people again. To my husband and gorgeous boys – thank you for understanding when I disappear into my office to write, and for celebrating with me every time I finish a book or reach a sales milestone. My children have become much more interested in my books now that I celebrate with a 'book cake' each time I have a new release!

I owe the biggest thanks to my 'dream team' editors, though – Victoria Oundjian and Sophie Wilson, with special thanks also to Sammia Hamer. Sammia, although you're on maternity leave, you will always be part of the dream team! You all know exactly how far you can push me, your ideas infuse my stories with so much depth, and I will forever be grateful to work with you all. I honestly thank my lucky stars every time I get to work on a book with you – thank you for believing in me!

I must also thank my long-time agent, Laura Bradford, for her support and advice, and thank you to my author relations team at Amazon Publishing, Nicole Wagner and Bekah Graham Pickering. Actually, I owe thanks to the entire Amazon Publishing UK team – thank you for believing in my writing and continuing to give me the opportunity to write the books I love. Also, a special note of thanks to copy-editor Gemma Wain – thank you for your attention to detail. Thanks also to proofreader Swati Gamble for being the all-important final set of eyes!

I also owe a debt of gratitude to authors Yvonne Lindsay, Natalie Anderson and Nicola Marsh. Our daily texts/emails mean the world to me, and it would be a very lonely job if I didn't have you all cheering me on and being there for me. Thank you!

The online writing community is such a supportive one, and I would like to say special thanks to all my Blue Sky Book Chat ladies for your constant support, and for letting me be part of the group. I would also like to personally thank Suzy (Suzy Approved Book Reviews), Annie McDonnell (The Write Review), Joanna (That Bookshop Girl), Susan Peterson (Sue's Reading Neighborhood) and Kristy Barrett (A Novel Bee) for your ongoing and dedicated support of my books. I know there are so many more of you who've supported me over the years, and please know I appreciate every post/mention/ review!

And finally, you, my readers! You mean the world to me. Thank you for reading my books – without you I wouldn't be able to do what I love. Your support means so much, and I hope that you continue to enjoy my books for many years to come.

If you'd like to connect with me, find me on Facebook and be sure to join my reader group! I love chatting with my readers and sharing book recommendations, as well as behind-the-scenes information and the inspirations for all of my characters.

Soraya x

ABOUT THE AUTHOR

Photo © 2022 Jemima Helmore

Soraya M. Lane graduated with a law degree before realising that law wasn't the career for her and that her future was in writing. She is the author of historical and contemporary women's fiction, and her novel *Wives of War* was an Amazon Charts bestseller. Soraya lives on a small farm in her native New Zealand with her husband, their two young sons, and a collection of four-legged friends. When she's not writing, she loves to be outside playing make-believe with her children or snuggled up inside reading. For more information about Soraya and her books, visit www.sorayalane.com or www.facebook.com/SorayaLaneAuthor, or follow her on Twitter: @Soraya_Lane.